THE
RAVENHOOD

EXODUS

KATE
STEWART

PAN BOOKS

First published 2020 by Kate Stewart

This paperback edition first published 2023 by Pan Books
an imprint of Pan Macmillan
The Smithson, 6 Briset Street, London EC1M 5NR
EU representative: Macmillan Publishers Ireland Ltd, 1st Floor,
The Liffey Trust Centre, 117–126 Sheriff Street Upper,
Dublin 1, DO1 YC43
Associated companies throughout the world
www.panmacmillan.com

ISBN 978-1-0350-1350-0

1 3 5 7 9 8 6 4 2

A CIP catalogue record for this book is available from the British Library.

Typeset by Palimpsest Book Production Ltd, Falkirk, Stirlingshire
Printed and bound by CPI Group (UK) Ltd, Croydon, CR0 4YY

Visit www.panmacmillan.com to read more about all our books
and to buy them. You will also find features, author interviews and
news of any author events, and you can sign up for e-newsletters
so that you're always first to hear about our new releases.

For my dear friend, Donna Cooksley Sanderson.
Thank you for the gift of your unwavering friendship.
Knowing you has brought out the best in me and
greatly enriched my life.

PART ONE

Then

Chapter One

"YOU'RE THE FRENCHMAN."

He replies with a faint dip of his chin, his hostile gaze blistering my skin with contempt. "You mind turning down that fucking calling card?" Each of his words curled by the thick foreign lilt, confirming I knew that much about him.

Dominic rarely, if ever, spoke French, which raised my suspicions about the nickname. But the man standing before me, and the air about him, suits.

A drop of sweat slides down his temple as I soak him in. Compliments to the tailor who cloaked him in a suit fit for a king. It clings to him, defining pure masculinity. Though his expression is hostile, it's his face that has me scrambling for words while my tongue dries up. This man is, without a doubt, the most beautiful man I've ever laid eyes on. Stunned, I can't help but drink in the thick, inky color of his hair, which is styled back in inches-long waves, not one out of place. The sharp outline of his jaw encases his flawless bronzed face. Below his thick, winged brows lies a natural black outline of thick lashes, which enhances the mix of orange-yellow flames dancing their way down my profile. His dominant nose wide, long, and swollen by the flare of his nostrils. His mouth more evidence his creator took his time, his lush lips symmetrical perfection. But it's the anger that seeps from his pores that has me battling the wits his unexpected appearance is stealing.

He's the devil you are never supposed to meet, dressed in Armani.

And a clear threat to me.

Snatching the remote from the table beside me, I furiously tap the volume button, sputtering, while searching for my bikini top.

"I didn't . . . k-know it was you. I d-didn't know there *was* a you."

"You weren't supposed to." His tone is acid, spilling from his lips into the back of my throat, making it hard to breathe.

Some fucking siren you are, Cecelia.

I dart my eyes around the deck, searching fruitlessly for my top before I cross my arms over my chest, humiliation burning my face. "Then why bother to make your existence known to me now?"

"Because, apparently, I can't do anything without those two imbeciles fumbling dick over head for—" his lips peel back from his teeth. Tack-sharp canines appear due to his . . . snarling?

"The enemy?" I shake my head. "I'm not your enemy."

His jaw ticks, his gaze littered with judgment. "No, you just benefit from Daddy's filthy money."

"Oh, good, that's a look of disgust in your eyes. I was worried it was something else."

"I don't fuck little girls," he drawls, his accent aiding in

4

his condemnation. "And I'm fully aware you're fucking your way through my crew."

It stings, but I don't flinch. "Only two of them, and from where I'm standing, it looks like you could benefit from a little side-action yourself. You're awfully tense."

Irrefutably annoyed, he shoves his hands in his slacks. "What the fuck do you want?"

"I want answers. I *want* to know my father is safe."

"I can't guarantee that."

"But *you* won't be the one to hurt him?"

His hesitation has my hackles rising.

"Physically, no. In every other way that matters, yes."

"And me?"

"You're not a part of this."

"I am now."

"No, you're not. I made sure of it." His smug reply sends a bolt of realization through me.

"You're the reason . . . *you're* the one who made them get rid of me."

Dom's words from just days ago have my gears turning.

"*We were trying to make a point, and we fucking failed miserably.*"

Someone from the Meetup got the message to him that I was here. Because this man in front of me is the *someone* they both answer to.

Silence lingers between us before the hostile stranger speaks up. "You were never supposed to be here."

"You knew about me. You all knew about me." Of course, they did. Rule number one is to know your enemy and their weakness. But to them, I was an estranged daughter and posed no danger to their plans—another one of the reasons why Sean was hesitant about bringing me in.

"Who are you exactly?"

Silence.

"So why show up here, *now*, and talk to me?"

He remains mute as I mull it over.

"Someone couldn't keep a secret."

Someone from one of the chapters had reported back to him, and that's why Sean and Dominic did what they did. They were trying to make a point to those in attendance at the garage the night they ostracized me—while relaying the message to the man glaring at me. To protect me.

Click. Click. Click.

"That's why *I* was the secret," I whisper. "You didn't know I was coming. You knew Roman and I didn't have a relationship." His eyes flare as a smug smile buds on my lips.

It's clear now why he's so angry. "You never expected me to show up here because it was a last-minute decision to come. I slipped through the cracks, and they hid me from you." A little thrill runs through me. "*You* don't know everything. How does it feel?"

He takes a menacing step forward. "You're out of your depth in ways you'll never understand, and you need to drop the tough girl act and *really* talk to me because I'm only giving you two minutes."

And I do. I drop all pretenses because I'm fighting for a lot more than my pride. "I'm not the disgusting person you're making me out to be."

"My opinion of you doesn't matter."

"I think it does. I think it does a lot. You're keeping me from my—"

"You can find someone else to fuck you, Cecelia." My name sounds abhorrent coming from his thick lips. He considers me a menace—a thorn in his beastly side, and most definitely a wrench in his well-oiled machine. But I slipped through the cracks, thanks to my eight-year hiatus, and they hid me from him.

And I can't help the thrill that runs through me at the thought.

"You may hate my father, but right now you're acting just like him, like a machine. A control-freak void of humanity with a God complex."

His nostrils flare. "Watch yourself."

"Or what?"

He towers over me, eyes flickering in warning. "You do not want to piss me off."

"This isn't pissed off? And who the hell are *you* to tell me what I should watch? You may have most of the cards, but you're missing mine. It would be in your best interest to play nice if you want my cooperation—my silence."

He doesn't respond, but the resolute shift in his demeanor is enough.

Those were the exact words that shouldn't have left my mouth. I can't be trusted at all now that I've said them. I betrayed Sean and Dominic by playing into this asshole's agenda. He's trying to poke holes in everything, flip it to prove to them they made a mistake in trusting me. Dominic would be so disappointed.

Dominic's words to Sean the day I left the house in a rage break to the surface.

"She's not strong enough."

"Give her time."

7

All of it, the trials they put me through. The infuriating back-and-forth between Dominic and me. All the time Sean spent teaching me what he believed, what the hood believed, while Dominic taunted me, twisted my words. From the time they decided to let me in, they've been readying me for a confrontation just like this. And it had *everything* to do with the man standing in front of me. While we were falling, they were preparing me for the shitstorm that is *The Frenchman*. His return was inevitable.

"I can keep a secret. I just want to know the plan."

"Just because you're here doesn't mean you get a part to play. *They* made a bad decision and *they* know it, and fucking them doesn't give you a say. And I know you won't tell anyone," he says with conviction, "but for the wrong reason."

"How is it wrong?"

"Because it's your loyalty to them," he jerks his chin toward the woods, "and your inability to separate your personal feelings, instead of embracing the idea that Roman has done some unforgivable things and deserves to suffer for it. So just let it go, like *they* are, and . . . live your life."

"Is that an order?"

"No, it's good advice," he snaps, "you should take it." I'm getting under his skin, which I would consider a good thing if I weren't at his mercy.

"I just want to see them."

"Not happening."

"I'm not a daddy's girl who's pissed she lost her playmates. Talk to them. They'll tell you about me. They'll vouch for my character."

His eyes rake me in revulsion. "I know enough."

I drop my arms, baring myself to spite him. I won't let

him shame me for something he knows nothing about, or make me feel uncomfortable in the skin I've spent a summer growing into. My effort goes unnoticed when his eyes remain bolted to mine. We stare off on opposite sides of the line he's drawn between us.

"You're really going to do this?"

"We live in different realities, and you were born into your side of things. I might not hold it against you if you drop it. Ignorance is truly bliss in your case, Cecelia. It would do you good to remember that."

"Even if we're estranged, which we are, I don't want him hurt. If you can promise my father's safety, I can help you."

"I'm not promising anything. He's got plenty of enemies who have nothing to do with us. It's business."

"Not for me."

"That's your problem."

"So what the hell am I supposed to do?"

He turns in the direction of the woods, dismissing me. "Go get your nails done."

Outraged, I reach for anything I can, finding purchase on my lotion bottle, and hurl it toward him. It nails him in the center of his back. He whirls on me and I yelp, backing up toward my chair until I'm forced on my ass. He jerks me up by the arm. What happens between us isn't chemistry; it's a white-hot fire filled with hate and resentment and a grudge that has nothing to do with me. This man isn't hinting around to anything. He loathes my existence.

"The next time you fuck with me, I'm going to fuck with you." His amber gaze licks fire down my chest before he tightens his grip. I keep my whimper on my tongue.

"You're making a mistake. You've waged war for people

just like *me*. Like my mother. Sean and Dominic are my friends over *everything else*, and I want to help them. They've been loyal to you. I don't even know your name! You may hate Roman, but I'm innocent in this. I knew nothing. I still don't."

"You *were* innocent in this, but you won't be if you keep pressing. You're too easy of a target." His insult strikes deep as he sprinkles salt on my new wounds. "You're too young and too naïve. You believed every word they told you, and at this point, you need to accept that they got what they needed from you."

Access. I was a means to gain access. My stomach drops as I remember the day Sean came back after our fight with a ready apology. Dominic went inside my house shortly after while Sean distracted me. I may be a fool, but . . .

"*I'm not a whore.*"

"*That's your conscience you're fighting with, not mine.*"

But after that day, everything changed. Maybe before I was a target, but after I was a decision. They let me into their world because they wanted me there. I'm certain of it. Sean confessed as much. He took a huge risk by bringing me in. Sleeping with me was sleeping with the enemy; letting me in on secrets kept me tied to them, and staying with me meant risking their credibility and position in the brotherhood.

If I ever needed proof of their feelings, I have it now.

"I care about them. *Deeply*. Just let me do my part."

"If that's true, stop being so fucking selfish. They're content with letting you go, and you need to woman up and do the same."

"You can't keep me away from them!"

"You know I can. Every door you knock on will not open.

No one will go near you. As of this moment, right now . . . you no longer exist. And you never did."

Rage like I've never known courses through me as I spew my venom.

"Fuck you, you backwoods fake-ass fucking Robin-Hood-wannabe son of a bitch!" I jerk my arm away and he lets me. "Get the hell out!"

He steps back, sliding his mammoth hands into his slacks, eyes blazing, voice arctic. "This is exactly why I don't want you anywhere near us."

I lift a hand. "Please, you're using the fact that I get a period as an excuse to eradicate me from the tribe? You and your group of vigilantes are supposed to be the do-gooders, right? We're supposed to be thankful to your sordid dick circle?" I huff. "Well, allow me to thank you on behalf of all of us pussy-wielding predators—" I exaggerate a bow—"thank you *so much*, but again, I'm not your enemy."

I lift my chin.

"They trusted me because they knew I was capable of handling it, and they made sure of it. They trusted me because I love them, and they knew I'd have their backs *because* of that love. Dismiss it all you want, but it's a driving force that will ensure my loyalty, not negate it, and help me to do whatever it takes to protect them as much as they are me. *And you.*"

Some sort of recognition flits over his features with my confession. Just as quickly, it evaporates. "You were never supposed to be involved."

"But I am now, so let me do my part."

"That's two minutes." He turns to walk in the direction of the woods, and I speak up because I know no amount of scheming will give me back his audience.

"I *do* love them. Maybe they screwed up, but what got me involved is their allegiance *to you* and your cause, everything all of you collectively stand for. They didn't expect to love me back, they expected to use me, but the fact that they weren't capable of deceiving me on that level is why I'm standing here fighting to be there for them. I'm still angry, but I understand. They made me understand. And maybe this had nothing to do with me, but it now has everything to do *with me*. Please. Let. Me. Help."

I wipe the weakness from my eyes and stare after him. He's magnificent and cruel, and far beyond anything I expected to face today. I was expecting my golden sun or my cool, dark cloud, and the thought of never seeing them again is too much to bear. I'm begging, and I shouldn't be. I should pack up and leave and kiss this whole town goodbye. Fuck my father and the bed he made. We have no relationship, and I could try to find another way, a safer way, to take care of my mother. But as the thought occurs, images of Sean and Dominic and the fear of the unknown cripples me. I can't bring myself to walk away. Not yet.

"I believe in this, in everything you're doing, in everything you stand for. I want in." It's the absolute truth, but I fear I've spoken up too late.

Back turned, he pulls my top from his pocket and frees it at his side before it falls to the deck. "I'll think about it."

Chapter Two

THE FIRST SIGN of autumn chill confirms his decision. And silence is my answer. It was always going to be no.

It's only been weeks since my confrontation with the hostile stranger, but it's the crisp air that plagues me with finality. No more summer nights beneath the stars with Dom; no more lengthy hikes with Sean. My love, affection, loyalty, and devotion mean nothing.

The end of the season marks the end of everything I've come to care about during my time here. It was just a little over three months, but I feel the change in myself, the change in my makeup. I'm so far from the curious girl I was when I arrived.

My reality is changing as rapidly as the foliage surrounding me in varying shades of brown, crimson red, and marigold. And in my state, I can't appreciate the beauty, only the message.

Summer isn't endless.

It's all over.

I started community college this week and threw myself into my studies. My shifts at the plant are more grueling now that Sean has quit—and he'd done so the minute after he left me in that office.

Just once I've given in to my curiosity and walked through the expanse of grass of Roman's back yard and into the wooded clearing—only to be met by utter silence. The picnic benches are gone, and the landscape's starting to rapidly grow over. It's as if it never happened. Aside from the new vegetation and the rustling of the trees, the space is void of life.

My tan has faded, and I know I've lost weight, my figure becoming gaunt as my heart shrivels, surviving only on memories from the months prior—months where granting smiles didn't feel like a chore.

It's my dreams that can sometimes bring relief. Dreams of long walks in a hazy cloud, of heated looks, of thunderstorms, and captive kisses. It's waking from them that leaves me raw, aching, grieving.

Melinda's been a surprising support, spending endless shifts updating me on all things Triple Falls, carefully avoiding conversation about those who I long to hear from the most.

Not that she would know.

Sean said he would make things right, but the pretense was one day.

One day.

A term so vague, so loose for interpretation that each day feels like a sentence.

The more days that pass, the more I realize it wasn't a promise or a guarantee, but more of a hope.

All of this heartbreak is because of two ghosts doing their job in haunting me. I've honored Sean's request. I never drive by the garage, never try to text either of them. It's pointless. They've made their decision and declared their loyalty. Our time together wasn't significant enough. *I* wasn't significant enough to cause a ripple in their agenda.

At least that's how their silence makes me feel.

My best friend Christy keeps me sane with long FaceTime talks of the future. Of our plans and the idea that, in a year, we'll resume them. It brings some comfort. This was only supposed to be a stopping point. As it turned out, it proved to be a leaping point, but right now, I have nowhere safe to land.

The longer they remain silent, the more my heart breaks.

I drift in and out of my days doing what I can, but every step, every tick of the clock weighs me down like a boulder in tidal waters. Every morning I shake off my dreams, determined to guard my heart, as if they haven't already ripped it apart. But the more leaves that fall, the more the pieces gather collectively, rattling in my chest.

I'd been a fool to think I knew heartbreak before, and maybe I have, but never have I felt I lost a piece of myself to it, until now.

I'm a drifter in my own life, living only for memories, for my dreams, reveling in the endless hurt, the ache of missing them, teetering on the edge of forgetting myself all over again. I came back determined to kick bad habits but hadn't expected to forgive them. I hadn't expected time to play the factor, to be the reason to let them go.

One day.

Today, I forced myself out of bed and mindlessly dressed, determined to try and spend a few hours outside of my head. Arriving downtown, I'm barely able to secure a parking spot before joining hordes of Triple Falls locals and tourists as they exit their cars with anticipatory smiles. Melinda has been talking about the apple festival nonstop, and when I round the corner and scour the square, I almost laugh.

It's a poor man's street fair at best. A small-town shindig made up of street vendors passing out tastes of local eateries and artists set up in tents with their works on display. It's a far cry from any large-scale city gathering, but upon entering, I decide it has its own charm. And of course, there are apples, locally grown and harvested. A quick glance at the logo on a tableside banner of the orchard Sean and I rendezvoused at for our midnight picnic levels me. The further I venture in, the more I regret coming, the walk back to the car becoming more tempting by the second. Memories of being worshiped between rows of angry trees surface, suffocating me, reminding me that I'm not the same girl I was when I arrived, and maybe I never will be. Instead of a quick retreat, I amble on the sidewalk along the rows of shops adjacent to the festival tents. I'm stopped short when a door opens as a group of guys walk out of a tattoo parlor. It's when I hear, "I know you," that I look up and into the eyes of a familiar face.

It takes me a few seconds to recall where I've seen it.

"RB, right?" He's taller than me by half a foot and towers over me with amused, warm, honey-colored eyes.

"Right," he says. "And you're Dom's girl."

"I . . ." I fumble, trying to think of an answer when my gaze zeroes in on the unbandaged ink sneaking up past his neckline—feather tips.

My eyes bulge as RB's smile goes wide, his eyes cooling considerably as his lips twist in condescension. He pulls at the soft white bandage, revealing fresh black wings gracing his arm, "Guess it's a good thing we don't all *think* like *you*."

Stunned, I try to come up with appropriate words, my demeanor brimming with mortification. He saw my fear that night, my hesitance, but mostly he saw me draw assumptions.

"Chin up, girl; don't cry about it."

I could give him a ton of excuses. I could mention that my fear stemmed from being in unfamiliar territory, from the unexpected appearance of a gun in Dom's lap, from their clipped exchange and the insinuation in their conversation, but none of it is good enough. I assumed the worst about both Dominic and RB. And I couldn't have been more wrong.

"I'm sorry."

A grin is his reply as he flexes his bird with pride. "I guess it makes a difference when you know I'm standing *beside you*. Respect to your boy, he saw it in me when we were *kids*."

Speechless, I try not to hang my head, and instead give him my eyes, hoping he can see the truth, that I am ashamed, that he's right. Once again, I've been schooled in a way that makes me uncomfortable, but I've learned it's the only way to grow. Sean taught me a lot over the last few months, but mostly he showed me the beauty of humility, and that's all I feel as I look up at RB.

One of his friends speaks up behind him, his arm covered in the same bandaging. "RB, we need to hit it, got shit to do."

Two new ravens.

And I envy them, because where they're going, I'm not allowed to follow.

I step up to the man addressing RB and hold out my hand. "Hi, I'm Cecelia."

He glances at my hand, amused before he takes it. "Terrance."

"Nice to meet you. Congrats."

He smirks, but there's no mistaking the pride in his eyes. "Thanks. You're Dom's girl?"

"Yes. Well, I was. I'm not sure anymore."

I look over to RB, my eyes imploring his, knowing wherever he is headed, he's going to lay eyes on the two men I'm desperate to see.

"I'm in no position to ask a favor, b-but when you . . . see them, when you see . . . Dominic—" I shake my head, knowing the message will never be delivered as I intend it. I haven't spoken to him since I discovered the truth about the death of his parents and my father's role in covering it up. "Never mind."

RB tilts his head, brows drawn, his light-brown eyes scanning me. "You sure?"

"Yeah."

"All right then, see you around?" he prompts, his question filled with insinuation before we share a small, conspiratorial smile.

"Hope so. One day," I say, hoping with all my heart that one day comes. That I can once again roam amongst the brotherhood freely, a privilege I'd taken for granted.

They walk away as I swallow the lump of remorse in my throat. And once again, the point hits home. As much as I think I know, I know nothing. Chest aching, mind reeling, I sidestep a stroller only to have cider spilled on me. A man two toddlers deep with no mother in sight apologizes while I brush the droplets off my arm.

"No worries," I assure, stepping off the curb onto Main Street. Herds of townspeople glide along the endless rows of vendor tents. Most all of them are wearing smiles, blissfully unaware that there is a war going on. That beyond some of their trees and state parks, there is a group of men fighting on their behalf so that the local economy can thrive, so the poachers don't get the best of them.

The longer I dwell on the last few months, the more my eyes open to what's been done and what's being done about it. A part of me wishes I could close them, erase what I now know, but doing that will erase my ghosts, and I'm still very much in love with them, now more than ever.

Even while my resentment grows for their absence and silence.

For everything they do, there is a reason. I can hate them for my unanswered questions, for making me doubt them, or I can trust what they revealed to me, what they begged me to believe, their admissions, and *in them*, before they vanished.

On sun-filled days I long for Sean, for his smile, his arms, his cock, and the laughter we shared. His warm, salty, nicotine-tinged kisses. The flick of his tongue on my skin. The slow winks he gave me acknowledging he knew what I was thinking. On stormy days, I long for my cloud to cover me, for the kisses that left me wanton, the hard thrashing of a tongue so wicked and smooth, for a half-smile that lights me up inside. For runny eggs and black coffee.

These men took me under their wing, taught by example, stirred my sexuality awake, and made themselves unforgettable. How am I supposed to move on from this?

For the life of me now, I can't go back to sleep.

Tears slip from my eyes as I start to unravel on the bustling streets while I force myself to try and adapt to the reality I've been tossed back into. Sniffling like an idiot, I navigate through the growing crowd in front of the town hall, where a band plays on an elevated stage blocking the entrance. A dozen or so couples, who look like they've been practicing all year, showcase their footwork, moving in sync as they dance in the street. I study the couple closest to me as they dance in tandem and smile at the other as if they're sharing a secret. And as I observe their wordless connection, all I feel is envy because I had that with both of them.

I had that.

And my secrets I'm forever obligated to keep. I'll never be able to share them. But I'll keep them because no one could truly understand their gravity or grasp their truth fully. The story itself would sound like some unrealistic, twisty, sexually provocative fairy tale with a bad ending, or worse, no ending at all.

When I got here, I wanted to suspend my strict morals and loosen my chastity, to thrive amongst some chaos.

I got my wish.

I should be grateful.

But I'm not, so I mourn.

And I can't do it here.

One foot in front of the other, I push through the crowd to get away, away from all of the smiles, and the laughing and the content people who have no idea about the battle I'm fighting not to scream at them to wake the fuck up.

Which would make me just another quack. The irony not lost on me. But if they only knew how much these men are risking daily, maybe they'd listen. Perhaps they'd band with them, join their cause.

Or maybe they're the intelligent ones, aware of the tyranny but purposefully choosing to ignore it. It wasn't long ago I was blissfully unaware.

The battle of good and evil isn't news. In fact, it's broadcast in plain sight every day. But at this point, even the news is unreliable, often projected in a way that requires deciphering fact from agenda-related fiction. But we choose to acknowledge what we want, and these people seem to have chosen wisely. Maybe my answer isn't to get away, but become one of them, to blend in and play ignorant to all that's wrong in this fucked-up world so I can breathe a little easier, so one day, I can mindlessly smile again. But as time passes, it's becoming more and more apparent that that's wishful thinking, because I can't go back.

The men in my life pried my eyes open, made me aware of the war they've declared. And I know now if I were faced with the choice, I would scream my decision—*all in*. Forever in.

On the edge of the crowd near an alley between buildings, my attention gets diverted to the band whose lead singer greets us, some ear-piercing feedback coming out of the mic before he apologizes.

"And now that we have your attention—" he chuckles as the sound clears before he cues the drummer—"let's start this off right."

As the music starts to play and the ring of guitar and bass kicks in, I blot my face and nose into the arm of my thin sweater.

I'm an emotional mess in the fucking street at the apple festival.

I can't do this. Not yet.

The lead starts to belt out some upbeat lyrics and I absorb them out of habit as he sings of being lost, falling on hard times, and encourages us to keep on smiling. I can't help my ironic laugh as another warm tear slides down my face, and I wipe it away with my sleeve.

Yeah, I'm out.

One day.

Turning in the direction I parked, I'm captured by a hand on my hip. I dart my gaze behind me just as the scent of cedar and nicotine surrounds me. A shocked exhale bursts out of me, and I use it to my advantage and take a huge inhale, melting into his chest just as warm breath hits my ear. "Good one."

His hand slides down to grip the wrist dangling at my side, and in the next second, I'm turned around and standing chest-to-chest with Sean.

"Hey, Pup."

Fresh tears fill my eyes as I gape at him, his sparkling eyes dimming when he reads my expression.

"What are you—"

Before I can get my question out, he snakes his arm around my waist and clasps his free hand with mine before leading us to the edge of the crowd.

"What in the hell are you doing?" I whisper-shout. He wedges his knee between mine and dips low, one bounce, two. I stand limp in his arms as he squeezes our clasped hands.

"Come on, Pup," he pleads as we start to gather attention. He rocks us in perfect time, dipping and swaying, urging me to do the same. "Come on, baby," he prompts, his smile starting to fade when I remain immobile, "give me a sign of life."

Butterflies swarm as he beckons me, impossible to ignore while rocking back on his heels with a sexy tilt in his hips. In the next step, I give in, letting the music fuel me as I dip with him and begin swiveling my hips. He winks at me in encouragement before he does a swift turn, gripping my hand behind his back and executing the move with ease. A few

onlookers next to us call out with words of encouragement
and cheers as a blush creeps up my neck. But this is Sean,
his superpower, and he's mastered it. So, I do the only thing
I can. I give in to him.

And then we're dancing, while he sings to me. His perfect
physique sways along to the pace-setting bass, just as a
harmonica chimes in. We rock along the crowded street, our
footing effortless as we collectively twist apart before falling
easily back together. We dance like we've been doing it for
years, not a couple of months. Clear pride gleams in his
emerald eyes when he sees me lighting up from within.
Mid-song, the music suddenly stops as do the dancers
surrounding us, and hands fly up as they collectively scream
the lyrics, a pause hanging in the air a split second before
everyone explodes back into motion.

I've never heard the song before, but I know I'll never
forget it—the lyrics far too ironic. They speak to me on the
innermost level. And I take it for the gift it is. It's here on
Main Street that we steal time and fall back into one another,
and just . . . dance. Together, we own our stolen moment
and ignore the fucked-up world around us, our circumstances, and the odds stacked up against us. And for those
short minutes of Indian summer, I breathe a little easier, and
the ache lessens.

Nothing matters but me and my golden sun and the love
I feel for him. I shake my head ironically as he struts us
around, defiant, daring anyone to try and mess with our
moment. It's then I know we won't let them, or anyone else,
ruin what we have. When the song ends, the crowd around
us erupts in cheers as he leans in and takes my face in his
hands. He bends briefly, a breath away before he claims my

lips in a kiss so sincere that the ache I just evaded gives way to agony.

Instinctively I know, today isn't *one day*.

"I gotta go," he murmurs in my ear, his hands pushing away the hair at my shoulder as his eyes beg for understanding.

"No, please—"

"I have to. I'm sorry." I shake my head and drop my gaze as waiting tears start to fall. He tips my chin and searches my eyes, devastation in his own. "Please, Pup, eat—" he swipes his thumb across my chin—"dance, sing, smile."

"Please don't go." Expression somber, he presses a gentle kiss to my lips, a sob erupting from me, breaking it all too soon. "Sean, wait—"

It's when he releases me that I palm my face, an agonized cry erupting from me as his warmth disappears.

Choking, I shake my head in my hands, unable to stand the clear rip tearing straight through my chest. My tears soak my palms as the crowd rallies around me, and I feel every step he takes away from me.

I can't let go. I can't do this.

Pulling my hands away, I look for any sign of the direction he went as I begin to push through the growing crowd, unwilling to let him leave me, unwilling to let that dance be our last because it will never be enough. My heart seizes when I lose sight of him. I turn in a circle searching in every direction, getting swallowed by a mob as they rush the stage. Struggling through swarms of bodies, I start to panic.

"Sean!" I scream, looking in every direction before I catch a flash of spiky blond hair and give chase.

"Sean!" I push through a family, nearly knocking down

a little boy with sticky hands full of candied apple. I right him and apologize before I dash through in the direction Sean went. Turning in circles, I spot a bench nearby and leap onto it, combing the sidewalks and nearby alleys.

"No, no, no!" Panic consumes me when I come up empty. Ears pricked; I search fruitlessly until I hear the faint but distinct rumble of an engine roar to life. I leap in the direction of it and run down an alley before I round the corner. It's there I slam into an invisible wall when I'm met with a silver stare. Dominic leans against Sean's Nova, his arms crossed as he drinks me in. Sean spots me from where he stands on the opposite side of the car, taking one last look at me across the hood before he climbs into the driver's seat. My gaze drifts back to Dominic as his eyes trail me from head to foot. Heart lurching, I take a tentative step forward, and he jerks his head, refusing me.

"Please," I whisper, knowing he can clearly read the plea on my lips as my tears fall rapidly. Emotions reflect in his silver eyes as he lets me in fully, his fingers twitching at his sides. I know he wants to erase the space, to erase the water pouring between us.

"Please," I beg, unable to handle the ache. "Please, Dom, please don't go," I cry out to him. I can feel the struggle in his refusal as he slowly shakes his head in reply. It's his eyes, not his posture that conveys the most. In his gaze I see longing, regret, and resentment for our collective positions. And it's enough. It has to be.

I hadn't imagined his affection for me. I hadn't imagined a minute we spent together. No one can cheapen or dismiss what we had. No one. And I won't ever let anyone take it away from me.

But I get no assurances from either of them as I stand there—bleeding out—and that's what terrifies me the most.

Dominic tugs at the handle behind him and opens the door while Sean keeps his gaze trained forward, either to grant us this time or because he can't look at me any longer. It brings me no comfort. I drink in Dominic one last time and let him see my tears, my love. Covering my chest with both hands, I close my eyes and mouth the truth.

"I love you."

It's when I open them that I see his raw reaction to my confession. He takes a step forward, his face marred with indecision a second before he snaps our connection and joins Sean in the car. And in the next breath, they disappear.

It's then I know whatever battle they fought to keep me in, they lost.

And "one day" may never come.

Chapter Three

THERE'S A SCENE in one of the *Twilight* movies where Bella remains unmoving in a chair—riddled in heartbreak—while staring out the window, watching the seasons pass before her eyes. And on my balcony, as the trees shed and deaden before giving new life to fresh blooms, I realized I'd lived the past three seasons of my life much the same way she did when she was deserted by love.

Love may have had its way with me last summer, but when the first snow began to drift toward the ground, it was my hate that grew. Hatred for a nameless man who's taken a large part of my happiness away by putting me in a state of exile.

Now when I ache for those who deserted me, I replace it with loathing for the fire-eyed man who gave an executive order to keep me in my respective place—which is nowhere.

The holidays came and went, and I went home. I spent winter break with my mother and Christy, all the while nursing my shattered heart, a heart filled to the brim with love without a soul to shower it on. And not once in that time did I regret a minute with either of them.

I was thankful.

I was grateful.

I knew myself better because of that experience with them. It wasn't just a summer but a season of discovery. I imagine most people go through life never exploring themselves as in-depth as I did. Those days of lust-filled trysts and nights I spent with my lovers beneath a canopy of green trees and twinkling stars reshaped me.

As the minutes, hours, days, and months passed, I didn't spring back to life. I simply went through the motions.

I kept my memories close, until one day I forced myself to start living again. School was easy, and my job was made easier the closer I got with Melinda and a few others in the night crew. None of the brotherhood spoke to me—none of them. Whether in town at a gas pump, or a chance meeting anywhere else, I was invisible to those who had the marking. I hadn't just lost my boys, I'd lost my friends too, including Layla, and everyone else associated with the brotherhood.

The bastard kept his promise. I've been completely on my own.

The more time that passes, the more I decide I'm better off. Any communication or association with anyone related to Sean and Dominic would only give me hope of a future that isn't coming.

At the end of spring, I've successfully completed my first two semesters of college with a near-perfect GPA and am now on the last leg of my year working for my father. I'm three-quarters of the way to honoring our deal with only a few months to go.

One summer left in Triple Falls, and I will be free of Roman Horner and my obligations to him, and my mother will be financially set.

Freedom is close.

Roman hasn't returned from Charlotte since our last exchange, and I don't expect him to. He hasn't made so much as an effort past a weekly email. As I suspected, he never lived here. If anything, this house seems to have been blue-printed as a shrine to his success.

By this summer's end, I'll no longer have to deal with the lingering anxiety about a possible face-to-face. Not only that, but I'll also have a large portion of his fortune signed over to me, and our ties will be severed.

Oddly enough, I'm in no hurry to flee Triple Falls.

The town and its people have grown on me. I no longer mind the monotony of my workdays. But now that the semester is over, my days off are my own again, and filling them is becoming a hard task.

I've been spending them wisely.

I hike, and often. Never on the trails that Sean took me to; I'm no longer a masochist in that sense. But I've grown stronger, my muscles no longer screaming after long treks in the woods and up mountain cliffs. I've brushed up on my French with my app, determined to eventually spend my summers abroad with the aid of a flush bank account. And now that the temperature has stopped lingering on brisk, I've resumed sunning, swimming, and reading out in Roman's courtyard.

I've allowed myself to dream up a new normal, having last-call beers with my coworkers and attending a few of Melinda's family functions just to pass the time. I'm trying hard to be a present friend to her, the way she has been for me.

But tonight presents a new hurdle. After eight months of painful silence from both my lost loves, I agreed to a date.

After a scalding shower, I line my lips shimmering-red while recalling Sean tracing them stretched around his cock, stifling the memory of the sounds he made, his pleasured grunts, his long exhale when he came.

"You have a date. A date, Cecelia." I close my eyes, hindered with memories of my last one.

Dominic's barely there smile crosses my mind as I vividly recall tracing his muscled skin with my bare toes in the front seat of his Camaro.

Cursing, I grab some tissue and wipe away the smudge in my lip liner.

"Date, Cecelia. Concentrate on your date. His name is Wesley. And he's polite, educated, and hot."

Not Sean hot. Not Dominic hot. And despite my immense hatred for him, no man on Earth is The Frenchman hot.

And fuck him for it.

Every time I think about that arrogant bastard, my blood boils. I may never get his audience again, but I refuse to let him have the power he once did over me. He took my happiness away without a second thought, passed his judgment and inhumane sentence before he strode away. Months ago, I would have gone along with any of his plans just to be near them. But time has been on my side. It's healed me. It's strengthened me and enraged me.

I dare him to cross my path because of the way he single-handedly ripped us apart.

But Sean and Dominic allowed it—and to me, that is unforgivable.

These grudges I hold close, they keep me objective, in hindsight. They also keep me angry and resentful—all tools I need for forward progress. One day, when I don't need the anger, I'll forgive them for the way they hurt me, for myself. But it's not happening any time soon.

Shaking my head, I concentrate on my eyes, going heavy on my mascara. My headspace is all wrong for this, and I know it. But I need this last step. I need to get back out there.

I've stopped waiting for "one day" in exchange for a "someday" and "some other".

And maybe that "some other" is Wesley.

On the vanity, my phone rattles with an incoming message. I buzz Wesley in, opting not to give him the gate code. Lesson learned on that front.

Filled with anticipation, I take the stairs in a new curve-hugging halter dress my favorite shop owner helped me pick out. Primed for possibility, I run my fingers through my hair as I reach the door.

I just want to laugh again without the sad pause of recollection at the end of it. Without erasing from my present by lingering in the past. I just want to feel some sort of closeness again, one that has *nothing* to do with the men who refuse to exit my dreams, the way they have my life. More than that, I want to see if I'm capable of feeling a flutter, an inkling, any sign of life other than acknowledging the beating my heart has taken.

Just knowing there is a chance will be enough.

"Please," I whisper to anyone listening. "Just a jolt, a whisper, *something*," I plea just as Wesley pulls up and steps out of his truck. It's when his brown eyes rake over me and flare before he flashes me a set of perfect teeth, that I know, for me, the date is already over.

*

Nothing.

That's what I felt. Absolutely nothing. Not during dinner, and not now when Wesley takes my hand in his while walking me back to his truck. Not a flutter, nor a single ounce of anticipation when he opens the passenger door and gently pushes my hair away from my face before leaning in.

That gesture triggers me, and I turn my head at the last second, unable to bear it. It isn't Sean's caress, and they aren't Dominic's lips. Wesley dips his chin and looks over to me.

"You've been hurt?"

"I'm sorry. I thought I was ready."

"It's okay. Just . . . I felt like you weren't really with me when I was talking at dinner, and I couldn't shut the fuck up."

"It's not you . . ." I cringe, and know shooting him would have been more merciful by the change in his expression.

He has the good grace to chuckle. "Ouch."

I want to crawl beneath his truck. Instead, he helps lift me into the cab and leans in. "It's okay, Cecelia, I've been there."

I gaze over at him, guilt-ridden. "I'll pay for my half of dinner."

"Just how much do you intend on insulting me tonight? And what kind of assholes have you been dating?"

Unforgettable assholes with a side of motherfucker.

"I wouldn't blame you at this point if you make me take a cab home."

"You're painfully honest, but I like that." He bites his lip, his eyes lifting to mine. "Painfully beautiful, too. I'll just be flattered that I was your first attempt. And maybe—" he shrugs—"we can try again sometime."

"I'd like that."

We both know it's a lie, but I rest easier in it as I click

my seat belt while he rounds his truck. A silence ensues when he joins me, messing with his radio on our ride back. I'm thankful when he finally speaks up. "So, was it someone from around here?"

"No. It's just some asshole I dated back home in Georgia." The lies are getting easier to tell. But the truth is not an option.

Wesley leaves me at my front door with a friendly hug and an offer to call him when I'm ready. As he drives off, I curse my faithful heart and slam the front door, aggravated with myself.

Disheartened, I haul myself up the stairs and into my bedroom. Sliding my sandals off, I pull my cell out of my purse and shoot off a message to Christy.

Project Get On With It was a complete failure.

Christy: Don't give up, babe. Whoever it is will be a Band-Aid right now anyway.

I'm still not ready.

Christy: Then you're not ready. Don't rush it. You'll get there.

What's going on with you tonight?

Christy: Netflix and chilling ;-). I'll tell you all about it tomorrow.

Go, girl. And you better. Love you. Night. X

I decide to make peace with my progress. I went on a date, successful or not. It's a start.

After plugging my cell in on my nightstand, I pull the

covers back, sit on the edge of the bed and run my feet through the plush carpet.

Attempting to live a "normal" life after two octane-fueled relationships is exhausting. All these months later, I still miss the chaotic nights, the mystery, the anticipation, the connection, and the sex. God, the sex.

I've given myself enough time to grieve. If my heart would just follow my head, I'd be so much better off. I run my fingers across my untouched lips and decide to opt for a morning shower to scrub off my makeup. Tossing the throw pillows off my comforter, I move to settle in with a new book and freeze when I see the metal pendant waiting on my pillow.

Wrapping my fingers around it, I bring it to eye-level, disbelieving of the weight of it and what it means before shooting off my mattress. My heart rockets into motion as I scan my room.

"Sean? Dominic?"

I walk into the bathroom. Empty.

The balcony. Empty.

Desperately, I search the house only to find all the doors are locked.

Not that that could stop them; it never has. The proof lies in my hand.

Hope soaring, I secure the clasp around my neck and dash toward the back door. Gathering my rain boots from the hall tree, I shove them on and grab the pocket flashlight from my slicker. Seconds later, I scan the courtyard with the weak beam.

"Sean? Dominic?"

Nothing.

I make a beeline for the woods, past the football field of newly cropped grass, the warm metal on my neck giving me the first inkling of hope amongst the wreckage. I'm nearing a sprint by the time I reach the small hill leading up into the trees and the clearing.

The sight that greets me there takes my breath away. Tall grasses sway before me littered with yellow-green light from hundreds of fireflies. They float from the brush into the thick branches, glittering like diamonds high above before disappearing in the beam of the full moon.

"Sean?" I search every corner of the clearing, scanning every shadow in the trees with the flashlight. "Dominic?" I call out softly, in prayer that one or both is waiting for me. "I'm here," I announce, searching the dark forest for any sign of life, the light in my hand doing little to aid me. "I'm here," I say, fingering the cut of the necklace.

"I'm here," I repeat in vain, to no one.

There's no one here but me.

Utterly confused, I turn in dizzying circles, searching, hoping, praying for any sign of life, and come up empty.

All the hope I felt just minutes before scatters on the wind, rustling through the tall, shimmering pines above me. But I don't dwell in the ache. Instead, I palm my chest and watch the symphony of light playing both above and at my booted feet, their melody soundless, but captivating. Entranced by the moon and light show, I thumb the raven's wing between my thumb and forefinger.

One or both has claimed me as their own.

Someone put the necklace on my pillow.

I call out for them once more.

"Sean? Dominic?" The air seems to still around me as an

inkling of a presence hits, *hard*. I go ramrod straight when a deep voice laced with French brogue sounds from feet away.

"Sorry to disappoint you."

Chapter Four

H E EMERGES FROM the shadows of the thick cluster of
trees to my left. I back away, clicking on my flashlight
and aiming the beam at him.

"What do you want?"

"Want? From you, *nothing*." Disdain drips from his tone
as he comes into full view.

With the help of my pocket light, I can see his face
clearly, not a single shadow clouding the smooth planes,
strong nose, or the angular cut of his jaw. Too bad I hate
him, or I could appreciate the beauty of his mask. I click
off my light, willing the shadows to swallow him, but even
in the darkness he shimmers in masculine beauty under
the brilliant moon and amongst the fairy-like bugs that
surround us. He's dressed much like he was when I met
him, save the jacket and skinny black tie. He looks
completely out of place in a button-down, slacks, and polished
shoes.

"What are you doing here? Dressed like that?"

"I could ask you the same."

I'm still dressed for my date, save for my polka-dotted

rain boots, in full makeup and hair. Equally as overdressed for a midnight stroll in the woods. "I live here."

"No, you don't."

"Semantics. And these aren't your stomping grounds anymore."

"I'll stomp anywhere I fucking want." His eyes are filled with the same flaming cruelty I remember from our run-in last year. His voice just as thick with condescension and grudge. And as easy as it would be to walk away, I want him to know that I've made my mind up about him, just as much as he has regarding me.

"You're disgusting. This air about you." I hold up my palm and wave it. "Like you have some right to act this way, to treat me any way you want to."

"Is this going to be a 'do unto others' speech? Because I guarantee you've fucked me enough by existing."

"You're ridiculous, and not at all worthy of a conversation."

"You forget who you're talking to."

"Yeah, well, you can tuck your cock back in, asshole. This isn't a pissing contest."

"You have a disgusting mouth."

"You're a prick and a bastard, and my mouth and manners belong to civilized humans, not entitled sociopaths with zero compassion."

He towers above me now, his scent invading. He's got both Sean and Dominic beat by a few inches. His build is monstrous, menacing, like he went straight from infant to man, no in-between.

"You're a little girl with a filthy mouth. And if I'm not worthy of a conversation, then why are you still arguing with me?"

"Good point. Go fuck yourself." I step away from him just as his hand shoots out and snags my wrist in a vise grip. I struggle against it, but his eyes aren't on me; they've zeroed in on the raven's wing dangling from my neck.

"What is this?"

I can't help my smile. "I think you know full well what *this* is."

"Who gave this to you?"

"None of your business. Let me go."

He jerks me closer and I drop my flashlight, clawing at the hand binding me to him just as his other reaches up to where my necklace rests. When I see his intent, I go feral. My free palm connects with his face, burning hot as I rear back to slap him harder. "Don't you fucking dare!"

I'm no match for the brute when he jerks me flush to him, shaking me like a rag doll, jarring me, before tossing me onto the grass and straddling me.

"GET OFF ME!" I screech at the top of my lungs, fighting him, dragging my nails along his button-down, unable to find purchase in his skin. He overpowers me easily as if he's fighting a gnat while he pins my wrists to the cool grass.

Hovering above, his eyes grow molten with fury. "Tell me right fucking now who gave this to you."

I spit at him and congratulate myself when it nails him on the jaw. He effortlessly gathers my wrists with one hand, pressing them into the ground before wiping the saliva off, on the shoulder of his shirt. It's then I see the flash of teeth and realize the bastard is . . . smiling, in a way that makes me nauseous.

"I've ended lives for less."

"You don't scare me. You're nothing but a huge body and an empty head."

His dark chuckle sends a shiver down my spine. "You don't even know you're wet yet." His heated whisper sets off new warning bells. "Maybe I should have waited until you discovered it yourself, until you slipped off your panties and agonized over it."

"Fuck you."

He leans in, the scent of spiced citrus and leather filling my nose. "Have you been lonely, Cecelia?"

"Get off me." I struggle against him, using every bit of my strength to no avail.

"Playtime is over. Who gave you the necklace?"

"If I knew, I wouldn't tell you."

Shit. Shit. Shit.

"You don't know." His full lips stretch with an infuriating smirk. "This is epic. You don't know which."

He leans in, his voice filled with another damning promise. "I'll make sure you *never* know." He grips the necklace as I fight with everything left in me.

"Don't, don't! Please, don't!" I beg, ripping at his hand when the metal clasp digs into the back of my neck just before it gives way and snaps. Enraged, I scream out at the loss. Fury-filled tears burn my eyes as he rips me in half with one single act.

"Why? Why? That was mine. He loves me!"

"Who . . . *who* loves you, Cecelia?"

"It's for me, for my protection! It's my promise!"

"Who do you need protection from?"

You.

But I don't dare say it. It doesn't matter if I give him the power to terrorize me or not; he's not a man to ask permission.

"These are your laws! You're not allowed to fuck with that. He chose me!"

"You're pathetic." He releases me and stands with the broken necklace and peers down at me. "You think a trinket can protect you? It means nothing."

"It means something to me!"

"You're a little girl with a crush."

"I'm a twenty-year-old *woman*, you ignorant bastard." I stand to face off with him despite the shake in my legs. "And I belong to him."

"Because he says so? You have no say. You're warped. And no, sweetheart, you don't. He's my brother."

"Your brother, my ass. He's just a boy you built a fort with before you reached puberty. You're what . . . breaching thirty? And still running around slaying imaginary dragons while playing *Lord of the Manor*."

"Believe what you want, but you've seen what we're capable of."

"Petty theft and throwing parties? That's no big feat." I'm lying through my teeth, but I don't want him to know just how much I do know. "And I *know* who I belong to."

He bends so we're eye level. "You sure?"

"I love him."

"*Name* him."

"It doesn't matter—"

"Yeah, yeah, you love them both. I've heard this speech—save your breath."

"You're going to pay for hurting me like this."

"You think so, huh?" He looks around. "And who exactly is coming to save you?"

I feel that truth's edge slice deep. He's right. Neither is

here to save me from this mad bastard. But they taught me well to protect myself.

As if he's reading my thoughts, he drops his voice, his threat clear. "I assure you I've gotten away with a lot worse." The curl of his French accent—combined with his open hostility—somehow makes his threat more dangerous. But I don't back away; I've let my hate fester for months, and I'm all too ready to unleash it.

"Why are you so angry, sir? Did I interrupt you killing and torturing small animals? It's Friday night and you have nothing better to do than stalk *little girls* with crushes? Who's pathetic?"

I gather my strength, straightening my posture, my anger boiling over. "You're nothing but a scared little boy turned control freak because he didn't get enough attention as a child."

One second, I'm standing; in the next, I'm off my feet and flat on my back. My heart stops beating as the breath is knocked out of me just as my mouth is brutalized by something resembling a kiss. He weights every inch of me as he attacks my lips, separating them with the thrust of his tongue. Frozen, eyes wide, his licks invade, and I sputter and choke. Fully in control, he keeps my kiss before stealing them all, erasing the last kiss Sean gave, and the one before it, erasing Dominic's torturous tongue play. And I fight, I fight clinging onto those kisses with everything inside me as they drift through my flailing fingers, and out of my grasp. The loss and hate fuel me as I try to turn my head and deny him, which he makes impossible.

With every stab of his tongue, he plunders, gathering me wholly, and with the next lick, takes me as captive. All at once, I'm thrust into a raging fire. The heat expending my walls until they collapse, smoke clouding me as I lay powerless beneath him engulfed by blue flames.

It's carnal oblivion I sink into as I lose the fight to regain my breath. His torturous licks are unforgiving as he feeds mercilessly on my mouth. A whimper escapes my lips as it consumes me, a raging inferno until finally it's snuffed out.

Until I'm snuffed out.

And reborn with a violent kiss.

A kiss that breathes life back into me, a life that's withered to nothingness during months of neglect and isolation. Beneath him, my treacherous body betrays me with the undeniable shift in intensity, the hunger starting low, unfurling through my limbs. My tongue meets his, dueling viciously, just as unforgiving as I fuck my enemy with my mouth, my thighs falling open as he shifts and thrusts his erection against my ravenous body.

Coupled outrage and lust has me fighting now for a different reason altogether, clutching him, clawing him, to bring him closer, puncturing his scalp with my fingernails as I angle my head to give him access.

Still struggling for breath, I steal his, our tongues battling as he licks into my mouth with dominance and abandon.

Insatiable lust overtakes me, and I get swept into the dark undertow allowing myself to sink within. Trapped, I feed inside the wave drinking in a new kind of air, renewed with a greedy mouth, my body swelling, opening, welcoming. I hike my legs around his hips as he glides his cock along my entrance. The thin material between us doing little to shield me from direct contact. Back arching, I'm pulsating everywhere. My breasts grow heavy, and my nipples draw tight.

Clit throbbing, I clutch him to me as he bruises and conquers, his touch void of any tenderness. But I'm fine with that because I know just a hint of it would ruin me.

Mortified by the thought, I rip my lips away and gape up at him.

"S-stop," I stutter out, terrified by just how much I want this. He ignores my useless words as I try again to wage war on the lust that's destroying me. He swats my fumbling hands and dips his head, biting my neck, and then my shoulder before taking the whole of my breast into his mouth, soaking the thin cotton beneath. My nipple peaks to stone as he pulls his head away, only giving enough time to lower the material with rough hands, yanking down my bra so my breasts are pulled taut in offering. He dips and sucks one into his mouth before I feel the bite as he pierces it with a sharp tooth.

A breath later, my skirt is lifted as his fingers press painfully into my thigh while I fumble with his belt. It's the clink of a buckle that has me freezing, and in the next second I'm abruptly released. Mouth gaping, I retreat, sliding back on my ass as his predatory gaze follows. I'm sure the horror of the act I just committed is written all over my face. Chest heaving, breasts bared, I shake my head furiously as he yanks me back beneath him easily by the boot. He dips and kisses me again, his tongue coated in metal, probing, exploring all the places he should never be allowed to reach, including those untouched. When he rips his mouth away, we face-off, our ragged breathing the only sound between us.

"Tu n'y connais rien à la fidélité." *You don't know the first thing about loyalty.*

Though unable to interpret this fully, I know whatever venom he's spewing is insulting. I move to slap him, and he catches my hand, biting into the flesh of my palm. I can't hold my whimper as he again thrusts his rock-hard erection against me, the feel of his length against my soaked clit dragging me to the edge. With the next thrust of his hips, I teeter on the brink of orgasm. "Tu ne peux pas échapper à la vérité. Tu me veux." *You can't escape the truth. You want me.*

He pulls me to kneel and does the same before he grips my hands, hooking my fingers on the band of his pants. Breaths coming out like we've just run a marathon; I glare up at him as he raises thick brows in challenge. "Your move."

I rip my hands away as he chuckles darkly. "I wonder how your *boyfriends* would feel if they knew you kissed me back."

I did. I kissed him back and more. Far more than that.

I wanted him.

There's no booze to blame, no scapegoat.

Inside, I wither and die. Outside, I kneel in a puddle of ruin as he shoots a smirk down at me.

"They'll hate you."

"Is that so? Tell me, Cecelia, where are they?"

He fastens his belt before pushing to his feet, leaving me kneeling before him. "I could've fucked you, and you know it. You can't be loyal even to those who you proclaim to *love*." His foreign lilt turns the word into something putrid, a complete opposition to its meaning. It's then he drops the necklace to eye level where it dangles from his fingers, wickedly taunting me. "Still think you deserve your declaration, *his* devotion?"

My chin wobbles, my lips painfully swollen, as I try to grapple with what just happened. "I hate you."

"I don't give a fuck."

"Please." I look away from the necklace he's holding in an attempt to right myself, my dress, searching for the dignity he stole. "Just leave me alone."

I can't meet his eyes. He knows he's won. And I'm not sure I would have been strong enough to keep my virtue safe with either of the men I swore my heart, my allegiance, to. For nearly a year, I've been committed to them. Honored our memories, remained faithful without any inclination that my affection was returned, until tonight, until I saw that necklace. And in a matter of minutes, I ruined it.

I ruined it by kissing a monster lurking in the shadows and letting him feed off me, off my weakness.

And I participated.

What the hell is wrong with me?

Am I what he's accusing me of? Am I just some stupid girl with a crush on two men she fooled around with last summer? Ten minutes ago, I would have said that was impossible and meant it with my whole being.

Now?

No.

No, I can't let him win. He's toying with me, and I won't let him dismiss what I feel to entertain some sick head game. I know better. I was taught better.

"It's a shame your date didn't go well, but you're going to have to find someone else to play with, Cecelia."

I don't bother to ask him how he got privy to that information, and it's clear he's in on every secret, including mine. His invasion of my privacy only proves he doesn't trust me at all.

He's been watching me. *Closely.* And I was a fool to think otherwise.

It's also a clear indication he still views me as a threat.

Thinking on my toes, I stand and close the space between us. My urge to fight is overwhelming, and so, for the first time in months, I fully let my devil out. I drop my gaze to the bulge between his thighs.

"You're still hard."

His amber eyes flare in warning. "Means nothing."

"You wanted me just as much. *Still do*. If I'm such a stupid, silly girl, why are you so anxious to take your *brothers'* place in my bed?"

"I was proving a point."

"Tell that to your cock." I slap his chest and glide my palm down his toned stomach. He doesn't flinch, but he doesn't move, either. Gripping him in my hand, I note the width, the girth, and train my features not to react. He would have torn me in half had he taken me as roughly as he kissed me.

I grip him harder and hear the breath leave him. A tiny victory I don't bother to celebrate.

"Before you go—" I stroke him roughly with one hand while sliding the other around his backside—"at least have the decency to let me know the name of my enemy."

He doesn't bother with a reply before stepping out of my grip. He swings the loose chain of the necklace in his palm before he pockets it.

"Just as well. I'm sure I'll have a hell of a good time finding out." His eyes narrow, dominance rolling off him.

"Do your worst," he taunts, all too comfortable with what he believes is his upper hand.

And that's when I step away and drop the leather between us. He flicks his attention down, and I revel in the light of surprise when his eyes widen at the sight of the wallet in the grass. Dashing out of his reach, I retrieve my pocket light from where I dropped it, lifting the ID into view.

"Jeremy taught me this trick," I smirk as I study the ID. "Charm them in the front while you fuck them in the back. I'm a quick study, Ezekiel Tobias . . ."

No. No. No. No!

"*King,*" he says, the victory once again his as he slaps the flashlight from my hand before ripping his ID from my fingers. "Tobias *King.* Dominic's *brother.*"

The truth stabs me like a dull blade.

"That's not . . . he would have . . . "

"Told you? No, he wouldn't. And now it's *your cross* to bear too. So, I wouldn't fucking disclose that information to anyone if I were you."

"I don't know anything."

"Sean told you plenty."

Praying to God I didn't flinch at his words, I toss my shoulders back. "I don't know what you're talking about."

"Oh, you don't? Is that why you inquired about your father's safety in our first conversation? Lying to me is not helping your cause. But damn near everything he told you is common knowledge in this town."

Sean also told me my father was enemy number one, which led me to the theory that my father is most likely the reason behind The Ravenhood.

Think of it as a promise.

A promise. A promise between two young orphans and their friends to exact revenge at just the right time. Dominic told me he was almost six when they died. Tobias isn't much older. Sean had said they'd been patient. Because they had to be; they had to grow up first, educate themselves, build an army.

"But you don't look . . ." There's not much of a resemblance aside from their hair and skin color. Where Dominic is sleek in his features, Tobias is hard lines and broad planes. I assumed they were related somehow due to the French connection, but never brothers. Sean had confessed at the plant that Dominic's mother was fleeing her ex-husband.

"You're half-brothers."

He tucks his ID back into his wallet, ignoring my question.

"I'm right, aren't I? You share a mother."

"Doesn't fucking matter—he's a weakness." His voice is lethal when he speaks, his warning clear. "And yours too, so if you mean what you say, you don't utter a word to anyone."

Anyone with a grudge could use Dominic to get to Tobias.

"*No one* knows? I find that hard to believe. You grew up here."

He's old enough to have left Triple Falls years ago. And he wasn't close. If so, it wouldn't have taken him so long to find out about me.

"You weren't here in the US. You weren't close. Were you in France?"

He remains mute, confirming my suspicions.

"That picture wasn't you; it's your father, right?" He's not even using a real picture in a government-issued ID? Or is it fake? This shit is something out of a spy novel, not real life.

"So, you share a mother? But you took Dominic's father's last name? Why?"

More silence. But if his mother fled France because of *his* father . . .

"I'm guessing your father is more of a monster than you are?"

"Watch it," he snaps. I've hit a nerve, a very big nerve.

"So, you were in France the whole time? Doing what?" I run my hands through my hair. "Jesus. How far does this go?"

"You don't want to know." He cocks his head. "We're not playing a game with toy guns, extra lives, and Monopoly money. We left the fort and torched any trace it existed a long time ago, Cecelia."

It all makes sense. He's remained faceless in a faceless and nameless organization because he's the man behind the curtain. I'm sure of it.

And in order to reign, if he is the mastermind, then there's definitely a pecking order. If so, Sean is the equivalent of a foot soldier, and Dominic is both brains and—by his behavior—the henchman.

But Tobias is the devil you meet only when you've fucked up to the point of no return.

There's a change in his tone, and it's grave. I take it at face value. This goes so much further than anything I could have imagined.

And I want no part of it. Not anymore. Not without them.

I've lost half my mind due to heartbreak alone.

"I can't pay for my father's mistakes. It's hard enough being his daughter. But I'm sorry, okay? I'm sorry about your parents. And for whatever part Roman played. It's not my place to apologize, but it's not my place to *pay for it*, either. Your war is with him."

I sigh, my limbs drained from the struggle. "I'm here for

my mother. I'm here to ensure she's cared for and will want for nothing. She's ill. I'm sure Sean told you as much." I close my eyes briefly. "Or maybe he didn't, but that's my purpose here, the reason why I'm still here. She's my priority, and I can't imagine losing her. So, I'm sorry it happened. But for the last time, I'm not your enemy."

Skin stinging from his bite, body swollen with desire, I shake my head in aggravation.

"I know you don't give a shit about me because you just ripped any amount of safety you yourself could guarantee from my neck. Jesus, this is so fucked." I walk to the edge of the clearing, intent on keeping what's left of my sanity. "I'm done, okay? I'm done. Just stay the fuck away from me." Gathering myself, I turn in the direction of my house.

"You're safe." His words stop my retreat and wrap around me like a balm. I turn to see him standing close as if he's silently followed me.

"Yeah, well, you'll have to forgive me if I don't believe you. The kingdom is all yours. I'll be gone by the end of the summer."

"I'll make sure of it."

Utterly exhausted, I let him have the last word. I feel his gaze on me the entire walk back to the house.

Chapter Five

DAYS LATER, I sit at my vanity gaping at my neck, and the puncture marks at the top of my breasts. I look like I was viciously attacked, and in a way, I was . . . until I wasn't.

The morning after our run-in, I spent an hour trying to cover the bite on my neck before I discovered the bruises on my wrists and called in. The bite marks have gone from red to purple to fading yellow, but they are still there, and I am nowhere near okay enough to fake it through a shift with Melinda.

I've been mostly holed up in my bedroom the last few days, unable to escape the constant replay of that kiss while deciphering all that was revealed to me.

Dominic's brother.

I kissed him.

But it wasn't just a kiss.

I betrayed their memory with that act, and that's hard enough to face, but my head is still splintering with questions. Behind that, guilt drags me along, a heavy weight continually tugging on the chain shackled to me.

Was it Sean or Dominic who claimed me? Both? And would one or both hate me if they knew I'd damn near screwed the bastard who tore us apart?

Does it even matter? It's been months and months, and they've given me nothing but a trinket. I've been dangling in the dark without a fucking thing to hold onto, and this is the thread meant to keep me?

It's not enough. Not nearly enough. My contempt for their continued absence has led me to a place of defiance. And maybe that's why I participated in that kiss.

I felt that thread start to unravel the second that bastard's mouth ravaged mine. I can still feel the pressure of his lips while the bones of the forest dug into my back. In seconds, his ferocious kiss turned me from a fighter into a willing submissive. And that made me question myself in a completely different way.

In the past few days, I've taken inventory, piecing together the parts I know while forming more theories. But no matter how much I try and piece it together—piece myself together—the longer I extend my sentence.

I need to let go. I have to let go. Now more so than ever.

Because it wasn't just Tobias's kiss that was the most damning, it's the fact that I should expect and demand more for myself. And the people in my life are making it hard for me to believe I deserve it.

When my father was alerted to my absence at the plant, I replied to his inquiring email and told him I had a virus. And with that, he was satisfied—unconcerned. He's no longer skirting the lie of a relationship. There's no point. He'll have me paid off soon anyway.

My mother's calls are also becoming less and less frequent.

I'm not sure if she's retreated into herself or not, but I can't bring myself to help her if she won't let me in. Once she's wealthy, maybe she'll try to get the help she needs. It doesn't change the fact that at twenty, I feel orphaned.

I allow myself to hate them both a little for it.

The longer this goes on, the more my relationships with each of them are starting to chip away at me.

Not a single soul on Earth, aside from Christy, cares about me enough to keep me close. Cares enough about me to make me a priority.

Maybe there's an exception in whoever sent that necklace. But even *he* hasn't been bold enough to step up and claim me, to come forward in backing his declaration, his decision. To fight for me. Not in the way he should.

And not in the way I need him to.

My self-worth is suffering at my own hands as well.

I can't shake the feeling that what happened with Tobias wasn't just a battle of wills with a man who is hell-bent on destroying me, but a closer look at my reflection.

I wanted him—*Dominic's brother*.

I wanted him.

So much so, that I loathe every part of me that he touched.

In the shower, I scrub my skin mercilessly to try and rid myself of all traces, welcoming the burn while aggravating the bite marks on my neck and breast. He'd actually broken through the skin around my nipple, and it was a tinge of copper along with betrayal that I tasted in his kiss.

Sick fuck.

But if he's sick, what does it make me? What does it say about me that I can't stop imagining what would have happened if I had given in? It's not just the way he kissed me. It's the intensity that bounces between us every time he's near me, and it's inescapable. I'd chalked up my initial reaction to him the day we met as a culmination of nerves and shock. I can't at all say the same now. This morning I woke up, my panties soaked because of a dream starring a man I loathe before I easily brought myself to a toe-curling orgasm.

Out of the shower, I don't bother to wipe the condensation from the mirror. I no longer want to see my reflection. Dripping wet on the marble floor, I search for the towel I swore I set on the counter and carefully tread to my room to retrieve another from the linen closet. Opening the door, I scream when I see Tobias standing, devastating and dangerous in another tailored suit, my missing towel dangling from his fingers as his eyes devour me in a long sweep.

Ignoring the rush his rapt attention brings, I point toward my door.

"Get out. Get the fuck out."

His blistering gaze continues to roam over me from the soaked hair at my neck to my breasts, illicit appreciation in his gaze before it drops to the thinly shaved patch of hair between my legs.

I turn my back to him, denying his view, jerking open my dresser, grabbing a pair of panties, and a long T-shirt.

"You need to leave, or—"

"Or what?" I feel him at my back. His warm breath hits the skin between my shoulder blades, and my nipples draw tight.

"Did I miss something?" I say, ripping a bra from my drawer. "I haven't said a word. I haven't done anything."

Slowly, he turns me to face him before draping the towel

around my dripping body and fastening it. Eyes locked, tension-filled seconds tick by before he steps away.

"We need to talk. Get dressed and meet me downstairs."

Pulling on a sundress, I cock my head when I hear the distinct clanging of pans downstairs. Confused, I take them two at a time before I hit the landing, crossing the dining room to find Tobias, in Roman's kitchen . . . chopping.

"What in the hell are you doing?" I demand from the doorway.

"Cooking," he replies dryly, keeping his eyes on his task.

"You do realize you're in Roman Horner's kitchen?"

He . . . grins, and I do a double-take. The sight of him without his jacket, his button-down rolled up at the sleeves revealing thick, veined, muscular forearms does unwelcome things to me.

"You're smiling about the fact that you're in his kitchen, cooking for his daughter?"

"I find it oddly satisfying."

He pops an olive into his mouth from an open container on the counter when the back door slams. I jump out of my skin and eye Tobias—who's completely at ease—just before Tyler appears in the doorway. "All good."

Tobias nods in reply, seeming satisfied. Tyler's eyes soften when he notices me standing on the other side of the island. I can't help the sting that starts behind my eyes when his dimple appears as he makes his way toward me. "Look at you. You only get more beautiful." I can feel Tobias's curious stare at our exchange from where he stands.

The closer Tyler gets, the more I notice the differences in

him. Though his hair is still close to a regulation military cut, he looks more of an islander at this point, his skin sun-drenched. There's a sparkle in his brown eyes that was absent the last time I saw him at Delphine's. He looks healthy and happy. I refrain from throwing my arms around him and asking all the questions I so desperately want answers to, the presence of the bastard only feet away stifling me to the point *I* feel like the outsider.

And that's the truth of it—I *am* the outsider.

The fact that they're in the same room feels odd, only reiterating that I showed up in the midst of something that started long ago. Not only are they acquainted, they consider themselves brothers. Whether we were close or not, Tyler's allegiance isn't to me. It's to the man standing across from me burning holes into the both of us.

Tyler stops a foot away, hesitance in his posture. "I've missed you, girl."

I snap my gaze to his, crossing my arms.

"Oh, now I exist? How convenient."

He sighs. "I know you're angry—"

"Angry?" I harrumph. "That's putting it mildly."

"Cee—"

I shake my head, unwilling to listen to his bullshit excuse. "Don't bother. What are you doing here?"

He winces. "Errands."

I dart my glare to Tobias, who matches it unapologetically, long seconds passing as he refuses to give me any explanation. Tyler reads the energy in the room and clears his throat, hitching his thumb over his shoulder. "I guess . . . I guess I'll head out."

Tobias nods. "I'll get with you later."

"All right, man." Tyler eyes me, reluctant to leave. "It was good to see you, Cee."

I don't bother to answer him; my hurt is front and center as he lingers a beat before he turns, his posture deflating. He's halfway across the kitchen when a rogue thought occurs to me.

"Was it you?" I look over to Tobias, whose jaw sets in a hard line before turning my attention back to Tyler. "You promised to be there for me, have my back. I considered you a friend."

"I do have your back. Always will." He stalks toward me and takes my hand. "And I am your friend," he swears, darting his stare to Tobias and then back to me. "No, Cee, it wasn't me. And trust me, I'm paying for it."

And I believe him. He was there from the beginning. The idea that he sold the three of us out is ridiculous and would be insulting if he hadn't turned his back on me.

"I know it wasn't," I admit begrudgingly, and swallow. I lift my eyes to his and resent the shake in my voice. "I'm so fucking mad at you."

"I know. So is he." He jerks his head toward Tobias. He leans in and presses a kiss to my cheek. "I'm sorry. And I just wanted to say thank you."

He gives me no time to ask him why he's thanking me before turning and striding toward the back door. A second later, he shuts it softly behind him.

A long, tense silence passes between us before Tobias resumes his chopping.

I run my fingers through my wet hair and secure it in a loose bun with the tie on my wrist. "What was the errand?"

He eyes the newly bared bite mark on my neck as he answers. "He swept the house and reset the security system."

"Dominic took care of that months ago."

He stills his knife. "Well, it's been done *again*." The sharpness in his voice matches the blade of the knife he's wielding—those poor tomatoes.

I take the stool at the island and can't help myself from asking, "Why are you here . . . doing this?" I gesture to where he works, expertly dissecting a cucumber. He stills his knife and looks up at me briefly before getting back to his task.

"We're going to have dinner and a conversation."

"Why?"

"Because I'm fighting hard not to become the monster you so easily bring out of me. This is business."

"What exactly are you hoping for with me? Friendship?" I snort, incredulous. "Maybe it's you who can't handle the fact that I despise—"

He lifts blazing eyes to mine. "Friendship, no. And I couldn't give a shit that you hate me."

"Then what?"

"Jesus Christ—" he slams the knife down. "I'm making dinner. You'll eat it. We'll have a conversation, and I'll leave."

"Fine!"

"Fine! Bordel de merde!" *Fucking hell.*

I stand and jerk open the fridge collecting two water bottles, slamming one down in front of him. "Here!"

"Fucking thank you," he snaps, uncorking the bottle.

Our eyes meet a split second before we both burst into laughter. And the sight of him in this state is blinding. And wrong, so wrong. I can't—won't—appreciate the mirth dancing in his eyes, the dazzling white of his perfect teeth, or the contrast of his dark skin against his crisp white shirt. I can't love the strength in his jaw or the definition in his shoulders or the sight of his belt on his trim waist. Within seconds, I'm back in that clearing, on my knees picturing myself unleashing him.

It doesn't take long to realize his laughter has faded out and he's watching the rise and fall of my chest, drinking in the look in my eyes. He stands like a sentry, still on the other side of the island as his gaze darkens.

Setting the knife down, he runs a hand through his hair and cups the back of his neck. His voice is low when he speaks. "What happened the other night was . . ." his eyes dart to mine, "chalk it up to curiosity."

"You mean that wasn't you? Sure looked like you."

"You don't fucking know me."

"I don't fucking want to."

He swipes his hand across the counter, drawing the chopped vegetables into a bowl. Another tense silence passes, and I don't bother to acknowledge the hint of guilt he's displaying. Even if he added the sincerest of apologies, it would never be enough.

"So, if it wasn't Tyler, it was someone from the Meetup who told you I was here. Is that how you found out about me?" He pauses briefly, seeming to weigh up whether to respond before he finally nods.

"The Miami crew; we're having allegiance issues with a few of them."

"Is it because of the driver who nearly killed Sean? The one Dominic made an example of?"

He shakes his head. "That only added to the existing problem. I became concerned when Dom told me what happened and then stopped checking in with me as often. My brother had never been that hard to reach. Neither had Sean."

"So, you broke the number one rule and asked—"

"They gave me no fucking choice," he snaps defensively. "I never had to until . . ." the implication lingers heavily before he drops it altogether with a harsh exhale. "My brother and I don't agree on a lot these days when it comes to his militant extremes. But I can't say I blame him for his reaction that night."

Tobias turns back to the stove and stirs the pasta, and I find it odd to see him in this domestic capacity. He seems the type of man to own a boardroom, a no-bullshit closer, who commands a meeting before he fucks his assistant after, her skirt hitched up around her hips as he thrusts into her while puffing on a celebratory cigar.

He most definitely doesn't seem the type to do menial tasks, like grocery shop. Then again, nothing is what it seems when it comes to these winged bastards.

"I can feel you watching me," he speaks up from where he stands, his back turned.

"Chalk it up to curiosity," I repeat his earlier words. "You went to the store?"

"That's usually the place you go to get food to cook."

"Smartass."

"I can feel you looking at that too."

Guilty, I dart my gaze away.

"You're awfully at ease in this kitchen. What if my dad were to walk through the door right now?"

He glances over his shoulder, offering me a dead stare that lets me know I should know better.

"Never mind, you probably know his morning dump schedule."

This time he turns to me, gripping the counter behind

him. "Your father is on a plane. And the only thing he knows about me is that I received a settlement he signed off on when he made me an eleven-year-old orphan. I'm sure he didn't give a damn what became of the two of us the minute he paid us off."

He was eleven, which puts Tobias somewhere around thirty-one.

"You're sure he's guilty?"

"I'm sure he covered it up. I'm sure he's crooked as fuck in his business dealings, and that's enough. But this isn't just about me. My motives aren't purely selfish."

"I never said they were."

"It's business."

"Business. So, I assume that kiss was business too?"

"It was to make a point, and you questioning it is the sole reason for our conversation."

"If this is a proposition, I'm not interested. You can take your business elsewhere. This conversation is pointless, as is your presence in this house. I've told you, it's not my place to pay for his mistakes, and you have no say in my life whatsoever. I owe you *nothing*. And this concludes our *business*, so you can see yourself out."

In a flash, he crosses the kitchen and painfully grips my jaw in his hand. "My *curiosity* stems from the fact I was lied to and gutted by the two people I trusted most in the whole fucking world. I think you know how fucked that feels. I'm pretty sure you've been there, *recently*."

A long silence passes before he speaks. "I've spent over half my life making plans and setting them in motion until you showed up—" He tightens his hold as my lips squish together. "I'm trying really hard here to have an adult conversation with you. I was angry, I'm still angry, and it's not going away anytime soon. But I'm going to do my best to try and talk this out with you because it's what *adults* do. So, I'm going to release your mouth, and you're going to do your best to work with me because, like it or not, we need to come to a *business arrangement*. At this point, we're both holding cards the other needs. And maybe, if you play nice, I'll give you some of the answers you seek. A conversation is what I'm asking for. Nothing more. If it was pussy I was after—" he pauses, his eyes dipping to my heaving chest—"I would've had it already. My patience is running thin, so I'm calling a temporary truce so we can sort this out before it gets any uglier. Blink once if you agree, twice for disagree."

Furious, I fight his hold and his eyes flare in warning.

I blink once.

He releases me and I work my jaw to get the burn out. "Jesus, you're a bastard." He rips his eyes away from me and walks over to the stove. "So, is this what you do to women? You break into their houses, assault them, and then force-feed them?"

He pulls a strainer from the cabinet and drains the noodles.

"I can't imagine how any woman puts up with this shit long-term. It's ridiculous. What kind of life can you build with someone based on lies?"

"Trust," he corrects sourly. "It's based on trust, not lies. And right now, I'm running short."

"You say trust. I say omissions and half-truths. At least that's what I got from it."

"Depends on who you're with."

"It's a good thing I'm not *with* anyone."

He doesn't so much as spare me a glance as he tosses the pasta under cold water.

"Your feelings make you a reckless loose end, Cecelia, which is really fucking bad for business. I told you when we met: you were loyal to them for the wrong reasons."

"You mean love. But that reason doesn't matter anymore. I'm moving on. I'm dating again. And you know that."

He looks over to me, skeptical brows raised.

I match his stance and lift my chin. "Wait . . . that's what this is about? Because I'm dating, trying to move on, you think that I'm going to spill your secrets to the next guy I sleep with?"

His silence infuriates me.

"Newsflash, I've been in far worse shape before now, I've been angrier, far more resentful and haven't uttered a word. Not even to the people closest to me. Your logic is ridiculous."

He doesn't flinch. "You were still waiting. Therefore, you were still loyal. Think about it objectively for a second. If you were me, would you put the fate of your entire fucking operation in the hands of an emotional lit—" he rolls his eyes as my expression hardens—"twenty-year-old *woman*?"

"Maybe you should have thought of that before you—"

He shakes his head ironically. "Took your boyfriends away? You keep proving my point. And if we're going by track record—"

"Don't you dare finish that sentence! I've been insulted by you enough to last a lifetime. You're a sexist pig."

"Say what you will, but *twice* I've seen you let your emotions overrule your judgment, and I'm not willing to gamble on that."

And then it hits me.

"This isn't a conversation. This is a *negotiation*."

He's here to strike a deal.

Not once in my time here have I ever taken advantage of my position. But I've learned well that everything comes with a price. And I seem to be the only one who's been paying it. Until now.

"You truly don't believe love and loyalty go hand in hand?"

"Two separate words with two distinct definitions. But if you look up the synonyms for love—" his eyes lock with mine—"I'm sure you'll find weakness amongst them."

"And what exactly is it that you think you have to barter with? You took away the only—"

He raises his brows.

My inheritance. "My mother—"

"If I move in now, it all goes. All of it. But I can't take that chance, can I?" He shrugs. "So, what's a few more months."

That's his card. He'll wait to move in on my father until I've signed for my inheritance. Sean told me he would try to hold him off, and I admitted to him just nights ago my purpose for being here, but no matter how he got the info, it's leverage.

Fuck.

It's time to show my card, but we already know what it is—my silence. If I speak up, I may be able to stop him from taking my inheritance, from getting his revenge. He sees it the minute I figure it out.

He lifts his chin. "Name your price."

"You really don't believe I'm capable of keeping my mouth shut without being blackmailed?"

"This isn't blackmail. And your real question is, do I trust you? Fuck, no. But don't take it personally."

I open my mouth to snap out a worthy retort, but he raises his hand.

"Let's save the insults for dessert. You need to really think about what you want."

I want him to pay, that's what I want. I want to strip him of some of his confidence, to humiliate him the way he has me. I want to hurt his pride and his feelings if he's capable of having them. And that's when the idea strikes me.

His eyes flare when he reads the price in my expression. "Cecelia—"

"Promise me my father's safety."

"You can't be serious." He curses and shakes his head disbelieving.

"It's the only thing I want. Maybe he does deserve whatever you do to him financially, but you yourself said you were never going to hurt him physically, so what's the harm in making you swear to it?"

"Like I said, he has other enemies."

"And you know of them?"

Another nod.

"Even better. You'll be the one to watch over him."

"You're putting way too much stake in your place, Cecelia. Either way, he's going down. The when is up to you."

I palm the counter and lean in. "You want to buy my loyalty? Then you wait until that money hits my bank account and guarantee my father's safety."

"You're asking too much."

"He's my father, Tobias. Whatever he's done, I assure you he's paying for it. The man is bankrupt in life already. His company is all he lives for. You take that, and I guarantee you will have taken everything from him. Just give him a chance to do something different with his life after you're finished with him." I circle the counter and look up at him. He towers over me, his posture rattling with anger, his eyes bleak. "You take his wealth and position, and he'll have nothing left. It's not like you can get revenge on a corpse. Consider it protecting your interest."

"I told you, this isn't just about me."

"But the victory will be much sweeter if you gain control as he is forced to watch."

It takes nearly a minute of staring off before he finally dips his chin.

"With words, Tobias."

"He's under our protection, from here on out, until we're done with him."

"Swear to me."

His eyes flare. "I'm not repeating myself."

"Fine. So now what?"

He nods toward the cutting board. "Dinner."

Chapter Six

TOBIAS SITS ON the floor across from me in his slacks and starched shirt, his hair slightly askew as he studies the pieces on the board before moving to claim one of my pawns.

Dinner was mostly silent, a battle of wills as he watched me eat. I didn't compliment him on his cooking or thank him, nor did I fight him as I consumed every last bite of chicken and Greek pasta salad, barely holding in my groan of satisfaction. I assumed he'd leave as soon as he got his way. Instead, he'd ordered me into the formal living room and declared we'd be playing chess.

He wiped the board with me on our first game, which is no surprise. I'd be bored to tears if it weren't for the company. I tuck that thought away as I try to ignore his effect on me from a foot away. It's been a struggle sitting across from him. I'm exhausted from fighting the constant crackle of electricity due to his proximity.

My hate for him continues to grow, along with my attraction. I'm in a constant state of anger and arousal with him near, his smoldering gaze always calculating, assessing, when I catch him watching me.

It's not intimidation or the power he holds. It's the intimacy I felt in that kiss and the fact that his words and actions contradict it in every way.

Twice I've caught him looking at me with the same curiosity, and twice he's kept me hostage with his amber gaze. But neither of us has said a word about it.

What's there to say?

Neither of us wants to want the other. Neither of us wants to feel more than hate and contempt, and yet the draw is so strong, so blatantly obvious, it's unnerving.

I'm all too happy to deny it until the bitter end of our arrangement. But the fact that he exists at all is still a revelation in and of itself. He's the essence of an enigma. If he hadn't come to me that day at the pool, I would have remained in the dark about him. The fact that Dominic and Sean hid him so effortlessly is alarming.

Well played, boys, well played.

These men are skilled in deception and disguise it as trust. But it's the bigger picture I see now when I think back to the beginning. And the fact that I'm not sure just how big it is.

"It's still unbelievable, you know," I say, moving a pawn only to have it swept away. He's been anticipating my moves, just as he has with every other one I've made since he came into my life nearly a year ago.

"How so?" He knows exactly what I'm referring to, and it unsettles me even more. Anticipating another's thoughts is a sign of shared intimacy.

I exhale a breath of frustration. I have to choose my words wisely. Instead, I opt for silence. These head games are grueling.

"In theory," he says, knowing I'm unwilling to mull over my word choice, "when you take what thieves steal, they can't exactly file a police report."

"I know that part, but do they ever retaliate?"

"Stupidly, yes, and *often*." He takes my knight. "And why is it so unbelievable? Haven't you seen enough?"

"In a way, yes, but . . ."

"But what? Too close for comfort? That's the beauty of it. You can't for a second believe what's going on in your own back yard, and that's the hardest realization to come to terms with."

"That's true."

His amber eyes flicker as he scans my face. "You know gangs exist, right? But you've never been in that environment. You've never witnessed a drive-by or seen an initiation, have you?"

"Also true."

He leans back and crosses his arms, pausing our game.

"Do you believe the Cartel exists?"

"Yes."

"The Mob?"

"Of course."

"Why, because you saw *Goodfellas*?" He shakes his head, a faint smile on his lips. "So why is it so hard for you to believe a group of people banded together for a reason they felt was justifiable enough to warrant extremes to try and evoke change?"

"It's just so . . ."

"When you were coerced in, you were just as ignorant until you saw for yourself."

"Yes."

"And you just admitted it's still unbelievable after the fact. So, would it be safe to agree your ignorance is shared with a large majority?"

I nod, mulling over what he's saying. "I believe so, yes."

"Seeing is believing for so many that it's fucking pathetic."

"So I've been told a hundred times."

He smiles but it's pride I see shining in his eyes. The pride of a teacher. "Sean."

You.

"Cartels are corrupt," I say, making my move, "and so is the Mob."

I lift my eyes to his. "And so . . ." *are you.* And they do it all—everything from blackmail and extortion, down to petty theft. The Ravenhood is just as corrupt, as lawless as any other extreme organization. "So, this is evil versus a lesser evil?"

He nods toward me to make my move. As soon as I do, his countermove earns him a greater advantage on the board. "How do you justify it? What sets you apart? The fact that you don't hurt innocent people?"

"If you don't think you're in danger, you're a lot less intelligent than I gave you credit for. The second we focus on taking someone down, we, in turn, gain bullseyes on our backs—all of our backs, no exclusions. There are no rules for innocents in wars like these. The casualties due to our declared wars all boil down to human decency. Whether or not our opponent has humanity enough to leave the innocents out of it."

He drives the point home by knocking my pawn off the board.

"Can we be done with this game?"

"No," he answers quickly, "I'm three moves away from winning."

I make my move, and he's already lifted his knight.

"The tattoos are pretty stupid, don't you think? Incriminating. How do you expect to keep this contained?"

"There will always be the burden of evidence for anyone to incriminate."

"Isn't that a bit arrogant?"

"No, it's not arrogant. There will always be the burden of evidence, just like there will always be an exception to every rule. I'm expecting it. I expect opposition. I expect retaliation. I expect to be surprised because of human nature—case in point, the interruption that is *you*. But make no mistake, America is a corporation, a business, Cecelia. Your father knows that, everyone in a position of power fighting behind the flag *knows* that. Roman isn't stupid. He's well-aware he has enemies, whether he can identify them or not. He's also aware that one wrong move could cost him everything, as *all* players are. And for every man positioned in a place of power or importance, there will always be someone waiting in the wings to seek weakness out, anticipate your next move, and attempt to take what doesn't belong to them."

He moves his knight forward. Checkmate.

"That was only two moves," I point out.

I don't miss the subtle but familiar smile that upturns his lips. When his gaze lifts to mine, and he sees my response to it, he draws his brows.

"What?"

"Nothing."

"You saw my brother when you looked at me just then."

"Why do you say that?"

"It's the first time you haven't looked at me like you wanted to fuck me or kill me today."

"I don't want to fuck you. But killing you sounds delightful."

"Maybe you'll get your chance one day." He flashes a different grin, one that's distinctly his, and I try not to swoon at the sight of it. Why does he have to be so fucking beautiful? Why couldn't he be a second-hand Dom? That I could deal with a lot easier. And the thought that I've been eye-fucking him and he's noticed is nauseating.

But I'm starting to understand the root of some of my attraction. When I look at him, I do see Dominic *and* Sean. When he speaks, I hear bits and pieces of them both. I must still be looking at him in that way because he lifts his chin, prompting me. "What?"

"You're the original quack."

He draws his brows. "Explain."

"Nope." He sits back against the fireplace draining the gin he helped himself to from my father's richly stocked bar.

"So, if you *know* it's just a matter of time before you meet a worthy opponent . . ." his eyes lift to mine.

Fearless. He's fearless.

He's expecting someone to best him at some point. He's expecting to pay the enemies he's stacking up with his life and the lives of people he's associated with, and he lives with this knowledge daily.

They all do.

They are, in essence, soldiers.

I resent the fact that I respect him for it.

Tobias stands and pulls his jacket from the couch. He slips

it on with his eyes on mine. I slowly stand, my mind racing as I grapple with all he's theoretically confessed.

"Safety truly is an illusion," I conclude, the rest of my blissful ignorance falling away.

He dips his head. "And the most powerful, but once you make peace with it, it's easier taking bigger risks to seek greater rewards. But that's no excuse to make a stupid move."

And it's the truth. In every aspect of life, safety is an illusion. I can lock this house up tight, but a storm could rip the roof from over my head. I could safeguard my heart and never let anyone in, but I would still feel the pain of isolation. I could make all the right moves every single day of my life out of fear, and with a sweep of the right hand, get wiped off the board altogether.

Every decision we make in life is a move, our opponent invisible. Whether it be the enemy of illness, or the enemy you sleep with, you don't get that knowledge until the opponent makes itself known.

His logic is that we're all pawns playing invisible opponents, and one wrong move or stupid decision away from revealing our enemy. Simply by inserting myself into this mix of dangerous men, I might have switched up my opponents and lined my life up differently. Up until now, I believed myself to be somewhat immortal, and Tobias just snatched that from me with the truth.

I suppose everyone has this kind of moment, but like everything else I've unearthed in the last year, my education came early. He must sense my fear because he takes a step toward me and thinks better of it before he turns and walks out of the room, shortly after, closing the front door behind him.

"Thanks for the dinner and mindfuck," I mumble, peeking out of the frosted, oblong window next to the front door just as he pulls away in a black sedan. On copilot, I lock the door and set the alarm, and a second after that, the irony hits me, and all I can do is laugh.

I made a bargain with a devil to keep his secret if he kept my father safe, but because safety is an illusion, it makes his end impossible to uphold.

And it occurs to me that my inevitable realization was Tobias's third move.

His true checkmate.

I shake my head as I warily climb the stairs to my bedroom. "Connard." *Bastard.*

Chapter Seven

CLEARING THE SLEEP from my eyes, I stretch out in bed, my latest dream coming back to me in flickered images before it plays out for me. They say dreams are a way for your subconscious to process things you attempt to avoid in waking hours. After years of recalling them, this I wholeheartedly believe. Last night I dreamed of the sun, but it was close, so close I could reach out and touch it. But the heat wasn't scorching. It was a welcoming warmth. It wasn't far, just a few steps out of reach. And then the clouds moved in seconds before bursting. I could feel the cool spray on my face just before a rainbow appeared in the distance. A few more steps and I could have reached them.

In a blink, it was gone, and I lay alone in the clearing, looking up at a lifeless sky. It was then my mother called out to me on the wind, to come home, but I ignored her pleas, searching for my missing sun.

A tear threatens as I toss the covers away.

Opening the French doors to my balcony, the morning greets me, a whisper of wind whipping through my hair as

I welcome the new summer day. If there's one thing I'll miss about living in Roman's mansion, it's the view.

It's the swish of water below that draws my attention to the pool. Powerful masculine arms wade through the water, causing a small, but strong tide in his wake. I hadn't noticed it before when he'd rolled up his sleeves, but the answer is clear as to why the markings weren't there now as I take in the deeply etched raven's wings inked along his shoulder blades, confirming his place in the royal lineup. I wish so much that I could rip them away, or somehow disfigure them. He's not worthy of having two brothers, blood-related or not, who are solely devoted to him.

And the added insult is that he's magnificent; rippling muscle and smooth skin as he glides through the water fluidly, his muscular legs propelling him across the pool. I take a minute to admire him as he turns to do another lap, his back coiling while the water cascades down his athletic frame.

Powerful, formidable, intimidating. He's a heartless, soulless predator.

And now he's invading, intertwining our lives just to prove his point that, temporarily, he owns me.

One of three phones rings where it sits on a waiting towel at the edge of the pool. I recognize two of them as the same model of the burner phones Sean used. I hear a faint "Oui?" before I make my way down to him.

By the time I get poolside, Tobias is furiously barking orders and cursing in a mix of English and French. I tentatively listen as he speaks with his back to me and can't make out much aside from the fact he's angry. His foreign tongue fluid, thick, sexy, enticing. His back goes ramrod straight before he turns to see me standing there, shamelessly eavesdropping. Snapping one last order, he cuts the call, discarding the phone next to the others before stretching his arms out on the side of the pool.

"Sounded serious."

"And what is it you think you heard?"

"Le pleck, le spit—" I upturn my nose and school my features in my best imitation of a French snob—"le plah, le bark, more spit, and merde."

We glare at each other for a second before he throws his head back and laughs. I completely ignore my urge to smile at the sound of it, instead crossing my arms and cocking my hip. "I'm not fluent. *Yet*. But watch your back, Frenchman."

His laughter slows and he shakes his head, a chuckle sounding just before his eyes roam me in amusement.

"So, what crises are you fighting today?"

"Don't concern yourself."

"I'm not concerned, but I am curious as to why you're here, again. Do you not have a home?"

"Plenty of them."

"Then why take up residence here?"

"Just taking advantage of my position. You should as well. The water is warm." He eyes me in my boy shorts and a cami.

"I'll pass. Seriously, can't you take your problem solving somewhere else?"

"There are two types of ways to handle problems," he starts, and I roll my eyes dismissively.

"Great, another lecture."

"And two types of people," he goes on, completely unfazed. "There's the one who will walk past that offending piece of lint or paper on the floor every single day and tell themselves they'll get to it. And those who will pick it up the minute they spot it. They'll figure out where it came from, trash it, and forget it was ever there. But, for the ones who walk by it every day, it will become a problem. It will start to fester. Another something they'll have to get to. Another pea on their plate. They'll start to look for it, its presence a nuisance, and tell themselves they'll get to it tomorrow. Until one day, it's more of a crisis of conscience than a pea."

"Let me guess. You don't have any peas on your plate."

One side of his mouth lifts in contempt before he speaks through thick lips. "I fucking hate peas."

"It's a piece of lint."

"Only to the person who picked it up."

"Confucius says 'pick up lint.' Got it, any more wisdom you'd like to impart before you *depart*? Can I count on your sudden and unwanted appearance *every day* now as well?"

"You can count on me being where I need to be until our business is concluded."

"Whatever. Now, if you'll excuse me, I've got better things to do than let you dip your finger in my head and stir."

"Don't be so quick to dismiss what I'm offering, Cecelia. We could learn from each other."

"You mean you can poke and prod me for more intel on my dad? Yeah, I'll pass."

"I know plenty, but the devil is in the details. Know your opponent."

"I'm not interested in learning more about you."

"The look in your eyes declares otherwise."

He doesn't smirk, not a hint of smugness in his tone, leaving no room for debate. Maybe he can sense my attraction just as easily as I can detect his. Just another reason he's the bane of my existence.

"You're a beautiful man, Tobias. I don't deny it. I'm sure you've used it to your advantage, and often."

He propels himself toward where I stand on the opposite side of the pool, his arms cutting through the water with ease as he zeroes in on me. Lust coats me from head to foot, but I don't make a move, nor do I bristle when he lifts himself from the pool, water flowing down his muscled skin as he towers above me, purposely invading my space. Seconds tick past as he sheds water, dampening me in more ways than one while my nipples draw tight. He misses nothing, his eyes dipping to my chest before they slowly lift back up to me.

"You want what I'm offering. You're just too stubborn to ask. It's on the tip of your tongue, so ask."

"I want nothing but your absence."

He draws closer, cold droplets of water pelting my chest and legs.

"You want my trust. That is something that I can't give you."

"From you, I want nothing," I turn on my heel and he grips my wrist to stop me.

I glare up at him as he blinks down at me while soaking my tank and shorts.

"I *can't trust* you. That's the miracle you seek. But it's far too expensive, and you can't afford it. But we *can* learn from each other."

"And what exactly is it that you think you can teach me?" I lift my hands and slide them along his shoulders and down his body, raking my fingernails over his damp skin, satisfied when I see him tense before I slowly lift my eyes to his. He grips my hands and squeezes them before releasing them.

"Like I said, we can *learn* from each other."

I scoff. "And what exactly is it that you think you can learn from a pea?"

There's a distinct shift in his gaze that has me hesitating before I dismiss it. This is just another head game I'm not willing to indulge him in. "You can't afford me either, Tobias. You're incapable of obtaining *my kind* of currency."

Tension coils in my belly as our breaths mingle.

"You have questions. Ask me, Cecelia."

I avert my gaze ignoring the surge in my veins. One second passes and then another as he leans in on a whisper.

"My proposal has nothing to do with the look in your eyes, but if I touched you, right now," he drawls out thickly, "the way you want me to *right now*, you wouldn't refuse me."

"Your game is becoming predictable."

"Yeah?" he whispers, "Maybe I'll up it." He leans in, his warm breath heating the cool drop of water at my nape. "Ask me, Cecelia."

I turn my head to keep him from reading me further.

"Have it your way."

The phone rings on the other side of the pool and we both glance in its direction before he turns back to me.

Shoulders tense, he steps out of reach and heads toward his phone as I head for the house. He's already snapping into his phone by the time I make it to the door. I don't have to look back to know his eyes are on me. I can feel the blaze from feet away.

Chapter Eight

Annoyed by the sight of the Jag in the circular drive, I enter the house preparing for battle only to hear a slew of heated French coming from my kitchen.

"Trouvez-le." *Find him.*

A brief pause.

"Pas d'excuses. Vous avez une heure." *No excuses. You have one hour.*

Tobias ends the call just as I come into view. He looks perplexed, furiously typing away on a laptop on the island. It's only been a few days since our confrontation at the pool, but it's clear he fully intends to take advantage of his position.

"Mind telling me what the hell you're doing here?" I make my way past him to open the fridge door to grab a water. I'm covered in sweat from my hike. He barely spares me a glance when he replies.

"Protecting my interest."

"You think you can manage that somewhere else, preferably far, far away?"

He scans the screen and slams his laptop closed. "Putain!" *Fuck.* Chest heaving, he picks up one of his cellphones from the counter in front of him before dialing. "Get the *new* here. Ten minutes."

He crosses the kitchen, grabbing a nearby bottle of gin and pouring a healthy drink into a tumbler full of ice. He circles it, deep in thought, with the ice cubes rattling as he swishes the clear liquid, one, two, three times before he takes a long pull.

"It's a little early for a cocktail, isn't it?"

Silence.

"Good talk." I roll my eyes. I'm halfway to the dining room when he speaks up behind me.

"You're wrong, you know. It's not people like you and your mother."

"What?"

"When we first spoke, you said I was fighting for people like you and your mother."

"Yeah, what's wrong with that?"

"Everything's wrong with that," he bites. "Everything. You want to single yourselves out."

"I meant—"

"I know what you meant. It's not just the blue-collar workers at your father's plant or anywhere else for that matter. That's secular thinking."

"Fine. I think wrong, I love wrong, my loyalty is misplaced, and I'm just an all-around fumbling idiot. Pardon me if I don't give a shit that I'm not up to your standards."

He again swirls the ice in his drink, one, two, three times before taking another sip.

"You're tracking my every move already. Do you really have to be present to do so?"

"I'm cleaning up the fucking mess that's been left for me."

"I don't understand why you're vetting me so hard. I don't know if you've been to a 'party' recently, but have you *seen* some of the people working under your fat thumb?"

He eyes me speculatively over the rim of his glass before he lowers it.

Just as he's about to speak, the doorbell rings and I roll my eyes.

"These aren't your headquarters. This is my temporary home. Find another place to do your evil overlord bidding."

He moves past me, ignoring my comment entirely before answering the door. A second later, RB and Terrance walk in.

"Hey, girl," RB greets me, just as Terrance speaks up looking between Tobias and me. "Thought you were Dom's girl. You're getting around, aren't you?"

Humiliation heats my face as he eyes me in a way that lets me know exactly what he thinks about me.

Tobias's demeanor shifts before he turns to me, his expression granite. "Give me your keys."

"What?"

He lowers his eyes to the keys in my hand. "Give me your car keys, Cecelia."

"Yeah, I don't think so." He walks over to me and holds out his hand, and I sigh before handing them over. He turns and hurls them at Terrance, who barely manages to catch them at his chest, a wince on his face from the sting. Tobias's tone is unforgiving when he speaks.

"Wash and shine her car—soap, sponge, water, and wax, and she better be able to see her fucking reflection in it when you're done."

I step forward. "That's not necessary, I—"

Tobias cuts me off with a look while RB glances over to Terrance with a 'you just fucked up' written in his expression. Tobias addresses RB next. "You watch him do it."

RB nods, regarding Tobias with distinct respect.

Tobias ignores them both as they glance around the foyer. "You're coming with me."

"Uh, no I'm not, I'm in need of a shower—"

"We'll be back in an hour," he tells them both, gripping me by the arm to escort me out. "No one gets past this door. Tyler will meet you here in ten."

"Got it," RB answers.

I rip my arm away just as Tobias rounds the driver's side of his Jaguar.

"I want to talk to Tyler."

"No."

"Well, I'm not decent," I snap, arms crossed in an attempt to hold my ground.

"This isn't a fucking date. And we're not done with our conversation. Get. In. The. Car."

We lock our eyes on each other for a second, then two, before I slide into his leather seat. Shortly after, we're flying down the lone road toward town.

"Want to tell me why you're giving anyone with ink access to Roman's house?"

Silence.

"You didn't have to do that back there, you know? I *can* take care of myself."

More infuriating silence.

"If disrespecting women is a hard limit for you, you might want to consider taking a closer inspection at your reflection."

He navigates the roads easily as I scowl at the side of his head, attuned to the fact I must reek after a two-hour hike, my skin sticky from dried sweat. My hair matted in a heap atop my head.

"Where are we going?"

He remains mute, relaxed in his seat as we drive another ten minutes until he whips into the parking lot of my bank.

"Making a deposit?"

He backs into one of the spots on the opposite side of the door facing the entrance.

"Let me guess, scoping for your next big heist?"

"Jesus." He shakes his head. "Just watch."

"What am I looking for?"

"Criminals. I want you to take a good look at that building and tell me when you spot one."

"Really? We're looking for criminals based on *appearance*?"

"Says the girl who just asked me if I've *seen* some of the people working under my fat thumb."

"I just meant—"

"No way to justify that statement. Now, based on *that line* of thinking, let's find some criminals."

An older man walks out of the bank; he looks to be in his eighties and holds the door for a younger woman walking in.

"Nope."

"How do you know? Because he held the door for her?"

"I don't for sure. But he doesn't look the type."

"What's the type? Everyone dressed in a hoodie? Everyone with tats? Who smells like pot? Sagging skinny jeans? Skin color? What about haircut? Can you tell by a haircut?"

"You've made your point." Heat travels up my neck.

"No, I haven't. Watch."

And I do. For several minutes I scrutinize every person walking in and out of the bank and dismiss them.

"You don't see one?"

"This is ridiculous. How am I supposed to know?"

"How about this one?"

A forty-something man walks out in a soiled work uniform just before he climbs into a utility truck.

"Clearly a hard worker. Looks local, and he's probably all about providing for his family. This is wrong. I get what I said was generalizing but—"

"Where's the criminal, Cecelia?"

"I don't know."

"What about this guy?" Tobias juts his chin toward a suit walking in.

"I don't know!"

"Then keep looking."

I search our conversation until I realize I've been looking at the people, not the building itself. "It's the bank, isn't it?"

"You think organized crime is as bad as it gets?" he says, staring up at the logo before turning to me. "Ask yourself this: why is a twenty-year-old employee feeling threatened enough by management to bring her elderly grandma into the branch to open a second bank account she doesn't need?"

"Because it's her job?"

"It's so her granddaughter can reach her eight accounts a day quota so she can keep her job. Because there were thousands just like her in small towns, who thought they were signing on to be a part of a well-known bank with a stellar reputation and, only a week or so in, found out they were dancing chickens. Every day they felt pressured to open accounts. A ploy by the powers that be to drive up stock prices to an untouchable status, to fatten an overstuffed cow because Midas rich wasn't fucking rich enough. Some resorted to opening accounts for *dead* people. This happened every day for years, all the while these people, these low-level employees, desperate for a paycheck, were being mentally abused to the point they committed criminal acts."

"*I* bank here."

"Then you're contributing to the problem without being aware of it. It all trickles from the top. If you think the bad guys are the ones selling dimes on the street, that's nothing compared to these fucking crooks. And the sad part is that some of the current customers wouldn't blink if it were brought to their attention, because it's someone else's problem. Their money is covered federally, so very few give a fuck if they're banking with a known and exposed criminal. But if enough of those customers cared, they wouldn't be getting away with it. But they did and still are. The higher-ups should have been crucified for what they did. There was a hearing. They paid a hefty fine, one that did absolutely nothing to hurt their bottom line. The CEO stepped down after the hearing, but no jail time was served, and here they are today, still in fucking business."

He focuses back on the bank, a clear look of disdain on his face.

"You want to find *real* criminals? Follow the money. Always follow the fucking money. I'm not saying none of it was earned legitimately, but I'm saying those who did earn it legitimately are grouped with those who didn't. It truly is a small world once you connect the dots. It's an incestuous mess. Everyone has fucked everyone at some point, and most of them stay in bed together for the same reason."

"You're talking about the one percent? The wealthiest."

"That's where it gets tricky, because that trickles from the top too."

"This really happened, and they got away with it?"

He slowly nods. "But most people are paying attention to Janet Jackson's halftime nipple peepshow or something similar because it takes the focus away from the real thieves."

"A distraction?"

"They create them and, at times, pay for them. The media is easily bought or influenced by the same people occupying the same fucking bed, and the world is kind enough to take care of the rest."

He turns the car over and takes off out of the parking lot. I study him while he drives and can't help the shift in my contempt. He's fed up. Not just for the plant workers in this town but for everyone within reach of the vultures who prey on all unsuspecting citizens, daily. And I've indirectly been in bed with this criminal since I was old enough to open a bank account.

"So, I close my account, and that's supposed to make a difference?"

"You close your account and you feel better about the part you play in it. You tell ten people about it, and maybe two listen and close their accounts. That's the hard way, the slower, more painful process, and in the end, they'll still win."

"So, what would you do?"

"Aim for the *head*, not the *foot*."

I mull it over and turn to him, his thick, dark lashes my

focal point. "If you don't trust me, then why are you so intent on making me understand?"

"We made a deal. I'm sticking to it. If you're asking if I have better things to do, the answer is yes, I fucking do. You asked about vetting, but I can count on one hand the people who know who you *really* are."

He clicks his signal at the stoplight and turns to me. "Those people at the parties, they all have a part to play that has nothing to fucking do with the foot."

Roman. My father is part of the foot.

"So, they're all looking for ways to get the head of the monster?"

His eyes linger on me for long seconds, taking me in in my shorts and tank before he floors the gas.

His business with Roman is personal, but he'd just told me in so many words that dear old dad is just the tip of the iceberg. I asked Tobias not long ago just how big this was, how far this went, and he just gave me a bird's eye view . . . from space.

Chess, again. But this time I studied up a little. I move to take one of his pawns and I catch the amused expression in his gaze when he realizes it.

"Best summer ever," I grumble as he swishes the ice in his glass.

"What will you do when it's over?"

"I'm sure you know of my college plans."

"I'm aware." He moves a pawn as a thick lock of hair falls across his forehead. I ignore the sudden urge to reach out and push it away. "But what will you *do*?"

"After? Not sure yet. Definitely not following my father's footsteps in the family business, not that you're giving me much of a choice."

"You couldn't care less about his company."

"Not true, I care a great deal about the future of his employees."

Silence passes as he swirls his rocks around before he speaks.

"Roman pulled a Zuckerberg just before he bankrupted his first business partner to gain control of their company. It was a small venture, but that move gave him enough monetary gain to play his first hand on a bigger gamble."

I sit back, stunned by his revelation about my father's dirty deeds. "When?"

"Years before you were born. This gained him his first enemy. Jerry Siegal. The irony? He's making his comeback by being just as fucking crooked."

I bite my lip and look up to see him watching me. "You're sure?"

Another swish of the ice, one, two, three times in his glass before he drains the liquid and stands.

"So, do you sleep in the woods?"

He slips on his jacket. "I might." He nods toward where I sit next to the fireplace. "Don't touch the board."

"Oh, goodie, you'll be back," I stand. "Can't wait."

He takes a menacing step toward me, and I take one back, turning my head to avoid his effect on me. With the lip of the couch touching my thighs, I'm out of space, and with his next step, I'm engulfed in flames, the paralyzing knowledge that if he so much as reaches out and touches me, my body will react. I hold my breath to keep from inhaling him in as he inspects me closely from inches away.

"What is it about you?" he asks, his voice close to a whisper. I take it as just another insult, an inquiry as to what Sean and Dominic saw in me.

I step to the side to give myself some breathing room, and he moves in.

"Can you just give me some leash? That's all I'm asking. Maybe knock before entering?" He leans in, his nose running along the side of my neck without contact, but the effect is the same.

"No." It's a faint whisper, but the message is received as if he'd shouted it. Shortly after, when the front door closes, I stand there fixed on the direction he went, my limbs heavy. He's infuriating, and fighting with him is starting to feel pointless.

That night, I dream of amber eyes and lightning bugs.

Chapter Nine

I WAKE THE next morning to the sound of a familiar voice drifting from the first floor. Aggravated, I brush my teeth while doing a once-over in my shorts and tank to make sure I'm covered. It's the addition of the second voice that has me taking the stairs two at a time. When I enter the kitchen, I'm struck by the sight of Tobias, suited and flawlessly polished, the scent of his freshly applied cologne the first thing to invade my nostrils before I lay eyes on Jeremy. He's busying himself by unwrapping a new laptop when he spots me and cracks a wide grin.

"Hey, you, been a minute." He darts his eyes back to his task as I cock my hip next to the counter and stare a hole through the side of his head. My thirsty eyes drink in his familiarity, and all it does is make my heart ache. His man beard has grown a little longer in the eight and counting months since I'd last seen him, and he's sporting his usual attire of dark jeans and suspenders over his T-shirt. Pinstriped suspenders *I* found at a thrift store and bought while shopping because I thought of him and considered him a friend. Late-night conversations between the two of us spring to the forefront of my mind, but I bat the emotion away and let my resentment take a front seat. Ignoring the amber eyes combing me, I make my way to the coffee pot and click on the small TV on the counter to catch the last of the morning news.

It's when I go to add my sugar that I find the box is empty. Tossing a glance over my shoulder, I don't miss the simper on his lips before Tobias lifts his mug, and I narrow my eyes at him.

Jeremy darts his gaze between us over the laptop he's just powered up. "I see you two are getting on well."

We both glare in his direction, and his chuckle is unmistakable. Temper flaring, I turn and open the cabinet above the pot and spot another box of sugar on the second shelf, just out of my reach. Lifting on my toes, I try in vain to grab it when I feel Tobias approach behind me.

"I've got it," I snap, pulling a spatula from the drawer and using it to hook the box before jerking it toward me. It gives easily, smacking me square in the face. Nose burning, I'm on the verge of exploding when an infuriating rumble sounds from Tobias's throat just before he steps away. Shrugging off my embarrassment, I prepare my coffee and ignore them both, keeping my eyes on the screen. Jeremy speaks up a minute later.

"How you been, Cee?"

Elbows on the counter, I lean in and turn up the volume.

"That mad at me, huh?" I can sense when they exchange a look behind me. I couldn't care less. But the burning at my back lets me know I may be revealing a little more skin than I should. I glance over my shoulder to see the source of my discomfort. Head cocked, Tobias is looking at me peculiarly before he darts his eyes to Jeremy.

"We good?"

"I mean, he only showed me how to do this once, but . . ." Jeremy glances my way, and I know who he's referring to. They're worried about the security of the laptop.

They share another wordless look as I go back to my coffee and pretend to watch the news. A few keystrokes later, Jeremy speaks up.

"I think we're good."

"Think or *know*?" Tobias replies in an unforgiving tone.

Jeremy sighs with exasperation. "It would help if you let me—"

"I'll figure it out," Tobias snaps.

"Too proud to reach out to your own brother, huh?" I say, with my back turned.

More silence.

"How is *he* these days, Jeremy?"

A pregnant pause. "I wouldn't know, Cee."

"Sure, you wouldn't."

A second later, I feel Jeremy beside me. I can't look at him. I can't let him see that his mere presence is weakening me. "We miss you, you know?"

"Do you?" I sip my coffee and swallow, unable to hide the bitter edge in my voice. "Nice suspenders."

He thumbs them in my peripheral. "You know they're my favorite."

"Good to know you give a shit about something."

"I do care about you." His sigh comes out more like a grunt of frustration. I'm sure his boss is staring right at him, a clear threat just feet away. He's tap-dancing between an apology for me and certain punishment. It doesn't seem like any of them are brave enough to go head-to-head with this asshole.

"Don't worry about me. You haven't in eight months."

"Come on," he argues, "you know we couldn't—"

"Want to know how I'm doing?" I turn my head and glare at him. "Well, you can relay to Sean I now know *exactly* what happens to caged birds."

"We're good," Tobias snaps at Jeremy, his intent to end our exchange clear. "I'll get with you later."

Not long after, the alarm beeps and Russell's voice sounds out from where he calls from the front door. "Hey, man, we have to open up in twenty. Mrs. Carter wants her shit checked out first thing this morning."

He's talking about the garage—a place I used to consider a second home. It's unreal what time and distance can do. It now seems like a lifetime ago. It takes some effort to keep from turning the corner and laying eyes on Russell. But I don't because he doesn't seem the least bit interested in seeing me. Maybe it has everything to do with Tobias and his menacing presence.

But it doesn't matter. These men aren't my friends. They're in on secrets I'm not privy to. Where once I belonged, now I'm just a liability.

"See you around, Cee," Jeremy says from by my side, but I don't look his way. I don't utter a word. And I can feel his disappointment before he turns and leaves.

I turn up the TV to drown out any conversation with Tobias. I'm relieved when he busies himself on his laptop. A few minutes pass before he pauses his keys when the anchor speaks up with a breaking bulletin.

"Last night, a known terrorist leader was killed in a successful operation led by the US Military. Shortly after the news broke, the target was portrayed by a major media outlet

as an *'Austere Religious Scholar'* leaving some Americans outraged, who have started to voice their objections on social media—"

"Bullshit!"

"Bullshit!"

Our shared reaction has me turning to Tobias, who stands equally as perplexed on his side of the counter. He runs a hand down his face in frustration as I turn back and click off the TV. We stand in silence for a few seconds before he turns and tosses his coffee in the sink. "This is fucking terrible."

"I agree; since when is it okay for reporters to humanize terror?"

"No, the coffee. You need a French press and a decent grind."

Baffled, I stare at his back, his shirt a light blue, fitted perfectly to outline his broad frame.

"Well, you've spoiled your French tongue. I'm sure you had a plethora of tastes to choose from."

He turns his head, before placing a palm on the counter and facing me with a cocked brow. "Are we still talking about coffee?"

"Of course, we are," I snap, perplexed. "And at this point, I'm surprised you haven't changed your address *here* for Prime Delivery."

His light chuckle fills the kitchen. I wrap my hand around my waist as he scrutinizes me from where he stands.

"You truly do care about them."

I inhale a breath for patience. "I told you a dozen times already. Our deal wasn't even necessary. *You're* the one who gave *me* the card to play. I would have kept my silence with or without our deal."

He lifts one side of his mouth. "Can't be too careful. You know. *'Hell hath no fury—'*

I slash my hand through the air. "'*A bird, unable to fly, is still a bird; but a human unable to love is an inexpensive stone.'*" I retort dryly and walk to where he stands, setting my cup in the sink beside him before lifting my eyes to his. "Like I said, you're incapable of *my kind* of currency." It's then I feel the spike, and it's unavoidable. His eyes flame brighter with each passing second as we face-off.

"Endearment, adoration, devotion, warmth, attachment; *also* synonyms for love." I turn to head upstairs and he jerks my elbow, pulling me flush against him. Electricity pings between us, stunning me for several seconds. It's both lightning and thunder without warning. Between his striking physical attributes, the burn in his gaze and his mouth-watering smell, it's getting impossible to play immune. The intensity of my attraction keeps shifting. The more I try to deny it, the more it rears its ugly head.

"No more bruises, please, I have a shift tonight."

He lessens his grip. "You bruise too easily. You think I don't understand you?"

"You don't know me."

He dips, his breath hitting my ear. "I *know* you." He brushes the loose hair away from my shoulder, and I'm barely able to control the shiver that slight touch induces. "And you're afraid of just how much I *do* know." He lifts a finger and runs it faintly along my collarbone. "You think it's love, but the truth is, you're an addict." He slowly trails the pad of the same finger up my throat before brushing it lightly across my lips. The shift in intensity is jarring as my limbs begin to tingle with awareness. "You're high right now. And that's all your currency is: a *high*." I jerk away from him and he crowds in, his eyes trailing from my pumping chest back to my lips before he steps away, collects his laptop, and strides out of the kitchen.

Chapter Ten

"*YOU'RE AN ADDICT.*"

The weight of that statement has blanketed me my whole shift.

"You sure?" Melinda asks as she gathers the last of our tubs together.

"Sorry, what?"

She looks over to me. Evident worry etched on her features as I recall our conversation. An attempt by her to set me up with her church's new youth pastor. She's no dummy—in fact, she's become an expert at gauging my moods. More often than not, she's bringing extra lunch on her shifts to make sure I'm eating. It's comforting to know she cares, her concern for me maternal.

"Yeah," I say, wiping down our workstation. "I'm just going to head home."

She pauses as we pack up. "Honey, it's been months and months. I just don't want you wasting away anymore."

Months and months. And today more than ever, I feel the weight of that truth.

"*You're an addict.*"

"I'm fine," I assure her. "I went on a date not too long ago."

This seems to perk her up. "Oh, yeah?"

"Yes. Great guy. And we're going to give it another go, sometime soon." The lie comes easily, but I feel no guilt when I see the relief in her eyes. Though invasive and maddening at times with her chatter, I've grown real affection for her and consider her a friend.

"That's so good to hear." She bristles. "Well, excuse me for saying it, but he's a damn fool. And I promise you he will regret it if he's not already. I can't believe he just up and left like that."

We both know the *he* she's referring to is Sean, but I dart my eyes away. When the conveyor belt comes to a halt signaling the end of our shift, she takes a step toward me and hesitantly pulls me into a hug.

I hug her back tightly. "I'm going to miss you, too."

She pulls back and grips my shoulders. "You won't miss my motor mouth." She laughs and nudges me. "But I'll sure miss your ear. How long do you have left?"

"Just a few months."

She winks. "We'll make it count."

I nod and manage to muster a genuine smile as she leaves the line to punch out. I trail behind her, my thoughts going back to this morning's conversation in my kitchen. To everyone close to me, I'm that girl now—the one who got her heart broken and retreated into herself.

Tobias sees me the same way—weak—but the irony is that it's people like Melinda who struggle daily to make ends meet, and my affection for her and those in our circle that keeps me silent, compliant. If I thought for one second

Tobias's plans included hurting her or the people I've come to care about, I would have blown the whistle long ago. But that's not the case. And despite my hatred for him, I know Tobias's plans include giving the power back to the people of this town.

And that plan I'm all for.

Does it make me a bad person if I'm willing to let my father suffer because of it? Maybe.

But this is the part I chose to play.

And maybe some of my disregard for his welfare has to do with the grudge that he chose his empire over me.

Maybe losing everything he owns will bring him some much-needed humility and give him a second chance to do something else with his life. Find a more meaningful purpose. I know for sure that humility has changed me in a major way. And these lessons I haven't taken for granted, even if I've been taken for granted in the process.

But if I thought Dominic was cold, his brother is far more callous. An impenetrable wall who thinks love is nothing but a nuisance.

Bad for business.

"You're an addict."

Anger flares as I gather my phone from my locker and check my messages to find one from Christy declaring she's on a date and will call me tomorrow. She checks in with me daily now. And I know some of it has to do with the fact that she pities me. She worries for me.

I can't even get my worst enemy to take me seriously because I walk around wearing my heartache like a badge on my sleeve, and it's become the bane of my existence.

I slam my locker door, aggravation snaking around me.

The people in my life are walking on eggshells, worried about my fragility. It's then that a sickening thought strikes me.

I'm becoming my mother.

An addict.

An addict.

Am I addicted to the high?

If I'm honest, that's a lot of what I felt when I was with them. They fed it to me at every turn. But then that's the crux of love, isn't it? It is very much a high, a high people thrive on. One that can rip your soul apart once you've lost it.

And maybe it's the chase of the high that has me breaking the rules tonight. It's been eight months without a word. And if I'm an addict, it's been way too fucking long without a hit. Physically, I can feel the added tension on the thin thread between the three of us now more than ever as I replay what happened in my kitchen.

Again, Tobias taunted me.

And again, I wanted *him*.

Guilty and cringing at the thought, I take the road that leads to the townhouse on the cul-de-sac. I haven't, not once, done the psycho ex-girlfriend drive-by, and it's past time I do.

It's when my headlights beam on a FOR RENT sign as I approach their house that I feel the thread give a little more.

Anger courses through me as I step out of my running car and walk over to the house, cupping my hands on the window from the porch to peer in. Empty. Not a trace of life. No trace of the memories made here.

All of it's gone.

On my walk back to my car, I realize the grass is at least a foot tall, which means it's been vacated for a month or longer. My gut tells me much longer.

Back behind the wheel, I tear down the road, blood thumping at my temple as I try to understand the why of it. Where is Tyler living now? I just saw him so he can't be far, which means they can't either. Sean had to know his request for me not to go looking would be too much to ask. And up until now, I've honored it because of "one day".

Furious with my findings, I drive through the roads I know by heart, intent on getting answers. It's when I hit the garage parking lot and slam on the brakes that I'm relieved to see the light on in the lobby. A sign of my old life, unchanged. Faint music drifts from behind the garage as Russell walks into view, eyeing me just before I step up to the door and rap on it lightly, knowing he saw me. When it doesn't open, I knock again, this time much harder.

"Open the door, Russell," I demand, my heart sputtering with the image of the abandoned house.

Nothing.

"Russell!" I step over and glare at him through the thick lobby window when my knock again goes unanswered. Russell cranes his head to avoid my livid gaze just as Jeremy joins him in the lobby. The second Jeremy sees me, he hangs his head.

"I just want to talk to you," I plead through the thick glass, knowing they can hear every word. In the next second, the light clicks off and Russell retreats to the garage. Jeremy holds the door to follow, pausing when he hears me speak up.

"Don't do this," I beg, pounding on the window. "Please don't fucking do this to me! Jeremy!" He stops where he stands, and I can see the sincere regret etched in his posture. "Please, Jeremy!" I watch as he cups his jaw in frustration, his eyes never lifting before he walks into the garage. I back away from the window, outraged, and that's when I come to grips with the truth I've been battling all day.

I *am* an addict.

I'm the pathetic girl who just can't take a hint, the one who refuses to let go.

If I'm being honest with myself, I've seen it in the face of every person who looks at me now—the pity and the concern. Their withdrawal has cost me my pride, my self-respect, and the respect of the people who know me.

It's cost me far more than any high is worth.

And it's past time that I remember how to kick . . .

Chapter Eleven

AFTER DRAINING SOME of the iced whiskey I helped myself to from one of Roman's crystal tumblers, I dive in the pool and emerge in the muggy night, the moon half-lit as I take a few laps around, loving the feel of the warm water on my skin as I work out some of my aggression.

Frustration runs front and center as I exhaust myself, trying to come up with any reason at all why they would take such great care to disappear. The deceit, the humiliation; I've made a fool of myself over two men who haven't bothered to show up for me in endless months.

And for what? The high?

Now all I feel is the crash, the inevitable burn. I tried for the last few months to convince myself that I was moving on, but in truth, I've been waiting.

I will no longer lie to myself, and I can't keep loving in vain.

Neither of the men I'd pledged my heart to have stepped out of the shadows to claim me.

I was delusional to believe that I had a future with either of them.

How strong could any of their feelings truly be with so much deception between us? What we had was beautiful in my eyes, but over time has been painfully proven to be one-sided.

It's been a little over eight months since I danced with Sean in the street. Months in which I've attempted to live normally. In hindsight, it had felt so real. That's what kept me hanging on.

But that's what addicts do, they deny the problem and coat it with excuses. And it's up to me to save myself.

So, I'm done.

I'm done with my unhealthy fixation on the two men who are undeserving of eight months of unreciprocated devotion. I no longer want to understand their motives or the cruel reasoning for their absence.

At this point, I just want to snap the thread and free myself of the burn of being in unrequited love.

Exhausted from my workout and lulled by the whiskey, I step out of the pool and under the outdoor shower to rinse the chlorine from my hair. Towel wrapped around me, I head upstairs and am halfway up when I sense that I'm not alone.

Annoyed, I round the corner to see Tobias flipping through the book on my nightstand. He's dressed in a suit, his tie loose around his collar, his hair perfectly combed back. I bypass him and drop my towel, heading toward my dresser to pull out some shorts and a T-shirt. I stop my hand in my dresser when I feel his gaze on me.

"Are you here on *business*, or is this about my *punishment*?"

He snaps the book closed. "You got the answers you expected. They made their decision."

And it wasn't me.

Acceptance. That's one of the five steps of grief, right? And so, I don't let the sting of his words penetrate my hardening heart. Instead, I search my drawers for clothes.

Seconds pass, and he stands mute, but I can feel his steady gaze.

Intent on nullifying his attempt at intimidation, I turn to face him and untie my bikini top before I let it fall away. The same top he held hostage to humiliate me the day we met.

"Anything else? Another lecture about peas, or pawns?" I stand, nipples drawing tight, water trickling from my skin and suit collecting at my feet on the carpet. He stands at the edge of my bed, seemingly unfazed by my nudity and brazen attitude before I slowly untie the bow at each of my hips, letting the material fall to my feet. It's nothing he hasn't seen, but I can see the surprise light up his eyes with the lift of my chin when I face him fully exposed. I refuse to let him bully me any longer.

It's time to snap the thread.

He ogles my naked flesh, his jaw tensing as he gauges the war I'm waging.

"I know who you are," he finally speaks, his voice tinged with the warning dancing in his eyes.

"Do you?" I challenge. "I don't think so."

He takes a step toward me, and I refuse to flinch. The air thickens as he unapologetically traces the hard lines and curves of my body with hungry eyes. The draw becoming harder to ignore the closer he becomes.

"Cecelia Leann Horner, born June eighth, nineteen ninety-five, five feet nine inches tall, a hundred and forty-three pounds." He takes a step toward me and then another as the water rolls in rivulets down my back. "Daughter of CEO Roman Horner, and Diane Johnston, never married."

He's visually devouring me as I feed on the gravity that threatens the closer he draws near.

"Is this supposed to impress—"

"A timid girl who grew up reading love stories and living vicariously through her best friend while her mother collected boyfriends and DUIs."

I hold my swallow as he takes one last step to tower above me, citrus and leather filling my nose. He raises a hand and cups my chin, sliding his thumb over my bottom lip before dipping the pad of it in my mouth, running it along my teeth. I turn my head as he leans in on a whisper.

"The picture of neglect, you grew up estranged from your absent father and made it your mission to care for your mother, all the while playing it safe. A good girl—that is until curiosity got the best of you and you skipped your junior prom because you were too busy giving away your virginity."

I turn back to face him, utterly shocked.

"Maybe because you felt he had waited an acceptable amount of time, not because you were seized by the passion you so desperately crave."

My eyes dart away as he bends to capture my gaze and holds it—holds me—hostage as my body responds to him, pulsating with a mix of anger and rapidly building desire as he caresses my face with a gentle hand while dissecting my life choices in a play-by-play.

"You drifted through your teens playing the role of the responsible adult in your household, and purposefully failed a final, placing you third in your graduating class from

Torrington High School. Either to avoid the spotlight to spite Daddy and go unnoticed for your perfect attendance and scholastic accolades, or to keep your mother from feeling guilty she couldn't pay an Ivy League tuition in case Daddy didn't come through. After all, it was much safer to stay under the radar and use your mother's mistakes as an excuse not to take any chances."

"That's enough," I snap.

I can't look away at all now as he analyzes my life, my decisions.

He moves in so I'm pressed to him.

"The silver lining? You used your mother's psychotic break as a reason to liberate yourself from being the parent while still gifting yourself the ability to play the martyr. Which leads us here. Where you claim to be for your mother's sake, but the truth is, being here gave you an *escape*. It gave you your first real taste of freedom."

Raw, stripped beyond my nudity, he grips my face in his hands.

"And now you're hiding again because taking chances and really living for the first time in your life didn't turn out the way you hoped it would. But I see you, Cecelia. I. See. You. You keep trying to give yourself, your heart, your allegiance away to anyone who will have it for reasons you can't understand, but it's so painfully clear. Your mother is a selfish narcissist, your father dodged his responsibilities, you feel that my brothers used you and abandoned you, and you're putting on a brave front all the while you're fucking dying inside."

He tilts my chin with his thick finger, as a lone tear runs along my cheek. I grant him the sight of it, the last of my weakness gathering before he gently swipes it away with his thumb. "You're sad and lonely, locking yourself up in this house day and night, and I shouldn't give a shit, but I know I'm partly to blame. I ransacked your life and—"

The crack of my palm against his cheek is sickly satisfying. He roars, gripping my wrists and pinning me to the dresser.

Eyes locked, I glare up at him a second before he slams his mouth over mine. It's noteworthy from his kiss that *he's high* from my pain, and all I've done is reward him with my reaction, my angry tears. He loves my opposition, and the sadness he's inflicting with these heavy truths—his angle to take me down, just as psychological as it is strategic.

I rip my mouth away, shaking my head, disgusted. "You're getting off on this, you sick fuck."

"Sadly, so are you," he counters, possessing my mouth again in a way I can't—don't want to escape. And I kiss him back because my body never listens. After all, he's right. My heart was begging for love in all the wrong places, lurching in any direction for a home. But it's not my heart he wants. It's my spirit he's intent on destroying.

He lifts his free hand to cradle my face and I grip his wrists, trying to tear myself away to no avail. He's stripped me bare, robbed me of more pride with his easy appraisal. I hate that he can see it so clearly, see *me* so clearly.

Or that he did.

Because I'm no longer the woman I was yesterday or even an hour ago.

His words come out in a whisper. "You are a fighter. I'll give you that." His lips inches away, he searches my eyes. "But you give too much for not enough. You trust too easily because you've been lonely your whole fucking life."

"Says a lonely king to the lonely little girl."

Our chests rise and fall collectively as we watch one another for long seconds.

For the first time in my life, I'm in the deep end and I no longer want to find my kick; all I want to do is drown . . . in my enemy. He's the way. The only way.

And once I do this, there's no going back.

It's as if he senses my decision when he lifts a hand to wrap the hair at my nape around his fist and pulls, exposing my neck. His breath hits a second before his full, warm lips land on my shoulder lapping the droplets of water away. Greedy, he draws them into his mouth as I tamp down the whimper on my tongue.

Snap the thread, Cecelia.

Leisurely, he moves across my collarbone drinking in more, savoring the water along my torso and down my stomach as angry tears threaten and I bite back a sob.

Determined to see this through, I sink my nails into his scalp as his hot mouth blazes a trail across my flesh. He devours, covering every inch in his path before he parts my thighs with his palms and begins licking at my core.

Fisting his hair, I cry out at the force in which he sucks, his thick locks tickling my thighs before his tongue darts out, separating me, spearing my clit with precision. And with one sure swipe of his tongue, I go boneless, my back crashing into my dresser as I throw my head back and begin to ride his face.

"Damn you," I pound his shoulders with open palms as his licks increase speed before he slips a probing finger into me. He eats me, his hunger fueled by my cries as I silently sag against my dresser, the knobs digging into my back. Soul aching, my desire for him consumes me as I begin to tremble uncontrollably. An orgasm threatens, and I deny myself, hating him, hating me, hating that nothing has ever felt so fucking good.

"Tu te retiens." *You're fighting.*

This much I understand.

He flicks his gaze up to mine as he works me with slick fingers. The sight of my wet heat coating his digits sets my blood on fire. "Je gagnerai." *I will win.*

Lust overtakes me as he drags me down to the carpet spreading my thighs wide while he hovers above. Silent, he commands my eyes as he lowers his head and begins a second round of assault. With the beckoning of skilled fingers and one more long pull on my clit, I detonate in his mouth. He rims my pulsing core as he draws out every bit of my orgasm with the lap of his tongue.

Chest heaving, he releases me to pull off his jacket before he slowly starts to unbutton his shirt. Eyes piercing, he reaches back to pluck a condom from his wallet before he tosses it next to where my head lay on the carpet. I flick my gaze to where it sits, a clear threat of where this is going if I don't stop it.

With this one act, it will break all ties, destroy us, and any lingering hopes I have left. From his side, I'm a threat and he wants me gone, and this is the way of ensuring I have no place, no future amongst them. It's up to me to stop it from going any further.

But I don't. And I won't. Because I no longer have a reason to hold on.

And because I *am* an addict.

A destitute product of my own imagination, of my own making.

Needy.

Sick.

Insatiable.

And with Tobias, it's like inhaling energy, each breath I draw grows heavy with it, pulling me further into him, into a place I've never been.

He unzips his slacks, unleashing his engorged cock, stroking it as I look on before he starts the slow roll of a condom. I catalog him, consuming every naked inch that my gluttonous mind is demanding I memorize. Dark olive skin stretches over his expansive and fully defined chest, a light smattering of hair is dusted between his pecs, and ribbed muscles line his taut abdomen and trim waist. An insanely deep V encases a trail of hair down his pelvis. Once fitted in latex, he lifts my neck in his palm, tilting my head to give me a clear view. He wants me to bear witness to the end, to his assumed victory.

And this, I refuse to deny myself, but for an entirely different reason.

He pauses briefly, a few seconds for any objection before he begins to press into me. Inch by thick inch, he takes up the whole of me and I lose my breath due to the stretch, the size of him. Cursing, he drives in further, watching intently as my mouth parts and a barely audible hiss escapes him. His features twist with restraint as his body vibrates with residual anger. And there's no mistaking it.

This is *his* revenge, on my father, on the brothers who disobeyed and purposely deceived him. On me for having an unknowing hand in it. And I'm letting him have it. I'm allowing my own degradation.

Once again, I give myself over to my devil, but this time,

this time is different because this time, I've already made peace with it on my terms. I allow him this purposefully, with every intention to see it through. And if I'm damning myself, I'm going to enjoy the burn.

He inches in and I cry out at the intrusion, the unimaginable stretch as he rolls his hips, slowly working himself into me. "Putain de merde." *Mother Fucker.* "Tellement serrée," *So tight.*

"Brûles en enfer." *Burn in hell.* The words pour from my mouth in perfect pronunciation, and my enemy's eyes widen a fraction before he drives into me fully.

It's then I feel the snap . . . and get consumed by the afterburn.

We collectively groan before he curses in a mix of English and French pulling back entirely and thrusting in again, burying himself. Connected fully, his hot exhale hits my neck as I claw at his shoulders, breathing through the discomfort, reveling in the stretch, and indescribable pleasure.

He palms my thighs, spreading them further before he drives in again, his eyes dropping to where we connect. I bellow, my body shaking, as he drags himself along every sacred place inside of me, drawing me out. Within a few more thrusts, I spasm, fighting it, but all it takes is a shot of amber flames and the press of his finger and I topple over the edge.

I revel in the descent, my orgasm taking over, my release streaming between my legs as an ecstasy-filled cry leaves my lips. Back arching, I convulse, cleansing in a white-hot fire that unfurls throughout my limbs as my body trembles in the aftermath.

His eyes slam shut, and he throws his head back, mouth

going slack as I milk his cock, the resulting turbulence shaking us both. It's when his hooded eyes open and latch onto mine, that he loses control.

And then we're fucking—hands clutching, gasps and groans mingling, sweat glistening off our slicked skin as he tears through me lust-crazed, possessed. Pain subsiding, I meet him thrust for thrust, fucking him with fervor until a second orgasm hits, taking me by surprise. I tighten around him as his eyes go molten.

"Putain, putain," *Fuck, fuck,* he curses, his hands covering my body, his touch pure electricity, as I begin to build again with every powerful drive of his hips. Sparks fire and ignite from cell to flesh as he pistons into me, the slapping sound tipping me over as another orgasm threatens. With its arrival, I bang on his chest, the friction too much. Jaw trembling, I come undone, pulsing around him as he picks up speed, his fucking unforgiving while he claims my body wholly. My hate fuels me as I scratch at his chest, determined to collect some of his flesh beneath my fingernails.

And with every sure and damning thrust of his hips, adversary or not, I know I'll never again crave the touch of another like I will his.

Trembling with this knowledge, my back arches again as he swells inside me on the verge. His hand tenses on my breast with the first pulse of his orgasm. His body tremulous as his eyes open with the onslaught. He stares down at me, gasping out his release, unmistakable terror in his eyes.

And I'm thankful for it.

I'm thankful for every vulnerable second of it because I see the recognition when he realizes what I already know.

He didn't want to feel anything, and instead, he felt *everything*.

We've just ruined ourselves with our hate for each other.

He palms the sides of my head as he stares down at me with something akin to astonishment. It's only a flicker of revelation, but it's there. His eyes drop as he pulls out of me and wordlessly grabs the towel nearby in an attempt to cover me. I bat it away, disgusted by his cowardice. If I have to bear witness to this, so does he. There will be no mercy on either of our parts.

"You have to live with it, too."

My words strike him exactly where intended as his face draws tight, all fear quickly becoming replaced by fury. But I'm not the one he's angry at.

He snaps to his feet, tossing the condom in my vanity trash before gathering himself in his boxers; his expression turns to stone as he begins slowly buttoning his shirt.

Flames fading, he eyes me, securing his collar when he speaks. "You should know better than to read into this. It's sex. And it was business. Don't take it personally."

I roll my head back and forth on the carpet unbelieving of his quick denial. "You really need to get over yourself."

He pauses dressing briefly, staring down at me. "I don't blame you, Cecelia. You were taught from an early age to be a fixer. To crave affection unreturned and somehow believe it will be rewarding."

He nods toward the battered library copy of *The Thorn Birds* sitting on my nightstand. "But that's the difference between a boy in a book or a movie and a man in the real fucking world. Some of us don't want to know the inner workings of your mind and heart, or throw away our pride, or tell you our secrets and confess our love. Some of us just want to fuck you until we tire of you and move on."

I pull myself from the carpet and don't miss his thorough sweep of my body. "Except you don't live in the real world. You decided to create one of your own. And you'll *never* tire of me. That's your punishment for betraying them, same as mine."

Face apathetic, he pulls at the cuffs of his shirt beneath his jacket and runs a hand through his thick black hair. "Belle et délirante." *Beautiful and delusional.*

This, I understand. "I guess I am. After all, I'm just a little girl *you* couldn't resist *fucking*." He wants to hurt me. I can feel it—the hate, the rage—he feels rolling off him.

He went too far, and I went with him, but for a completely different reason.

But I'll share in the punishment.

And I'll crave my enemy.

Because that's what we are.

"I'm not the only one who's delusional," I counter, grabbing my towel and securing it around me as his eyes narrow to slits. "And you're insane if you think I'll ever want to know the inner workings of your heart and mind." I grab his suit jacket from the floor and toss it in his face. "Don't take this *personally*, but get the hell out." His eyes flame just before I turn and slam my bathroom door behind me.

I stand on my balcony and pull on the joint, gazing at the horizon in the distance, welcoming the calming effect with every inhale.

In seven weeks, I will be free. Free of Roman's watch,

free of his position in my life. In seven weeks, I'll be far out of Tobias's reach as well, his scrutiny and his judgment. I have two of the most powerful men fighting for control over me while I occupy space in this town. Until then, I'll give Roman and Tobias what they demand of me to pacify them both until I leave, but it'll be on my terms.

Because I no longer feel the weight of the pendulum swinging overhead.

Tobias had planned to finish me off with our shared act of betrayal, but unbeknownst to him, he liberated me.

Sweet freedom.

Violet clouds move over the end of another day as I tap out the joint I managed to roll with some of the weed I stole months ago from Dominic's bedroom. I don't know why I took it, but as I exhale the last of the smoke, I'm glad I did.

I run my hand along the back of my neck, where a small scar exists from where Tobias ripped the necklace from me. He'd cut my skin, and a scab had formed. And I'd picked it, to remember it happened, to remember that once, someone cared enough to claim me, to call me their own even if it was short-lived.

But the necklace and the meaning behind it means nothing to me now.

It can't. Tobias broke that connection, snapped the thread in half. And I allowed it, so I no longer feel tethered to them.

It was clear what his agenda was, but I had one of my own.

All I feel now is justified; justified in moving on, and ending my wait.

If they came now, they would be way too late. Even so, I will never want them the same way. All my foolish notions and hopes ended the night I let my enemy fuck me on his adversary's floor.

And though I do loathe Tobias, with every fiber of my being, I'm okay with the revelation it brought. I crossed a line that my mind and body agreed to and ignored my heart, all for this bittersweet relief.

So, while my flickering love fades for two men, my lust flames for another. And the best part? I don't have to *feel* anything.

Shame, remorse, and guilt are my new enemies.

With no apologies, I'm making my own rules to eradicate my weakness.

I may hate him, but he was right on so many fronts.

By pinpointing my shortcoming, he unshackled me from the heart that continues to weigh me down.

A heart that has proven to be worthless.

No one wants it, and I gave it way too freely. It's made me reckless and weak. And so, I'll stop supplying it with hope and lies. I'll deny its existence and stupid aspirations. I'll let it wither, try to take away its strength, and any power it holds over my decisions. And until my time here is served, I'll allow myself to become my father's daughter—cold, cruel, deceptive, calculating, and unapologetic.

But it's the acceptance of *one thing* that truly sets me free.

My heart has no place here.

Chapter Twelve

"WEAKER GIRL" BY Banks thumps through the cabin of my new Jeep as my freshly cropped hair whips in the wind around me.

New wheels and new hair, to go with my new mindset.

Reinvention is a powerful thing.

I'm determined now more than ever to take my control back. Over myself, my emotions, my direction, and my decisions.

As the days pass, I find myself less concerned with the moral high ground, and more concerned with my next move.

Because this isn't chess we're playing. This is a different game altogether.

I spent the last week celebrating my liberation at Eddie's bar. Small towns being what they are, according to Melinda, I've built quite a reputation in only a matter of days.

No doubt as a fast girl.

She spent last night's shift at the plant trying to convince me I needed saving and was welcome at the church any time to confess my sins and cleanse myself of all my wrongdoings.

None of that appeals to me.

I don't want forgiveness.

I willingly slept with Tobias knowing it would snap the thread.

And it worked well, maybe too well.

Not only did I decide to let my devil out, but I've convinced myself to let her reign. Love and end game don't factor in my participation.

That line of thinking will serve me well when it comes to the bastard who tried to debase me on my bedroom floor.

But it's my craving for the devil I'd let into my bed that I want to erase now.

"Fast girl, indeed," I agree as I race toward the square before whipping into a parking space at the store in front of my favorite dress shop. Tessa greets me with a welcoming smile, her eyes bulging when she sees my hair and the grin I'm sporting.

"Girl, you look incredible." She walks over to where I stand sorting through a rack of dresses. I've already spent a fortune today but couldn't care less that I'm redlining my bank account. Deliverance can do that to a girl. I'm out of fucks to give. I run my fingers through my hair, which feathers right back into place due to the sleek cut.

"Thanks, I'm still getting used to it."

"It suits you," she says, joining me at the rack.

We've become fast friends since I started frequenting her shop, which seems to be thriving, maybe due to a little aid from the brotherhood. But she hasn't mentioned anything about it; she wouldn't. Even if she had, I'd keep my involvement out of it. I don't want credit—the fact that she's doing well is reward enough for me.

I glance around the bustling store at a group of women pulling dresses from the various racks. "Looks like things are going well."

"You have no idea. It's amazing what can happen in a year."

"Oh, I believe you. And that's so good to hear." Tessa runs her fingers through her hair as I compliment her on her dress. She's a beautiful, petite, champagne blonde with doe eyes. The thought occurs to me then; well, Tyler occurs to me. Briefly, I entertain the idea of playing matchmaker, though I'm still pissed at him. But I've got a soft spot for Tyler despite the role he's played. And the sadness in his eyes the day we visited Delphine haunts me. He's in a good place now, or seemed to be when last I saw him.

"Are you seeing anyone?" I ask in a whisper as one of the women picking through dresses eyes me. I wink at her, gauging the judgment in her eyes, no doubt due to my recent scandals, before directing my attention back to Tessa.

"No boyfriends, no," she answers. "Not really much to choose from around here."

"I might have someone for you."

She perks up. "Oh? Please tell me he's not a local."

"He is, but he's been in the service for years. He's a little older than you, so I doubt you know of him. He's one of the good ones."

"Yeah?"

I nod. "Yeah."

"Well, send him in for a dress for his mother."

"I may just do that."

"Does he have a name?"

"Trust me. You'll know him when you see him." And

maybe she has; he is the Friar after all. Then again, I know nothing of the day to day of hood business anymore.

"Really? That hot?"

"That hot."

"I'll be on the lookout."

She looks me over as I again sort through the rack. "I know that smile. Who are we dressing you for tonight?"

I pull a dress from the rack and lift it to my collar, eyeing my reflection in a nearby floor-length mirror before I turn to her.

"*Me.*"

"Well then. I have just the dress."

I wake to the clink of ice against a glass, and a whiff of gin, spice, and leather. A second later, my bedside lamp clicks on, filling the room with a soft yellow hue. Tobias sits at the edge of my mattress, invading me with his presence. He's impeccably dressed in a single-breasted suit, his strong jaw flexing as he drinks me in, his eyes blistering orange-gold. He jerks the covers back, revealing me in my new curve-hugging dress that shows a touch of side boob. I'd gone sans panties tonight as I sipped whiskey on one of Eddie's bar stools. Every time I enter his bar, he greets me with the stink eye, but he's been serving me, and I've been generous with my tips—a sort of silent agreement.

Far different from the one I have with the man shooting flaming daggers at me from where he sits at the edge of my bed.

It's been over a week since Tobias ravaged me. Stupidly, I'd assumed after that much time had passed, I'd seen the last of him.

Gauging by the look in his eyes, I was dead wrong.

I stare back at him from where I lay on my stomach, my head facing him from where it rests on my pillow.

Slowly, he raises his hand and collects a lock of my newly cropped hair before rubbing it between his fingers. Where it was close to waist length, it now rests just below my shoulder in mixed shades of light and dark brown. He drops the lock of hair and runs his palm along the expanse of my back before covering the curve of my ass and stopping mid-thigh to squeeze.

"Rough day?"

"You didn't fuck them. *Why*?" I know exactly what he's referring to. My bar trysts. Though I entertained the idea of giving my body away to a nameless, faceless man to try and erase Tobias, to erase them all, I couldn't do it. Not out of loyalty, but because I knew it would only degrade me in a way I could never face my reflection again.

Instead of inching myself further toward the edge, I decided to white-knuckle my belief about my time with Sean and Dominic last summer. That I had been a girl in love and shared my body with two men I deemed worthy. The reckoning that it meant far more to me than it did to them was still a hard pill to swallow, but it's my self-respect that took the front seat.

For Tobias, I have no beliefs. He's the embodiment of a lone wolf. And I'm all too familiar with the phrase "a wolf loses little sleep over the opinion of sheep".

In his presence, that's all he thinks I am. Prey. Prey to play with. A new toy to pass the time. A business decision.

I'll play sacrificial lamb to make him believe he's gotten his victory, but I will never play into his judgments about me, nor will I fuck faceless men to prove him right. In me, he will find no more satisfaction.

The only belief I have about Tobias at this point is that we're a treacherous mistake.

He stares at me with expectancy to answer his question, and I give him the same damning silence he and his brothers have given me countless times before.

"Do you still believe they're coming for you?"

He flips me with his hand, smoothly turning me from back to front for better access, running his knuckles along the side of my breast, his eyes lingering on my skin before they lift to mine. "Or is it because you wait for me?"

"I despise you."

"That means nothing. You could have gone anywhere. Instead, you chose to prowl around the bar I own to try and make your point."

"You may have taken a great interest in learning everything about me, but I assure you, I couldn't give a shit about you, who you fucked at your junior prom, or what bars you own. Nor do I care about the psychology behind why you act the way you do."

He stops his hand and raises his brows in mild surprise. "Someone's in a mood."

"Blame it on the hormones rather than the backbone. I guess that's easier for a sexist like you to believe."

"Pussy-wielding predator," he chuckles darkly. "I have to admit, I almost laughed." He's had more than one drink, and I assume it's the excuse he's allowed himself to be here.

"That's not who I am, as you well know, but feel free to make all the assumptions you want about me."

He sets the glass down and leans forward, his nose running along my collarbone. "Have you been smoking weed?"

Daily.

"Who would have thought?" he muses, ghosting his lips along my jaw. My nipples spike to life as I try not to inhale his scent. I don't want to be wet. I don't want to react. "And what message were you trying to send?"

"It has nothing to do with you."

"Did you think I would come for you? Stake my claim?"

"I wasn't thinking about you."

"I don't have to give chase. I have you."

"You'll never have me. Not in the way they did."

His eyes flare and I grip his hand just as he snaps the strap of my dress.

"I just bought this, you bastard."

He doesn't so much as flinch as I sink my fingernails into the flesh of his hand while he lowers the fabric to cup my breasts.

"Under my *fat* thumb," he muses, lifting the bodice before he slides his thumb along my stomach, and down, past my pelvic bone and through the thin smattering of hair, inching lower before pressing it against my clit.

"You hate me," he presses harder and I wince, releasing his hand before he licks the pad of it and resumes his touch, massaging me in dizzying circles. "I have some hate for you, as well." He exhales a gin-infused breath. "But you've given me a sort of gift. I never imagined I'd be here under his roof, touching what he treasures."

He pauses his movement when I let out a self-deprecating laugh. "You're sadly mistaken if you think I'm anything close to his treasure. He's incapable of feeling anything. Just like you." Instinctively, I buck my hips against his touch and close my eyes. "Why just months ago, Daddy told me he didn't love me over lamb chops."

His finger stops altogether, and he withdraws it.

I open my eyes to see him staring raptly. I tilt my head, nothing but malice in my voice when I speak. "Don't act so surprised, I told you his only child is his company. Did you think I was bluffing? That inheritance he's granting me is a payoff. A payoff for every recital he missed, for every father-daughter dance he avoided, for every Christmas morning he skipped, for his *absence*." I pull his hand back to my center, spreading my legs wider to grant access. "My mother put together my first bike, built me my treehouse. My mother did those things. So, like I told you, I'm here to collect, for *her*. Unlike you, every word I breathe isn't a lie."

I might as well have slapped him, judging from the look on his face. He earns a lazy smile from me due to my victory. "You really didn't think a monster like Roman Horner is capable of a pesky emotion like love, did you?" He stares down at me deathly still. "Like I said, you're one and the same."

His expression has my blood boiling. "Don't you fucking dare pity me, Tobias—play your part. In case you forgot, you're the *bad guy*."

"What is this?" he asks, leaning in, his tone laced with suspicion. "What are you doing?"

"Doing? Nothing. I was sleeping, but apparently that's not happening anytime soon, so . . . " I nudge his idle hand and close my eyes. A breath passes, then another, before his hand resumes covering me in a soft caress. I open my eyes, irritated by the unwelcome tenderness in his touch. It's when

I see sympathy that I reach back and slap him, wiping his expression away. In a flash, I'm being pressed into the mattress, my wrists in his grip as he snarls at me, nose to nose.

"Stop. Fucking. Hitting. Me."

He smashes his mouth on mine, slipping his tongue past my teeth with my first moan. Mouths molding, I rip at his shirt as he buries his face in my neck, lowering his hand to push his fingers inside me, finding me soaked. He groans as he rims my pussy, sliding a second finger to the circle of muscle behind it. I yelp into his mouth and grip him behind the neck while he probes me in an untouched place.

He breaks from me, his fingers smoothly going in and out as he watches my reaction to his touch. Eyes ablaze, he withdraws and stands to rid himself of his clothes. Breasts exposed, legs open, I lift to my elbows to watch.

I'm barely able to manage another clear thought when his cock springs free from his boxers, bobbing heavily in front of me. I do my best to control the display of my hunger as he draws me to the end of the bed and wraps my hair around his fist, before bending to kiss me. Fire ignites in my core as he thrusts his tongue in, over and over until I'm moaning and reaching for his cock. I pump him in my hand when he pulls back, his eyes hood as I lick my lips, lust drunk from his kiss.

"Suck," he orders, and I gape at him—the audacity of this man. His eyes are unyielding as I barter with my devil, eyeing the head, my mouth watering. Stalling, I glare up at him and squeeze him from thick base to engorged tip. He's dripping, and I find satisfaction in that.

It's my move.

I continue to pump him with my hand as he traces my hot-pink stained lips with his finger before pushing one into my mouth and then adding another. On impulse, I suck as he curses before replacing his fingers with the thick head of his cock, and sliding it in.

"Putain." Fuck.

I choke on the fullness of him as my jaw burns while I furiously try to fit him in my mouth. His amber eyes are ensnared as he watches, bewitched. I struggle with his size, hollowing my cheeks, opening my throat. He's too big, and I'm barely able to cover half of him as he begins to pump his hips. Clawing his thighs, I try my best to get him in, his jaw flexes at my effort, his eyes hooding while his lips turn up in smug amusement. The man is ridiculously hung and no doubt aware of it.

Relaxing my jaw, I lift to my knees and dive, finally able to get him in as a trail of saliva drips between us. The sight of it sets him off as I choke on his length, his girth, and his hands start to roam. My teeth rake his silky head as he orders me on all fours before turning me so that he's stretching me with his thick fingers while he feeds me his cock. My jaw burns with every thrust of his hips, but I'm rewarded by his mingled breaths and filthy words.

I pull away, allowing myself some breath and fondle his balls, pumping him in long strokes. He runs his fingers along my jaw, and then across my lips. He's in no hurry, he plans on taking his time.

My core tightens around his fingers, my orgasm building while I stroke him, pleasure him, a man I despise beyond words, all reasoning.

But I love the feel of him in my mouth, the sight of him

bare and under my power. I stroke him, suck him, playing with the fire that has done nothing but burn me since the moment I knew of his existence. His girth bulges in my mouth just before he pushes me off my knees and jerks me to the edge of the bed, spreading my legs before lining our bodies up, his intent clear.

"N-no." I back away from him, sputtering and jerking my head, denying him. He stills me and grips my throat, the pads of his fingers digging in. He moves to hover above me, tracing my lips with his tongue before feeding alcohol-laced words into my mouth.

"You have an IUD, and I'm not fucking anyone else, Cecelia. I'm no threat to you." Retrieving his pants, he pulls a condom from his wallet and tosses it on my stomach before jerking me back to position and spreading my thighs wide. "I'm taking my punishment." Our eyes meet with his confession. "As long as this is happening, it's only you."

And I can't help myself. I watch as he slides his thick tip through my folds, pressing it to my clit, teasing and torturing us both. Condom still resting on my stomach, I make no attempt to retrieve it as he runs his head up and down my slick center, the head of his cock glistening.

My move.

He allows only a moment more for any last objections before I answer with the faint lift of my hips.

A soft gasp leaves me as he fills me, our gazes locked on the stretch as he claims me in the most intimate way. Once seated, his eyes narrow to slits as both our jaws go slack.

I hate that I love the way his eyes burn bright as he watches my reaction to him. I hate that somewhere deep inside, a voice is dying to break free, the one that never wants this to end, and that the voice belongs to me, to my darkness, to the sick woman inside me that can't get enough of this evil bastard.

He drives in again, his palm gliding up my body before he tightens it around my throat.

"Call out to me," he orders, his voice laced with restraint. "We might as well enjoy hell together."

The feel of this is overwhelming; too carnal, too personal, it's just entirely too much, and it's driving me to the brink. His thrusts deepen, and I begin a quick climb, the pressure of his fingers around my neck fluctuating with every roll of his hips.

I rip at his hand as he denies me air, the intensity building with every squeeze and release. My need growing the heavier his hand becomes.

"Call out to me," he grits out as he slams into me and I hold onto his hand, unable to steady myself. I'm teetering on the edge of darkness when he pulls out and taps the top of my pussy with his thick head.

My body writhes beneath him, my center aching from his absence. He wants to absolutely break me, brainwash me, brand my body, train it to crave him—and only him.

Why can't he just be satisfied with what he's taken already?

He presses in again, his chest rippling with restraint, his thick voice full of command.

"Call out to me, Cecelia."

"No."

He's taken everything else. I won't give him this. I can't give this man more of what he so clearly doesn't deserve. He searches my face, seeing the truth of it, and slams into me, and I bow off the bed, my body convulsing in pleasure before he bends, claiming my mouth. He fucks me with his tongue, suffocating me with his kiss, his hand still wrapped around my throat. It's torturous, agonizing bliss. When he pulls away, his strokes pick up as I crest again and he squeezes, cutting off my air supply just as I explode around him. My body succumbs as the tidal wave of ecstasy washes through me, and the minute my throat is released, I moan, rippling with the onslaught before I unhinge.

Shivering in the aftermath, he laces our hands and pins them next to my head. Our mouths collide as he pistons inside me, the slapping sound of skin again driving me to the brink. When he feels me tighten around him in anticipation of another release, he rips his mouth away. I climb and climb as he keeps me pinned, his eyes locked in on my lips. Just before I come again, he releases my hands and scoops me into his hold. Lifted from the mattress, his forearms cradle my thighs, his arms hooking through mine while his fingers dig into my shoulders, anchoring me to him. And within a few thrusts, I erupt, biting my lips, holding his name on my tongue, coming so hard I see black. Utterly sated, I go limp as he lays me back on the bed, gripping my chin in his hand and forcing my eyes to his as he thrusts once, twice, and succumbs.

I see it, that immense pleasure in his gaze as he fills me with his orgasm, a long groan erupting from his throat before his eyes close and he collapses at my side.

He takes great care not to touch any part of me as he regains his strength. I turn my head and study him as he stares up at the ceiling, seeming lost in his thoughts.

Long minutes pass and I feel the fatigue set in, and oddly enough, sleep begins to beckon me. Sometime later, I open my eyes to see him watching me.

Briefly, he lowers his stare to my bare flesh before he darts it away. "This was a mistake."

A sarcastic laugh erupts from me. "You *think*, Tobias?" I shake my head. "Be honest and admit tonight was just as purposeful as the *first*. If I have to own it, you do too."

"You sound a lot like Sean." He weighs my answering expression. "That pleases you." I see the disdain in his eyes. He's jealous, or something close to it. And it's territorial jealousy at most because there's no way this man cares for me.

"You can't tell me who to sleep with."

"I don't have to. You won't fuck anyone but me. You proved that to yourself. And I don't share all the beliefs of my brothers." Women. He doesn't share women. His eyes flare in warning. "From here on out, I strongly suggest you don't test me on that."

"Well, let me think of a response." I pretend to mull it over. "Screw you. You don't own me. And you're crazy if you think I'm taking orders from you now just because of this."

"But you won't." His confident smirk is infuriating. He moves to get up and I position myself back in bed as he pulls on his boxers.

"You aren't staying. I don't want you here."

He glares at me from where he stands, one arm through his T-shirt. "What in the hell makes you think I want to stay here?"

He lifts his slacks and fastens the buckle, the loose hair cresting across his forehead, distracting. His business dress is a contrast to the jeans and T-shirts I'm used to, and I briefly wonder which I'd prefer under different circumstances.

But with Tobias, I'm grateful I still feel nothing but hate and lust. And the softness in his eyes tonight with my confessions only angered me. He set out to hurt me. He made sure of it. But he himself gave me the power to remain immune to him.

"Tu me crains autant que tu me détestes." *You fear me as much as you hate me.*

I've been desperately trying to brush up on my French, and though I'm nowhere near fully conversational, it's slowly coming back.

He looks down to where I lay, shaking his head while he buttons his shirt. "Jésus, toujours aussi délirante." *Jesus, still delusional.* "I have you the only way I want you. And your French tongue is shit."

"Yet you understood me, and I've made my point. You're a *tool*, Tobias, in every sense of the word. Close the door on your way out."

I can feel his eyes on me as I turn my back to him, pulling the covers over my naked body. And when he leaves, he leaves the door open.

Chapter Thirteen

I CAN FEEL him.
Everywhere.

And though I've washed my sheets, I swear I can still smell the lingering spice of his presence permeating my bedroom. I don't check my rearview but I know I'm being followed, my every move being watched. If I'm honest, I felt it long before the past few weeks.

I don't bother trying to pull anything stupid. It won't be long before I claim my life as my own. I've started to form some plans for my future and to secure my place in my new life. I have to be smart about every move. With every punch of my timecard, I keep up my end of the deal with Roman. On the day I clock out for the last time, I'll arrange a life-changing transfer to my mother. As for myself, I'll make use of the money, but know it won't make a dent in my state of mind other than the fact I won't have to stress and worry about how to obtain it in the future.

That aside, I want more for myself than inherited wealth. Every day I feel a little bit stronger, like I could turn this around and try to cover the surface of the scars I've collected, no matter how deep they still run.

I've been diligent in serving out the rest of my time here without incident, passing on beers after work and gatherings at Melinda's while researching majors as summer passes me by. It's a night and day difference from my last summer, but I refuse to dwell on it. Daily, I push away the thoughts of the men who ruled me for endless days and months, and the latest addition to the mix is becoming the most challenging to ignore. It's during the night when my subconscious takes over and I dream vividly, and the morning after, where I'm forced to relive each painful moment, cursed with the gift of dream recall.

The hangover from them can take hours and sometimes a full day to get through. I allow the burn because it's my hope it's a part of healing—that they'll strengthen me.

Your heart has no place here.

Where I thought I'd been growing wings last year, they've all but disappeared at this point. My consolation is that I'm more focused than ever on what happens when Roman's control clock ticks out.

I consider applying for college far away on the other side of the country, or maybe in a different one altogether. With an abundant bank account and a decent GPA, there are no limits to what I can do. I can start all over, gain my full education at a more reputable school. I've only been a student a few months, and though I like school, my education in Triple Falls has been a collection of very hard lessons.

However, my fire has returned front and center, and I won't stop this flicker of hope, not for anything; it's my driving force. My only regret is that I continue to lie while

FaceTiming Christy and make up excuses to keep her at bay, to keep her safe from my situation. I purposefully deceive her with each conversation, only allowing her to know a percentage of the life I now live. Her new and distracting boyfriend, Josh, is my saving grace. If it weren't for him, I'd be in much hotter water.

But I don't want Tobias anywhere near her, and I refuse to speak of him. He's business for me now, and I'm handling him. He doesn't deserve the acknowledgment as a presence in my life.

I'll live with and deal with my business decision, *alone*.

But it might be best to stick to our core plan having already applied to UG. Maybe being back with Christy will help mend our broken connection. Going back to her may remind me more of the woman I was before I had too many secrets to keep.

And I keep them. No one will benefit from me breaking my silence, and more than that, many will suffer.

Perched on my bed, I begin to fill out one last-minute application, just in case, when I feel him darken my doorway. With Tobias, I've come to realize I have a twisted sixth sense.

He lingers at the threshold as a hint of his earthy scent fills my nose. And I despise my body's initial response. My fingers are still flying over the keyboard when I finally acknowledge him.

"I'm on my period," I announce dryly, not bothering to look his way. "And I don't want to see you."

He remains where he stands, his suited silhouette in my periphery.

"I said—"

"I heard what you said," he snaps, "and you don't get to

decide when you see me." He stalks toward my bed and jerks my laptop from me, collecting my phone from my nightstand and stacking it on top of my computer before striding out of the room. The slam of a door in one of the guest bedrooms lets me know where I can find it once he leaves. He, like Sean and Dominic, refuses to let me have anything electronic near us while he's here. More than once, I've realized my things are missing once he's left the house and have to thoroughly search to find them—the bastard. He has absolutely no regard for my privacy, down to what birth control I use. This devil is swimming in my details.

"I was working on that! It's important!"

His deep voice echoes from down the hall. "I'm not going to fight electronics for your attention."

"Sounds familiar," I drawl dryly. "And no one asked you to come here!"

I lift my eyes when he comes back into view, despising the surge in my veins when they connect. "I think you've made your point. How long do you think I'll let this go on?"

"What makes you think you can stop it?" He strides back into the room, tossing a box on my bed, and I blink at it.

"Whatever it is, you can take it back."

"Just fucking open it."

"I'm not your whore, don't bring me gifts."

He jerks the bow on the box, speaking through gritted teeth. "Open it."

I unfasten the ribbon and open it to see it's a new negligee and matching silk robe. Expensive. I toss it at his chest, and it lands at his shoes.

"For someone who was so intent not to be labeled

Daddy's princess, you sure are acting like the bitchiest noble of them all."

"You want me to be grateful to you?" I shake my head. "Your arrogance is truly astounding." I dart my eyes to his offering. "Take that with you when you go."

In the next second, my hair is fisted around his thick fingers as he pins me, his eyes firing bright with annoyance. I turn away from him, the burn in my scalp strengthening as he rights me where he wants me. I sigh, giving in, my body coming alive with him so close. "Just leave. I've got nothing to offer you."

He squeezes my jaw, so my lips part a fraction, and I glare at him.

"Please tell me you aren't *that* disgusting."

"You're making it very easy to be *that* asshole."

"I don't want your gift, or *you*."

He pushes me down onto the bed and presses his forehead to mine. "I came to apologize for ripping your dress."

"Are you going to apologize for ruining my relationships, invading my privacy, busting my necklace, biting me, kissing me, fucking me?"

"No."

"Then why apologize for anything else?"

"Good point." He dips and kisses me, and I fight him. I fight him, my fire coming back in waves as he presses his body against mine, laying on top of me, stealing my breath, and rattling my senses until I succumb. I grip him to me, destroying his hair, running the thick strands through my fingers. And I kiss him with the same fire, with the same passion I felt to fight just seconds before. Because I hate him, I hate that I think about him, I hate the threatening gnaw I felt in my icy chest the minute our eyes locked. I hate that I thought the gown was beautiful and imagined him fucking me in it. And I hate that I love the way he kisses me.

It's possession and now bordering on obsession, and it's not what I'm supposed to feel. I won't allow it. I bite his lip, and he bites mine in return, and then we're moaning onto each other's tongues. With him this close, I can't do anything but feel him, want him, and he knows it.

He pulls away and I lunge for him, latching onto his throat, suckling his neck, inhaling his scent and loving his sounds as he runs his hands down my sides.

It's then I realize I've been waiting for him, and worse, hoping for him to show. It's no mystery to me why he feels so familiar. Because I know him, and the reason I know him is that the essence of who he is was fed to me in bits and pieces by Sean and Dom. Ironically, a large part of me is drawn to him because last summer as I was falling for them—in a way—I'd been falling for Tobias too, his ideals, his ambitions, his agenda, his take on life. I tear myself away and collapse on my back, frustration brimming as I turn my head to avoid his gaze. "Just leave. Nothing good is coming out of this. And this wasn't a part of our deal."

He dips and kisses the hollow of my throat, and when he gets no reaction from me, he tenses, his exhale audible. "Maybe I am sorry for more than the negligee." If he's feeling remorse, it's much too late. He can't have a heart. He's never supposed to have a heart. He's not allowed to, and neither am I.

"Please don't." A long silence passes as he stays suspended above me. I feel his need, our yearning for the other ricocheting between us. He's becoming familiar, and it's terrifying.

This was not supposed to happen.

We are not supposed to happen.

We cannot happen.

I refuse to let us happen.

"I ransacked your life out of anger . . ." he swallows, and I shake my head.

"Don't plead your case to me, Tobias. I know why you did what you did. You felt just as betrayed, but we took it a step further, and we can't undo that now. No amount of apology will ever make this right. You did what you set out to do, so fucking deal with it." I turn my head and gaze up at him. "We are just business."

His face ripples with ferocity as he lifts himself to sit. "You think this is about your fucking love? This was an apology you turned into melodrama. It's a nightgown, not a declaration." A light sting of rejection tints his face, and I know I've struck another nerve. "You think I won't fuck you if I feel like it?"

I plant my bare foot on his chest from where I lay, my jean shorts riding up my thigh. "Then fuck me, Tobias, call my bluff. Go ahead, you mean, silly monster," I taunt, wrinkling my nose. "Let's get fucking dirty and turn this into a real shitshow."

He scoffs. "You're being ridiculous."

"Of course, I am." I lift to sit. "I'm just a stupid little girl."

He grips my jaw, his eyes dropping to my lips. "I said lonely, not *stupid*."

"Lonely people make stupid decisions. Allowing you into my bed is proof. Apology not accepted; get out." I pull a school brochure from the mail pile on my bed and begin flipping through it.

He's silent for long moments before he speaks.

"You drew the right conclusions. I knew about you. It was my decision, my call, to keep you out of it. I'm the one who hid you."

He pulls the brochure from my grip and tugs my hand to rest between his. "I'm the one who made the decision years ago to keep you out of it. I failed you. I got distracted, and I dropped the ball. I promised myself long ago that no matter how far I decided to go in bringing down your father, you wouldn't suffer for it. I was never going to let you pay for his mistakes."

I try to rip my hand away and he hauls me toward him, so I'm forced to look at him. "I failed you. Not Sean, not Dominic. *Me.* And when I found out you'd been pulled into this . . . and just how far—" ire laces his voice when he speaks—"I was too late. So, when I told you, when I *tell* you, that you were never supposed to be a part of this, I mean it. I failed you, Cecelia. I handled it in a way that I'm not fucking proud of. In a way that could potentially destroy everything I've been working for over half my fucking life."

We sit, face-to-face, the draw becoming undeniable as he releases me and scrubs his face with his hand to sit at the edge of my bed. He's made it impossible for me to sympathize, but I understand his frustration, his fight, the need to believe that we are a cataclysmic mistake. Neither of us is to blame for the attraction we feel. Much like the last year of my life, as cliché as it may be, it just happened.

And we wanted it to happen, but for our *own* selfish reasons.

But I would be a fool to believe him. He's done nothing up to this point that rings sincere.

And it's not my place to comfort him. Because in the wreckage that is Cecelia Horner and Tobias King, we are still reeling, clinging to our purpose as enemies and our loyalty to the people we love. The same two people who can never know we happened, because if those men do care for me, it will cause nothing but destruction.

"You haven't told them."

Silence. The battle is clear in his expression, with himself, and the question he can't bring himself to ask me because he has no right.

But it's me who says it out loud.

"You don't want them to know."

Tobias stays silent for several moments, his reply low. "It would make you an accomplice, not the victim, which you are, and I don't think I can live with that."

"I knew exactly what I was doing."

He jerks his gaze to mine, and I know I've probably said too much.

"Well, I didn't," he admits in a rare show of vulnerability.

"You didn't force me. And if this is a secret I decide to keep, make no mistake, it will be *my decision*. It will be *my* decision to keep it from them, not yours." It all boils down to that. The very foundation I'm standing on, the foundation he's built his life around; secrets and lies and a bond with his brothers that trumps everything else.

Can I keep another secret?

Do I want to?

Do I want to lessen Tobias's punishment? Do I want to guilt myself anymore for sticking to the principles I've been taught by the very man who ripped the safety of them away from me?

Do what you want, when you want, no regrets.
Sean's words.

I study Tobias, trying to weigh if this is just another ploy by him to do his bidding.

"It doesn't matter," I say. "Look around. Do you see them here? You're the one . . ." I inch away from him, disgusted with myself. "You almost had me." I shake my head. "You almost had me." I move to get off my bed, and he stops me with a hand on my thigh. "I'm not buying it," I declare. He's just another opportunist taking what he can get from me. His continued presence baffles me, but I'm sure there's an agenda behind it. There has to be. He's made it his mission to be the only man in my life purely for spite against his brothers.

He leans in, his knuckles brushing my cheek. "I know what you're doing, and I don't blame you."

"I don't know what you're talking about."

He forces my gaze to his, calling my bluff with a single look. But the fact that he knows me well enough to know I've checked out, irks me.

But if his confession has any truth to it, then he's been trying to protect me. That's why he didn't tell his brothers. It wasn't the fact that I was hidden; it was the fact that I was *discovered*.

The bastard now wants me to believe his black heart was filled with good intentions, despite the way he's treated me.

"Question everything," he says softly, reading my thoughts. "I don't deserve your trust, either."

"Now, *that* would be a miracle."

He exhales, sliding his thumb along my bottom lip. "But you're right. This is your decision. This card is yours, and it's your highest one to play. I'll respect your decision on however and whenever you decide to use it. I won't fight you on it."

"Are you forgetting something?"

He draws his brows.

"*You're* the great continental divide. They've ceased to exist for me, Tobias." My eyes narrow and I jerk away from his touch. "What are you not telling me?"

"A lot."

"Get out."

"I wish it were that simple."

"It is. You stand, you walk out that door, and you don't come back. And you cease to exist for me too."

He leans in, making it impossible for me not to see him. "I wish I could. I would. I'd leave you here and never look back."

"Then what's stopping you?" I snap.

He swallows and stands, pulling me to my feet, and stupidly, I allow it. Tentatively, he trails his knuckles from the valley between my breasts down to the button of my shorts.

"Tobias," I object, stopping his hands.

"Allow me this," his eyes implore mine. "Please?"

A word I never thought would ring sincere coming from his lips. I remain silent, watching him with clear accusation as his expression remains earnest while he pushes the shorts past my thighs, and grips my hand to help me step out of them. Slowly, he lifts the hem of my shirt before easing it over my head and leans in pressing a kiss to my bare shoulder as he unclasps my bra, discarding it onto the growing pile on my floor. Bare in nothing but my simple cotton panties,

I cross my arms over them, thankful I opted for a tampon this morning, my cheeks heating before he gently pulls them apart, his eyes gliding down my body in an appreciative sweep.

My pulse kicks up as he retrieves the gown from the floor and lifts my arms before he pulls it down, the silk caressing me as it slides down my frame, where it hangs mid-thigh.

He steps back. "Exquise."

I bite my lip as the atmosphere swirling around us thickens just before he plucks his wallet from his pants and tosses a few hundred dollars on the bed behind me. He sees the insult his action causes and palms me flush to his side, his thumb sliding along my hip when he speaks, his voice heated.

"I didn't know where you got the dress, so I couldn't replace it. But the negligee felt like you. Soft—" he presses a kiss below my ear—"sensual—" and another—"delicate." He pulls back to weigh my reaction before licking along my bottom lip, "beautiful." He releases me and steps back, eyes searing me before he turns and leaves me staring after him, covered in silk, thoroughly seduced, and utterly perplexed.

Chapter Fourteen

I RINSE A day of work away, opting to call Christy tomorrow. I don't even know what to tell her at this point. I've been in a daze, just going through the motions since Tobias left me with his confession. Even Melinda has left me alone with my thoughts as I made it through my last few shifts on autopilot.

More and more, I've become attuned to my surroundings after my shifts at the plant, fearful at times despite those flanking me to get to their cars and back home. Even though I know I'm being watched, and am under Tobias's protection, I sometimes get a sinking feeling. More and more, my dreams are becoming nightmares, and more often than not, sleep is starting to evade me. Whether it be guilt for the part I'm playing in my father's downfall or the lover I've taken, or the scary truths that have been revealed to me, something is off.

I'm to the point where I trust nothing and no one.

I told Tobias he feared me as much as he hated me, but with the way he left me days ago, it's clear he's attempting to turn the tables and paint himself in a better image.

I refuse to believe him. He's far too deceptive for his

apology to have been authentic. I have to chalk his sudden change in behavior as an attempt at more manipulation. There's something he wants, and I have to figure out what it is and whether it's worth it for me.

His sudden change of heart is too convenient, too far-fetched to consider. He was convincing, I'll give him that, but I will not fall victim to him or his performance. Fool me twice.

I will not be played again. No matter how much I desire him.

The more I think about my conversation with him, the more curious I become about his fear of us being discovered.

Would they even care at this point?

It's been nearly nine months of utter silence.

But something in Tobias's confession alluded to the fact they would care—very much—about us sleeping together. And still, days pass without a word, without a trace they exist.

During our conversation at the clearing, though, Tobias couldn't be sure. He assumed that necklace came from Dominic.

Why?

What is he not telling me? That's what I have to figure out.

But his admission to me was ammunition against him, and he said he wouldn't fight me on it. He gave me a grenade and put my finger in the pin with the option to pull. I don't see that playing to his advantage from any angle unless he thinks he can manipulate me into keeping our secret.

Or maybe confessing is exactly what he wants me to do.

Maybe that's his motive.

The man is a walking mindfuck.

I'm in the midst of rinsing out my conditioner when a sudden but distinct electricity spikes my awareness.

Clearing my eyes, I peer through the glass door and spot Tobias standing just outside of it, gloriously naked while unmistakable thirst is evident in his expression. The second our eyes connect, all my thoughts fall away as my libido takes the wheel.

Might as well enjoy hell together.

He opens the door and steps in, just as I reach for him and our mouths collide. His kiss is ruthless, his tongue delving into every corner of my hungry mouth, and I return it with equal fervor. In seconds he's inside of me, his mouth latched to my neck as he furiously fucks me against the heated tiles until I go limp in his arms just before he jerks his hips and stills, emptying inside of me. "Putain. Putain. You feel so fucking good," he rasps, just before he draws my lips into a dizzying kiss. I drag my nails down his back and through his hair when he jerks away from my touch. It's then I see that his hair is soaked, and it's not from the shower spray. A drop of crimson hits his shoulder and I gasp when I realize he's bleeding.

"What in the hell? You're hurt!"

I raise on my toes to inspect the wound and he gently pushes me away.

"I'm all right."

"You're bleeding. Tobias, this looks bad."

He reverses us, the water hitting his scalp and coming out tinged with pink between our feet at the drain. He runs his hand through his hair as I struggle with him to get a closer look.

"What happened?" I battle with him until finally he relents, sitting on the shower bench so I can inspect him. The inch-long gash at his crown could use a stitch or three.

"You need stitches."

"It will heal."

Once he's rinsed off, he follows me out of the shower and stumbles before bracing himself on the counter.

His eyes close as he pales.

"You've lost too much blood."

He chews his lip with his teeth. "I'm good."

"Sit down. *Now*."

"I'm fine."

"If you pass out and crack your head, I *will* leave you to die."

"No, you won't, that's not who you are." He grips my hand and glances at me, his smile faint.

"Sit the hell down."

He does, as I do my best to towel him off.

It takes every bit of strength I have not to press my lips to his skin as I do.

That's affection, and maybe it's his helplessness that has me wanting to do something so intimate.

I bat that notion away Louisville Slugger-style. I've shown him enough kindness by tending to him.

I will not be the fool again.

He watches my every move as I pat the water from his body before ordering him to sit on the edge of my bed.

"You think fucking me was smart, considering?"

"I think fucking you was worth the added headache you're giving me."

I roll my eyes as he tries to pull me into his lap.

"Tobias, you're seconds away from passing out. Stop, you're white as a sheet."

He shrugs. "Better than having one draped over me."

"That's debatable."

I don't miss his grin. "Maybe you don't hate me so much anymore."

"Not debatable."

I collect his clothes from my floor and see the collar of his shirt is covered in blood, along with the back of his suit jacket.

"How long have you been freely bleeding? You've lost a lot."

He nods toward his clothes. "Burn them."

"I'm afraid my incinerator is on the fritz." I bite my lips to stifle my laugh.

He rolls his eyes. "Bag them. I'll take them with me."

I lift the clothes in jest. "So, this is all covered in incriminating DNA, all I need to take you down, huh?"

Nothing about that amuses him.

"I'm joking."

He's not.

"You already have all you need to take me down."

We stare off, his newest confession throwing me until he winces.

I cock my hip and palm it. "You *need* stitches. It's still bleeding. Don't you have some sort of dirty mob doctor on the payroll?"

A chuckle erupts from him. "You've seen entirely too many movies, but it's not a bad idea. It's not deep enough, and it *will* close tonight. I'll settle for a nurse with a horrible bedside manner instead."

"Fine." I roll my eyes. "Stay there." Dressing quickly, I go to the hall closet and pull out a trash bag and the first aid kit. I bring it back to the bedroom and spray his gash with antiseptic. I can't help my giggle when he lets out a whimper as I press a bandage to his wound before ordering him to hold it.

"Big baby."

"It fucking hurts," he says, his posture wary as he holds the bandage to his head.

"I'll get you something to put on."

He grips my hand. "No."

"This isn't debatable, Tobias."

Downstairs, I head to Roman's bedroom and check his medicine cabinet, grabbing a couple of Vicodin. Searching his drawers, I find some unused boxers and a T-shirt before I stop in the kitchen. Back in my bedroom, I hand him the painkillers and juice. He swallows them down before studying the clothes in my hands—the clothes belonging to a man he despises.

"They're clothes. You can't walk around naked."

"Says who?"

"Don't be ridiculous. The boxers are still in the package."

He doesn't say a word as he opens it and slips them on, along with the T-shirt. I extend the napkin, holding the quick sandwich I made, a croissant and Swiss cheese.

"Here, eat this, a Frenchman's delight."

"Not hungry."

"Eat, or you'll pass out."

He takes it from me and shoves half the croissant in his mouth, chewing slowly, his eyes never leaving mine.

"You're acting like a brat. Like Mom just forced you to

get a buzz cut. Just say thank you. You won't hate yourself as much."

It's faint, but I hear it when I switch off the bathroom light. "Merci."

"So, is this some sort of scare tactic? Because I'm leaving soon."

"No, this is a rough day."

"Retaliation?"

He sips his juice, completely ignoring the question.

"You know, your brother did the same shit." I roll my eyes. "I wonder where he got it from."

I pull my comforter down and sort my pillows while he finishes his sandwich. He sits there as if he's confused about how he got here. I am too. Instead of questioning it, I lay our used towel on the pillow next to mine and gesture for him to lay down.

Instead, he stands, crumpling up the napkin in his hand while walking into the bathroom. A second later, I hear running water.

"What are you doing?" I ask from the edge of the bed.

"Brushing my teeth."

"Are you serious?"

I hear a mumble around the toothbrush, "Swiss cheese breath is the worst."

Laughter bursts from me. "You better not be using my toothbrush."

"There was a spare in the cabinet."

A few seconds later, I see the flicking of the light once, twice, three times before he climbs into bed with me.

"Better?" I press my lips together.

He rolls his eyes. "Laugh it up."

When my smile dies, we lay there silent, facing the other on our pillows.

"Why did you come here? I'm not your girlfriend."

"No, you aren't." His voice is wary, as is his stare; he's exhausted.

"So, are you going to answer the question?"

"No."

Up close, I take in the slight wave of his damp hair, his thick midnight-black lashes, the smooth planes of his face, his mouth. His top lip a more masculine cupid's bow, slightly smaller than the bottom. He returns my stare, his eyes roaming my face, and equally as probing.

I'm the first to speak.

"What's your game?"

He fires right back. "What's yours?"

We lay there, silent, eyes challenging.

"I won't ever be able to believe a word you say, Tobias."

"I don't expect you to."

"So why bother, after treating me like total shit, you suddenly have a conscience? Suddenly I'm worthy of—" I wave my hand around—"whatever the hell you're doing?"

"Treating you with respect? Like I've wronged you? Like I've mistreated you horribly and I'm apologizing for it? I'm not a monster, Cecelia."

"Debatable."

He sighs. "As I said, I don't expect you to believe me."

"I don't, and I won't."

His eyes dart past my shoulder, a deep line forming between his brows.

"Are you okay?"

He focuses back on me.

"Te soucies-tu vraiment de moi?" *Do you really care about me?*

"Tobias, I'm not fluent."

He clears his throat, but the question seems to pain him. "Do you really care?"

"I asked, didn't I?"

"You should hate me."

"I do."

"No, you don't. You want to, but that's not who you are. You want to believe the best in people."

"Is that so wrong?"

"No." He swallows. "It's not."

"Just bad for business," I conclude.

A faint dip of his chin before his eyes gloss over.

I lean in, unable to help my smile. "Pills kicking in, huh?"

A little smile forms on his lips, which in turn tugs at the edges of my heart. And in that moment, his words ring true. I've been looking for the good in him. But I can't trust him, which leaves us nowhere. He sinks into the bed a second later, and my smile grows.

"Ohhhhh, you're high as a kite." I straddle his lap before leaning forward and pressing my nose to his. "All doped up."

He grins up at me, his smile so blinding that I feel that familiar flap of wings.

His grin starts to fade as I peer down at him. He slowly lifts from where he lays and kisses me, his fingers stroking my face in a way that has me turning my head to ignore my reaction. It's far too intimate.

"Don't do that." I lift to climb off his lap, and he stops me with his hands on my thighs.

"Do what?"

I change the subject. "Are you going to tell me what happened?"

"You're better off not knowing."

I pull back and nod. "I thought that would be your answer. Can't give me an inch, huh?"

I don't miss the ironic twist of his lips as he gently lifts his hips, his growing erection letting me know precisely what inches he would readily give me.

Rolling my eyes, I take my place beside him and click off my lamp. We lay in the dark, inches away, untouching. We've never been in bed together, not in the domestic sort of sense. And I curse my stupid emotions for feeling what I shouldn't when he begins running the pads of his fingers along my arm.

Utter fucking disaster.

Minutes pass, as I stay quiet beside him. His touch lulls me into a state, a minute before he pauses his fingers.

"Why did you sleep with them both?"

"Whoa."

I click the light back on and slide to sit at the head of the bed, peering down at him. If his pupils are any indication, then he's been pulled way under. Those painkillers must be potent, or he's a lightweight. Otherwise, he would never let me hear the hint of jealousy in his voice. And it is undeniable.

"Why do you want to know?"

I get a half shrug. "I'm curious."

"No, you're not; you're judging me. And it's none of your business."

His voice is faint when he speaks. "Je n'en ai aucun droit."
I have no right.

"English, Tobias."

"I have no right. Answer the question."

His voice is so raw, as if he's been mulling this over and it pains him to ask. What do I have to lose by being honest? Nothing. This man knows me. He sees me more clearly than most others I've known for most of my life. But only because he's studied me as his opposition.

"Sexually, for me, it started like a college phase. I'd only slept with two other boyfriends before I met them."

"You weren't in college."

"It's an expression."

"I know the expression," he replies with an edge. But the look in his eyes isn't condemnation. It's curiosity.

"I know I'm not the first woman they shared, so don't think relaying that will make a damn dent in me. And don't be such a prude. Wasn't it the French who coined the term ménage à trois?"

His eyes narrow to slits.

"Come on. I've been on the receiving end of you. I know you aren't a saint."

"I'm not."

"Then why does it matter?"

He stares at me with expectancy.

"If you get this from me, I want something from you." He opens his mouth to speak, and I lift my hand. "And it's got to be good. A real confession."

He smirks, his expression boyish, and I soak it in, knowing all too well this is a side of him he rarely reveals. His guard is down, even if it's drug-induced. "When I was twenty-one, I slept with every woman in the June edition of a French lingerie catalog."

Maybe I didn't need that confession.

His lips turn up at my reaction.

"Don't look at me like that. I'm not jealous, I'm . . ."

"Judging?"

"No. But exactly how many girls was that?"

"It was a boutique."

"You aren't joking."

He slowly shakes his head, and his lips press together like he's trying to hide a threatening smile.

"How is that even possible?"

"I was bored."

"You were . . . bored."

"Yes." He shrugs. "But it was just the once." His accent makes his comment almost comical. Almost.

"So, what, the other eleven calendar months didn't appeal to you?"

"It was a college phase," he supplies blandly.

"Well—" I clear my throat—"there you go." I move to turn off the light, and he stops me.

"That answers nothing."

Positioning my legs to sit criss-cross style, I sit and scowl at him. "You really want to know?"

"I wouldn't ask if I didn't want to know."

"Don't you already? Aren't you the one who mapped my life up until now—my motives?"

Silence.

I gaze over at him as he adjusts himself on the pillow, his sculpted arm bulging as he does. I uncap the water on my nightstand with the image of Tobias, ten years younger, alone in a hotel room with naked lingerie models.

And in a sick, possessive way, it turns me on.

His eyes light in recognition as he dips his hand between my thighs, and I swat it away. A knowing chuckle leaves his lips, and my cheeks flame.

"Let's just go to bed." I again move to reach for the lamp, and he grips my wrist in a silent order. I meet his eyes and sigh.

"Fine. When I got here, I realized no one knew me. It was a chance to reinvent myself. So I decided to live it up and let myself go. Like you said, I was pissed at Roman for stealing a year of my life and feeling a bit rebellious. I gained my freedom as you so cleverly pointed out. When I met Sean, it was as if the universe had handed me an invitation. It was an instant attraction with him. We clicked both physically and spiritually, but Dominic hated me from the start."

He looks up at me in silent urging—permission. I'm a fool for freely giving the devil more of my details.

"I trusted Sean because he took his time, he earned it from me, so when he said he recognized my attraction for Dominic and told me he wouldn't judge me if I acted on it, I permitted myself. I trusted Sean enough with my body and heart to explore with him. I was already falling for him and had a hate/lust relationship with Dominic. After it happened, we just . . . grew into more. I got to know them both inside and out, and neither one of them made me feel bad about it. We all just sort of fell into place, together."

Tentatively, Tobias lifts his fingers to brush the damp hair away from my shoulders, the act so intimate. I shiver involuntarily, trying desperately not to get lost in the look in his eyes.

"I will say, it went against my nature, it bothered me a lot more than I let on—at first—but the more we grew, the more I couldn't imagine . . . didn't want to think about giving either of them up. And they didn't force me to choose. We were all okay with it. In fact, we were happy, until they . . ."

Tears threaten, and in a flash, I'm back in that garage, living some of the most painful seconds of my life. Tobias grips my chin in his hands. "Until they what?"

"They called me a whore in a roundabout and very fucked up way. Have you ever heard the song 'Cecilia' by Simon and Garfunkel?"

He shakes his head.

"Well, it's about a promiscuous girl, and the lyrics are degrading. That's how they ended it with me. They played that song when I showed up to the garage and humiliated me *publicly*, to try and get the message to you that they were playing me. So, they tore me to shreds in a way they knew would work. And it did. *I* got the message, even if you didn't. I don't think I've ever known pain like that, *ever*."

"Je suis désolé."

"In English, Tobias."

"I'm sorry."

I want to believe him. Everything in his expression, his posture, tells me he's sincere, but I can't. He has to understand I *can't* believe him.

I bite my lip and briefly contemplate coming clean with the rest.

He lifts the pad of my pointer finger to his lips and kisses it, in an attempt to tell me my secret is safe. I know the safer bet is to shut this down, but I continue anyway.

"Looking back now, I know some of the sexual stuff was me waging war on the wallflower I was before I got here. You were right. I played it safe. I rarely took chances. I colored in the lines. When my father told me he *tried* to love me, I think it cut much deeper than I could heal. I'm not saying I went out and purposefully sought to sabotage myself, but it sure as hell didn't stop me from acting on impulse. I will not blame it on him, or my new-found freedom. I fell for them. Both of them. And the best part about it was that Sean and Dom refused to let me apologize for it. They refused to let me degrade myself. It was the safest I've ever felt with anyone because of the way they embraced me. I don't regret it. I will *never* regret it. And I'm not ashamed of it. As for loving them, you *know* them. These are the people closest to you, right?"

"Oui."

"So how could I *not* love them?"

We stare off until he gives me a faint dip of his chin. Refusing to look for or try to decipher any further reaction, I click the light back off and lay my head on my pillow facing away from him when he sounds up next to me.

"I will never speak of this to you again." This time, I hide behind his native tongue. "Es-tu jaloux?" *Are you jealous?*"

"Non." *No.*

I disregard the uncomfortable and unwelcome sting his quick answer gives. "I was honest with you."

He pulls me to him, my back to his front as he rests his head on my pillow, his warm breath hitting my ear. "So was I. Je ne veux pas n'être qu'une phase pour toi."

"English, Tobias. Please."

Silence.

And in seconds, he's asleep.

The next morning, I wake to see my phone lying on the pillow next to me. I unlock it, and when the screen lights up, I realize my email has been checked, the most recent from my father.

It's a summons—a summons to sign for my inheritance, *tomorrow*.

Tobias saw it. Which means our deal ends the minute the ink dries.

Once that money is safely transferred to my new bank account, we have no more business together. I'll be free, and he'll be free to move in on Roman.

Chapter Fifteen

STANDING IN THE middle of my bedroom, I make a quick decision to pack an overnight bag, drive to Charlotte and get a hotel to prepare myself mentally. I don't want to smell him on my sheets or study the drops of blood on my comforter while I mull over the feelings that threatened with our intimate exchange.

Dismissing what happened between us last night is the smartest move. It felt like there was a definite shift in our hate/fuck relationship. But I have to reject any idea that it was more than a late-night confession between two enemies calling a temporary truce.

But what if he had meant every word, every kiss, every touch? He had absolutely no motive to be so deceitful. He had no reason to confess or ask the questions he did, to touch me the way he did. To look at me the way he did.

He's fucking with you. Sign the papers, punch your time-card, cash in, and go back to Georgia.

The second after I sign the papers, there's a good chance I will never see Tobias again.

And good riddance.

Right?

I have no way of reaching out, no way of contacting him. Much like the men before him, when our arrangement ends, I'll once again be locked out.

This is a purposeful advantage on his end. And what would I say to him anyway if I could?

Somehow, he's slipped into more than my bed. He's managed to occupy my thoughts too. But at this point, I can still make it safely away from him without adding another scar.

He's a liar. His words, his looks, his touches—all lies. He wants me as his ally for his agenda. Nothing more. I don't even know where he lives.

We are business.

"Don't be a fucking fool," I scold, throwing a suitable pair of slacks and a silk blouse along with the heels I chose into my bag.

After packing up, I lock the house up just as I get a confirmation email from the hotel of my reservation. Once buckled in my Jeep, I shoot a quick email to my supervisor at the plant and put in for two days of paid time off. Honestly, I don't give a damn if I'm fired. I'm surprised Roman agreed to sign early, considering I still have a little over six weeks left to fulfill my end of our arrangement.

It takes me around two hours to get to Charlotte. I took my time on my drive, knowing I have nothing to look forward to once I get to the hotel.

Tomorrow I'll be a millionaire, but for some reason today, I feel bankrupt.

Any normal woman would be charging up room service, popping bottles, or one-clicking a new pair of heels. Or, at the very least, building an impressive shopping cart.

All I feel is dread.

Sitting at the edge of the bed, I run a finger along my lips when memory kicks in.

Tobias woke me in the middle of the night with his lips, his tongue, before he took me.

And he didn't just take me, he consumed me, hooking my thigh on his hip before pushing inside me from behind. Blood surges between my legs as my chest heats and my face flames.

"Call out to me, Cecelia," he murmurs, pumping into me slowly, his strokes deliberate, filling me as he sucks my fingers into his mouth before guiding them to where our bodies meet, pressing them to my clit, drawing out my orgasm.

"Damnit!" I stand and pace the room before running a hot bath. Lowering into the scalding water, I wince at the sting between my legs before laying a washcloth on my face.

Days ago, I wanted him as far away from me as possible. I was still toeing the line between lust and hate.

I cannot feel for this man.

It's better that it ends now.

It's already over. No goodbyes necessary.

And maybe the waiting phone on my pillow was his way of saying it was over as well.

Fine.

We live on opposite sides of the universe. Our worlds are completely different.

"He doesn't feel a fucking thing for you. He can only play you if you let him." And now, with our arrangement satisfied, he'll disappear just as suddenly as he came.

Good. Good riddance.

After leaving Triple Falls, I'll go off to school, graduate, and dominate the field of my choice. And maybe, one day, I'll marry and have children.

But it's the pounding at my temple, and the gnaw in my chest that refutes that type of future. Do I want that life?

All my best-laid plans now seem simple-minded, if not a bit boring and predictable. My focus before I moved to Triple Falls had been solely on just making it through with Mom. I always dreamed of the day I'd gain my freedom, but I didn't plan past that. Now that day is almost here, and any plan I've come up with recently doesn't seem like enough for me anymore.

Pulling myself out of the bath, I dress in my pajamas and sip whiskey from the small flask I packed before I dial my mother. She answers on the second ring.

"Hey, baby girl. What are you up to?"

"I'm in Charlotte. I've got a meeting with Dad in the morning."

"Oh?" She lingers on the line.

"Mom, I'm signing tomorrow."

"You don't sound so happy about it."

"Money doesn't make me happy."

"It's good you found that out early. But a lack of it sucks."

"I mean, I hated it when we were broke, you know? When you worried yourself sick, but—"

"We did okay, didn't we?" I can hear the smile in her voice.

"Five bucks' worth of gas and tater tots."

"I miss you, kid."

"I miss you too. But I called for a reason."

"Okay."

"Look, I know what you're going to say, but I need your bank account info."

"What, honey? No. That's all yours. It's meant for you."

"And I want no part of it. The son of a bitch is a multi-millionaire and made us do without for years paying the bare minimum while we scraped by. It'll be my money and therefore my decision. I want you taken care of. And I want you . . . to see someone."

"You want me to see a shrink?"

"Yes. If you think it will help. Yes . . . I want you to get help. I think you need it."

"Wow. Subtlety is no longer your strong suit. What happened to my sweet little girl?"

"I'm sorry." I sip my whiskey, thankful for the burn and the numbness that follows. "I didn't mean for it to come out that way."

"Tell me what's wrong."

"Nothing, I'm fine. We're talking about you."

"Then I'm fine."

"Will you stop with that shit, Mom?"

"No, I will not."

"I am fine. I'm just . . . tired."

"Same guy?" The insinuation in her voice brings all my wandering thoughts of Tobias to a crashing halt. Even if it's my head he's invading, he's got me vulnerable. I hate that she can hear it.

Just like that, all my shields snap back into place.

I'm done. I'm done thinking about him. I'm done fantasizing about him.

"Mom, we'll talk about this some other time, okay? I'm going to wire you some money as soon as the funds are transferred. Life-changing money. *You* be happy about it."

"You know I can't take money from you."

"Then take money from *Roman*."

"He's truly not the cold-hearted man he makes himself out to be."

"It's much too late."

"I don't want his money, Cecelia."

"What *do* you want from him?"

I can hear the flick of her lighter, and her exhale. "Nothing. He gave me the best thing he could ever give me."

"Why won't you talk about him? If you're so determined that I give him a chance, then give me a reason to."

"Because he's your father."

"Not good enough. Does he think you tried to trap him? Is that why he's been so stingy with his money?"

"You mean baby trap him? No, no, nothing like that."

"Then tell me what it's like. I really would like to know. Don't you think I deserve to know?"

"There will come a day when I'll explain things to you, but for now, can you just try to be patient with him?"

"No." I'm adamant. "My patience has run out. He's given me nothing, and I'm only here . . ." I cut myself off mid-sentence. I don't want her to ever know I spent my time in Triple Falls to make sure she's taken care of.

"Parents love their children, Cecelia, even if some are incapable of showing it the way they should."

"Why are you defending him? I don't get it."

"I just hoped you living with him would change things."

"He lives *here*, in Charlotte. I haven't seen him since the fourth last summer."

"What?! Jesus, Cecelia, you've been alone in that house this whole time?"

"Basically. Kind of. I've made . . . friends."

"Cee, how did I not know this?"

"I didn't want to bother you with it. Nothing you can do about it anyway."

I hear her sniff.

"Mom, don't cry. I'm fine. A few more weeks and I'm out of here. I'm coming home. I'm going to UG, so you'll see me all the time."

"I feel terrible."

"Don't. This is why I didn't tell you. There's no reason to feel guilty. He doesn't, I'm sure."

"He does. I know he does."

"I think we're talking about two totally different people."

She sniffs again, cursing under her breath. "Damnit, Roman."

"Mom, send me your info, okay?"

"No. What kind of mother would that make me? Me and Timothy are doing just fine. We're thinking about buying a house on the lake."

"Well, now you can have it—Roman's treat. And then you can go to Mexico and celebrate with a margarita in hand. We've never taken a vacation. Promise me you will. Promise me. And promise me when you get back, you'll see about talking to someone."

"Cecelia—"

"This isn't up for debate, Mom."

"Jesus, bossy. What's gotten into you?"

"One too many," I reply, knowing she'll understand.

"Talk to me."

"I'm not ready, okay? And I don't think you would believe it if I told you. I'll be next in line if your shrink's any good."

I stand and open the curtain to my hotel room and get a

clear view of my father's building across the street. My father owns a skyscraper, and Mom and I ate mac and cheese with hot dogs cut up in them to make it through to her next payday. She'll never have to do that again unless she's feeling nostalgic or gets high. That knowledge alone is worth every trial I've gone through this year.

"Please, Mom. Please let me do this for you."

"I can't, Cecelia. I'm sorry. It feels wrong. It *is* wrong."

"It's not."

"I'm hugging you so tight, kid."

"Mom, wait—"

"I love you."

I sigh, deciding to fight her on this another day. Technically, I don't even have the money yet. But I will win this battle. "Love you too."

I take another nip of whiskey and lay back on the bed. A different bed in a different world where I don't masturbate to thoughts of the boogeyman. A world where things aren't so complicated, where I'm free to do as I please.

And suddenly, freedom doesn't seem so appealing.

I don't sleep at all.

Chapter Sixteen

M Y FATHER JOINS me in the conference room where I've been waiting for nearly an hour before he takes the seat next to me. I sip my water, feeling his eyes on me as I stare down at the stack of papers on the table, still unable to grasp the enormity of what he's giving me fully. "How are you, Cecelia?"

"Fine, Sir," I reply, straightening my posture in my seat.

"How is the plant? Better with the improvements?"

"It's good, Sir."

"Did the lawyer brief you on what you'll be signing for today? Do you understand—"

"Yes, Sir." I fight the urge to thank him, but I never asked for it. When I finally lift my eyes to his, I see he's regarding me carefully.

The last time I saw him, I'd snubbed him, too pre-occupied with the men in my life, and too resentful to take him up on whatever he was offering that day. The conversation with my mother had me thinking all night of ways to try and approach this, but I decide to go with brutal honesty.

It's now or never.

"Please help me understand this."

"Understand what?"

"You," I reply simply. "Why do this?"

He drops his gaze to the paperwork. "I told you why."

"So, this is a payoff? Because you didn't want to raise me?"

His flinch is barely visible, but I don't miss it. "This ensures you'll be financially secure for the rest of your life and, if managed properly, beyond the lives of your children."

"Why care about them if you don't care about your *own* child?"

His eyes soften, but there's a hard edge to his voice when he speaks. "I've explained this to you."

"No, you haven't. You said your parents were WASPs and drunks and squandered their fortune and that you weren't raised in a loving environment. But I'm not asking for a hug, Roman. I want to know why."

He bristles but gives me nothing else, and I have half a mind to stand and leave him with his filthy fucking fortune, but it's my mother's terrifying blank stare that keeps me sitting here, ready to collect. She's in a good place now, but what if she goes back to where she was? Though it would be the ultimate fuck you to deny his fortune and walk away, I can't. I can't do it.

"I'm sorry I failed you, Cecelia."

"That's twice now you've admitted you've failed me, and once you admitted you tried to love my mother, love me. But those are apologies and excuses without real explanations. 'I'm sorry I failed you' is not an explanation, and I've heard that quite a bit recently."

"Maybe it's the company you keep."

Insinuation clear in his tone, I look over to him. "What's that supposed to mean?"

"Are you still parading around town with misfits in old muscle cars?"

"You'll be happy to know that I've upgraded. This one drives a sedan, but *he*, too, is temporary. The men in my life don't have a tendency to stick around long," I snark. "I'm sure you know how that is. I've heard emotional attachments are bad for business."

"They usually are, yes."

It's there, staring at my father in a boardroom fit for twenty that I have a moment of absolute clarity. I no longer have to figure out what I'm going to do with the rest of my life. I see it clearly as I gaze on at him, my purpose, my future, and it starts in this room.

"Well then, let's just put this personal crap in its respective place for the moment, and get down to business, shall we?"

Roman doesn't hesitate as he stands and opens the door for his waiting staff.

Just short of an hour later, I'm a multi-millionaire.

The minute the door closes behind the team, Roman stands up with a ready excuse. "I have a meeting."

"I'm sure you do, but I'll just need a minute more of your time." I stand and face him, splaying my hands on the table. "I want you to be the first to know. I'll be taking care of my mother financially from here on out."

He doesn't so much as cringe with my confession, which is so far from what I expected.

"I have no issue with that. It's your money; do what you will with it."

It was my only punch to throw, and he's robbed me of

it. It's all I can do to keep my mouth closed. "What in the hell do you mean you have no issue with that?"

"Exactly what I said, Cecelia. I wish your mother well. Will you still be attending UG?"

I grit my teeth. "That's my plan."

"I'll see to it that your expenses are covered. I'll have my assistant find you an apartment off-campus."

"You just gave me millions of dollars and a thirty percent stake in your company. I'm sure I can manage to pay for tuition on my own."

"It's my privilege as your father to see that your school is paid for."

"You haven't earned the privilege of calling yourself my father," I snap, unable to hold my anger back any longer.

"I see. I really should get—"

"Nice doing business with you, Sir," I dismiss him and turn to gather my purse.

Roman opens the door briefly and then closes it before taking strides over to me. He stops a foot away, commanding my attention. He assesses me with a cool expression that I'm sure intimidates the hell out of any opposition, but I refuse to back down. But it's in his eyes, my eyes, I see a hint of regret. I swallow the lump in my throat as a burn threatens behind my eyes.

"Your mother did an outstanding job of raising you. You're well-mannered for the most part. You have respect for authority. You're a highly intelligent and beautiful young woman. You will go far. I have no doubt you have a bright future ahead of you."

Eyes glistening, I do my best to control the shake in my voice. "No thanks to you."

"She made her choices, and I made mine."

"Choices. You mean abandoning your daughter? If that was a choice, you sure made it seem like an easy one."

Silence. The most infuriating silence I've ever endured.

"She deserved your mercy. She's suffered horribly."

His eyes gloss over briefly before he straightens his posture. "Say whatever it is you want to say. I'll allow it, Cecelia. If it will make you feel better."

"Maybe it's *you* who wants to feel better, but I refuse to let you off easy any longer."

"Good. I hope you hold the men in your life to a higher standard."

"*Any* man would be better than the coward *you* are."

This time his flinch is visible, and I'm pissed I find no satisfaction in it. "Anything else?"

"You should know I only did this for her. To care for her long-term because *she's* the deserving parent."

"I see." He squeezes his fists briefly at his sides, and I go all-in.

"Last year, when you came home, that day—"

"I had no right to impose—"

"Demand the right," I rasp. "Fight for *me*. For once in my goddamn life, fight for me. Fight for *your place* with me."

"Cecelia, I made choices, hard choices, and I've only had your best interests in mind when I made them."

"What does that even mean? It's not supposed to be a choice. Daddies are supposed to love their little girls. They're supposed to be their world, their life, and I seem to be worth more on paper to you than I am standing right in front of you. Help me understand."

"This money wasn't meant to be an insult—"

"Why? Just tell me what I did? Was it her? Do you hate her so much you refused to get involved with me because I remind you of her? Tell me why you can't be the father I deserve. Tell me why you can't love me. Tell me why she so clearly still loves you!"

He repeatedly swallows as I come unhinged.

"This is it, Roman. This is it. I saw something that day you came to me. I'm giving you that moment back, right here, right now. This is it. Do you hear me? Fight for me," I cough on a sob. "I want a father, not a fortune."

He stands completely motionless. His eyes cast down as all my foolish hopes leave me. Nothing. Not a word, not a single thing I asked for, just a portion of his fortune and his damning silence. Inside I hollow out as I declare war on my emotions while desperately trying to scrape together what's left of my dignity.

"Okay," I swallow, wiping my eyes. "Okay. But you should know you ruined her."

His eyes glaze over again, and I can feel the shift in him despite his cool demeanor. "You broke her heart, and you should know you were the first man to break mine, too. But at least with her, it was a clean break—" I shake my head— "but you've been breaking mine for twenty long years. I sometimes think it was a curse to inherit her heart, but I'm thinking now it's much better I didn't get yours."

"I want nothing but—"

I slap my hand on the table. "The best for me? Well, I guess I appreciate that." I shake my head, disgusted. "Business concluded, Roman." I thrust my hand in his direction. "Shake my hand."

"What?" He stares at my outstretched hand and visibly pales.

"This was a business deal, was it not? I'm not seasoned yet, but I'm pretty sure that's the way you conclude a business deal. A handshake to seal the deal. I accept your terms. I-I accept your payoff, Mr. Horner. Consider it money well spent."

"This was not meant—"

"Yes, it was. Shake my hand."

Shoulders sagging, he places his hand in mine, and it's all I can do to keep my knees from buckling. My motives with this act purely selfish, because it's the first and last time I'll ever hold my father's hand. "Now look me in the eyes," I rasp out, "and say goodbye."

When he lifts his eyes to mine, I feel no satisfaction. "Say goodbye, Roman."

"Cecelia, this is ridiculous."

I rip my hand away.

"You deserve every damn bit of Karma that comes your way. And there's a beauty to Karma; you never know when it will come back to bite you in the ass."

"I'll take that into consideration." He clears his throat, his voice hoarse when he speaks. "Have you said your piece?"

Tears I can no longer hold glide down my cheeks, and I nod. "Yes, Sir. That will be all. Do you feel better?"

"I understand you're upset but—"

"Goodbye, Roman."

It's me who walks toward the door this time with a folder full of payoff in hand. His voice is barely a whisper when he speaks up behind me. "Please keep me updated on your progress at school." I glance back and see remorse shining in his eyes a second before he rips them away.

"Go to hell."

Chapter Seventeen

Though I have another night paid for at the hotel, I drive home, because I feel safer there. If I'm honest with myself, I feel safer on Tobias's watch, and safer in my short time with him than I felt with my own father in that board-room.

On the drive home, I thought of a thousand better ways, better things I could have said differently, but I made my point, and my point didn't matter. Not at all.

After leaving him in that room, I didn't shed a single tear, not one in the elevator, nor when I retrieved my bag from my room or on the drive home. But the burn starts to become unbearable as I pull up to the house and once again recognize it for what it is—a lifeless structure, an imitation of a life that doesn't exist.

A home that will never house a family.

I leave my bag in the car, sluggishly taking the steps up to the door before I hear the faint purr of an engine. I turn back to see Tobias's Jag speeding down the driveway. Emotions warring, fists clenched, I turn just as he rounds the drive and skids to a stop.

He exits the car, dressed to rule, and takes purposeful strides toward me, stopping at the foot of the stairs. I cross my arms as he sweeps me from heel to head, his eyes filled with something akin to worry. But I'm too far into my head to try and decipher what it could mean.

"I can't do this with you. Not today, Tobias. Not today. Just give me today."

He bites the edge of his lip, not budging.

"Why are you here?" I demand, my voice betraying me with a rattle as I take a step toward the stairs. "The papers have been signed. Our business is concluded, Tobias. You won. The kingdom's yours for the taking. Go get it. I won't stop you." I school my features, feeling the tiny fractures start in my chest.

No. No. No. Please heart, don't do this to me.

He swallows, shoving his hands in his slacks, his eyes dropping.

"Leave! Damn you, if you have one decent bone in your body, leave right now. Whatever you need, it can wait."

His eyes slowly lift to mine as I press my hands to my stomach, willing myself to keep it together just a little longer.

"You got what you wanted! It's all over. I'm leaving soon. No more trust necessary. So, go! The board is all yours."

He remains silent, continuing to watch me slowly start to unravel.

"Did you come to gloat? Well, you shouldn't; I'm a very wealthy woman now, don't you know?"

"Cecelia—"

"You win! You win!" I spread my arms and thrust them high above me. "All yours. Do your worst."

His features twist as he takes a step up and then another.

I take a retreating step toward the door. "Don't. It's all over. Check, in favor of the king. Just one more move and he's done."

He slowly shakes his head.

"Jesus, you've bankrupted me, I have nothing and *no one*, but I've got a hell of a lot of money. I don't need anyone. I don't *need* anyone! Did you hear me? I want you to leave!"

Silence.

"Don't pretend to care about me. It's insulting!"

He cups the back of his head and exhales, regret etched in his face, his posture. Guilt.

My jaw goes slack when I realize where it's coming from.

"Oh my God, you heard it, didn't you? You heard every word." I huff and shake my head incredulously. "You couldn't even give me a moment I deserved. Just one moment of privacy, just one."

I bark out a laugh, my eyes shimmering with humiliation. "Wow, you must think I'm so fucking pathetic. Is that why you're here? To tell me how pathetic I am. Then do it. Do it!"

I rip off my heels and fling them at his feet.

"Did I disappoint you? Did you come to tell me this isn't what grown-ups do? How they handle *business*? Well, don't waste your time. You've made it perfectly clear I'm not a worthy adversary. Go! Go take him down. We're done here."

A long silence passes as he doesn't move, his eyes pleading, unflinching.

"Say something! Say something, you bastard, say anything, but make sure at the end of it is goodbye. I don't want you. We're nothing. Nothing but business. Leave!"

He stands there mute, guilty, his expression filled with pity, which only infuriates me.

"You're halfway there; you've ruined his daughter, time to aim for the head. Take him down. Please," I beg, my resolve crumbling, "take him down."

He moves toward me, climbing the steps as I back away toward my door.

"No, don't you dare!" I turn to flee when he reaches me, pulling me into his arms just as the levee breaks. "I hate you," I cry, my sobs muffled as I bury my face into his neck. He runs his hands through my hair, hurried words leaving his lips.

"I'm so sorry, Cecelia. I'm so fucking sorry." The soothing lilt in his voice only makes me cry harder, and I fist his jacket as he lifts me off my feet, leaving no space between us.

"Just breathe. Okay? Breathe," he whispers as I sob into his neck, my face stinging with tears, the burn unbearable.

"He p-p-aid me off, Tobias. He paid me off."

He grips me tighter to him, as I weep freely in his hold. After several minutes suspended in his arms, he sits on the steps of the porch, situating me along his lap as I unload twenty years of rejection.

It's there on my father's front porch, in his nemesis's arms, that I find solace. Tobias murmurs into my ear, alternating the press of his lips between the top of my head and my temple while his warm hands glide up and down my back. Unbelieving that the man intent on breaking me is the one who's mending me; with the stroke of his hands, the gentle kiss of his lips, I pull back and gaze over at him, utterly at a loss. With tender thumbs, he wipes the black smudges from my face. And we just . . . stare at one another.

"I didn't think I'd see you again."

Silence.

"Were you in Charlotte?"

He slowly nods.

"You followed me there?"

Another nod before he presses his forehead to mine.

"He doesn't decide your worth. *No one* does. I know that doesn't make it better, but he doesn't deserve you."

I bite my lip as twin tears glide down my cheeks.

"And we both know I don't deserve your forgiveness, either."

"Tobias, we can't—"

"Shhh. Not now," he soothes before pulling me tighter to him like he's comforting . . . a little girl.

I wonder if he still sees me that way, especially now, in this state, throwing a tantrum. I wonder if he could ever understand if I put a voice to my thoughts. If I admitted from what I've been taught from his pupils, his brothers, from what *he's* taught me, in a twisted way, he's become more of a father figure than my own. My cries die down, and when he tips my chin, I become lost in the licks of tender flames.

I sniff, smoothing down the lapel of his jacket. "I don't know if you're a very bad man who does good things or a good man who does very bad things."

His voice is raw when he speaks. "What do you think?"

"I think I'm crazy for attempting to try and figure it out."

He exhales, running his knuckle along the trails on my cheeks.

"With you, Cecelia, I realized anger can make you just as reckless as any other emotion. And yet here I am, doing very bad things to a *very good* thing," he whispers, just before he claims my salty lips.

Chapter Eighteen

I WAKE ON the couch from a deep and dreamless sleep where Tobias had carried me after my breakdown. There he held me against his chest as we sat there wordlessly. I can't remember closing my eyes and drifting away, but coming to, I find myself covered with a blanket, my head resting on one of the throws. Slightly disoriented while I rouse, I hear faint, melodic French music drifting from the kitchen. When I reach the threshold, I see Tobias uncorking a bottle of wine. Without looking my way, he pours two large helpings into stemless glasses before he turns and extends one to me.

"Just in time for the show."

Curious, I take the offered glass along with the hand he extends and follow him to the back door. Silently, I trail him with our hands attached while the insect noise increases, sounding on all sides of us. The air rapidly cools as we walk, the sun slowly dipping behind the mountains beyond, taking the bulk of the heat with it. The grass feels cool and dewy against my bare feet as he leads me up the small hill and into the clearing.

"Une table pour deux." *Table for two.*

He lays his suit jacket on the ground and gestures for me to take a seat. I'm still in my tweed slacks and wrinkled blouse, my heels long forgotten. He's still dressed in suit pants and the button-down I stained with my tears. He sets his wine down and removes his shoes and socks, planting his feet in the grass to ground himself.

We sit for long seconds just sipping and taking in the view.

It's when the violet sky starts to blacken, illuminating the full moon that the lightning bugs begin to play a soundless melody around us. With the next sip, my shoulders roll back, and I start to sink into the earth below. Completely at ease, I lean into his side, trying my best not to read into the words he spoke earlier, the softness in his eyes, the tenderness in his kiss. But I'm too drained emotionally to keep my guard up. And far too numb from the day's events to let myself overanalyze, to protect myself further from the damage he could—in my weakened state—so easily cause. And I can't bring myself to give a damn. He was there for me at a time I felt utterly alone in the world, and for that, all I can feel is grateful.

For endless minutes we just follow the lights from the ground to the expansive tree line above. The night sky becomes littered with twinkling stars as we're transported into a different world. I've never in my life seen anything so breathtaking. That is until I turn to the man sitting next to me, watching me carefully.

"I like your view much better," he whispers.

"What do you mean? You have the same view."

"No, I don't. But I'm starting to see it again." He tenses and lets out a long breath. "At this point in your life, you're experiencing many things for the first time. And in a way . . . I'm jealous."

I lift a brow. "That's an awful lot of honesty. How much wine have you had?"

One side of his mouth lifts before all amusement disappears, and he tears his gaze from mine.

"T-thank you for today."

"Don't," he says, just as soon as the words pass my lips. He lifts his chin just as the light around us intensifies. "Look." As if on cue, the fireflies seem to multiply by the hundreds, and it's nothing short of whimsical. It's as if we're surrounded by unearthly light. Reading my thoughts, he speaks up, his voice slightly mystified.

"This place. Right here. Is magical."

I scoff. "You're too much of a realist, too practical to believe in magic."

"It's practical magic," he counters, "see, because here, we can catch light." He reaches out and snatches a lightning bug, which beams in his palm as he speaks. "No decisions to make, no burdens, no debts to pay, no deals to strike, not here, not now."

"That's convenient."

"Ah." He opens his palm, and the bug takes flight between us before floating away. "Now, *there's* a magical word. Because if there's something you want, here, all you have to do is dream it up, and then you just reach out and take it."

"Maybe it's the wine and the view, but right now, that doesn't sound so far-fetched." I take another sip. "So, I take it this place is significant for you?"

He nods. "This place *made* me. It holds every secret I have."

I glance over at him as he keeps his focus on the shimmering trees above. Briefly, I close my eyes, letting the rest of the stress of the day fall away. It's the hurt that remains, that will probably always remain, but for the moment, it's a bearable throb.

His voice is coarse, saturated with the past when he speaks up next to me. "One of the scariest moments of my life was when I figured out that I knew absolutely nothing that *someone* hadn't taught me. That's when I was at my most humble, my most vulnerable. When I realized just how much I needed people."

"When was that?"

"The night I lost my favorite teachers." He swallows, as if he's in pain, his words coming out chalky. "That night, when Delphine came to tell us that our parents weren't coming back . . . I stood, walked out the front door, and kept walking. I don't remember how I got here, but I knew I was searching for something, I needed *something*, and somehow I ended up in this clearing, staring at these trees, searching the sky for answers."

"So, this is where . . ."

He turns to me, his thick hair disheveled, new stubble on his jaw. "For me, this is where it started for *me*." He swallows. "It became a sort of church at first, a sanctuary. Wild, overgrown, and untouched. I was drawn to its purity. Over the years, it was like this place summoned me. At first, this is where I grieved because I didn't want Dom to see. Eventually, I came to map out my future, clear my head. Night after night, when Dom went to sleep, I would run the nine miles to get here. Sometimes when Delphine passed out, I would take her car."

"So, that's why you were here that night?" The night I ran into the forest calling his brothers' names. The same night he kissed me, sending me into a tailspin.

He shakes his head ironically, his expression somber. "This was *my* place. I don't know if fate plays a role in life, but I knew when I found it. Somehow, I knew this place was meant for me."

He plucks at a piece of grass next to him, before rubbing it between his fingers. "That's why I wasn't at all surprised when Roman started building his fortress only a few hundred yards away from where I was charting out my future *and his.*" I try and picture Tobias here as a young boy, newly orphaned and utterly alone in the woods, staring up at the night sky. The image I conjure up tugs at every corner of my heart. To be so young, to have lost everything in a blink: it's unimaginable.

He sips his wine, his swallow audible.

"I can still remember Papa putting a voice to his big dreams. His plans for us, the way he advocated for this place, willing us all to imagine along with him, in this new world, this new life he so believed in, that turned and robbed him of his every dream, of his life. So when I lost them, I pushed the world away. I trusted no one. I was so angry that I shut myself off completely. And the more I learned about the world he believed in, the people he blindly trusted, put his faith in, the angrier I got." He watches me carefully. "My purpose began to change as the years passed. I made no room for anything else. And since then, I've been doing exactly what I set out to do. Every plan I made *here*, I put into motion. Every decision I made *here*, I made happen." He turns to me. "Yet somewhere along the way, I forgot to look around, look up, to focus anywhere but on my task. I got so determined to see my own plans through. I tainted this place. I shared it for the sole reason of carrying out my purpose. After a few years, it was no longer my sanctuary because my ambitions had turned it into a war zone. That's why I like your view. You're seeing it right now, the way I saw it for the first time."

He takes another healthy sip of wine as I absorb his words and decide to offer some of my own.

"I believe in fate," I declare, "I truly do. I felt it earlier today in that boardroom. I was at my most vulnerable as well when something clicked inside of me. It was like a voice I've never heard. And for a few seconds, I saw my future so clearly, so vividly. I don't at all think it's a coincidence that I came to Triple Falls, or that I've had the experiences I've had in the last year. It was like all of the hell I'd gone through made sense specifically for that one moment." I turn to him. "Not long ago, you asked me what I was going to do, and today I saw it."

He fixes his attention on the ground and nods before we collectively sip more wine.

"You're so young." He looks over to me before pulling a piece of hair free from where it's stuck on my lip. I open my mouth to object, but he presses a finger to it to silence me. "I don't mean that in a condescending way. But when you live long enough, you won't see things as absolute, the way you do now. You've got simple solutions for complicated problems. But the more you learn, the more jaded you'll become. The more you'll question your decisions, regret some of your choices. Just don't let them change you. Don't ever forget the way you felt in the boardroom today. No matter how much life you live."

"I won't."

He bites his lip briefly before he speaks.

"I don't regret it, you know, I really don't. I helped Dominic with his homework. I got my first job at fourteen bagging groceries so he had a new bike on Christmas morning." He lifts his knees and drapes his forearms on them. "I made it my mission to try and rear him like Papa would have. To give him everything I could. I can still remember so clearly the day I taught him how to shave. I was honored when he asked me." He smiles, really smiles. "He hadn't hit his second growth spurt, so he was a full foot shorter than me."

"So, you were more of a father than a brother," I conclude.

"I wanted it," he quickly adds. "I did. Beau was a good man. And I wanted to give Dominic as much of his father as I could. I wouldn't trade those memories for anything. I just . . ."

Guilt. I can feel it oozing from his frame, along with all that he's not saying. He lost his own life raising his brother and setting his plans into motion. He doesn't seem to know who he is without his purpose.

And that's when I know we're both lost in a similar way. I've pegged him as well as he had me.

Because, in that respect, we are a lot alike.

It occurs to me that the night he broke me down, ripped my life apart so intimately, it wasn't because he knew the details; it's because he understood the sacrifice. We both have— and still are—put off our own lives to take care of the people we love. He's just been doing it far longer than I have.

"Dominic and Sean are the only two people I've ever fully

trusted." He runs his thick fingers through the grass. "It's not their fault." He shakes his head. "I get that. They didn't know how much it would . . ."

"Hurt," I finish for him. "How much it would hurt you."

"But that's not on them. It's on me. I expected them to be just as dedicated on every level . . . I expected too much."

Never in a million years would I dream of seeing his side of things. Never did I want an explanation. Never did I want to see his black heart start to beat red. But it's here I understand him, his logic—and even worse, I empathize.

"You still trust them, Tobias. And you know you can."

"I do trust them—with my life. But I just . . . I was jealous." He takes a sip of wine and glances at me. "I still am."

"Tobias, you can change it. Right now. You can make a decision—"

I shift my gaze to his, but the look he's returning has my tongue going dry, the words failing me. Swallowing, I tear my eyes away as I draw steadying breaths.

"I have a place," his tone is faint. "It's near Saint-Jean-de-Luz. My biological father took me there when I was very young. It's only a flash, an image of being there, being happy. That's it—a blink. But I went back a few years after I graduated college, and I felt it. It's the only other place on the planet I've felt as at peace as I have here. So, as soon as I could afford it, I bought a piece of paradise right on the water and began building. It was finished a year ago, and I haven't set foot in it."

"Why?"

"Because I don't deserve it."

"That's ridiculous."

"No. It's still a dream, and it's untouched. It's my finish

line. I have to earn it to get there. I'm not done yet. But, if I'm being honest, I'm scared of going there."

"Why?"

"Because when this is over, I'm going to have to find a way to live with myself, with the things I've done. The things I'll continue to do. Because this is my only plan."

He turns to me, his expression haunted. "But I dreamt it up here, all of it, right here where we're sitting. Saint-Jean-de-Luz exists. And it's there when I'm ready for it. And now I'm sharing my place with you, so—" he implores me with the sweep of his eyes—"what is it that you want?"

"It may seem silly, but I want Paris."

"That's too small, too easily attainable. Think bigger."

"I want to have a say."

He nods as if he understands. "Then you'll have a say."

"I want my own kind of sanctuary."

"Then you'll have it. Keep dreaming. Keep planning. Dream a thousand dreams and then make a thousand things happen."

He pulls the wine from my hand and sets his glass down next to it.

"Poof." I smile, the wine thrumming through my veins. "Just like that."

"No." He pulls my hand onto his thigh and flips it over, sliding his palm along mine. Dizzied by his touch, my body springs to life as he strokes my hand lightly with the pads of his fingers. An inch of his thick hair sags across his forehead, and I itch to touch it when his brows pinch together. "After you dream, plan, that's when the work begins. And that's where it gets the most complicated, your plans can get convoluted, your dreams may get watered down and grow more distant, seem out of reach, and sometimes, sometimes you lose sight of what's important and hurt the people who rely on you. Others might get hurt in the process." Our eyes lock with his confession. "And when that happens—" he swallows—"it might make you question who you are and just how far you will go."

No matter how much I want to, I can't look away.

"Cecelia." His voice dips and my name has never sounded so beautiful coming from a man's lips. I sit mesmerized by all he's revealed, unbelieving this is the man I met. "I'm sorry, truly, for the things I've done to you. What happened to you today—"

"It had nothing to do with you. And I don't want to talk about it." I still his hand, frustrated with what he's beginning to stir within me. If I'm not careful, he'll succeed in resurrecting my starving heart with his words, his touch. "And you're making it seem like it's already game over for you, when it's not. You're still young enough to change your plans. You have a lot of life left to live. You can still dream here. Hell, you could walk into that house in Saint-Jean-de-Luz tomorrow if you wanted to."

"No, I can't." He flips my hand over, separating my fingers before lifting them to his lush mouth and kissing them one by one. Sparks ignite and fire licks up my spine as the electricity between us begins to move. Thrumming with anticipation, his voice hypnotizes me as I watch him press each of my fingers to his soft lips. The sight of it sets me on fire. "You see, my plans, my decisions, have backed me into a corner. But in this place—" he lifts simmering eyes to mine and cups my face as if he's holding the world in his hands. My instinct is to look away, to recognize the lie, to pinpoint the deceit. But I don't, I can't, because I feel every word he's saying to my core. "Here, there are no outsiders, no threats, no pasts, no one else. There's nothing but *us*." Choked by his honesty, by his openness, he runs his thumb along my bottom lip, his eyes dipping briefly before he brings them back to mine. And in them, I see him so clearly for the first time. "And because of you, I see this place again for what it truly is. It hasn't lost any of its magic. I just forgot how to look for it."

Eyes locked, he bends, his lips so close, gaze imploring. And I can't deny him, or myself, because he's speaking the truth. Since the day we met, we've been drawn to the other. Though we were born of anger, resentment, and betrayal, it's been there. And through the fog of all of it, we were familiar.

"I know you, Cecelia, because you *know* me, and it's here, in this place, that we recognized we've known each other all along."

He presses a feather-light kiss to my lips, sliding his hands back to cup my head before opening me with decadent pressure. Savoring the wine off his tongue, I whimper into his mouth as he takes his time, exploring, licking, relishing. Effortlessly, he lifts me to wrap around him, his mouth drawing on mine, robbing, consuming, the gravity holding us firmly in place as I kiss him back without reservation. When he pulls away, I can see nothing but satisfaction in his eyes. He might have recognized it first, but the reflection I see is undeniable.

I see you, Cecelia, you keep trying to give yourself, your heart, your allegiance away to anyone who will have it for reasons you can't understand, but it's so painfully clear.

Clear to him, because he's been living in the same sort of self-imposed exile, but instead of offering his heart up, he's locked it safely away. Breaths mingling, chests heaving, we face off as understanding passes between us.

"What is it that you want, Tobias?"

He pins me beneath him, pressing my wrists to the grass, his hair tickling my chin as he gazes down at me.

"A selfish moment," he whispers softly before he captures my mouth, drawing me into the most damning and selfish of kisses.

Chapter Nineteen

I WAKE LONG before the sun, fully clothed and wrapped in an inferno. Tobias sleeps silently next to me, his arms wrapped around me protectively, his chin burrowed into my neck. I slept through the night, buzzed on wine, in the safety of his arms since we'd wordlessly returned to the house. He didn't undress me. Instead, he turned off the light and pulled me into him.

And it's in this same position that I manage to untangle us without waking him before I take a long shower, putting on my favorite stark white sundress that looks more like something from the Edwardian era. Layers of silky white material tickle my calves while the bodice hugs my curves; the inch-thick straps lay loosely off my shoulders. I grab my favorite hardback and head toward the garden, nabbing a thin blanket to ward off the morning chill. Nestled in the queen lounger beneath a trellis covered in wisteria, I watch the show, the sun rising on a different world I'm now a citizen of, my thoughts drifting to the man who lays comatose in my bed.

Under the haze of a new day's sun, I lose myself and

spend hours reading while soaking in the world around me.

Fresh blooms warm a few feet away, scenting the air as I flip the pages of *The Thorn Birds*. It's my favorite book, or at least it was when I was younger. It was the first hit to my addict's heart, and therefore the strongest. I stole it from the library the last summer I spent with my father and never returned it. It's the story of Ralph, a priest, and his Meggie, a little girl who was groomed by him and who grew up to fall in love with him. But their love was impossible. When she was young, he told her of a bird who leaves the nest searching for the sharpest thorn to impale itself on so it could sing the sweetest song as it dies, living solely for the purpose of finding that thorn so it could sing, just once, in its lifetime.

But his story to her at such a young age was a preemptive strike if not predictive, and her heart didn't listen. Meggie describes her love: her devotion to Ralph was like crying for the moon. Because it's impossible to capture, impossible to keep.

Meggie could never have Ralph in the way she wanted, and he could never give up his life's purpose for her. Therefore, Ralph was also Meggie's thorn, and she spent her life searching for the time to impale herself upon him just for the chance to sing. And then it happens, they have that sinful and secular moment where the world stops, time ceases, and love wins.

I always stop reading when they're together, because I know the ending, and I'm happiest in the midst of their song. I savor it.

Partway through the novel, I stand and walk on the soft

green carpet beneath my feet, admiring nature's handiwork. Endless rows of rose bushes line the center of the garden, and I stop every few steps to run my fingers along the delicate petals and breathe them in. It's like a dream—the breeze, the smells, the pink haze of early morning—and I'm fully intoxicated. For a moment, I pity Roman. I'm positive he's never spent a minute out here simply enjoying his life. He could, at any time, make a decision to enjoy the fruits of his labor, to appreciate the palace he haunts, but he lives his life too engrossed in harsh reality. Numbers and power rule him. And I'm convinced his is a miserable existence.

I don't want that for myself. Not ever.

And one day, I'll need to forgive him. I'll have to forgive him, for myself. But this morning, the pain is starting to gnaw at me, and I can still feel the humiliation, the arrow precision sting of his rejection—the unexpected balm to my pierced heart sleeping in the bedroom above me.

The last twenty-four hours with Tobias have been surreal, and I'm way too terrified to trust a single memory. I run a finger over my lips thinking of the way he kissed me, held me, like I was precious, like my every thought mattered. Palming my face, I try to push those thoughts away, and I can't help but recall our conversation.

"Dream a thousand dreams."

In the last year, I've learned a different way to live, and I don't think I've ever embraced it the way I can now.

With my epiphany yesterday, I know my future consists of big moves and big decisions. I want the experience of it all. Otherwise, what's the point?

A peace washes over me as I remember the future I'd mapped for myself in that boardroom. A decision to live in the now, even knowing what I know. Risk and reward. No regrets. I've decided on my part to play.

I'm strolling along the hedges admiring the walls of honeysuckle draping them when I sense him. I look up to find him standing in the corner of the courtyard, staring at me.

"Hi."

He stands silent. His undershirt wrinkled, the material clinging to him like a second skin stretching over his chest, outlining his powerful frame when he stretches. Black boxers accentuate his insanely cut, muscular thighs. He's completely disheveled. A far cry from the stylish terrorist I've come to expect darkening my door. And as messy as he looks, he's more agonizing to gaze upon. We'd stolen a moment last night. A moment to be selfish, to give in to what we both wanted, and it wasn't purely physical. It was a long drink for two thirsty people. And we'd savored every drop, but we're skirting disaster now. Still, I can feel it, the gravity, the ache, the need building for him, and he's only feet away.

I run my hands along more of the delicate blooms. "It's beautiful out here, isn't it?"

More silence, and it's unbearable. My heart gallops as the air around me stills. Tension coiling, I can feel his gaze on me, my neck pebbling with the weight of it. I can't bring myself to look him in the eyes. Because if I do, he'll know.

"Hard to believe such a bad guy owns such an extraordinary place." I can hear the sadness in my voice. I was honest with Tobias that night he questioned me. In my time here, I've experienced a slow snap. From the time my dad confessed he couldn't love me to the time we spent yesterday in his boardroom, it's felt like one drawn-out and agonizing blow. Though it's been hard to admit it, I came here with a hope that's now obliterated. My father and I are beyond repair.

Roman's rejection has made me a very sad and lonely little girl, and I'd been acting like one, dragging my battered heart around and begging someone, anyone, to tell me it is worth something.

"You were right, you know," I say, running my fingers over the blossoming wall of honeysuckle again. "I've been a sad, lonely little girl for a long time." I smile, though my eyes are glistening. "I couldn't understand why he couldn't, didn't *want*, to love me. I understand that's just a blood tie now, and I'm a responsibility. Nothing more. But I won't apologize for growing up thinking I deserved his love or for growing up period, and the choices I've made doing it. In believing in it. Because . . . how can love be a mistake?" A warm tear runs down my face as I finally look up at him. "Even if it's not enough, if it's more trouble than it's worth, if it does me more harm than good, even if everyone I give myself to denies me, I refuse to believe it's a mistake."

He stalks toward me, his eyes unwavering as I swallow, bracing myself for impact. "Sometimes . . . s-sometimes I wonder if I'll ever grow up enough to know the difference between what I romanticize and what's real."

He reaches me, and I keep my eyes averted as another fast tear forms and falls.

"How do you do it, Tobias? How do you keep your heart out of it?"

He lifts my hand to cover his chest, and I lift my eyes to his. It's in his gaze I see the same vulnerability and fear that shone in them the night he realized he'd damned us both.

"Please don't do this to me," I beg, knowing if this is another game, another mindfuck, I will not survive it.

He bends so we're eye-level, as his heart pounds against my palm.

"There's something you need to know." He swallows, his frame rattling as he covers my hand on his chest, the beat beneath quickening, smashing against my palm as if trying to break free.

"Your heart is not *your* weakness, Cecelia. It's *mine*."

Slowly, so slowly, he bends and presses his full lips to mine. And with this one act, the rest of my self-preservation ceases to exist.

Because of him, because of his kiss. A kiss just as raw, just as honest as it was last night, but far more meaningful than any other we've shared. I grip his wrists when he palms my face, tilting my head before he dives deeper. The burn starts behind my eyes as my innermost fear is realized, and I dive headfirst, living fully in the seconds and minutes that replace everything I thought I knew about love.

He explores my mouth with gentle licks, his tongue coaxing mine, drawing out a whimper.

My heart pounds in distinct beats as I rip myself away.

"Please—" he cuts off my plea with another searing kiss and another, and then another until my fears quiet.

He pulls my chin with his thumb, parting my mouth further, opening to me and licks in discovery as I wrap what I can of myself around him.

Slick with need, I squeeze my thighs together as he teases me, drawing me further into him. He does this over and over, dizzying me to the point of insanity. At his mercy, I wrap around him as he kisses me, and kisses me, his tongue sweeping me into this moment with him, erasing every line we've drawn. When he pulls back and gazes down at me with hooded eyes, it's not lust that has me gasping.

It's the truth he lets me see. No amount of lies or contradictory actions on his part can ever take this away. He dips again and takes my mouth, a confession on his tongue, and I meet him, kissing him back, telling my own.

And it's then I allow myself to fall, further and further into the biggest secret of my life. A secret I've known longer than I will ever admit.

I'm falling in love with my enemy.

So be it.

Our tongues tangle in the most erotic and passionate of dances. Eyes closed, I savor the affection and clutch him to me, drinking, consuming as he feeds my starving heart. He answers every question I've ever had, with each sure stroke of his tongue, and brush of his fingertips.

I don't need words or promises. His kiss makes them irrelevant.

Hunger rumbles low, and with every thorough brush of his tongue I become more ravenous to expose everything we've hidden beneath our thin veil of hate.

He bends, lifting the hem of my sundress, and I extend my arms above my head and keep them raised as he pulls the material off, leaving me completely naked in the middle of the sun-soaked garden.

His eyes explore me from head to foot; he runs fingers along my skin, his palms covering me in his reverent touch, an apology for all the violent touches before. A tear drips from my chin and he whisks it away with his tongue before sweeping me into his arms and setting me on the lounger. Wordlessly, he pulls off his shirt and boxers between kisses. Shaded by a canopy of wisteria, I drink him in, as we exchange one kiss for another, the next more intoxicating than the one before it. He pulls away, gazing down at me, his palms caressing the top of my head with a gentle sweep.

"Why, why couldn't you just leave me alone?" I rasp out, utterly helpless to the emotion he's stirring within me.

"C'était trop demander." *It was too much to ask.*

He stares down at me, hands roaming over every inch of flesh within his reach, his eyes and lips worshiping, his heart pounding against mine, demanding acknowledgment. The kiss turns fevered as our mouths call a truce and begin to make promises we can never speak because, if we do, we will no longer be enemies.

But in glimpses of his fiery depths, all of it's gone: his contempt, his judgment, his anger, his resentment, all of it replaced with tenderness, longing, and blatant need. He slides his warm hand down my stomach before pressing thick fingers inside me. Every brush of his lips causes eruptions throughout my chest and all over my body.

Our visual connection remains unbroken as he moves to hover above me. Cradling him between my legs, I cup his jaw. Once he's readied me, he lines us up and, without hesitation, pushes his length into me, claiming me fully. Flattening his chest to mine, he drives in further, and I lose every ounce of my breath. His cock is rooted so deep, I'll never be able to forget the way he feels.

He grinds into me, burrowing further, embedding himself as he peers down at me, eyes beseeching, begging me not to look away, to accept him, to accept *us*, and our fate. He pushes my knees apart further before he slowly, so slowly, begins to move.

My world shifts as he gently rolls his hips, his gaze never wavering as I take all of him in, while he brands my body; a declaration, a possession.

It's belonging I feel with every slow thrust, every kiss, every look, every breath that passes between us.

We let ourselves go, our mouths molding with the perfect exchange, moaning and gasping at the way I fit him, and the way he fills me so completely. His lovemaking is ecstasy in the purest form. I shudder in his arms, in the completion.

Pulling him tighter to me, I cry out as he surges into me, his mouth covering the whole of my breast, his teeth grazing my nipple as he rears back and drives in again, hitting the end of me over and over, purposefully staking his claim.

"Je ne peux pas aller assez loin." *I can't get deep enough.*

With every slow thrust of his tongue, every possessive push of his hips, he damns us, the confession in his eyes narrating our story, our ill-fated fortune as star-crossed fools, sharing a merciless love neither of us can ever deny, but can never keep.

On the brink, I break our kiss, look him in the eyes and call out his name as the rush overtakes me. It's the sound of his name coming from my lips that sends him over, and I feel him pulsate just before he buries himself and pours into me.

Bodies slick, he burrows deeper, a thin veil of sweat covering him as he trembles in my hold, emotion shining in his eyes, twisting his features. He's completely exposed and lets me see him in his most vulnerable state, and I've never seen anything so perfect.

He presses his forehead to mine, as we share several collective breaths. I stroke his back with my fingers as some of the high disappears from his eyes, and the truth sets in. He dips to kiss me, and I feel him start to retreat as my heart begins to sink with the weight of our secret.

When he pulls away, the loss rips me apart as I hold in a sob, and he turns from me to sit on the edge of the lounger, his shoulders sagging forward, stretching the wings along his muscular back.

The sight of the bond he made with his brothers draws tight. It's there, the answer, the reason for our beginning and the reason for our end—a bond made from love. A timeless bond a different love could never break. A bond that exists with his brothers and his reason for being.

He can never choose me.

He will never choose me.

I can never ask him to.

"We can never be," he says softly from where he sits.

"I know." I lift to sit as he slowly stands and picks up my dress, handing it to me. Gathering his boxers, he glances over his shoulder, his eyes filled to the brim with guilt. "I can't make you any promises."

"I haven't asked for any."

"This ends now. It has to, Cecelia. It has to."

"I know."

It's anger that takes hold as he jerks on his briefs. I brace myself for the pain of his absence, for more heartache as he retrieves his shirt from the ground. I've had my heart broken before. I'm all too familiar with the feeling, but there's a raging now in my chest with a strength I never imagined possible.

Briefly, he stops dressing, staring at me with the undershirt around his neck before pushing his arms through. Tortured eyes meet mine, and I see his defiance, not against me, but against the stars lining up against us.

Utter fucking disaster.

"I don't want to fucking leave. I don't want to argue. I don't want to hate myself. I don't want to blame you. I'm tired of being angry at them, but damn them and . . . damn you, Cecelia, you were never supposed to know them, you were never—" his face twists with fury as my heart seizes— "you were . . ." He jerks me to stand, pulling me against him, anger rolling off his frame, anguish in his eyes.

"Yours. I was always supposed to be yours," I say as he nods and crushes me with his kiss.

Chapter Twenty

"TELL ME ABOUT her," I say as Tobias folds his hands over my stomach, peering up at me. He's gloriously naked, his beautiful ass in full view behind him. Even with his declaration in the garden that we can never be, he's prolonged that decision. Since then, we've spent our day christening the house in new memories; talking, eating, playing chess, swimming, and alternating between fucking and making love. We're both in denial, refusing to deal with the inevitable.

"Please, I want to know."

"She was . . . beautiful, funny, full of life. Headstrong and strict when she needed to be but surprisingly gentle. She loved her wine and taught me to cook. She was such a good cook. In the kitchen is where we spent most of our time together. She could always make me laugh, no matter what mood I was in. She was my best friend . . . my everything."

"And your stepfather?"

"Beau *was* my father."

"Okay. Don't suppose he was moody?"

This earns me a look that has me laughing.

Kate Stewart

"I have to be just as cunning," he defends without apology, "just as ruthless, and you know why."

"Are you saying there's some sort of charming flip personality? *Do* let me see it."

He slaps the side of my ass and I yelp. I swear my heart stops when he smiles at me.

"Jesus, Frenchman. I think I've broken you."

He exhales and drops his head on my chest. "I'm human, Cecelia. I didn't start this with intent to be . . . the way I have to be. I have to know a criminal mind to think like one. I have to command respect, loyalty."

"Well, you seem to have succeeded there."

"There's no other way to go about it. But that's not why I'm in this. I don't need power. It's a necessity. And I didn't go into this looking to get rich. That's also a necessity, the cost of the ante. I'm just as disgusted by some of the human products of money and power as you are, but it has to be a fair fight in order for there to be a fight."

I swallow. "I know."

"I've kept a lot of secrets in my life, easily, and without a second thought, but with my mother, it was damn near impossible to lie to her. She had this tone she used, and it worked like a truth serum on me. Within minutes she could get me to break. I thank God she's the only one. And sometimes I'm grateful that she's not here anymore to get the confessions out of me. Because I'm not sure she would want to claim me as her son if I was honest with her about the things I've done."

His eyes flit with emotion before they gloss over in thought.

"My mother swore my real father was a horrible man, but I think, maybe, he was just misunderstood."

208

"Why do you say that?"

"I have a feeling."

"Or a secret?"

"A feeling," he insists.

"Well, look at us," I pipe up, "with our Daddy issues."

"At least I had a man willing to step in where he failed." He runs a hand down my abdomen, eyes lowered, nostrils flaring. He's angry for me.

"I'm okay," I say, running my fingers along his jaw and over his shoulders. "I really am okay. It's time to suck it up and move on. But not one of my thousand dreams will include him."

"You think you are okay, but the truth is, that's a blow you'll feel in some degree for the rest of your life." His eyes flame. "I've never wanted to kill a man in cold blood as much as I did him yesterday."

"You don't *ever* have to be that guy."

"I will take him down, Cecelia." It's a promise. Probably the only one he will ever be able to make me.

"You don't have to do that, either." His gaze goes from rolling embers to accusatory within the same second.

"I didn't mean it like that. Tobias." He lifts, and I force his eyes back to mine. "I didn't mean it like that. I'm not condoning what you're doing either, but I'm not going to try and talk you out of it. I would never ask you to."

His stare turns incredulous. "How can you still feel *anything* for him?"

"I feel sorry for him."

"That's *feeling* something."

"I'll pity him when you're done with him, too."

He pushes me back to hover above me, his hand covering

where my heart lay before he presses a kiss to it. "I've been such a bastard to you."

"Yes, you have."

"Don't forgive me."

"I haven't and I won't." I fist his hair, pulling his eyes to mine.

"You're trying to forgive me," he says. "And I don't deserve it."

"Probably not. But I understand the game, and no matter how hard I try, I can't stay angry because I know the reasoning behind some of what you do. I know how naïve that seems, but we weren't just fooling around last summer, I was made to understand what this is about. I respect what you're doing." I roll my eyes and draw my next words out reluctantly. "I admire you for it, a lot more than I've let on."

He nods, threading our fingers, his eyes unfocused.

"It's been my life for so long, at this point I'm not sure if the man I am now and the boy who took it on still agree on much. And Dominic is so much like I was. And he's only getting angrier. We've earned enough capital to go legitimate, but he likes the hunt too much. And he loves the street games. We've been arguing a lot about the way he handles things here."

"What is it you want to happen?"

"Too much for a lifetime. I'm not sure how far I want it all to go."

"Meaning?"

"I've said too much." He drops his head and rolls it back and forth on my stomach.

"You said you need a vacation. I really don't think that's equivalent to spilling trade secrets."

"Let's change the subject."

"Let's not. Let's talk about Saint-Jean-de-Luz."

"Leave it alone," he warns, his tone going cold.

"Wow. Okay, that was a fast regression." He lifts to hover above me, leans in to kiss me, and I turn my head.

"Don't you dare think of denying me," he growls, pulling my lip with his teeth.

"My, my, Frenchman, how demanding we are."

He runs his erection along my thigh. "You called my name," he murmurs, getting lost as he lines himself up with my entrance. "Fucking beautiful."

"You're just a gauntlet of emotions today."

"I'm losing my fucking mind—" he narrows his eyes at me—"and you're the reason."

"Now I'm to blame?"

"Take it. Please take it," he says softly. And I nod, just before I float away in his kiss.

Chapter Twenty-One

"I T'S VANILLA."

"It's cinnamon," I counter as he pulls the milk and eggs from the fridge.

"I hate cinnamon," he grumbles.

"Hate is a strong word," I argue as I start the coffee, grinding the beans for my new French press.

It's become a morning ritual. He cooks for me, and I watch him while goading him for kicks. He stands in nothing but black boxers, his hair still damp from our shower. The bulge of his ridiculously thick thighs along with his impressive length and muscled ass strains the fabric where he stands only feet away. The sight of him tempting from any vantage point.

He woke me up this morning with my wrists secured in his hands, his head between my thighs. An apology for his day-late return from a "business trip". I'd waited, restless, worried, especially with the image of his last injury fresh in my mind. He only spent two days away, but the wait felt like an eternity. And I endured it just for another stolen moment. With his wicked tongue, he apologized profusely until I'd verbally mouthed my forgiveness, and he only let me go when I shuddered beneath him.

Then he teased me mercilessly until I begged him to take me. And when he did, all playing ceased, our eyes locked, and he tore through me equally as starved. He kissed me with so much fervor, that I forgot myself, forgot that we were wrong.

In those minutes of his tender and apologetic lovemaking, as he hovered above me, gripping the top of my mattress and thrusting into me like it was his birthright, I just knew no other man in my life would ever know me so intimately, or could ever reach inside me the way Tobias has.

When we're together, he makes it easy to forget the dangerous game we're playing. To forget that we've been stealing selfish moments for the last three weeks. Three weeks that we've spent playing house in Roman's mansion.

It's been just the opposite: it's unparalleled bliss. I haven't regretted a minute. Foolishly I'd tucked my heart away for safekeeping only to turn around and gamble the whole of it on a man I still can't fully bring myself to trust, despite all his confessions. My heart is weary, and I will not fault it for being cautious.

But it's not as if I have a choice. With Tobias, it was never a decision. He's obliterated all my barriers save one, and in giving in, I've been thrust into a living dream.

My sensibilities have been warring lately as I toy with the idea of trying to trust him, because my heart can't stop the free fall it started since the night he confessed the one thing he wanted is me, is us, and more selfish moments. And like him, I'm choosing daily to play ignorant to what that means.

We're ignoring the cracks in the ground of our foundation, tap dancing over them while consistently giving in to the pull and getting lost in the other. We're kinetic when we're together, magnets drawn continuously to the other.

Since we've given in, I've memorized him. The faint mole on his cheek, the weight of him when he's on top of me, the depth of his kiss, the curl of his tongue, his salty sense of humor, his quirks, his fetishes. He's become an expert at gauging me, just as capable of goading me, of finding my buttons. He sees our similarities, because he studied his opponent, considered me an obstacle before setting himself free to indulge. And that's the hardest part to get past. Because if some part of him still considers me business . . .

Yet, that's damn near impossible to believe at this point. Inside Tobias, I've discovered the heart of a romantic. More than once, he's surprised me with gestures fit for a queen. He's spent endless hours while I work my shifts preparing multiple-course French feasts and pairing them with wines for before and after we dine to share in our place, another of our daily rituals. Days ago, we got caught in a storm in the clearing and made love through it.

He'd fed me his dizzying kisses as we lay in the grass, drinking from each other's skin. After, we stayed up until dawn, playing chess as he spoke to me about his favorite frequents in France. Sharing just enough to keep me intrigued but not enough to uncover the secrets he guards.

And therein lies the real problem.

He's all but mastered my anatomy both inside and out. He quenches my desires while fueling my insides. But his greed doesn't seem to be for my benefit alone. It's as though he's living out some of his thousand dreams with me.

It's the idea that eventually we're going to have to stop playing ignorant to what's happening between us that keeps me on edge. I don't want to find out once again that I'm the fool.

Aside from that. I'm leaving. Soon. I'm heading back to Atlanta in mere weeks.

I'd almost broached the subject last night after we shared another pricy bottle of Louis Latour. And as I lay in the grass cradled in his arms, I could feel the tension in him, the hesitation.

"Are we ever going to talk about this, Tobias?"

He turned me to face him, and I could see the revelation he was holding, but instead, he kissed me, stoking our fire higher to blind us both from the flaming truth.

Instead of protesting, of demanding a real conversation, I released my relieved breath onto his tongue and kissed him back.

And it's here we remain, selfish, untrusting, greedy.

What could possibly become of us?

But I gladly pay the price for every minute spent with him, because the alternative, our inevitable end is too crippling, too painful to acknowledge.

"I'm cooking," he smarts, ripping me from my wayward thoughts, "so it's the chef's choice."

"Well, I want cinnamon." I search the spice rack and grab a bottle, breaking the seal.

"No cinnamon."

"You're so damn bossy."

"Chalk it up to a side effect of my line of work," he snarks, expertly whisking the batter into submission as I taunt him with the bottle.

"How about three shakes?"

He stills his movements and looks over to me, and I swear I see a bit of heat spread over his face.

"Three swishes of the tumbler before you take a drink. Three taps of your toothbrush against the sink. Three flips of the bathroom light. Three flicks of your pinky before you move a chess piece. Three pumps of body wash. Happy three seems to be your number, Mr. Touch of *Just Right OCD*."

I flip the top to the cinnamon as he sets my profile ablaze with his glare. I flick my eyes to his, a knowing smile on my lips. "You tried, Mr. King. You really did. You masked it as well as you could, but I didn't miss it. And, honestly, I find it endearing you have these tics."

He raises a thick brow, his ink-black hair still drenched from our shower. And there's very little more alluring than a soaking-wet Tobias. I'd proven as much a few seconds after we stepped out of the shower.

Before I remembered my dream.

The raw stab the image produces has me wincing as I move toward him, shaking the bottle in taunt.

"Don't you dare," he threatens, slowly backing up.

"But I love cinnamon." I push out my lower lip.

"That's your problem."

He cradles the bowl protectively away from me, still whisking as I prowl toward him.

"Don't test me, woman."

"Fine, I won't put it in the food."

"Glad you're seeing things my way." He watches me as I shake three dashes of the spice into my palm before I lift it, and blow. Tobias wheezes as a cloud of cinnamon covers the side of his face, momentarily blinding him. Cursing, eyes flaming with the promise of retribution, he slams the bowl down and lunges for me just as I leap out of reach. Giving chase, I barely manage to get through the back door and yelp when his fingertips brush my hip just as I clear it.

"You better fucking run," he roars behind me as I sprint past the pool and dare to glance back. He's hot on my heels, eyes dancing as he gives chase. I'm barely able to make it through the garden when he manages to hook me around the waist on the lawn.

I yelp his name when he twirls me around like a ragdoll, my feet dangling in the air before he lowers me to the grass and begins rooting into my neck as I choke on spicy fumes.

"Damnit man, you reek."

"J'adore la cannelle," *I love cinnamon*, he retorts snidely, shaking the residual water in his hair across my neck and chest before coating me with the powder, creating a paste across my flesh as I frantically try to push him away. It's when he pulls back that he robs my breath, his eyes bright, his smile so blinding, I shudder beneath him. It's when my smile dims with the image that's been screwing with me all morning that he draws his brows.

"What is wrong with you today?" He scrutinizes me beneath him, his eyes probing. "Are you still mad at me? I told you it couldn't be helped."

"No."

"What is it then? You've been giving me hell all morning."

I gaze up at him for a few seconds before I dart my eyes away. "I might have had a dream."

"This is about a dream," he says in the same breath.

"I told you," I sigh, pushing at his chest to no avail. "I've explained this. They're real for me."

"But they aren't real, Cecelia. And you can't hold a dream against me."

"Says you, and it *felt* real." I can hear the ache in my own voice. "You locked me out of my own bedroom."

"You had a *dream* that I locked you out of your bedroom, and you're mad at me?"

"Yep."

He narrows his eyes. "There's more."

"Nope, that's the gist of it."

"You're lying."

"I'm not."

He reaches between us, gripping my thigh and squeezes.

"S-s-stop. I c-can't breathe inhaling all of this cinnamon. Get off me. I'm hungry."

His fingers begin traveling to the hem of my sleep shorts before inching toward the promised land. "I can do this all day," he assures, unflinching when I pinch his skin. "Tell me, what was I doing in this dream?"

"Non." *No.*

"Non?" He leans in, darting his tongue along my bottom lip just as his finger faintly brushes over my clit. I moan, and he captures it, kissing me breathless as he sinks more of his weight onto me, pinning me to the grass.

"Damnit, man, you're suffocating me."

"Tell me, and I'll set you free."

"No."

He resumes his touch, suckling my chest and teasing me without reservation.

"You're a cruel and evil man," I rasp out, digging my fingers into his scalp.

"Word of the day, *soumission*." He muses as my hips buck due to his touch.

"Submission? Dream on, pal."

"Have you forgotten already? *One* finger." He licks a trail from my neck to my ear. "And I'm pretty sure that was a tear I licked off your temple."

"You're never going to let me forget that, are you?" He licks his finger in threat.

"Tobias," I mewl, hearing the husk in my voice. "It was just a dream."

"Ah, but I've been paying for it. At least enlighten me on what I'm guilty of in your land of make-believe."

"You were mean to me."

He pins my wrists and leans in as I struggle. "Mean to you?" He rolls his eyes. "That you can handle."

"Breakfast," I remind him.

"It can wait," he retorts.

"You were starving."

"It can wait."

"Tobias, damnit, let me up."

"You're your own worst enemy right now."

"Debatable," I say, lifting to bite his chin, and he dodges me easily. "This is bullshit. You outweigh me by nearly a hundred pounds. I'm utterly helpless."

"Guess you better find some leverage. Or you can just tell me what I was doing."

Briefly, I entertain headbutting him and get a smug grin.

"It will hurt you more than it will me."

"Get out of my head."

"Gladly, it seems to be a scary place today. But only after you give me what I want."

"Fine." I close my eyes. "There may have been lingerie models behind you when you slammed the door in my face."

Heat creeps up my neck and I peek up at him with one eye open. He stares down at me a second before bursting into laughter.

I push at his chest. "It's not funny."

He dips his head and nuzzles me. "Oh, mon bébé, are we jealous? No wonder you rode me this morning like you were trying to tame a horse. Going for the gold, huh?"

"It's not funny." I shove at his chest, my heart lurching as I again picture him eyeing me with a slew of half-naked women behind him before he shut me out. Gazing up at him, I feel the stretch of my own reluctant smile as he glitters down on me with affection. It's this look, the look on his face now, that keeps me breathless, a relapsed and happy addict.

"Maybe I'll get used to cinnamon, for you." He sips a little of the spiced water on my neck with eager lips before making me painfully aware of the difference between the first time he kissed me and now. Everything has changed.

Everything.

He works his sinful mouth, sliding his flavored tongue against my own, and he kisses me and kisses me while the sun warms our skin. "You think adding cinnamon to breakfast will make up for the horrible things you've done?"

He shrugs. "You mean the fiction you've made up?"

I shake my head and dodge his next kiss as he chuckles. "I would not do that to you, mon trésor."

My treasure.

The man just called me his treasure. If it was a slip, he's not regretting it, nor is he taking it back. In fact, he's staring right at me without an ounce of second thought. It shouldn't surprise me, not after the recent events of the weeks we've spent together. But every day he sheds more light on parts unknown, and every day I find myself more surprised in the best way.

Words evade me as we stare at the other unspeaking, giving in to our natural gravity, the magnitude far too strong to fight. And now that we've acknowledged it, embraced it, fed on it, there's no turning back.

Because the truth is that I no longer hate Tobias King.

I'm in love with him.

My insatiable need for him flows like lava through my veins, spurring the ache, one I know, soul-deep he's the only one capable of sating. Seconds pass as he recognizes what I'm not saying. I look up at him, imploring him not to exploit my weakness, but what's mine, he claims is his own.

"It hurt," I confess.

"Your dream?"

"Yes."

He frowns. "Ce qui te blesse, me blesse." *What hurts you, hurts me.*

"Do you mean that?"

He places my hand to his chest to let me feel the truth. His heart hammers against my palm as my own heart toes the ledge, carefully peeking down at the endless stories below and weighing the risk before shaking its head at me.

Not yet.

It's trust we need, and it's all backward, but that's our nature, and if I'm honest, it's all we lack. Well, that and the thousand other secrets he's not letting me be privy to. Those matter.

So even if my heart is playing masochistic daredevil, my head is doing its best to keep me above water.

He lifts from me, easing my comfort, and in turn, I cradle him between my legs. We're filthy, in need of another shower, but I wouldn't trade a second of this stolen moment, because I can feel the reckoning coming. And we've put it off for far too long.

"Ask me anything," he whispers, pressing his thumb into the corner of my mouth before tracing my lip as his cinnamon-coated hair hangs between us. "Ask me, and I'll tell you."

"We're not business anymore," I whisper, partly a declaration, part question. We're chest-to-chest as he slowly shakes his head.

"No, we're not."

I can't bring myself to ask him, and so I don't. Instead, he leans in and presses his lips to mine before he speaks. "You warned me not to fall in love with you. You said you wouldn't make room for me."

"You told me you wouldn't," I remind him, my soul soaring with his confession.

He leans in close, his nose brushing mine. "Then I guess that makes us both lia—"

"Well, *brother*, would you take a fucking look at this? Are you seeing what I'm seeing?"

Tobias tenses before going ramrod straight, his expression sobering as he pulls himself to kneel a second before I jackknife, my pulse skyrocketing as I turn from where I sit on the ground and lift my gaze to meet the livid eyes of his brother.

Chapter Twenty-Two

BESIDE DOMINIC STANDS Sean, and at the sight of them, I'm thrust into a reality of the worst kind. I stagger to my feet as I dart my disbelieving gaze between the furious eyes of two men who, not long ago, I pledged myself to. Two men I swore I couldn't, never wanted to live without. Two men who ceased to exist after leaving me begging for them in the street as they drove away.

Dominic's gaze drips acid, peeling me away layer by layer as he takes the two of us in, dressed in nothing but unmistakable guilt. Sean's expression is equally as damning, his jaw set, his eyes blistering us both with rage.

Tobias stands and takes a step away, distancing himself from me, but it's way too late. Trembling, filled with dread, I face them both, speechless, as they collectively batter the two of us from where they stand, their posture threatening in a way I've rarely been privy to.

Dominic is the first to speak. "So, I would say we should catch up, *brother*, but I can see what you've been up to. Or should I say who you've been *into*."

"Where have you been?" I rasp out, my eyes drifting from

one to the other, soaking in the changes. Dominic's hair is cropped close to his head, his physique bulging with new muscle. Sean's hair is tucked under a ball cap and he's bulked up just as much. Even their demeanors seem different. And judging from their collective expressions, it looks as if they've survived hell and just been refused the chance to tell their story.

Dominic leers at me from feet away, his silvery gaze laced with disgust as if it pains him to look at me. My heart lurches in every direction as I sink into the ground, stunned by their sudden arrival.

"Where have we *been*?" Sean hisses before he darts his gaze over my shoulder. "Want to answer that for her, Tobias?"

He takes a menacing step forward, fisting his hands at his sides, opening and closing them as he shifts his stare between us as if he's not sure which of us he wants to strike first.

I turn toward Tobias. "What's he talking about?"

Tobias closes his eyes as Sean speaks up. "I guess it's a good thing we caught that early plane, isn't it, Dom?"

Tobias's expression cools considerably. "Don't play innocent, Sean."

"Innocent? No, I'm not fucking claiming that." He snaps his fingers sarcastically before pointing at Tobias, his voice filled with condescension. "What was your speech before you sent us off? We needed to get our heads right. So, you sentenced us away for ten fucking months to be Boy Scouts and pay for our crimes. And what did you do?"

"What do you mean you caught an early plane?" I ask Sean, who looks at me in a way I never imagined possible. He ignores my question and takes a step toward me. "I asked you to trust me. I told you I would make this right."

"Trust you? *Trust you*? You gave me *nothing*, which is exactly what you left me with. Both of you," I say, darting my eyes between them.

"So, you fuck my *brother*?" Dominic speaks up, his voice lethal. "Pretty cold, baby."

"Watch it," Tobias warns, as Dominic's eyes drift over to him.

"I suppose I should congratulate you for keeping it in the family."

"Don't you dare!" I swallow in an attempt to wet my dry throat, unbelieving of the difference in the appearance of the two of them. They look every bit like soldiers. It's only in their eyes and expressions that I see traces of the men I knew. "This didn't start the minute you left, or anytime soon after. I grieved for you both for months and months without a single thing to hold onto, without a word from either of you!" I look to Sean. "One day didn't come."

"What in the hell do you think this is?" He runs a hand down his jaw.

"Too late! Too late. I had to move on. You gave me no choice. I was losing my mind wondering if I should even bother. You asked me not to look for you, but I did, and you moved out of the townhouse, quit the garage, you both left without a trace. What was I supposed to believe?"

Neither of them speaks up about the necklace. Both would be hard-pressed to admit it now, probably because of the man standing beside me, and now I'm sure I'll never know.

Sean's voice booms, scattering my thoughts. "We were fucking forced away! Cut off from the world for keeping *you* from *him*. For doing exactly what he's been doing!"

I turn to Tobias. "Is this true?"

"It's true," Dominic snaps, his tone as cutting as his silver gaze. "And since when is *his* fucking word money over ours?"

"Since you left me with nothing!"

"Fuck this," Dominic says, turning on his heel.

"Don't, Dominic—" I move toward him, and Tobias stops me—"please don't go," I beg. Eyes watering, I plead with him as he goes completely rigid, his back turned to the three of us. "Please, just tell me the truth."

"The truth." He slowly turns, his voice hoarse. "The truth is, Cecelia, you and I have both been played, but me, by my own fucking blood!" He charges toward Tobias, the wrath in his face unbearable. Tobias steps between us, pushing me back a few feet, readying himself.

This only fuels Dominic as he lunges for his brother, and Sean catches him around the chest just before impact, speaking rapidly in his ear. "Don't. Not here. Not now. This isn't the place. We'll deal with this our way."

Chest fracturing, I look helplessly to Tobias, whose eyes are zeroed in on his brother. In them, I see shame and a hell of a lot of guilt. I shake my head furiously at the revelation. "You mean to tell me you've been waiting this whole time to come back to me?"

Dominic fights Sean's hold, ripping at the arms circling his chest, murder in his eyes for his brother. "Yeah, we've been fucking waiting, waiting for the okay to come home! Fuck you—" his face falls as he stops his struggle, and I crack in half at the agony in his eyes. He shakes his head as Sean steadies him, whispering to him furiously.

Dominic taps Sean's arms. "I'm good. Let me go." When Sean releases him, Dominic grows eerily calm before he steps toward his brother, his voice filled with venom.

"Notre mère aurait honte de toi." *Our mother would be ashamed of you.*

It's then I note Dominic's accent is heavier, more polished. Tobias's was just as heavy when I met him.

"France," I speak up in a whisper. "You sent them to France."

All three of them turn to me as I look over at Tobias, who helplessly looks back at me as I piece it together. "That's what you've been hiding."

That was his secret. And our relationship was always a ticking time bomb. He knew they were coming for me.

He knew.

"You sent them to France. You made them leave, leave *me*."

Tobias hangs his head. His voice defeated when he speaks. "I was going to tell you, tonight."

"How convenient," I whisper hoarsely, feeling every bit the fool I am.

Dominic speaks up. "You are no brother to me. Everything you stand for is a lie."

Tobias scrubs his face, clear offense in his tone when he speaks. "I've done this one thing, for *me*, which doesn't change the fucking thousand other things I did before it, for *you*. I've spent most of my life paying my dues, paving the way while you two had your fucking fun." He steps forward, his eyes pleading. "Tout ce que j'ai toujours fait, c'est prendre soin de toi." *All I have ever done is take care of you.*

"Je te décharge de ça maintenant, et pour de bon." *I relieve you of that now, and for good.* Dominic smashes his palms together as he speaks and separates them as Tobias flinches with the blow of his words.

"Tu es en colère. Je comprends. Mais cela ne signifiera jamais que nous ne sommes pas frères." *You're angry. I understand. But that will never mean we are not brothers.*

"It means nothing to you. You proved that." Dominic eyes me, and I can feel the onslaught of his words before he speaks them.

"Quand tu la baises, frère, sache que c'est moi que tu goûtes. Tu peux la garder." *When you fuck her, brother, just know it's me you're tasting. You can keep her.*"

"Elle parle français," Tobias snaps. *She speaks French.*

Dominic smiles at me, his eyes void of the soul I know and love. "I know she does."

"Of course you would go there, Dom. Of course, you would. That's your go-to, isn't it? Say it in English. You. Fucking. Coward. Call me a whore in a way I fully understand. That's me, isn't it? Nothing but a whore. Not the woman who loved you unconditionally despite the way you treated me in the beginning and deceived me before you left me in the street crying for you. I was faithful to you until I had no choice but to let go and move on. But that doesn't matter, does it? Because all that matters is that I'm not yours to fuck anymore."

Dominic lowers his eyes as Tobias and Sean stare off. Sean's eyes glisten when he speaks. "I didn't think you were capable of this. Not you."

"I'm no more guilty than you are," Tobias defends weakly. But he's got no defense. He sent them away. He sent them away purposefully, expecting to break us. He and I are the only ones who know he had no intentions of us happening, at least at first, and they will never believe him.

But he did send them away. He sent them away to break our hearts because of his anger, his jealousy, and his agenda.

It's then I realize Tobias has been admitting this betrayal to me for some time now. The guilt he's displayed, his words about his actions all have to do with this inevitable fallout. It brings me not an ounce of comfort. I'm still reeling as Sean's eyes scour me, and I feel the need to cover myself. I've never been so ashamed to be in my skin.

"Stop looking at me that way!" I say as tears glide down my cheeks. "Go ahead, call me a whore too, or better yet, don't bother; I see it clearly in your eyes." I clench my fists. "I was left dangling in the dark for damn near a year for you." I lift my chin. "Fucking hypocrites, both of you. I played by *your* rules, Sean. No apologies, remember?" I look between them both. "And the fact that you can't stand by what you preach doesn't make me less of a woman. It makes you both less of a man. You are the ones who told me to take what I want when I want it. I guess the rule only applies if what I want is *you!*"

Sean bites his lip, a lone tear falling straight from his eyes to the hand that now holds his ball cap, and I die at the sight of it.

"I waited for you. I made myself sick. I cried for you both every night for months. I waited and waited, and you never came for me. And I didn't know." I glance at Tobias, who looks like he's about to explode, but he keeps his eyes focused on his brother.

"I didn't know. Sean," I plead with him, "you know me."

"I thought I did," he replies hoarsely.

"You couldn't even trust me enough to tell me where you were going."

"That wasn't the deal we made," he swallows, eyeing Tobias, who's deathly still as he darts his gaze between the three of us, swallowing repeatedly.

This is what selfish does, Cecelia. This is the mess selfish creates.

"Sean, I didn't know." I step toward him, and Tobias intercepts me, unwilling to let me past his barrier as he addresses Sean.

"She was your toy."

Sean cocks his head. "You don't know what the hell you're talking about. And what is she to you? A means to an end? The ultimate revenge against Roman? And there we were feeling guilty, carrying out your fucking orders, and you go and gut us like this? What was this meant to be? A taste of our own medicine? Nah," he says, nothing but contempt in his eyes, "for you, it was misery loves company, right?"

Tobias steps toward him, his face riddled in a mix of jealousy and guilt. "I didn't overstep. The punishment goes for anyone who fucks up. You know that." He exhales. "It wasn't my intention—"

"That's a lie. You wanted her the minute you saw her. Don't forget, brother, I know you. You saw what we saw. Except you knew how we felt about her because we fucking told you." Sean snaps out his arm, pointing at him to stay back. "You asked me if she was worth it, and I told you she was. If you take one more step toward me, I'll forget our past, and I'll fucking end you."

"Remember your place," Tobias snaps, his tone molten.

"You made this personal, and you lost my loyalty in the process." Sean shakes his head. "This is on you." I can physically feel the break between the three of them as Sean addresses me.

"Cecelia," he whispers, the lilt in his tone breaking me apart as he brings his hazel eyes to mine, drawing me back to a time when things were so much simpler. A time where I could love him freely, reach out and touch him. "You were the first goddamn person I thought of every morning and the only woman I have ever dreamed about. And if you would have waited for me, I would have given you the *opposite* of nothing."

Tears fill my eyes and spill over as my heart reminds me exactly which parts were mapped by him. "I wish I could have believed you."

"I wish you would have believed *in me*, too."

"Sean, I—"

"You love him." It's not a question, it's a statement, and I feel all three stares on me as I lower mine. A long, tense silence follows before Dominic turns and heads toward the gate. Finally able, I lift my eyes to see Sean glance at Tobias behind me before running his hand through his hair and pulling on his cap. He turns his red-rimmed eyes to me before he gives me a solemn nod. "I guess we both fucked up. Take care, Pup."

I cup my mouth, sobbing into my hand as Sean joins Dominic where he waits, sparing one last look at me before they walk out of the gate, the loud clang of it slamming behind them making me flinch. I push the tears away from my eyes, unable to move and nowhere near ready to take a single step in any direction.

I stand there for endless seconds, unbelieving of what just happened before anger wins, seeping into my every pore as I turn and face Tobias.

"They *told you*." My voice rattles in my throat on the verge of explosion. "They *told you* how they felt about me. You knew it. They told you, and you sent them away."

"Cecelia—"

"You led me to believe they were done with me. Why? Because you were jealous? As if that's an excuse. Jesus, Tobias!"

"You know I didn't mean for us to happen. I stayed away for eight months before our run-in. I had no intention of laying a hand on you."

"Until you did. The whole time they were coming back for me. They wanted me! They loved me!"

"And what kind of relationship would that be?"

"It was up to us to decide." I shake my head, incredulous. "What have you done?"

His eyes dim as he looks on at me, utterly lost.

"I was going to tell you. I was trying to figure out a way."

"Oh, I know, you've been apologizing every day. I just thought it was something else, not this. Not this."

"I was going to tell you. They weren't supposed to fly back until next week."

"And you telling me was going to make it all better? You're nothing but a selfish, manipulative, fucking liar!"

"I didn't know we were going to happen."

"You *made us* happen. I'm so done with this. I'm so done with this. Please leave." I point in the direction they went.

He charges toward me and clamps his hands on my shoulders, his eyes firing with temper. "Stop and fucking listen to me."

I jerk from his grip. "Get your damn hands off me. Fuck your rules. They loved me, and you knew it! You played us. All three of us. You did what you set out to do. And there's no excuse good enough to justify what you did." I fight his grip as he tries to pull me to him. Words catch in my throat as I freely bleed out. The looks on their faces will haunt me for the rest of my life. "If this is what happens to people who give you their love and loyalty, I'm going to have to pass."

"Stop it." He felt that blow to his core because I can feel our foundation crumbling beneath our feet. We never had trust, so it's giving easily.

"I never trusted you fully, so there's that." I glare at him. "I don't ever want to see you again."

He grips my arms, his voice barely audible. "If only you meant that."

"What did you do?" I whisper.

"I did what thieves do. I stole you!" he roars, gripping me tighter. I refuse to look at him. I can't because I played my part in this too. My knees start to give out as the image of the two of them flashes through my mind.

"Watch it, Tobias, you're getting emotional," I say lifelessly. "That's bad for business."

I can feel his pain, his devastation, but I refuse to acknowledge it.

"Just . . . give me a chance to talk to them."

"Go. Talk to them. Handle your *business*. But say your goodbyes now, I won't be here when you get back."

"Don't even fucking think about it," he whispers so vehemently that I feel the weight of his threat, but it's desperation that leaks from it.

"You don't deserve them. You don't deserve any of us. You said you would up your game. That's what I've been thinking in the back of my mind this whole time. Remember? I told you that you were getting predictable, and you said you would up your game." I shake my head. "And boy, did you deliver."

"This was not a game. And we are not fucking business." He grips my chin, his jaw set as his eyes flame with determination and hurt as he forces me to face him. "Twenty minutes ago, you knew all too well who you belong to, and *with* and you still do. Tell me *I'm* a fool to believe it."

"You said we can never be."

He presses in. "We. Fucking. Are."

I glare up at him, my eyes overflowing. "I'll never forgive you. They'll never forgive you."

"I know." He bends to catch my gaze. "I may be the villain you fell for, but that doesn't make me any less the villain. *Stay*. I'll be back."

I stand in the middle of my yard as he disappears into the house. A heartbeat later, I hear his Jag turn over. He speeds away as my legs give out where I stand in the yard, utterly destroyed.

It strikes me then that I've never known all-consuming love until this day, until him, and I'm positive I will never know it like that again. I found my truth in love just seconds before it was ripped from me. A curse, a damning fate, to be in love with a man I was supposed to view as my rival who instead stole my heart.

And he's just destroyed any trust I might have had for him by laying down all of his cards, and only because his hand was forced.

After hours of staring up at the clouds, I pull myself from the ground, walk upstairs, and begin to pack.

Chapter Twenty-Three

I WAKE UP in a haze surrounded by drawers full of clothes. My French doors clang against my bedroom wall as the summer breeze drifts through. With the next wind-induced crash against the wall, it's clear why I woke. They're still wide open because I spent the majority of the night blaring George Michael's "Father Figure" throughout the house and back into the woods. I'd been furiously tackling my task of packing when it popped up on one of my playlists, one of my mother's old favorites. As I listened while ripping through my belongings, it occurred to me just how fantastically fucking fitting it was. A song so utterly symbolic of my relationship with the man who deceived me to my very core, who preyed on my weakened heart at just the right moment, claiming my weakness as his own. And for a brief time, gave me everything I felt I've been deprived of. Everything I've ever wanted. He played into every one of my romantic fantasies, declared us kindred spirits, worshiped my body, took great pains to handle my heart with the utmost care, pulled me into a living dream and kept me there until I was completely saturated with him, in him, while permeating himself into my fucking soul.

So, for the man who played me so well, I turned it up just to acknowledge his victory. I spelled it out with each lyric that I knew exactly on what level in which he deceived me.

The deepest.

I might not ever have fully trusted Tobias, but I believed enough in his lie to give him the rest of me.

But play he did. And he won with a checkmate to shame all others.

Whether it was deception or not, I may never know, but what I do know is that man now owns it wholly—in a way I can never get back.

"I did what thieves do. I stole you!"

And oh, how he succeeded.

Leave, now, Cecelia. Now.

This time it surprises me how effortless it is to check out. I won't fight it. In fact, I embrace it. I'm no longer capable of holding my own in these types of high-stakes games. And with him, it seems I never had a chance.

Groggy, I shift in bed, wincing at my discomfort.

I don't, at all, remember falling asleep, but I lay amidst my destroyed room filled with nothing but open bags and newly purchased suitcases I'd ordered last week in preparation to move home. I'm determined not to leave a single thing behind, because once I cross that threshold, and drive out of the gate, it will be for the last time.

I didn't expect Tobias to come to me last night and I wasn't disappointed. For all I know, I played DJ, only aggravating the birds whose chirping now sounds distorted outside the doors. Still fighting, I wipe at my eyes, trying to clear the fog away.

When I'm finally able to keep them open, I lay confused on how I landed in a dead sleep in the center of my bed, my folded clothes intact. Continuing to fight to get my wits, I struggle to raise my limbs. It's when I manage to lift from where I was comatose that I feel faint and resume my position back on the mattress to catch my bearings.

What in the hell?

Seconds later, an annoying sting beneath me has me lifting to check for sharp objects. Coming up empty, I reach for my cell phone on my nightstand for the time to see I've slept the day away and have only an hour until my shift.

That is if I was going back to work.

Which I'm not.

Instead, I shoot an email to my supervisor that takes me minutes, not seconds, to compose due to my blurred vision.

I won't be coming in. Not tonight, and not ever. I won't even give my father a heads-up about leaving early because I owe him no explanation. I'm only a few weeks shy of fulfilling my obligation of our agreement and what loyalty I had for him no longer exists. To hell with him.

To hell with them all.

As of this moment, I'm granting myself early parole. Normalcy sounds just peachy at this point—bland, blissful. Determined to get home by nightfall, I try to lift again and groan out in frustration.

"What in the actual fuck?"

I repeatedly blink as I grapple with the gravity holding me down. I've never in my life been so tired.

Struggling to stand, I stumble back and steady myself with my hands on my mattress, feeling hungover even though I didn't have a drop to drink last night. Which is ironic because there's no better time to indulge than when your ex-boyfriends appear like bloodthirsty fairies after months of heart-shattering absence, busting you just as you're declaring your love for their brother.

"Ha!" I shout to no one at the utter insanity of it all. Oh, the stories I'll *never* be able to tell. Who in the hell would believe them anyway? I'm hard-pressed to, and I lived it.

But will I survive it?

That's a determination I'll have to make at a later date.

Determined not to completely crack until I'm in the vicinity of Atlanta, I try again to lift the fog.

I must have passed out folding laundry, emotionally exhausted. But from the looks of it, between packing and staring at the walls, I managed to get enough done so I can leave in a matter of hours if I hustle. But it's my body that betrays me as I'm forced to sit back down to control my spinning head. It's been years since I slept that hard. And thankfully, I can't remember a single dream.

Determined to right myself, I freeze when I feel the burn due to the stretch of my skin at my back, just before I hear the faint rustle of something behind me, something attached to it. And that's when the burn sets in. When I reach back to palm my shoulder, the movement again draws my skin taut, causing the discomfort to spread. Searching with my fingers, my eyes bulge when I feel the edge of the slippery pad attached to it.

What in the fuck?

Jerking my T-shirt over my head, I toss it to the floor and hobble toward my vanity determined not to faceplant. It's there I discover there are *two* pads taped along my shoulder blades.

What in the fuck!

I don't have to lift them to know what's there, but I have to see it for myself. I manage to reach the edge of one of them with my thumb and slowly peel it off, bold black ink clear in the reflection.

Raven's wings.

"Oh my God," I gasp as I manage to lift the other side. Reeling, I study the unmistakable mark while shaking my head in denial.

Last night, I wasn't emotionally drained, I was fucking *drugged* and . . . branded.

Branded!

Marked by one of the sadistic liars who claimed to love me.

My first thought is Dominic, but Sean was just as angry, just as hurt, maybe even more so.

Is this my punishment?

Or is this a display of how much power they have over me?

Tobias would never take the choice away from me. He's too level-headed, less emotional. He wouldn't do this to me, especially after the way he deceived me.

Or would he?

"I may be the villain you fell for, but that doesn't make me any less the villain."

I wouldn't put it past any of them at this point. But this only makes sense for the one who thinks he has a point to prove. Who in the hell actually believes they own me? Truly owns me enough to mark me as his possession.

Not only is it sick, but it's also against the law.

But who am I kidding? I invited these criminals into my

life, between my legs, and into my heart, and they've fucking branded me.

A permanent mark—a very visible and *permanent* mark. One I damn sure should have had a choice in. And why? So, I can't hide behind my secrets anymore?

I still know nothing. Not enough to incriminate any of them, not really. All this time, I've tiptoed around their borders, respected them enough not to push too far, too hard, and for what?

I must have dozed off while packing, and that's when they stuck me, *drugged* me.

They came like the thieves they are under the cover of night and marked me, labeled me: a label that screams one thing and one thing only—*mine*.

This isn't real. This can't be real. I study the tattoo on my back, disbelieving that this is my reality.

And I'm so done.

So fucking done.

Done with the questions, with the struggle, with the understanding, the mystery. I'm so fucking done wondering, waiting for answers while forever dangling in the dark.

I'm just . . . done.

And tonight, when the moon rises high in the sky above, I'm going to declare fucking war.

Bass thumps from behind the bubbled metal doors as loud laughter sounds out. They're all here. Mindlessly partying while I stand a marked woman, completely set adrift on an island of rage and bitterness. I lift the first bottle and toss it, hitting my mark when it shatters against the door. The music clicks off, as the second one sails into the air, smashing to pieces at the foot of the door. Tyler is the first to go into the lobby. I can see his lips move with his report as one of the metal doors slowly lifts, and I hurl another bottle at it.

"Jesus, fuck," Sean says, flinching as some glass hits him as I hurl another and another. His eyes flare with anger as he surveys the damage I've already inflicted. All of their tires are flat. No one will be following me tonight.

It's surreal to see them all standing there, gawking at me like I've lost my mind. Jeremy, Tyler, Dominic, Sean, Russell, even Layla, who ghosted me along with the rest of them but regards me now with wide eyes. For so long, I felt like I'd imagined my time among them. But the gang's all here and a few others I didn't expect to see. Some fare with similar tattoos to the one I now wear, one of them with her eyes locked on Dominic, who discards a joint as he surveys the damage in his parking lot.

Sean takes a tentative step forward as my eyes meet Dominic's behind him. His features impassive as he surveys me.

I can't believe I let myself get wrapped up in these liars, these manipulative thieves who stole me from myself.

"Cecelia," Layla speaks up, her voice on edge. "Baby, what's going on?" She turns her gaze on Sean and Dominic. "What did you fuckers do?"

"Don't bother," I scold her dismissively. "Don't pretend to give a damn about me now."

"You know I didn't have a choice."

"Oh, bullshit," I glare at her. "You had a choice. You chose them. And guess what? You deserve them."

Guilt runs clear in her blue eyes. "I'm sorry."

"Save it. You've all made your point. I think it's time I made one of my own." I lift the five-gallon can, adding the rest of the contents to the puddle in front of me.

"What the fuck are you doing?" Sean asks, taking a step forward, just as I lift a different kind of bottle, the rag inside soaked.

"Jesus Christ," Tyler says, his eyes bulging. "Cecelia, what the hell are you doing?"

"Who did it?!" I fume as Sean starts toward me.

"Take another step before I get my answer, and I'll light this, and we'll all see where it lands. Don't fucking push me, Sean!"

"Put it down," he barks as I try to ignore the sight of him and what it does to me. Seeing them again is surreal.

But I've been a fool far too long.

"Who did this to me?!" I scream, no longer able to keep our secret. No longer able to hide what's been done.

"Is this what you consider loyalty? You want me? Well, here I fucking am! You want extremes? You want devotion. Trust me. I'm dedicated to this. And I learned from the best. Fucking test me." I lift my chin in defiance. "Speak up, and you can come and get your fucking prize."

I strike one of the Zippos I stole from Sean when we were together, and he jerks back.

"Cecelia, don't!" Sean's panicked eyes dart back to Dominic, who starts to move toward me, his steps sure as he pushes through the crowd.

"Bitch has lost her mind," one of the girls says from the garage. "You must've dicked her too good, Dom."

A few guys I recognize from one of the meetups chuckles, but no one else is laughing, especially Dominic, whose eyes flare in irritation as he moves toward me at a leisurely pace.

"What the fuck?" One of them speaks up, catching on to the damage done. "She slashed our fucking tires!"

Dom holds up his hand, silencing them all with the flick of his wrist.

"I swear to God, Dominic, I'll light this place up," I say, my voice steady. "Stop!"

He does, his eyes cold, dull, lifeless, familiar boredom schooling his features. And it hurts, it stings, it's as if we never existed.

"Why?" My jaw shakes with anger. "Why?!"

I twist, just enough so they can see the clear marks on my back and watch them both carefully for reactions. Neither gives me a single tell. I can only calculate this was just another one of their plans to mess with my head.

"Cowards! You're both fucking cowards!" I shake my head, rage boiling over just as phones begin to go off at random around us. Tyler lifts his to his ear as Dominic and Sean both start to slowly walk my way as if cornering a stray cat. "I was *never yours*, and I never will be. Stay the fuck away from me!"

"Dom!" Tyler shouts, running to his side with the phone before putting it to his ear. A second later, Dom grips it and drops all pretense walking toward me in a blur just as I light the bottle and toss it down in the puddle of gasoline. Dom lunges, but the flash of flames separate us, giving me just enough time to dash to my Jeep. Dominic reaches the hood, slamming his fists on it just as I peel out. My heart hammers wildly against my chest as I race down the roads, screaming as I beat my hands against the wheel.

And under the cover of night, I disappear.

Chapter Twenty-Four

IARRIVE HOME near dawn, feeling safe enough to avoid any visitors so I can make my exit. Limbs heavy, back stinging, I'm exhausted from hours of driving aimlessly, my body sore from countless minutes spent staring into the dark road ahead, directionless. I have no idea what it's going to take to move on from here, but I'm leaving. Not tomorrow, or the day after, now.

I have the money.

I've lost my fucking sanity for it, but it's over. This ends today. The toxicity of the relationships I've formed is making me venomous. I'm so far from the girl who pulled up to this house a year ago.

Securing the house, I set the alarm, knowing that anyone who wants inside *can* and *will* get to me. Walls and doors mean nothing to these men, and at this point, I'm sure none of them will stop me from leaving. Because maybe now they see me as a poison too. We've hurt and betrayed each other. There's no coming back from that. And Tobias's absence, his silence, only confirms that once again, I've played the fool. I might not know what love is, but I now know what it isn't.

I push all thoughts of Tobias away as I pull the packed suitcase from beside my bed and begin loading another. I should have been packed before I hit the garage, but I was too angry to come up with a better plan. Instead, I counted on arriving home at the late hour, expecting that anyone looking for me would give up when they saw I didn't return home. It's when I hear the disarm of the front door that I know that my plan backfired.

I'm not alone.

Fear cripples me as I stand in the center of my bedroom, waiting. Never did I fear these men before, and never did I ever think they would hurt me.

Nor did I think they would push back over a couple of tires.

Okay, *a lot* of tires. Every tire in the parking lot.

Tires that will cost them a small fortune to replace. In the grand scheme of things, it was a psycho ex-girlfriend move. And that spectacle made me look like the guilty one when I'm anything but. But who marks a woman without their consent?

Lunatics in a power struggle. I'm forever branded because of them, because of their selfishness.

I blink and see Dominic standing in the threshold of my bedroom. A gun tucked in his waistband with the tip of a silencer attached to the end of it.

A silencer.

Swallowing, I eye it and take a step back, and he holds his hands up.

"Cee." He shakes his head as if my reaction is ridiculous. "Come on."

I'd shown my ass tonight, made myself look unstable. Unreliable. Emotional. A liability.

"I'll pay for them. All of them. I-I was angry." I take another step back, and he chuckles incredulously before pulling the gun out of his jeans. I hear the thump of it land on the stairs as he makes his way into the bedroom. "No gun, okay?"

"W-what are you doing here?"

He eyes my suitcases and then brings his silver gaze back to me. I can't control the shake that overtakes me, nor the panic that starts to rapidly consume me.

"I'll pay for them, Dom. I swear. I won't say anything. I'm leaving, see?" I nod toward my suitcases.

"Come on, Cecelia," he scoffs. "Really?"

"I was angry. But I d-didn't t-tell anyone."

"Why are you shaking?"

"I can't believe anything you say." I eye my cell phone where it sits on my nightstand, and he shakes his head dubiously.

"I'm not here to hurt you."

"I don't know you."

"Yes, you fucking do. You know me," his tone is guttural, full of disappointment, and it throws me.

"Now you care about me? A few hours ago, you looked at me like I meant nothing to you."

He blows out an exasperated breath. "Well, I'm a bit fucking ripped up at the moment. And you do know me."

"I don't know anything. I'm not a loose end, okay? I won't say anything to anyone. I haven't told a soul, Dom. I swear."

"Jesus," he says, scrubbing his face with his hand, his expression turning sick with worry. "What have we done to you?"

I swallow. "I just want to leave now." I do my best to control the shake in my voice as a tear spills over. "C-can I please just go home?"

He studies my expression, and nothing but hurt shines in his eyes when he steps toward me, and I flinch.

"Did *he* tell you to come here?"

This time he's the one who flinches. "Please tell me you don't think that of me. I could never hurt you."

"I don't know what to think anymore." I cup my mouth holding in my sob. "I don't know what to believe."

"Jesus Christ, I think this hurts more than coming home to find you with him." He hangs his head before bringing his eyes to mine. "Cecelia. I would never, ever, fucking hurt you. Not for anything or anyone or any reason." He takes a step forward. "Come on, baby, look at me."

I shake my head.

"Damnit, Cecelia, look at me. Right now."

I lift my eyes to his.

"*See* me. It's me."

My heart seizes when he takes another step forward, and another and I stop my retreat, his name bursting from my lips in an anguished cry just as he pulls me into his arms. We clutch each other as my fear subsides, and I realize just how far I've fallen down the rabbit hole.

"Goddamnit," he whispers, pulling me tightly to him, his voice riddled with ache, "I'm so sorry. I'm so fucking sorry. Have we twisted things so much?"

I clutch him to me, pressing my face into his neck as he covers me with his hands, running them along my back and down my arms. "What have we done to you?" His voice is full of emotion as he pulls me tighter to him, and I inhale his faint but familiar scent.

"I just . . . don't know what to believe anymore."

"We fucked up so bad with you, believe that."

He pulls away and stares down at me, his eyes searching mine, his tone desperate. "Tell me you know deep down we aren't those guys?"

I shake my head, unable to form words.

"Cee, that's not us."

"Last night, I was drugged and tattooed. Are you sure you're not those guys?"

"Jesus—" he cups the back of his neck—"you're right. I can't blame you for thinking the worst, can I?"

He exhales a breath and pulls out his burner phone from his jeans before sitting at the edge of my bed. Tension begins to brew as he looks over at me.

"Ten months," he says as I study him just as carefully, feeling every single day of the space those months put between us. "We should have told you we were coming back. I wanted to. Sean wanted to keep to the deal we made with him to prove Tobias wrong. He didn't think . . ." He exhales a loaded breath, "I guess it doesn't matter now."

I lower my eyes to the carpet as he clasps his hands between his knees. A long silence passes before he speaks up.

"He's right, you know. My brother spoke the truth. He's spent half his life setting things up, always in the background, doing everything he could to fucking get this thing together. To make sure we were taken care of." I look him over and see the exhaustion in his posture, in his eyes. "He was telling the truth."

"I'm not sure you know the meaning of that word. That any of you do."

"You wanted in," he reminds me. "This is in."

"Not this way," I counter. "And not at this cost."

"I told you more than once you didn't want the truth. Why do you think I tried so hard to push you away at first?" One side of his mouth lifts. "You were so fucking perfect." His eyes cloud with memory. "Standing there in my yard that day, and after . . ." he shakes his head. "I wanted to hate you. I tried so hard to hate you."

"Didn't notice."

We share a sad smile.

"We always knew the truth would be the end. We always knew that keeping you in the dark was the only real way to keep you. You were amongst liars, thieves, and killers," he says softly, "way too fucking good for any of it, and I think we clung to you because you represented everything we wanted to protect, but could never be."

"I never saw you that way. Not ever."

"Until tonight, huh?" He hangs his head. "Even if we're trying to do right, we aren't saints, Cecelia."

The familiar pang of my name on his lips stings me, and I breathe through it.

"I'm no saint either. You made sure of that. I was a game."

"No—" he tugs at my hand so I'm standing above him—"never, you were never that."

"Tell me why you're here."

"You didn't miss me?"

My eyes instantly water. "Every day, rain or shine." I huff and slap the tears from my face. "Jesus, why can't I hate you?"

"For the same reason I can't hate you."

He eyes his phone and sets it down before a sad smile tips his lips. "I haven't seen him look at *any* woman the way he looked at you. I've never seen him light up like that. I knew it the minute I saw you together. I knew that we were fucked. Sean did too."

"It doesn't matter."

"It does. I can hate him all I want for taking what didn't belong to him, but it's true."

"We didn't mean—"

He jerks his chin. "I can't hear that right now, okay?"

"Well, I'm not a possession. Despite the fucking branding on my back. No one has that right over another person. This is supposed to be about free will, remember?"

He laces our fingers. "You make that hard to remember. And we were too late." He looks up at me, and all I see is hurt. "We were too late."

"So, you guys fucking mark me? Throw a fit and fucking mark me?"

He squats and leans in, pressing his forehead to my stomach. "I can't do this now. I can't . . . just . . . make him happy."

"I'm leaving, Dominic. Right now. That's what I'm doing."

"You may be, but we both know he won't let you go."

"He doesn't have a choice."

"I'm sorry," he whispers, nuzzling my stomach before looking up at me. "I'm so fucking sorry for all we've put you through. I want you to know that. We all are."

I swallow. "I might be pissed at you, too, but I'm sorry about the cost to you. I never got the chance to tell you I'm sorry about your parents."

"It wasn't your fault."

"I don't understand how you could—"

He snaps his gaze to mine. "Be with you?"

I nod.

He stands, and time stops when he cups my jaw. And it's just me and my cool dark cloud. We lock eyes for long seconds. "That's one question I can answer," he whispers, his eyes piercing as he leans in, "yes."

"Yes, what?"

"Yes," he strokes my face. "I've been in love."

The words strike hard, and I burst into tears at the sound of them.

He grips me in his hold before pressing a brief kiss to my lips and pulling away. "But she went and fell in love with my brother."

He brushes a tear from my cheek as I look up at him. "I swear to God, I didn't want to. I clawed his eyes out for as long as I could."

He gives me a weak chuckle. "I believe that." He clears his throat and eyes the suitcase behind me.

"I'll never forgive him," I say, the ache intensifying.

"I'll leave that up to you."

"Will you?" I ask.

He sighs. "He's my brother, hell, in a way, he's been like a father, too. I don't know, Cee. It's been a fucked-up couple of days." He scrubs his face. "Come on, let's get you home."

"Not without answers, first—"

His phone goes off, and he lifts a finger to me before he reads the text and his eyes fly to mine. "Fuck."

The look on his face has me paling. "What is it?"

He jerks his chin to quiet me before he races out of my bedroom.

I move to follow him and freeze when Dominic speaks up from the top of the stairs.

"What brings you here, Matteo? It's a little late for company."

Chapter Twenty-Five

"WHAT BRINGS YOU here, Matteo? It's a little late for company."

I race to the threshold of my room and look over Dominic's shoulder. Running through my thoughts, I search and search, dread coursing through me when I recall my conversation with Sean at my first Meetup.

"That's Matteo and Andre, The Spanish Lullaby."

"Why are they called The Spanish Lullaby?"

"Use your imagination."

Matteo's eyes meet mine over his shoulder, and his lips lift in a sick grin as he answers Dominic. "Business."

Dominic stands ramrod straight, his back to me, violence in his posture, and protectiveness in his voice as I duck away from Matteo's lethal gaze.

"Aren't you playing on the wrong side of the fence?" Dominic asks.

"Money doesn't care."

"You need to turn the fuck around, and don't ever let me catch you out of Florida again. It won't end well."

"You tapping that?" Matteo asks, batting away Dom's

threat. "I was thinking of sampling." I'm sure Dominic's eyes scream murder when Matteo speaks up again, clearly amused. "Pussy's that good, huh?"

Matteo has to be pushing around three hundred pounds, a lot of it muscle, his hair as greasy as his clothes, his thick nostrils flaring as he eyes me with a look that turns my stomach as his knife comes into view. A hunting knife at least nine inches long. Panic zings through me as I turn and scan my room for anything I can use and come up empty. I step out onto the landing behind Dominic as he speaks up.

"Cecelia, baby, get back into your room, *now*."

The door across the hall opens and Tobias appears, a similar gun in hand as the one Dominic discarded when he steps out, his eyes sweeping me with relief before he glances down at Dominic.

"What's good, brother?"

"Got this handled," Dominic replies, his voice lethal. "Speaking of brothers, Matteo. Where is yours tonight?"

"You know him." Matteo shrugs. "Probably out at the club."

"Actually, he's in here, resting," Tobias says, jerking his chin over his shoulder. "You should join him."

I peek over Tobias's shoulder, and he shakes his chin subtly. I school my features.

Don't fucking react.

There's no one in that room, which means the other half of the Spanish Lullaby, Andre, is somewhere in my house. Have they been here the whole time?

Just as the thought occurs to me, Tobias's eyes drift past me and widen, and he lifts his gun, training it just above my shoulder.

"Come to me," Tobias says in a steady voice as I leap into

the clearing between the two doors. Tobias jerks his chin in an effort to get me to back up more, and I plaster myself to the wall behind me just as Andre appears at the threshold of the bedroom door, where I was just standing. There's a knife in his hand similar to the one Matteo has. Fear paralyzes me as Andre gazes on at Tobias with black eyes.

"Oh, looks like he showed up after all," Matteo says with a sickening lift to his voice.

"I must have been mistaken," Tobias says in a dull monotone.

"Don't worry, we have more joining the party," Matteo assures.

Just as he says it, the doorbell rings, making me jump out of my skin.

Ding dong. Ding dong. Ding dong.

Matteo hollers out something in Spanish, and the noise stops.

"Out of respect, we wanted to try and handle this like gentlemen," Andre says to Tobias by way of greeting.

"Appreciate it," Tobias says, matter of fact.

"Least I could do," Andre says. "After all, you're the one who brought me in."

"And look where that got me." Tobias's tone goes icy as he looks on at Andre with disgust. "What the fuck are you doing, Andre?"

"Things are getting a little too light down south."

"So you take a fucking contract that has to do with my *personal* interests? Not a good decision."

"Gotta get paid," he says as if this is an everyday occurrence. And I'm guessing for him, it is. "I don't blame you for your interest," Andre says, eyeing me.

"Don't even look at her, you greasy motherfucker," Tobias barks.

"You've seen what I can do with this," Andre threatens, "let's not get offensive."

"Tobias," I whisper hoarsely as a veil of fear-induced sweat cloaks me.

We're not playing a game with toy guns, extra lives, and Monopoly money.

As much as I've witnessed over the last year, as much as I've been warned away, I realize I've been spared to the point I still felt like the danger was in an alternate reality. This is what they've been trying to avoid all along. And now I'm living in my worst nightmare. I could very easily die tonight, and so could the men I love.

It doesn't get more real than this.

"Let her go, and I'll pay you twice as much," Tobias says to Andre.

"Deal," Matteo says quickly. "We'll take your money, bro."

"Andre," Tobias spits in warning. I look over and see Andre inching toward me. "Don't."

Andre stops and gives Tobias a sheepish grin. "Been a long, long time, man. I almost didn't recognize you in that suit."

"You like it?" Tobias smiles, and it's the most dangerous thing I've ever seen in my life. He's going to kill them, *both of them*.

"Where is Daddy?" Andre whispers to me. "His car is here."

My eyes shoot to Tobias, and I try to read him for the right answer and get nothing.

"I d-d-don't know. I just got home," I stutter out. I hate

that I can't get myself right. That I can't mirror the two men with steady hands and strong voices defending me, protecting me.

"I don't think I'm satisfied with the terms of this agreement," Dominic says, his voice steady.

Andre cocks his head. "How so?"

Tobias looks to me as I begin shaking uncontrollably.

I read his expression.

Easy, baby.

I've never been so fucking scared in my life.

Ding dong. Ding dong. Ding dong.

Tobias darts his eyes to Matteo, his gun still trained on Andre. "Want to answer that?"

Matteo speaks up. "Trust me, man, you don't want me to open that door."

Tobias nods. "I can have the money to you in minutes."

"Like I said," Dominic hisses, "I'm not happy with this deal."

It's then I see Dominic's gun tucked in Matteo's jeans. He's unarmed. He didn't make it to his gun in time. And it's because of me. If he'd had it, this would already be over. Bile climbs up my throat as I try to steady myself against the wall behind me.

"It's the only deal to be made, brother," Tobias snaps, a warning in his voice.

"Cecelia," Dominic says, in the intimate tone he used with me in the days we spent together, alone.

"Dominic," Tobias implores, a jagged fear in his voice.

"I'm talking to Cecelia," Dominic counters.

"Yes?" My eyes spill as Tobias darts his apprehensive gaze between his brother and me.

"After this, you want to watch a movie?" Dominic asks. "You can make that cheddar popcorn I love. We can crowd under that blanket that smells like . . . what's that smell?"

I choke on a fresh wave of fear. "Lavender," I say as more tears stream down my cheeks.

"Yeah. And I'll let you watch a chick movie because all I really want to do is watch you watch it. Your face gets all dopey when you get love drunk."

"Must be some good shit if she's whipped you, Dom," Matteo snarks, his vacant eyes lifting to me.

"We love rainy days, don't we, baby?" Dominic's voice drifts up as he takes a step toward Matteo.

"We do." A sob escapes me as I cripple under the tension. To my right is safety—Tobias—to my left, certain death. And death is much closer. If that blade reaches me before Tobias's bullet, I'm first. But if he doesn't make it to his brother in time . . . it's a choice that Tobias has to make. Save his brother or me, and Dominic is making it for him, trying to throw himself on the grenade.

"We don't fucking negotiate with terrorists." Dominic tilts his head in challenge, and Matteo only grins, his canines dripping acid. He outweighs Dominic by at least eighty pounds, but Dominic has speed and incredible strength. He wouldn't need either if I had trusted him earlier. If I'd believed him. I'm the reason he doesn't have his gun.

"Dominic," I whimper as he takes another step down the stairs toward Matteo.

"What is it, baby?"

"S'il te plaît, ne fais rien de stupide. Je t'aime." *Please don't do anything stupid. I love you.*

"Je sais." *I know.*

"Dominic," Tobias orders gruffly. "Stand down, right fucking now. We're still talking."

Dominic takes another step toward Matteo. "Care to dance?"

"Honored, my friend," Matteo replies.

"Make it a good one."

"Dominic, no!" Tobias yells just as Dominic lunges for Matteo.

Tobias charges forward a second before Andre reaches me with the blade, batting me back before he takes Andre down with a point-blank shot to the head. Tobias clears the whole of the railing, stumbling in his landing just as Dominic lands a solid right to Matteo's face. I hear the crack of bone as blood sprays from Matteo's nose.

Tobias is just a few steps away from his brother when Dominic rears back and kicks Matteo in the chest. Matteo falls straight back, bypassing the stairs, his back smacking into the landing. Dominic leaps toward where Matteo lays before he makes a fast turn back in our direction, meeting Tobias midway and knocking him out of the way just as the air splinters with the ping of bullets.

The plaster next to my head explodes as I scream out. Dominic is leaping toward me, his eyes bulging when the second shot rips through his abdomen. The third shot hits Dominic in the thigh just as he cups his stomach falling to his knees before jerking forward when a fourth shot pierces his shoulder just as Tobias pushes him out of the way.

Tobias roars, turning and unloading his gun on Matteo's lower half before crashing into him at the foot of the stairs. Another shot pings the air landing somewhere in the foyer. Leaping to my feet, I race to Dominic just as his eyes cloud over and his mouth opens, clear agony written all over his face as he reaches for me. I make it to him in seconds, and he pulls me with him before he stumbles back, landing against the wall and sliding down, leaving a trail of blood behind him. Matteo cries out below us, and I see only a glimpse of him before the side of his face disappears, and he lands in a lifeless heap on the floor.

Dominic coughs as I cover his wound with my hands and look up into silver eyes.

"I'm sorry." I press my hands to his stomach as his eyes dart left and right and blood begins to coat his beautiful lips.

"Hang on. Okay? Hang on."

Dominic pulls at my hands and coughs again, just as Tobias meets me where I kneel. "Go," he rasps out, his face drawn due to the pain.

Ding dong. Ding dong. Ding dong.

We all turn in the direction of the door and know the clock is ticking. We have seconds.

I press onto Dom's stomach and he winces, every breath challenging him as his eyes drift between us.

"Hold on," I say, desperately trying to stop the blood leaking from his stomach. "I'm sorry." I press in harder, and he cries out in misery.

"I'm sorry, baby, I'm so sorry," I murmur, pressing my forehead to his as Tobias unties his belt and wraps it above the bullet wound in Dom's thigh. Dominic jerks as we struggle to address his injuries, and that's when I see his leg is soaked. "Go," he rasps out, his eyes rolling up as he battles a fresh wave of pain.

"Goddamnit, goddamnit, Dom," Tobias exhales, anguished, while he inspects Dom's shoulder, pressing his hand over the bullet wound in his leg.

Dominic covers my hands with his and squeezes them faintly before his eyes lift to his brother. His pain-filled words coming out chopped. "Nous savions tous les deux que je n'allais jamais voir mes trente ans, mon frère. Prends soin d'elle." *We both know I was never going to make it to thirty, brother. Take care of her.*

Dom coughs again, more blood lining his lips, a grimace twisting his beautiful features. "Go," he coughs out. "Please," he wheezes.

"No" I shake my head furiously as his eyes drift to mine. "Sorry, you can't go, Dominic, because I dreamed your future up for you. Hang on, and I'll tell you all about it." I press into his wound and look him right in the eyes. "Don't you dare leave me here. I want that date with you."

Skin slick with a glaze of sweat he gazes at us both, and the next time he coughs, I hear the gurgle behind it, his struggle. I continue to press against him as he releases my hands, finally relenting to let me help him.

Tobias presses his forehead to his brother's, and I hear Dominic's faint whisper to him. "Frères pour toujours." *Always brothers.*

"Mother greet you," Tobias replies. "Father keep you. I love you, brother."

It's when Tobias mewls and drops his head that I look up.

And I realize Dominic is gone, his eyes clouding over before they fixate in a place I can no longer reach him.

A gasp leaves me, and my heart stops.

"D-D-Dom," I choke out before looking to Tobias. "W-w-we didn't get enough t-t-time to help him! We didn't get enough time. Oh my God, Dom."

Tobias coughs out incredulously, tears spilling down his

face as I clutch Dom to me. "I just got you back." I pull him to me as he sinks further down the wall, his arms limp at his sides, all signs of life leaving his body. I lower my head to his chest, and I don't know how much time passes, but it can't be much because the doorbell is ringing again, and I know our time is up.

I glance over to see Tobias and see his eyes trained on the two of us. Physically, I feel him start to withdraw as his gaze drifts from me to his brother.

Ding dong. Ding dong. Ding dong.

Collectively, Tobias and I snap our heads in the direction of the worthless barrier that separates us. Half of the defected Miami crew is probably behind that door. In minutes it will all be over, and my only thought is—good—because I don't want to be anywhere in a world where Dominic doesn't exist.

Tobias gathers both guns before grabbing his brother beneath his arms and dragging his lifeless body up the stairs and into my bedroom. I follow, sobbing hysterically as he sets Dominic down on the carpet next to my bed, and I move to sit beneath him, cradling his upper body in my lap while stroking his beautiful face. I run my fingers through his thick hair and over his jaw, but his gaze remains somewhere far past the both of us, and I can't look away.

The front door bursts open just as Tobias kicks the bedroom door closed, and our eyes meet when the sound of gunfire sounds out in all directions below.

Which makes it a fight.

They're here. The rest of the brothers are here.

We needed a few minutes at the most. A collection of seconds. That's all Dominic needed to have a chance.

Darkness cloaks me as hell unleashes around us, and I

sink into a state of disbelief as I cradle Dom in my arms and succumb to the undertow, fully submerged, drifting deeper in when a bang sounds outside the bedroom door. But it's Sean's voice that pulls me back onto the bedroom floor. "Tobias?! Dom?! You in there? She with you?!"

"We're in here," I yell a second before Sean bursts through the door, fully armed with three vests in hand and strapped with guns at his back. His eyes dart between us, evident relief in his face before he sees Dominic laying lifeless in my lap. A cough escapes him, and his eyes immediately glass over as he crosses the space in two strides before falling to his knees in front of us, dropping the vests on the floor next to me. A hoarse curse leaves him as he lifts his eyes from his best friend to me as I sob over his body.

"It's my fault," I admit as I look up to see Tobias at the foot of my bed watching us. "When he showed up, I was afraid he was here t-to hurt me, so he ditched his gun on the stairs." I look between Tobias and Sean. "It's my fault he didn't have his gun."

"Cecelia, don't," Sean says, his voice breaking as I look up at Tobias.

"I didn't know they were here, Tobias. I didn't know they were here because he didn't tell me. I didn't know what was going on. He didn't tell me, Tobias. I didn't know!"

"He didn't think he needed it," Tobias whispers hoarsely. "Because *I* already searched the house once and told him it was clear. I don't know how they got in."

"Don't," Sean says, looking between us, "you don't do this now. Neither one of you pulled the fucking trigger." He slowly stands and stares down at us both, and in a blink, his expression goes granite, his eyes shining with vengeance. He looks over to where Tobias now stands, and I look up and into his amber eyes to see him utterly destroyed.

"What's your call?" Sean asks him as Tobias eyes me, then his brother, and then me again.

"Tobias, what's your call?" Sean repeats.

"No one leaves breathing," Tobias says without another thought, his eyes locked on me before he turns to Sean. "Give me everything on you." His voice is void of humanity as he holds out his hands.

Sean hands over one of the guns on his back along with a few magazines as Tobias looks down at where I sit with Dom, all traces of mortality leaving his face. I gaze down at Dominic and stroke his hair before pressing my lips against his forehead, his temple, before closing his eyes with my hand.

"Sleep, prince," I say softly, biting my lips as my hot tears pelt his face. I lace my fingers with Dominic's and close my eyes. "I'll find you again. I'll find you in my dreams. We'll have so many rainy days. I'll find you—"

"Cecelia," Tobias snaps out my name in a way that has me jerking back to lift my focus to him.

In seconds, he draws me in, eyes blazing before he speaks. "You leave, and you *don't* come back. You *never* come back." His order is definitive, leaving me no room for any argument or response. He turns to Sean, lowering a vest around his neck before securing it and nodding toward me. "Get her out of here. She's parked past the tree line." I'm too far inside my head, inside the despair clouding me to understand his words or the full weight of their meaning. Tobias walks over to the bedroom door, takes one last look at me before he disappears out of sight. Sometime soon, in the future, I know the damage from his words is going to be caustic, but all I can do is gaze back down at Dominic before I carefully clean the blood away from his lips.

More gunfire sounds around us in all directions, just as Tyler's voice booms from beneath my balcony. "Sean! All clear!"

Sean's eyes dart to mine from where he stands next to the French doors firing twice into the yard. "Cecelia, we have to go."

Shaking my head, I grip Dominic to me. "He's still warm."

Sean kneels before me a second later as I stroke Dom's cheek.

"We have to go, Cecelia." He gently lifts Dominic from my lap, and I cup his head, tenderly resting it on the carpet before pressing my lips to his. A sob erupts from me as Sean pulls me from him. And then we're on the balcony, dawn threatening on the horizon while I study my blood-covered hands.

Sean lifts and lowers me over as far as he can to drop me to where Tyler waits, catching me easily, just as gunshots ricochet near the side of the house. Tyler springs into action, pinning me against the brick behind him while lifting twin Glocks and pointing them in all directions. When another raven appears, Tyler looks back, scanning my clothes, and me, a question in his eyes.

"Dominic," I sob out in reply. His face falls, and he swallows, eyes gleaming just before they clear.

"How many?" Sean asks, drop-landing next to us with my purse and one of my sundresses spilling out of the top of it.

"I counted ten cars when we rolled up," Tyler says,

nodding toward the tree line as more brothers emerge, running toward the house.

"No one leaves breathing," Sean repeats Tobias's orders, and Tyler nods in understanding.

I turn to Sean. "Sean, where is Roman?"

"He's not here. He's safe."

"But they said his car is here."

"He's safe," he assures, stepping up to me and handing me my purse before he turns to Tyler.

"Get her out of here. She's parked past the tree line."

Sean looks over to me, hazel eyes flitting with emotion a second before he thrusts me in Tyler's arms. "Go," he whispers hoarsely, and with that, he stalks toward the house. "No, not like this, please," I call after him. "Sean!" I scream, my heart disintegrating, fear consuming me that this may be the last time I see him—that I see *any* of them. He ignores my plea, and the second he enters through the back door, a shot sounds out, ringing in my ears. Tyler muffles my scream while gripping me firmly around the waist before dragging me away.

"Please, Cee, please, we have to go," he shouts as I crane my head in the direction of the house. He stops, cupping my shoulders and shaking me, drawing my eyes to his. "I need you to soldier up, *right fucking now.*"

I immediately stop my fight, swallow hard and nod. He grips my jaw to keep me focused on him as more gunfire sounds just inside the house, drawing closer.

"I need five minutes," Tyler pleads. "Give me five minutes. You can do this." I nod just before he grips me by the arm and takes off at a dead run. I follow, letting the adrenaline take over as we zigzag on the outskirts of the large yard until we reach the trees. A few more ravens emerge racing past us, not sparing us a glance as we sprint in the opposite direction just as the morning sun breaks through the base of the pines. Tyler scans the woods. His head cocked, his posture rigid, his military training appears to take over as he keeps me quiet and plastered to his side.

Safely, he navigates us to a break in the trees and roadside as we collectively catch our breath. My Jeep is parked at the side of the road, and behind it sits Dominic's Camaro.

Tyler pulls the dress from my purse and turns facing the woods, keeping guard as I peel the blood-soaked clothes from me. When I'm redressed, he gathers my clothes and turns to me, slapping a wad of cash into my hand. "Cash only until you reach *home*. Get in and do not fucking stop until you reach Atlanta. Do not speed, do not drive erratically, and as soon as you're there, find a place to wash off. No one sees you until you're clean. You were not here, Cee. You were *never* here. Got it? Wait for my call."

"Tyler, I can't leave like this! I can't leave them!"

"Cee, let me get back to them."

I nod as he pulls me to him in a tight embrace before releasing me.

"Go. *Now*."

In a blink, I'm thrust behind the wheel of my Jeep, and in the next, Tyler disappears behind the trees. Shaking uncontrollably, I turn the engine over and put it into gear, the sight of the car I pass as I floor the gas has me releasing a guttural cry.

The road begins to rapidly blur as the sun climbs into the morning sky, shedding light on a day I know I won't survive. It's all I can do to keep the wheel straight.

Dominic is gone. Gone.

There's no coming back from this. From losing him. Not ever.

"God, please." I bang my hands against the wheel as agony rips through me while I re-live the last minutes of his life.

I did nothing.

I stood frozen with fear as I watched them fight for me. I watched Dominic die to protect me, and I did *nothing*, nothing at all to help them, nothing to help myself. I just stood idly by and screamed. I reacted like a coward.

We both know I was never going to make it to thirty, brother. Take care of her.

"P-p-lease, G-G-od, p-p-please don't take them! Please!" I race away with the taste of Dominic's blood on my lips, coating my hands as I drive past the county line and exit onto the highway toward a future I no longer want.

PART TWO

Now

In visions of the dark night
I have dreamed of joy departed—
But a waking dream of life and light
Hath left me broken-hearted.

—*A Dream*, Edgar Allen Poe

Chapter Twenty-Six

Cecelia age 26
Nine hours ago . . .

"*To the Bride and Groom.*"

Champagne glasses rise around the small restaurant as I clink flutes with Collin. A serene smile graces his handsome face as he squeezes my hand while covered plates are ceremoniously set before us.

When the cloche is lifted, I glance down to see lamb chops with mint sauce and rosemary potatoes. Just as I start to voice my protest, a familiar, masculine scent invades my nose. My breath catches as I inhale deeply while my eyes drift to the sun-drenched forearm in front of me. Beneath the rolled-up sleeve of a crisp white button-down, an unmistakable dark ink pattern lay etched into his golden skin. My gaze lifts to meet recognizable hazel eyes, but the face, it's all wrong.

"Congratulations," the waiter drawls, his voice covering me in warmth. My eyes gaze back to the tattoo just as he pulls away. I call out to him, and he hesitates at the kitchen door

273

*and turns to me, his muted features becoming more recogniz-
able as the seconds tick past. I know this man, intimately.*

"*Wait,*" *I croak out, chest tightening unbearably when the
chatter around me drowns out my pleas as he disappears
through the service door.*

And that's when I feel him.

*Slowly, I stand and take inventory of our guests who all
seem to be oblivious to the shadow that's entered the room,
casting a dark hue over the rich, warm light from the dripping
chandeliers. I'm thankful they're all ignorant to it, because
if they notice the shift, they'll be afraid, but I'm not. And I
want nothing more than to see the source.*

*Collin rattles on to my left in conversation, and I know
he can't sense my reaction. I'm safe. My secrets are safe in
this cool cocoon. My eyes scan the party. Everyone is here;
our coworkers and friends, Mom and Timothy, Christy and
her husband, Josh, and their two boys, one of whom my
mother holds tightly to her while keeping Christy busy in
conversation. My attention shifts to the double doors on the
other side of the room. Tiny sparks of light flash behind the
sheer curtains in a dizzying pattern. I know I should be
afraid, but I feel nothing but safe alongside the cool shadow
who beckons me, covering me in goosebumps while urging
me toward the door, toward him. Anxiously, I scan the room
once more for any reaction and am relieved when I find none.
These people don't know. They can never know.*

*Slowly, so as not to alert anyone, I walk through the divi-
sion of round tables and the back doors just as a breeze sweeps
up the leaves at my feet, creating a wind tunnel that envelops
me. I can see the veins running along the center of the foliage
as they dance and sway at arm's-length, and a giggle bursts*

from my lips. Mingled scents grow thicker in the air, engulfing me in sheer happiness.

They're here. They came for me.

The doors close behind me with the next gust of wind, and I step into the clearing as a swarm of lightning bugs comes into view. They glow around me, lighting my skin in a green-yellow hue. I reach out for them and capture one in my hand. Its wings buzz against my palm before it sets off again, leaving neon residue on my skin. I swipe it with my thumb, but it remains. For these few seconds, I feel a peace I haven't in years—the sensation a lot like coming home.

I search through the flurry of light, smiling wide until I feel the lingering shadow begin to move toward the clearing and into the trees.

"Don't go! I'm here!"

Just beyond where the cloud drifts, a dark figure steps out from the shadows, his expression blank, his amber eyes lifeless, as he gazes back at me. I open my mouth to speak, but the increased buzzing drowns out my words. I scream into the void between us, and his expression doesn't change. My chest burns with emotions as tears start to escape me, my voice going hoarse as I furiously plead my case. He has to hear me this time.

The waiter appears beside him, with an empty tray in hand, tucking it into his side. He glances back, and I strain to see his expression, but I can't make it out as the swarm of fireflies dance around the two of them. Just behind them appears a silhouette, dark jeans, black boots, a black shirt, and a faint but distinct twist of lips. Heart lifting, I take a step forward and both men move to block him, protecting him, from me.

"I'm not afraid anymore!" I assure them, searching each of their faces for an acknowledgment.

The lightning bugs begin to slow to the point I can count the beat of their wings, see the tip of their glowing bodies, make out every detail. The waiter turns his back, moving to retreat into the shadows as I cry into the thick wall of light between us.

"I love you! I love you! I'm sorry I wasn't ready before, please, please don't go!" My voice cracks and bleeds as a string of frantic words pour from me. "I'll do better. I'll be better. Don't leave me!"

Desperate to erase the space, to get a closer look, I swat at the fireflies, my eyes devouring what I can as I reach out, but the weight of the lace of my dress holds me in place, rapidly pooling at my feet, and anchoring me where I stand.

"I'll do better. I'll be whoever you need me to be! Please. Don't leave me. Please don't go!"

Tears and flashes of light blind my vision until I'm able to focus on a pair of flaming eyes in the center of the chaos. His strong jaw sets as he scans my dress before his eyes lift to mine. He slowly nods, and I know it's in acceptance. I scream out at the loss as he turns his back on me.

"Don't go. Please don't go! Don't leave me! I love you!"

One by one, they begin to retreat into the thick brush as I will my body forward, fighting against my restraints, but it's the dress rendering me immobile, making it impossible to get to them. Gripping the train, I furiously begin to rip at the lace, but the material refuses to give. "No! Don't go! Don't leave me!" The party roars at my back, and the heavy buzzing resumes just as the fireflies begin to disappear.

"Wait!" I scream as fiery eyes meet mine one last time

before they begin to fade into the darkness. "Don't leave me!"

The leaves kick up again, robbing me of all vision just as the doors behind me shatter.

Jackknifing in bed, I sob into my hands, unable to handle the unbearable pressure in my chest. Gut-wrenching cries leave me as tears flood my cheeks while my heart screams for relief.

Relief that's not coming.

It's never-ending, the feeling of loss, the unimaginable pain. It hasn't faded, and I know it never will. I cry uncontrollably, unbelieving that at, one time, I thought the ability to remember my dreams so vividly was a gift, a superpower.

It's anything but.

I was just there, with them; they were in reach, so close.

Heaving and choking, I grip my sheets and scream out in frustration as I try to clear the haze. It's then I see it, hanging on the back of my door, taunting me, damning me. Tossing away my comforter, I launch from the bed, unzipping the bag and ripping the dress free. Agony fuels me as I grip the lace with my fingers, only feeling satisfied when I hear the tear of the fabric when it gives in my hands. Sinking to the floor, I ravage the dress with my fingers. Every rip brings a sort of liberation as the helplessness leaves me. Here I can rid myself of what weighs me down. It's here that I can free myself to get to them.

It's here that I know I never will.

Seconds after I destroy my wedding dress, reality sets in.

I'll never be free.

As long as I dream, and as long as these dreams can destroy me, I'll never be free.

Studying the ruined dress in my hands, I bury my face in it to muffle my defeated cries.

I could try to rationalize this act in a thousand ways but can only draw one conclusion.

I'm mourning a future I can no longer allow myself to have.

As long as I keep our shared secrets, as long as my questions go unanswered, as long as the heart I have keeps beating, the more I'll lose myself inside my web of lies. Full of despair, I stare into space, my heart refusing to give me an inch of release. I don't know how long I sit in the wake of my own destruction, but I get lost in between my dream and reality, intent on feeling every part of the aftermath.

It's the sound of the front door and the familiar call of my name that has me scrambling to get my ruined dress back in the plastic garment bag before tossing it into my closet. For years I've been rationalizing these dreams. For years I've denied my emotions, compartmentalized them, tucked them away while telling myself that perspective and release will eventually come. For years I've promised myself that rationalization and reasoning will one day allow me to make peace with my past and lead to some semblance of salvation.

But it's simply not the truth, and time has proven as much.

And so, when my fiancé pushes open our bedroom door to see the wreckage of those empty and unfulfilled promises, I do the only thing I'm capable of—I stop lying to us both.

Chapter Twenty-Seven

T<small>IME DOESN'T FLY</small>—<small>AT</small> least it hasn't for me. It ebbs and flows between the parts I want to remember and the minutes I would give anything to forget. The flow is tricky, especially between the past and present. I've got to tread carefully around it because I can get swept-up between the parts I romanticized and the brutal reality of what transpired. When I left Triple Falls, that was very much the case for me.

It took some time for me to see just how wronged I'd been in my time here, and just how manipulated I was. A few years after I left, I got angry to the point I forced myself to face the excruciating truth.

No matter how much they proclaimed to care for me, I was used by the men in my life in an inexcusable way.

I should never have let them have so much power over me.

I should have been stronger.

I should have fought a lot harder for myself and for what I deserved.

I shouldn't have let them keep so many secrets from me.

To this day, the woman in me still ridicules the girl I get glimpses of in my reflection.

I resent that I still dream of them so often, dragging myself through our memories, which only aids in maintaining my self-made prison. I hate that, in the waking hours, I'm a woman intelligent enough to rule my life in all areas with an iron fist, but when I dream of them, I'm too weak to bring myself to begrudge them for their collective crimes against me, the way I should.

Anger should win, but it doesn't. It never has.

Most people mourn intending to move forward, but some part of me knows I grieve in my sleep to keep my memories close, and they come to me vividly, aiding in deconstructing the world and walls I try to resurrect day by day. But it's a different world and has been since I left. Over the years, I fought hard to earn my self-respect back, while nightly I was forced to give in to the whims of my heart.

A battle I fought since I left.

A war I lost last night.

So, today I'll let myself go and ride the drift, let the flow consume me. I'll live in the past, unpacking my memories, trying carefully to not give absolution to those who don't deserve it.

But it's the loss that stifles my progress. It's always the loss.

Because no matter how much I resent them at times, I was lucky in a way few get lucky.

I was loved in a way few get loved.

So, naturally, it forever changed me.

Parking at the edge of town, I exit the car in the freezing wind, the clouds covering the day in grey, the gravel crunching beneath my booted feet as I make my way toward the entrance at the foot of a small hill.

Though my time here is limited, I've purposely sabotaged my future to the point I'll have zero direction once I leave. It was on the drive back to Triple Falls that I realized my course was always going to be in reverse. Even with all the milestones I've accomplished, with all the living I've been forced to do, sadly, and deep down, I feel the best part of my life is already over. When I lived here years ago, I constantly dreamed of a future. My purpose here, now, is to suspend time and concentrate on then.

All I have of them now are the remnants of our time together. Over time I've realized all that happened in those months I spent with them was enough to seize and lock my heart away. And it's the battle between my temples that gnaws at me, my unyielding loyalty that refuses to let me forget while the rest of me begs to be set free.

But it's truth I seek, and I'm steps away from it now, feeling the full weight of our collective mistakes as I enter the small cemetery, the creak of the waist-high iron gate making my presence known. A few steps into the secluded yard, I find him and kneel, pulling off a glove to trace the bold letters on the top of the heavy stone.

Prince Déchu
Fallen Prince

It's been over two thousand days since his departure, since he was stolen from us, from me, leaving an irreparable and permanent hole in my heart. I can still recall the curl of his dark lashes when I closed his eyes. I can still remember the weight of him in my lap as I cradled him to me, the feel of his lips when I kissed him goodbye. No matter his crimes against me, all I feel for him is love, longing, and gratitude.

He died to protect me. He died because he loved me, but damn him for not knowing how hard it would be for me to try and live with it. His sacrifice has left me—more often than not—feeling unworthy of such a love. But love him I did. Wholly. For all that he was and the gift he gave me with his selfless sacrifice.

If only I'd trusted in him enough to believe his love was the truth, he wouldn't be here.

Of all the mistakes I've made in my twenty-six years, the only one I can't live with was being fearful of my protector the night I lost him.

If only.

Seeing his grave only makes that night more real, our conversation and his parting words more precious. He took sure steps toward his demise, his only request to spend a rainy day with me. A day I would give anything to have shared with him.

"I wish you would have taken me with you," I manage through a voice full of ache. "But, I guess, in a way, you took us all with you."

The image of him the first time we locked eyes flashes through my mind.

"You terrified me," I sniff, as my eyes water and begin to leak with the budding ache. "You were such a *motherfucker*."

When I met Dominic, he had barricaded himself behind his purpose, the brotherhood. Still, somehow, I'd managed to be the one lucky enough to find the undetectable space in his armor because he'd let me.

"You are in."

His words from our last date. I can still hear them so clearly.

Pressing my hand to my forehead, I do my best not to fall apart as I speak.

"You left before I had a chance to tell you about the future I dreamt up for you. Maybe it had a little of my dreams mixed in with it too. Maybe it was a daydream for us, but it was a good one. It wasn't a plan so much as it was a place. A place filled with music and laughter, books, and long kisses, and endless rainy days. It was a place where you didn't have to hide your smile anymore."

If only.

Cupping my mouth, I stare down at the stone as a soft sob escapes me.

"I pray now, Dom. Often and for you. Sometimes I pray selfishly, but just for the chance to see your face in my dreams. You never let me see you, not fully. A hint of your profile here and there, but it's not enough—" I choke on the words—"but I keep trying. I keep chasing after you." I'm convinced I haven't seen him fully because I haven't voiced the one thing I want so desperately to ask him for. And the hardest part is, I know the answer is up to me.

"Please, if you can, let me see you," I choke up, a gut-wrenching cry bursting from me as I wipe the tears from my cheeks and kneel to press them into the freezing ground where he lies beneath the stone, permanently, a truth I'd give anything to change.

I'd imagined none of it. That, I already knew, it's the mere sight of his stone that makes it more real. I'd fought my way back to some semblance of sanity without an ounce of proof of what happened that night, and finally I have it, but it doesn't comfort me. Instead, it's an excruciating ache. One that will never leave me. I never got a chance to mourn him properly. Not the way I deserved to, not as the woman he loved and who loved him in return because everything became distorted before he was killed. But I am thankful for the minutes we spent together, even if they were precious and few.

My eyes drift to the grave next to Dominic's, and I address the woman who rests by his side, having joined him just months later.

I swallow as I think of the fear in her eyes that night we met and wonder if, when she died, she was afraid.

"Tell me, Delphine, did you find the back door? Did your nephew open it for you?" The wind kicks up, and I shiver in my jacket, thinking for the first time in a while about my own mortality. I'd come face-to-face with it just before I left Triple Falls. I don't fear much of anything anymore, and I'm determined to see my thousand dreams through.

My eyes drift over the cluster of headstones.

The whole of Tobias's family rests here, and if I have any fear at all, it's the thought of *his* mortality. That one day, he'll take his place beside his family.

I avert my gaze back to Dominic's grave, and another rush of grief strikes me, and I tamp it down, refusing to let it consume me so soon. I can't go into this grieving, or I won't survive it.

Not yet.

"Repose en paix, mon amour, je reviendrai." *Rest, my love, I'll be back again.*

Chapter Twenty-Eight

FOLLOWING THE ROUTE home, I adjust my rearview as flashes of the day I fled come back in torturous waves.

The gunfire, the smell of my fallen love's blood, and the feel of it on my hands on the drive home.

The adrenaline disappeared after the first hour or so, leaving my limbs aching before giving way to utter devastation. They were the most agonizing hours of my life.

"You leave. And you never come back."

I left a war zone not knowing if the men I loved were alive, if they were hurt, if they blamed me, or if they'd forever hate me if they survived. But those damning orders made me feel as if I were the poison, the cause of all that had gone wrong.

The details of that drive are still murky from one hour to the next. Once I got to Atlanta city limits, I stopped at a bustling gas station and turned down my visor to see Dominic's blood smeared on the corner of my mouth. I found an old—inch full—water bottle left in my car, using my fingers to clean what I could from my face. I peered back at my reflection and saw bloodshot eyes and dark circles, my skin pale and clammy. When the bottle was empty, I raced inside the station, my hands tucked beneath my armpits as I kept my head down. I locked myself in the bathroom. Inside, I relieved my bladder before facing myself at the dirty sink, fully expecting to see what I felt. The only thing out of order was the stain on my hands, the blood of a man who pledged his love for me only minutes before he took his last breath. I turned my hands over and over, wanting to keep the stains, to keep the only part of him I had left, as sick and irrational as the thought was.

Unrelenting tears dripped from my chin as I scrubbed the caked blood from beneath my fingernails, watching the tinged pink water go down the drain.

When a gentle knock sounded a foot away, I quieted my cries and splashed cold water on my face. When I opened the door, I was greeted by a woman in a collared shirt and tennis skirt holding a little girl in a matching outfit. They'd smiled at me in greeting, and the shock of seeing them so neatly polished, so unassuming, their eyes alight with so much life, easy smiles on their faces let me know just how far down the rabbit hole I'd traveled. Instinctively I returned that smile, knowing it was a new mask. I remembered hating the feel of it, it didn't fit, and from that day forward, I was stuck with it. That smile was the first lie I told after leaving Triple Falls.

Cecelia Horner died that night, the totality of her naïve innocence eradicated along with all her silly and foolish dreams in a reality where she was made painfully aware that evil exists, lurking in the shadows just waiting to prey on innocents just like that little girl in the Polo. The girl I used to be.

A reality where the wrong side often wins, where bullets are real, and the people you love can take their last breaths, and you could be the one to bear witness while their light goes out right in front of you.

And I asked for it, to be a part of it all because I was too greedy loving men who continually warned me away, and I refused.

Dominic died.

For all the questions I asked, for all the begging I did, I got few answers. I got secrets and a story, both I would never be able to share. The punishment behind the knowledge was unbearable. I knew I'd have to use the mask every single day for the rest of my life because I could never let anyone see what's behind it.

I had to forget that girl existed.

For endless hours I sat in my car on top of a parking garage overlooking the Atlanta skyline, a world away from the small town that changed everything I thought I knew about life and love. My phone clutched in my hand, all I could do was pray to a God I cursed just hours earlier for taking my dark angel. Prayed that Tyler would keep his word, prayed that the people who had become a part of me made it through the day, hearts beating, still breathing.

The wait was unbearable and riddled with anxiety. Struck by nausea, I opened my door, spilling the contents of my stomach onto the cement next to where I parked. Once the wave passed, I wiped my mouth and resumed staring at my cell phone, willing it to ring when I got a notification of an email from my father.

Cecelia,
I was delighted to have gotten your email yesterday that you've left early to prepare for the coming school year. I'm

pleased to find you have enjoyed your time working at the plant. I'll consider our agreement satisfied due to the good news and your dedication to further your education. Attached is the address and contact information for management concerning your new apartment in Athens. I do hope you see this gesture as intended with my congratulations. I will see to it that all your expenses are covered for the duration of your stay.

Please keep me updated on your performance at school.
Roman Horner
CEO Horner Technologies

Gesture as intended?

I read the email over and over in disbelief. After, I searched my sent items to find it was a reply to an email sent from my account hours *before* I confronted Sean and Dominic about my tattoo. A response to an email *I* never sent.

An email that gave me an alibi, placing me in Atlanta before a gunfight broke out in his home.

Roman knew. He had to have known what was happening.

Just like Tobias and Dominic knew Miami was coming.

The clues started trickling in the more I X-rayed that night and started piecing them together.

The first was Dominic's sudden appearance moments after I got home, that along with the fact that his car was parked outside the clearing and mine had been moved to sit next to it, probably minutes after I pulled up and resumed packing.

And I was always the last to know.

That's where some of my residual anger lies. If Dominic had only told me what was happening, if he had trusted me . . . but it was my reaction to him that had him handling me with kid gloves. But keeping me in the dark is what caused Dominic to make his fatal mistake—tossing his gun on the stairs, leaving him defenseless while Tobias quietly searched the house for the threat.

Tobias must've been the one to send that email. I assumed that was one of the reasons why he never came to me as he promised. He was planning my exit strategy, giving me an alibi for my whereabouts in case things went south, in case the authorities got involved.

It was Tyler's strict instructions that hammered that point home. He'd given me cash so there would be no trail as to when I traveled. *"You were never here."*

Tobias was always a step ahead of me while keeping me in the dark.

But other pieces perplexed me. No matter how hard I tried, I couldn't make them fit, no matter how many times I flipped them and tried to push them together.

Even if Tobias had unlimited resources to right the damage to Roman's house from the wreckage, there's no way Roman wouldn't notice. Clearly, he'd played his part in covering it up, which enraged me to no end. Was he that intent on keeping his nose deceptively clean? He had to have known something. Had to. Matteo said Roman's car was parked in the garage.

But how?

Or was a similar car used to lure Miami in?

Either way, Roman must have known.

The day I left was the day I knew they hadn't lied about Roman Horner and his filthy business dealings. It was all the proof I needed to believe the man was as corrupt as they had portrayed him to be. His hands were just as bloody as far as I was concerned, but I was done with him before that night. I'd already written him off.

But that day, sitting on top of that garage, fatigued and sick with worry, I pushed the mystery aside, eaten alive with grief and indecision all the while fighting the urge to drive back to North Carolina.

Time was cruel, and I spent it absently watching the grid-lock on I-285 move at a snail's pace. People were leaving their jobs and going home to eat dinner and watch TV. *Normal* people doing normal everyday things, and I couldn't imagine going back to any semblance of normal with the taste of my ex-lover's blood still lingering on my tongue.

When my phone finally rang, and I saw a familiar area code from a number I didn't recognize, I couldn't answer fast enough.

"Hello."

I listened intently for several seconds as they passed, my chest filling with unimaginable dread at what news waited on the other end of the line.

"Hello, please, hello?"

Several seconds later, I heard the distinct open and close of a Zippo. That sound had a sob bursting from my lips. Sean.

It was the sound of ice rattling in a tumbler, one, two, three times, that had me sobbing hysterically behind the wheel. Two distinct sounds they knew I would easily recognize.

They're okay.

They're okay.

"Please. Please . . . talk to me." When silence rang clear on the other end of the line, somehow, I just knew the

damning quiet was because of Tobias. And words would never come.

"I'm sorry, I'm so sorry. Please, somebody, talk to me. I'm sorry." *The silence lingered as I tried to search for words until a familiar voice finally spoke.*

"Hey, Cecelia, sorry about that."

"Layla, I, I, I . . ." *I sobbed so hard I gagged, rolling down my window and inhaling deeply to try and calm myself.*

"Oh, babe," *she sighed,* *"it's just a move. You'll be fine. We're all fine here."*

We all were anything but.

"All of you?" *I asked breathlessly.*

"Yes, I swear to you, we're good. And you will be too." *She continued a clearly rehearsed speech.* *"And we're all going to miss you, but we're glad you're moving on. It's a shame we'll be so far away."*

"Layla—"

"Don't get upset, honey. I'm sure you'll make new friends wherever you land. You're a tough girl. You'll be on your feet in no time."

"I can't do this," *I cried into the line.* *"I c-c-can't."*

"No choice, sweetie, you're growing up, and you have school to finish and this great big life to live. We'll all be on the sidelines, cheering you on. I'm so glad you left this shit town and are never coming back."

"I can visit." *The question lingered as harsh whispers were exchanged in the background, but I couldn't decipher them.*

"No reason to, baby . . . My boys are leaving me today, and I don't know how long they'll be gone."

They're leaving, and they'll be untraceable wherever they land. A thousand-pound weight sinks in my stomach.

"And I hope you know, you're better off there." It was a warning, and she'd delivered it with the gentleness of a mother's love. *"There's nothing good going to come out of you coming back here. You don't want to end up a dried-up old lady working at the plant, anyway. And we only want the best for you."*

"Layla—"

"I gotta run, but I just wanted you to know that I'll miss you."

When the line disconnected, I screamed at the loss. Neither Sean nor Tobias wanted to speak to me.

It was all over.

My future had been decided, my ties cut; they didn't want me to come back. I had no choice in the matter, no say. And I'd lived that reality before.

Thoroughly unhinged, I shattered over and over again at the finality of it all. It was never going to end well, but that parting had ripped some of my humanity away from me.

I moved to Triple Falls a teenager, wanting nothing more than to challenge myself, to give in to my wild side, and create some stories to tell.

By the time I stood in my new apartment in Athens that night, I was a woman who'd been unearthed by deception, lies, lust, and love, whose essence was shrouded by life-changing secrets, full of stories I could never share and never, ever tell. In keeping me safe, in architecting my future, they'd left me to wither and rot with those secrets.

Between the painstaking lengths my boys went to and the first-class ticket my father bought out of hell, all I wanted to do was go back and let the flames consume me. But in protecting me, in all the trouble my presence caused, all they asked in return was for my absence and to keep their secrets.

And I did.

Baptized by fire, I wore my mask until I grew into it, I kept our secrets, following their orders to the letter while trying to resume some semblance of a life.

And eventually, I did that too.

I far exceeded my own expectations, but time has been nothing but a noose, giving me the rope an inch at a time. And now that I'm here, I refuse to continue the charade. It's far too much to ask. And so, I'll demand answers and seek them in full from the man who owes me the explanation.

And I'm not leaving without one.

It's my last promise to myself as I drive down the lone road leading to the forgotten house.

Chapter Twenty-Nine

A N EERIE FEELING washes over me, and I expect nothing less as I gaze on at the grand estate from the gate as freezing rain begins to pelt the hood and windshield of my Audi. The house is far more intimidating underneath the grey sky. But I know a majority of my contempt is due to the history that lives within the walls.

Pulling up, I swallow hard and step out. Leaving my bag in my car, I grab the envelope from my purse that the management company sent me years ago along with the new key, security instructions and a schedule for those in charge of maintaining the late Roman Horner's estate. I palm the heavy key in my hand as I walk up the steps and turn back toward the driveway. Though the wind whips heavily around me while the stinging rain infuses the cold into my bones, I'm graced with a glimpse of my past, an image of a golden man waiting at the hood of his Nova, boots and arms crossed, a smile playing on his lips. The gilded tips of his spiked halo, lit by the sun as his eyes danced with promise and mischief. And just as soon as the ray appears, it's gone.

Taking a calming breath, I turn and unlock the door,

pushing it open and standing frozen at the threshold baffled by the sight that greets me.

The interior is no different than it was the day before I left, though I can only imagine the damage done that morning. I'm fairly certain the walls house shells of bullets in between sheetrock and touched up paint. But all traces of that horrible night are gone, as if I imagined it.

If only that were true.

"No one leaves breathing." I shudder as I think of the look on Tobias's face when he gave that order. Tyler said Miami had pulled up ten cars deep.

If the ravens succeeded in carrying out that order, there had to have been a significant body count. And then there was the brotherhood side. I didn't know them all personally, but I hated to think they'd lost more brothers that day.

Odds are, they did.

I'd accused Tobias when we met of being a petty thief who threw parties trying to downplay the extent of what I knew, all the while they kept me cornered, shielded, and safe from the ugly truth of the reality of what the war they waged entailed.

Dominic had admitted as much to me the night he died.

"You were amongst liars, thieves, and killers."

And as many times as I was told, I still had to see to believe. And that night, I became a believer in the worst imaginable way.

But I understood their logic. They never wanted me exposed to it, so they distracted me, kept me ignorant to it for as long as possible because *they* didn't want me to see *them* for who they really were—dangerous criminals whose bad deeds ran more along the lines of corporate theft, black-mail, racketeering, espionage, and if forced, retaliation that included bloodshed.

They were never cold-blooded killers, but they all had blood on their hands, and I share in that secret now.

Though I searched the web for endless days of any report on what happened in this house, I came up completely empty. Not a word was spoken, no reports on any media outlet, not even an obituary or service announcement for Dominic, which infuriated me.

I have no knowledge of what transpired after I left, but it was covered up in a way that is unfathomable to me.

For months I checked the papers, the web, searching for clues, arrests, anything pertaining to that night and drew a blank. I also checked Miami papers as well and got nothing. Not even in the nearby counties. It was eight months later that I finally stumbled upon an obituary for Delphine, who'd finally succumbed to her cancer.

And after that investigation, I checked out. I had no choice. My health and sanity were at risk by that point, and I had to give in and do their final bidding.

I had to try and move on, start to live some semblance of a life.

I'd spent months and months between grief and anger in the waking hours before I made a decision to try. I never returned Roman's inquisitive emails on my well-being or progress at school, avoiding him altogether until the day he died of colon cancer two years after I left.

Not once after had I tried to contact anyone in the brother-hood. I knew it would be pointless. Anger and resentment had helped me with that task.

I played along for the sake of self-preservation, despite my eyes being pried wide open by what went down here.

It was the decision of preservation that helped me forge ahead and finally yanked me from the spiral. But shortly after, the dreams took over, threatening to destroy every bit of progress I made.

I'm declaring a new war by coming here, and I need to be ready. It's not just my sleep I want back. I'm not certain of exactly what my motives are. But my dream last night set this into motion, so for now, I'm going with it, knowing the truth will never really set me free, but maybe it will close a few doors, and I'm hoping it's enough.

Shaking off the freezing rain and unease of being back at this house, I take a step in and close the door behind me as history threatens to come at me from all sides. I shiver in my jacket and rub my arms, making my way over to the thermostat and cranking it up. Peeking over the couch in the formal living room, I note the chessboard still intact sitting where it rests on the lip of the fireplace. Unbelievably, the pieces are set up from the last time Tobias and I played.

"Your move," he prompts after taking another of my pawns.

I sip my wine and gaze at him bathed in the amber light of the few candles I lit when I came downstairs after my shower. We'd shared an intimate smile when I'd spotted him from where he'd stood, uncorking a bottle of wine. After lathering myself up in juniper lotion, which I learned was his catnip, I'd chosen an off-the-shoulder, thin sweater, and nothing else. I don't own any lingerie, except for the night-gown he bought me that I decided to save for our last night together, which will be the night before I leave for school, which I refuse to think about. The clear approval of my choice shines in his eyes as he sweeps me appreciatively while passing me my wine before we take our seats. The board rests diagonally on the fireplace, where we sit across from the other, very little space between us. The game itself, I still find incredibly boring, but the beauty and mystery of the company I'm playing with make it more than bearable. And if I'm truthful, it makes for some intoxicating foreplay.

"Is there another game you would ever play?"

"Non."

"And you never watch TV aside from the news?"

"I do when I'm sick."

"How often do you get sick?"

"Once every three to five years."

I roll my eyes. "I don't suppose we'll be bonding over any sort of binge-watch then."

He glances over at me, the touch of vulnerability evident in his gaze. "Is that what we're supposed to be doing?"

His question is serious. As naïve as it is for a man his age. Over the last week together, I've learned that much like his brothers, the man truly doesn't at all run in any circle, or include any norms of his life that would indicate standard "American" living. Though he went to school abroad, he was raised in the States for a long period of time, but it doesn't seem to have rubbed off on him in the McRib way, which is crazy ironic for a man with his finger on the pulse of current events. A man who is so in tune with the world yet so far removed from it in a personal sense. One, he's very much a hermit and a creature of habit. His OCD making his routines hard to deter from. Two, he lectured me endlessly when I told him I was craving said McRib. In fact, he went full-on French snob. I barely got away with a peanut butter and jelly sandwich and now have to hide my junk food.

The man's indulgences include expensive coffee beans, his food must be nothing less than fine dining standards, and his wine choices—though delicious—are very, very, expensive. And every one of his suits is designer and tailored, that much I knew, but I have yet to see a repeat in the two months he's taken me hostage. While his tastes may be a little over the top, I don't at all fault him for spending his money on the finer things because he didn't grow up in a house like the one we're occupying. He grew up enduring a "wrong side of the tracks" type of lifestyle answering to an alcoholic aunt who considered cockroaches a part of the family while trying to play father to his little brother.

He hasn't lived a charmed life, and I'm happy that he gets to not only experience these things but demand them for his daily life. If he's selfish about anything, it's these little indulgences that bring him joy. He's complicated, yet simple. And he doesn't seem to require the stimulation of the average man. He seems to consider most things an experience, not music, but a single song, not food, but a feast, not wine but a tasting. And sex, that he takes even more seriously. For him, it's an art form, and one he's mastered beautifully.

"What?" he asks, flicking his gaze to mine while contemplating his first move.

"I don't hate you anymore." I don't miss the slight lift of his lips. "You smile, but I really did hate you, Tobias."

"I know." His smile only grows.

"You love my opposition."

"You're the only woman in the world who's good at making me really angry."

"I'll take that as my first compliment, and that's quite a lot of honesty there. Sir, are you drunk?"

His lips lift even higher. "Maybe a little."

I narrow my eyes. "I knew you polished that half a bottle off while I was in the shower. I hadn't imagined seeing it. Stingy."

"Sorry," he says unapologetically.

It's so insincere, I laugh. "Oh, I can tell just how sorry you are, thief."

He makes his first move.

"Nous entraînons-nous ce soir?" Are we practicing tonight? *I ask when I push a pawn into play.*

"Peut-être." Maybe.

"Où vas-tu m'emmener?" Where will you take me? *I ask, licking my lips clean and savoring every drop.*

"J'étais en train de penser à te pencher sur ce canapé." I was thinking I would bend you over that couch. *"But if you keep looking at me like that, we won't make it that far."*

I roll my eyes. "Je voulais dire en France, pervers. Où m'emmènerais-tu en premier?" I meant in France, you pervert. Where would you take me first?

"Easy," he says, frowning at the board, "The Eiffel Tower."

"En français, s'il te plaît." In French, please. *"And that's the last thing I expected you to say."*

"Why? Isn't that what all those traveling to France dream of seeing first? Who am I to deny you?" He reads my deflated posture. "You had something more personal in mind?"

"Your favorite places. And I wouldn't mind going down

memory lane with you. Seeing where you went to school. Meeting some of your college friends."

"I don't have friends."

"Not one?"

He sits back against the fireplace. "I don't have the type of friends to look up and have drinks with when I'm there. Not in that way." *There's a hint of melancholy in his voice, and I understand why it's there. He was far too busy playing grown-up to have a life of his own. Been there.*

"So, you never kicked back, relaxed? Aside from banging lingerie models?"

"Non."

"Well, I'll be your friend," *I say easily.* "I'll be your best friend, but that requires far more effort. At some point, you're going to have to tell me where you live, let me snoop through your bedroom, and tell me about the first time you got your period."

This earns me a dead stare just before he takes another of my pieces. I scrunch my nose in frustration. "I'm never going to get good at this."

"Because you don't want to get good at it. I'm going to beat you again. But the good news is your French tongue is no longer complete shit. Though it could use some improvements."

"Oh, yeah? I'm pretty sure you love my tongue by the way you were sucking on it not too long ago."

Face inscrutable, he nods to me. "Your move."

"I'll let you win."

He lifts burning eyes to mine. "Why?"

"Because I want you to win, so our tongues can negotiate your last statement."

"There you go, mixing business and pleasure. You'll never learn."

I drain my glass and set it down before lifting on all fours.

He shakes his head. *"We're still in a match."*

"I just said, I'm letting you win."

"No," he says sharply. *"And I'm going to win anyway. Get your ass back in your corner. I'm into this game."*

"You win," I say, my thin sweater gaping in the front as I lean in, giving him a clear view of my bare breasts all the way down to my navel.

He doesn't spare my girls or me a glance as he focuses on the board.

"You're really going to play immune?" I rasp out, covering some of his upper half where he sits with one leg stretched out and one leg drawn up, his forearm resting on the fireplace his other on his knee.

"Now, that's a game you are horrible at." I can hear the amusement in his voice as I latch my lips to his neck and suck. *"I can always tell when you're turned on."*

"Oh, and you think you've mastered it?" I taunt.

"I know I have."

"I'm calling your bluff," I drape myself around him despite his rigid posture, sliding my fingers through his hair and raking my nails along his scalp before tugging lightly. He doesn't give me any leeway as he remains hunched over the board while I try my hand at seducing my king. I don't initiate often. I don't have to because the man is just as much of an addict as I am.

"So," I whisper, licking the shell of his ear. *"If I were to pull your cock out of your pants, right now, and start sucking*

you the way you like it, right now, the way you want me to, right now, you wouldn't react?"

"Non."

I bite his earlobe, hard, and he doesn't even grimace.

I pull away frowning. "You're never going to let me win, are you?"

"Non." He turns to me, dipping his eyes briefly as if I'm a stranger on a park bench before turning back to the board. I drop my jaw, insulted, but don't make a sound. I don't miss the slight upturn of his lips just before I slide my hand down his chest and palm his crotch.

Bingo.

He's rock-hard. Immune, my ass.

"Well played, Tobias, but unfortunately, you've got a very big tell."

"That is unfortunate," he grumbles "and an unfair advantage."

In a flash, I'm pinned beneath him, a yelp escaping me as he leans in running his nose along mine before I look up at him through my lashes.

"But in the spirit of full disclosure, you should know that every time I look at you, Cecelia, I want your attention, your lips, your tongue, your body. You have infected me with your sickness, and now I'm an addict too."

"I knew it!"

He tugs my sweater down suckling my nipple, eliciting a moan from me. "And while I do appreciate your beautiful face and your pretty peach nipples, it's this," he presses his palm to my chest, "and the fact that you use it as your mouthpiece. That is what is most alluring to me. I've never met a woman so willing to brave her own destruction for just a little truth."

Fully drawn into him, he gazes down at me as I stroke his jaw. "But I will never let you win. Not ever, not once, not out of mercy or due to a cease-fire. Not ever. And I don't ever want you to let me win either."

"Why?"

"Because if and when you stop fighting me, that's when I'll know I've lost."

He kisses me and pulls away, his expression going grave. "And you will hate me again one day, maybe soon or maybe later in the future, but you will."

I frown. "You're so sure?"

"Yes, and only you will be able to tell me why."

"Tobias—"

"Come with me," he murmurs.

Staring at the chessboard from the foyer, I can clearly see the two of us and the way the rest of the night played out. A night I've replayed over and over in my head. Just after his confession, he'd stood and taken my hand and I'd silently followed him up the stairs and into my bedroom. That night, he'd taken me so fiercely, with so much intensity, I'd practically convulsed in ecstasy, my jaw shaking as I'd called out his name. It was the best sex of my life.

But it was both an apology and a preemptive strike. At least that's the way I see it now. And the fact that I see one of the most beautiful nights of my life as one of manipulation only fuels my contempt for him. But it was one of the many apology attempts he made before the bomb dropped, and he destroyed three relationships.

When I left, or was forced to leave—after the initial shock

wore off—I began to experience the blinding pain of losing him and all I thought we had. Even so, I told myself I was leaving him, and I was. He deserved it. What he did was unforgivable. But somewhere deep down, I had hoped he would come for me. My twenty-year-old heart probably would have forgiven him. And the kicker is . . . if he had come back to me, I would have fought him, more furiously than I ever had.

It's funny in retrospect just how you figure things out. Especially when you fell for a criminally deceptive man.

And where would that twenty-year-old heart be now if he had come back, if it had forgiven him?

But it's my twenty-six-year-old heart who never got an explanation, nor an apology, and will never forgive him.

But like all things that happened, it didn't play out the way I wanted it to or expected. He never came after me because he had again banished me.

My eyes drift to the dining room where I shared uncomfortable dinners with Roman. Tobias wasn't the only man to break my heart in this house.

Why did you come back, Cecelia?

The more memories that surface, the more I'm beginning to realize just how asinine it was to forsake a life that was, for the most part, working for me.

Breaking it off with Collin was inevitable. But to re-live these memories, and purposefully?

It's already too painful, and I only got here an hour ago.

Exhausted already from a day of confrontation, I head to the wet bar next to the kitchen, shooting up a silent prayer, and it's answered when I find it well stocked.

I uncap one of the bottles and pull down a rocks glass.

Tossing back the whiskey, I savor the taste, remembering the first time I drank it at Eddie's with Sean. That now seems like a lifetime ago.

But it wasn't, it was here, in this place. And some part of me knows they are too. They probably never left. Another lie they told, to keep me at bay.

At some point, I'll have to make my presence known if it isn't already.

But not today.

I glance around the kitchen and past the set of windows that give a clear view of the pool and loungers.

Memories again threaten just as the liquor begins lacing my veins. The house may be freezing, but my blood is warming. For the first time in years, I need to allow myself to indulge in my recollections instead of fighting them. I have to let my mind continue to drift during my waking hours if I want to see this through. With another sip of whiskey, I climb the stairs to my old bedroom, stopping short where Dominic's body lay the last time I saw him.

"Yes."

"Yes, what?"

"Yes, I've been in love."

The sight of the new carpet devastates me as much as the sight of Dominic's grave. He deserved so much more than a silent burial. Needing air, I walk across the room and open the French doors leading onto the balcony, remembering all too well that it was my escape route the morning I fled. Closing my eyes, I can picture Sean's grief-stricken face as he lowered me to Tyler while shots rang out around us.

If I hadn't been here, I would never believe any of it happened.

Exodus

What the fuck were you thinking coming back, Cecelia?

The only conclusion I can draw is the same I did last night. I can't out-live these memories. Moving on hasn't happened in the six summers that have passed.

There's no help for this, no psychiatrist who can shrink this away without the full truth. There's no pill to prescribe to help me forget.

There's no priest I believe in enough to confess our collective sins to. There's only a God I have taken issue with, who I'm not sure has ever heard me, and might not consider me worth listening to.

It's always been up to me to sink or swim. And I've been in the deep end for years without an inch of cement to grab onto while the kick slowly drained from me.

I chug more of the bottle as the grey sky greets me and I take in the view in the distance, the cell tower blinking at me as if to say, "welcome home".

Chapter Thirty

Hours later, I wake with a slight hangover, my head thumping as I realize the rumble of my cell phone on my nightstand is what woke me. The silver lining is that I can't remember a single dream I had in the last few hours. It's when I see the name flashing on the screen that my celebration is cut short.

"Hey."

"You were sleeping? You promised you would call when you got there."

"I'm so sorry."

"You should be." Guilt nags at me when I hear the plea in his voice, "Cecelia, please come home."

"Collin, I can't. I'm sorry. But I can't." I lift from my bed, disoriented, and decide I'm far too sober for this conversation.

"Can't or won't?"

"Won't. I won't deceive either of us anymore." Grabbing the bottle and my tumbler, I take the stairs two at a time, opting for a little hair of the dog over ice. I have no issue with rock bottom. I'm comfortable here. On the rocks might be the safest place for me for the moment, much safer than walking around lying recklessly to those I love.

But the reality I've thrust myself into is hell on Earth. It was so much easier to lie.

"Tell me why this is happening," he urges me gently. "Just come home so I can try to understand. You just left."

"I gave you an explanation." I press my tumbler into the fridge door, adding some ice and pour a generous helping of whiskey. "Collin, I won't ever come home."

"I don't believe you. This is some . . . mental break, some . . . episode."

"You're not wrong, but it's not a case of cold feet. I wish it were."

"You aren't thinking clearly. What we had was real. No one is that good of an actress."

"I wasn't acting. I was . . . masking. I wanted it to work. A lot of the time, I believed it was." I take a healthy sip of the whiskey and glance at the clock as it flips just past midnight, bringing an end to my first day in purgatory.

"So what if you were promiscuous when you were young. I'm no saint. I don't give a damn if you slept with half that town."

"Are you wondering if I was faithful?" I swallow, as a guilty tear sneaks out of me.

"You told me you were."

"And you believe me?"

"Yes."

"But you won't for long. You'll wonder if I was honest about that too, and then you'll resent me for it."

"I won't. If you'd just come home—"

"Stop. This is beneath you, Collin. I do love you. I always will. I'm so grateful to have been loved by you."

"So, you just decide it's over and I'm supposed to accept it? Are you purposefully trying to destroy me?"

"I know how cruel this seems, but I want you to know the truth of what I've been battling for years. The guilt I constantly feel, knowing what I'm doing is wrong. Please trust me when I say next to Christy, you're the closest person in the world to me. But you don't know me fully, and if you want honesty, neither does she."

"Jesus, Cecelia, I don't understand," his voice cracks and I feel it, the sharp stab of pain that I'm causing, again I fill up my tumbler. The reality of losing him is taking a toll.

"Collin, I've come to realize I'm broken that way. I lived too much. I experienced too much when I was too young. It was intense, and it made me . . . think differently, crave life differently. That's the most I can explain it. I'm capable of monogamy. I've been faithful to you physically. It's just . . ."

"You think I wouldn't understand. You don't want to tell me what you want because you don't think I can give it to you?"

"I know you wouldn't want to know this side of me. And I don't want you to see it. That's not who you fell for."

"Stop telling me what I know about you!"

His anger is warranted, and so I let him have it. I put this train in motion and I need to see it through. He gives me a minute of silence before he speaks up.

"So, are you with them now?"

"No." I hate that's his conclusion. "Not at all. That's not what this is. I'm not sure I'll see him."

"Him? Just one? I'm so confused."

"I was upset last night, and maybe I explained myself horribly." I wince, knowing no amount of whiskey will ever help this confession. "I told you when I was younger, I was in a polyamorous relationship for a few short months."

"Yes."

"But my feelings ran deep, Collin, really deep for both men, and after it ended, I fell in love with another, and he's the one who I haven't let go of. But full disclosure, I still have lingering feelings for them all."

"Is this . . ." I can physically feel the gap splintering further between us, "is this what your dreams are about?"

"Yes."

"Jesus, Cecelia."

"It was one year, one year of my life, but it changed me. And I haven't been able to fully move on since because of how that time with them altered me and how it ended. And that's the reason I've never been able to give you what you need, what you fully deserve."

"I'm no less guilty of having lingering affection, feelings for the women in my past. I've had moments, here and there. It's all part of it."

"It's more than that, Collin. The unreasonable part of me still exists in a time I can't erase or can never go back to. Because no matter how hard I try to forget it, it won't let me." I take another sip, and then another, terrified of admitting more of the truth. "I've been hiding things from you."

"Like what?"

I grapple with the words and know the impact they'll have.

"I deserve the truth," he demands.

"You do." I close my eyes and bring the glass to my lips, taking a long drink and bracing myself. "Sometimes, after we have sex, I fantasize about them while you're in the shower."

Over the line, I hear a pained breath leave him, and know I've just butchered his pride.

"Do you masturbate thinking about them after fucking me?!"

I confirm with my silence. It's cruel, but necessary, though I'm not about to drill it into his head. I have to get through to him. I don't want to draw this out. And I don't want to give him hope where there is none.

"Bloody hell, Cecelia, you thought about them while we were in our bed?!"

Him. But I don't correct him. I want his anger. I deserve it. Because my admission isn't fabricated. It's the absolute truth.

The more I reveal to him, put words to years of thinking it, the more I realize I'm doing the right thing. I was about to marry into my own lie.

"Collin, my sexual depravity aside, I can't love you the way you deserve."

"Whatever you think you lack, it's in your head. You make me happy."

"And at times you made me happy too, you know you did, but I can't marry you. I've been lying in different degrees since we met. I'm sorry. I'm so sorry, Collin. I already miss you. I'm already regretting this, but this is the truth, and I'm so tired of fighting it."

"I'm not a fucking prude, Cecelia. I'll give you any fantasy you want."

"It's not just about sex, Collin. My heart was never in the right place, just . . ."

I palm my face, my lips shaking, my voice anguished as I ruin a relationship with a man who's done nothing short of worship me.

"I'm still in love with the memory of another man and have been since I was twenty. It's clear now, I'll never stop wanting him, and I've failed at every attempt to hate him. I had hoped so much to move on—and with you—I tried, I tried so hard, but I failed. I failed us both."

"And you don't know if you'll see him? What future can you have with a memory?"

"One that's not deceptive to *you*. One that doesn't hurt *you*. I don't care about my happiness anymore so much, but I refuse to ruin yours. I've been selfish enough in my thinking. Find a woman who would move heaven and earth to be good to you. Find her, and one day, maybe you can forgive me. One day, maybe you'll say you'll try to forgive me."

"You've ruined my life."

"No, walking down that aisle and being emotionally unfaithful would have ruined your life."

"You're not giving me a chance to fight!"

"Because I'm certain, Collin, I'm certain. Please hear me. It's over."

As expected, he hangs up, and I hang my head, setting my tears free. My fate is sealed. There's no back, and there's no forward. I've been physically monogamous for years, just not emotionally faithful to the men I've dated. In one way or another, they all failed in silent comparison. I'm still strung out on the highs of my past because I never closed the door, fully let myself grieve, which left me in a constant state of limbo.

At this point, I would rather be alone than a liar.

I came back to declare war on my memories, to draw my lines, and I'm already disgusted with just how relieved I am by reclaiming, owning my dark side.

Maybe my scales are harder to see than Roman's were, but we've got far more in common than I initially thought. I'm more than capable of being the villain.

Villain.

I guess it takes one to love and loathe one.

And I've become a convincing one at that.

And in Collin's story, I will be.

Furious with the easy comparison, I scroll through my phone and press send. He answers on the second ring.

"You know, you're about four years too late for a booty call."

"Hey, Ryan, sorry, I know it's late."

"What's going on? Neither you nor Collin have been answering my calls. And thanks to you both for not bothering to show up for work today, it was a shitshow. I had to push meetings."

"I'm sorry, something came up. I'll explain later."

A brief silence.

"Should I be worried?"

"Ryan, I need your help."

"Name it."

"How soon can you get here?"

"Where is here?"

"I'm in Triple Falls."

"You're finally going to sell?"

"His business, his house. I want nothing more to do with him. It's past time."

"You sure?"

"Positive. Is the last offer still on the table from a few months ago?"

"I'll check. If so, I'll rearrange some meetings. I can be there by noon tomorrow."

"See you then."

"Are you going to tell me what's going on?"

"I'll explain when you get here."

"I'm on my way."

"Thanks, Ryan."

Tossing the phone on the counter, I pour another two fingers in the tumbler.

"To you, Sir." I lift my glass before tossing back my dinner.

Chapter Thirty-One

*M*Y BODY VIBRATES *along with the sound of the motors as they whiz past me on the narrow road.*

The wind kicks up as they speed by, and I wave, teeth chattering, shivering in the cold, before looking into the direction they're heading.

Fear slams into me when I see the road ending abruptly in the distance. There's nothing but darkness past the tree line.

"Stop!" I scream as they continue to blast by. Furiously, I wave my arms in warning and point to the road ahead, but I know they can't hear me. Flailing, I move to step out onto the road just as the Camaro comes into view. I attempt to call out to him, but I can't. Instead, his name comes out muddled off my tongue. "Stop!" I step out into the road to give chase, but they're too far gone. I'm too late. It's too late.

I jerk awake as one of the French doors crashes against the wall, a gust of wind covering me as I whimper, and slam my eyes shut, starting a slow count to even my breathing and steady my heartbeat. A hot tear escapes as the dream freshly implants in my psyche. Another icy gust of wind has me scrambling from the bed to shut my balcony doors on a drab, cloud-littered sunrise.

After a long, hot shower to warm me up, the Advil finally starts to kick in. Sucking on a water bottle, I hydrate while I pick through my old closet and the wardrobe of a twenty-year-old me. Apparently, my things had been carefully unpacked after they restored order to the house. Moving the hangers aside one by one, I pause when I spot the crumpled dress on the floor tucked in the corner of the closet. Fingering the straps, the rest of the pale-yellow dress falls limp in front of me, faint stains covering the bodice.

A dress still soiled from our watermelon fight, the night I confessed to Sean I was in love with him.

"I take it back."

Throat stinging, I press the fabric to my face in hopes of breathing in any trace of him and am disappointed. After we broke up, I couldn't bring myself to wash the dress. The ache gnaws at me as I carefully fold it and stick it on the shelf above before heading downstairs and hauling my suitcase in from the car. Taking my time, I restructure the closet with my temporary wardrobe. I don't know how long I'm staying, but with last night's decision, I know it will take some time to get it all done. And it's apparent I need some semblance of order.

The last thirty-six hours have been a mess. I splintered within hours of arriving here. I'd confessed unthinkable things to my ex-fiancé who didn't deserve it. I'd said too much. I can't fall back into old patterns or I'll lose focus. My emotions may have gotten me here, but my sensibilities need to kick in and help me navigate the rest.

After unpacking, I head downstairs with my rocks glass and the half-empty bottle of whiskey. Still a bit disoriented from hitting the bottle so hard, I stumble in my footing and drop the glass which shatters on the kitchen floor. I gather a broom and dustpan and begin sweeping the shards up when a faint but distinct smell wafts into my nose.

Dropping the pan, I stare down at the cracked glass in disbelief. I lift one of the larger pieces and sniff.

Gin.

I would know this scent anywhere. At times, I can still taste it on his lips.

Big Brother is watching you.

Racing to the small pantry that houses the security equipment, I rewind the last twenty-four hours to around the time I arrived. But it's only my car in the driveway that appears on screen, and it's only me that enters the house. I was alone last night.

I palm my face and sigh.

The dream, the dress, the surfacing memories, along with the lingering alcohol, have definitely set my imagination off. I'm already a prisoner of this place and the way it's haunting me.

I decide to preserve some dignity and toss the glass into the trash.

My mind is playing tricks already, and I'm not going to entertain it.

I opted to meet Ryan at his hotel in the lobby and spot him typing a mile a minute on his laptop. I called him in because he's one of the best corporate lawyers in the country and the biggest asset in my company. He's also highly protective of both me and my best interests. He glances up at me over his screen in greeting and gives me his signature panty-dropping grin. He's ridiculously good-looking in an all-American way: an athletic build, thick wavy, sandy-blond hair, and ocean-blue eyes.

Despite being my most trusted business partner, he's also an ex-boyfriend from college. We dated for a few months during my junior year before he grew tired of the space I purposely put between us, refusing to let him get close. He eyes my dress, and I don't miss the way they linger. Despite my rough morning, I managed to pull myself together today, choosing my favorite "I've got this" spiked black boots. I paired them with a sleek black pencil skirt and form-fitting, popped collar blazer that reveals a respectable amount of cleavage. I left my hair down and curled it in waves before applying a full face of makeup, lining my eyes black and shading my lips deep red. The same red of the trench coat draped over my arm.

Ryan stands from the small two-seater he was lounging in and towers over me before pulling me into a hug. As always, he's impeccably dressed. His hair combed back neatly. I can feel the stares of the two women standing at the front desk. He's got a natural knack for drawing attention, but at the moment, his is on me. "You look beautiful."

"Thanks, but I feel like hell."

His thick, dark blond brows V. "Not sleeping well?"

"Not really, no," I confess as I glance around the boutique hotel.

Traffic bustles in and out of the lobby as I take in the posh furnishings and artwork. He's staying at one of the few inns on the square that's been newly purchased and renovated.

"This is nice."

"It will do," he says, looking me over curiously. "You want to tell me why the sudden change of heart? You've refused to entertain any offers or even talk about this place."

"I have my reasons."

He closes his laptop and pushes it in his dark brown leather satchel, the same one he used in school. "Always so damn secretive."

I shrug. "Every woman needs some element of mystery, right?"

"It's not annoying at all." He deadpans. "And not at all the reason why I dumped you. I am curious as to how Collin got in. It's because he's British, it's the accent, am I right?"

His smile fades when he reads my expression at the mention of Collin. "Really, Cecelia? Even *I* had a hard-on for him."

"I don't want to talk about it." I turn and make my way out of the double doors, and he stops me out on the sidewalk, gently tugging my coat from my grip before helping me into it. "I'm sorry," he whispers softly. "That was an asshole thing to say."

"It's fine. It needed to happen." He stares at me expectantly. "I'm okay, Ryan. Come on. I'll drive."

He follows me to where I parked my Audi and climbs in the passenger seat before glancing out the window at the bustling square.

"This town is . . . charming. You grew up here?"

"Yes and no."

"Jesus," he grumbles, "It's like you're trained to be evasive."

If he only knew. I turn to him. "I came here for a year when I was nineteen. I never really lived here."

"A full answer. I'm impressed."

"I wasn't that bad." I turn the engine over and glance his way to see a face filled with skepticism. "I wasn't."

"You vetoed Valentine's day and told me to start sleeping with other women the night I told you I was in love with you."

I pull away from Main Street and take the few turns leading us away from the square toward the plant. "I wasn't ready for all that. And I didn't want to lose you as a friend."

"You were already the one that got away by the end of our first date."

Though he's being playful, maybe I wounded him more deeply than I originally thought. But he was supposed to be the party guy, capable of showing a girl a good time, and I was in desperate need of that.

"I never expected us to get serious," I say honestly.

"Then you should have dumbed yourself down and worn frumpy sweaters."

We share a grin at a stoplight. "I'm glad we stayed friends."

"Yeah, well, now that your gold standard and disgustingly charming English gentleman is finally out of my way, we can negotiate adding benefits."

"You're ridiculous."

"I'm not a complete animal. I'll give you time to mourn," he says matter of fact, scrolling through his phone, "how about a week from Tuesday?"

"Shut it. We need to get our heads in the game. Tell me about the offer."

"The terms are simple. The offer is killer, despite the recent drop in share price. It's pretty open and shut. We're meeting their lawyer at two."

"That was fast."

"The majority shareholders have already signed off on it."

"The offer is that good?"

"That good. If you use the money the way I think you're going to, we'll be able to do a lot more. But are you sure you want to do this?"

"Yes. Why do you keep asking me?"

"Why now?"

"Because I've avoided it long enough." I take a turn onto the familiar road and a smile graces my face as it stretches out before us.

I can feel Ryan pause next to me. "What's that smile?"

Rolling the windows down, the wind whips through the car along with the whisper of a memory, of a voice.

Eggs—runny, coffee—black.

"Music," I say softly, turning up the radio, "loud."

"What's that?" Ryan says, flipping through his cell.

"Cars," I finish glancing his way before flooring the gas, "fast." Ryan's eyes bulge, his jaw going slack before I turn my attention back to the road and open it up. Racing down the straightaway, I feed on the exhilaration as the hairs on my arm start to rise.

"Cecelia?" Ryan's voice rattles with anxiety.

"Yeah?" I manage through a laugh.

"What are you doing?"

The lyrics of "The Pretender" by Foo Fighters blasts through the car. I shake my head ironically and shift. If it's memories I'm unearthing, then I plan on doing it right. I've faced the boogeyman, hell, I fell in love with him and survived. I survived a lot more than that.

It's time to unpack.

I glance over and answer him honestly.

"We're blowing the dust off." We shoot forward, and Ryan lets out a ladylike shriek.

"Cecelia, slow down before you make me a praying Christian!"

A laugh bursts from my lips. "Hang on."

"Oh fuck, oh fuck, oh fuck," Ryan mumbles in pure fear next to me just before we skid around a curve on all fours. I correct the wheel, downshift, and stomp on it, plastering him back in his seat.

Ryan slaps one hand to the dash while gripping the oh-shit handle with the other. "Yep, I just tasted the omelet I ate this morning."

I can feel his stare on me as I let loose, soaking up the adrenaline, feeling anything but numb. I take another turn that has us edging the shoulder briefly before I find purchase on the cement.

"Cee, what is happening right now? Is this some sort of cry for help?"

I grin, shaking my head like a lunatic, letting the music fuel me. "We're waking up ghosts, Rye, and it's way too late for help."

"Waking up ghosts, huh? Well, I'll be honest, I'm not interested in becoming one of them, and I'm too fucking pretty to die so young. Slow the fuck down!"

My answering laugh is maniacal, and I can feel the fear rolling off him. "Relax."

"Not fucking likely." He cranes his neck to look behind us. "Are we running from someone?"

"Not this time." I take one last turn, and we fishtail into the entrance of the plant. With ease, I whip us into a parking spot and glance at Ryan, who's varying shades of white. Grinning, I glance up at the building and feel no apprehension. I can do this. I can free myself. I've got the strength to try. And if the stars are kind enough to align for me, maybe I can forgive myself, forgive them, and finally move on. "I think I'm ready."

Ryan dry heaves next to me. "I'm going to need a minute."

Chapter Thirty-Two

I SIT AT one of the conference tables adjacent to the lobby as Ryan guides me through the proposal page by page. Once he's satisfied, he takes the seat next to me and hands me a pen. "Initial here, and here."

He flips another as I scan the lines. "We discussed these articles earlier in detail. By signing this, you agree to the terms of sale."

I'm about to gain a fortune, and nothing about it excites me, aside from the good the money can do. I've done well enough on my own, but this move will make me a ridiculously wealthy woman. Along with the stock inherited on my twentieth birthday and because of Roman's untimely death, I became the majority shareholder of Horner Technologies. His colon cancer diagnosis was swift, as was his death, leading to what I imagine was an undignified end. All the money in the world couldn't help him as he withered away, overlooking his kingdom. I don't know the details, and I didn't bother taking part in a last-minute attempt to try and mend our relationship.

I didn't shed a tear the day I got the phone call from his

hospice nurse, nor did I attend his funeral. I keep expecting that guilt to kick in; so far, it hasn't.

Now I just want to be free of my obligation to him and his distorted idea of a legacy along with a name that stands for everything that broke us—power, money, and greed.

Sometimes I wish I would have remained asleep, blind to his evil deeds, and those of others like him. But I made the most of my knowledge using it to start a campaign against CEOs with the same delusion of legacy. With Collin, I started a nonprofit with an emphasis on social welfare and employee association programs. A direct opposition to Roman's career path. Not only that, I also used his riches to fund the startup. And under the umbrella of the foundation we've got a vast number of lawyers, Ryan included, who've made it their life's mission to expose and seek justice on corporations, just like Horner Technologies, and bring them to their knees for shitty business practices.

We've been wildly successful.

Amid my crisis of conscience, I've decided to set new plans into motion. When we arrived at the plant, after a brief tour, we secured a conference room, and I dropped the bomb on Ryan. After a two-hour yelling match, he agreed to draw up the paperwork so I could sign over my rights to the foundation to Collin. After this sale, I'll wire a substantial amount of the proceeds to keep it going for years to come. I'm proud of the legacy we created in such a short amount of time, but with all of the pain I've caused my ex-fiancé, it's a gesture of consolation. Collin has been by my side since the beginning. But by his side I can no longer be, and I trust him completely to do what's right with it.

With the stroke of a pen, I can start over in whatever way

I choose. And maybe it's for the best if I pack up sooner than later. Perhaps this was a fool's errand. It was an emotional decision to come, but at least I can use this as an excuse to do some good. But it's my heart in the driver's seat now as I click the pen and press the tip to paper, pausing when I see the logo underneath the buyer's signature line. The company name was undisclosed with the offer, but there's no mistaking the emblem glaring back at me.

A raven.

"What's wrong?" Ryan senses the shift in my posture as my eyes dart between him and the lawyer, whose name evades me as he hovers a few feet away, making sure all T's are crossed. Ryan leans in on a whisper. "I looked into it when we got the offer. The company is legit, and the CEO is just another billionaire who saw a business opportunity."

"Where is he?"

Ryan frowns. "He?"

"Tobias King," I finally voice the name of the secret my heart's been screaming for six long years.

The lawyer clears his throat, his gaze lingering on Ryan for backup he doesn't get before he turns to me. "Ms. Horner, I assure you my client has—"

"I'm sorry," I interrupt. "Your name?"

Clearly offended, he gives me a clipped reply. "Matt Straus."

"My apologies, Mr. Straus. But he obviously wants me to know." I trace the wings with the pad of my finger. "Legit," I say, stifling a laugh as his lawyer speaks up.

"Ms. Horner, the board has already signed off, this deal is in motion—"

"I'm aware of that, Mr. Straus. But it's dead in the water

without my say so, and I will not sign off until I've spoken with Tobias King. *Privately*."

Ryan feeds off my vibe, his face going resolute as he eyes the lawyer with expectancy. And I love him for it. Ryan's a shark, and that's why he's here.

I push myself away from the table and cross my arms. "I'm firm on this."

Mr. Straus sighs, pulling his cell phone from his pocket and excusing himself. "I'm not sure he'll go for it."

"Oh, he will," I assure, which gets me lingering looks from both men before the door clicks closed behind him.

Ryan turns to me.

"What are you doing?"

"Trust me."

"I do, but I'm going to need some clarification. We don't want any surprises. You know this buyer?"

"Yes."

"How?"

Mr. Straus comes back into the room before I can answer. "Mr. King will be here in twenty minutes."

It takes everything I have to keep my voice even. "Today?" He's here.

Tobias is in Triple Falls.

My mind flits back to the idea that I wasn't alone last night. Oh, how he fucks with *me* just by existing.

I was ready to confront him at some point in the near future, but today, now? My nerves start firing off as I stand and walk over to a row of large windows.

"Please excuse us," Ryan says, his eyes still on me.

Mr. Straus nods. "I'll be just outside. I'll send him in when he arrives."

Ryan replies with a quick "thank you" and closes the door behind him. Our eyes connect for a beat before I dart them away.

"Finally, a secret you can't keep. It's written all over your face. Who is he?"

"Someone I didn't think I'd ever see again."

"Clearly he wants to see you."

"Not true. He wanted this to be a quick sale. His name is nowhere on the offer."

"He knew you could dig and figure it out. He made it too easy."

"He knew I would see, but he's made it clear he doesn't want to see me."

"So, this is the one that got away from *you*," he says, sidling up to me as I move my attention back to the windows. "Cecelia, what's going on?"

"I'm not sure." But I am sure he still wants Roman's company. This was always supposed to happen. But Tobias hasn't touched it since I left.

"Do you trust this man with the company?"

I nod.

"Then, why do you look so terrified?"

"Let's just say the last time I saw him—it didn't end well."

"He's offering you a lot more than it's worth."

"That has nothing to do with me. It had to be an offer I wouldn't refuse."

"So, we're dealing with the Godfather?"

That crack doesn't even get him a smile.

"Are you sure you want to do this?"

"Positive. Look, don't worry. He wasn't a fan of my father. But he's not trying to gain this company with ill intent. My guess is that he plans on making it employee-owned."

"I see." Another pause, and I still can't look at him. "Is any of this, you coming back here, selling the company, and Mr. King, any part of the reason why you broke it off with Collin?"

I don't answer.

"Wow, now I'm really intrigued."

"Don't be. He's just a man who wants to own the company, this plant in particular. He's got his reasons, and he'll do right with it."

"Well, I sure as fuck don't want to leave you in a room with him if you're afraid."

"I'm not afraid."

"Cee—" he grips my hands in his, forcing me to face him. "You're shaking."

"It's cold in here."

His eyes narrow, calling bullshit.

"It's just been a long time."

"You're sure you can handle this?"

No.

"Positive. Ryan, please do me a favor and give me a minute alone."

When he hesitates, I shake my head. "I swear, I've got this."

"Okay, I'll be just outside that door."

"Thank you."

When the door closes, I move toward the window and stare into the trees on the other side of it.

Over six years without a word, and this is all I get? Years of silence, and he expects me to hand it over without a fight?

His audacity only feeds my residual anger. I understand his grudge, for Roman and for me, but this move only adds insult to catastrophic injury.

For years my father monopolized the city's welfare, and it's only fitting that they fought back. Tobias was always going to be the one to give it back to them. I was so young then, I never really saw the bigger picture, but his plans haven't changed. Small town justice was always his gateway to corporate warfare.

And I can't even hold a grudge for it. It's brilliant. From an alliance formed when they were just teenagers to the bittersweet victory of today, he seems to have done everything he set out to do. Everything.

His day of reckoning has finally come. And ironically, I'll be the one to gift it to him.

But not without seeking some justice of my own.

When the door opens and closes some minutes later, I keep my gaze out the window but can feel his hesitance from feet away.

"Well done, Tobias, but you had to know I'd figure it out."

Silence. A long minute of quiet followed by another. I can feel his eyes on me, my spine prickling in awareness, my heart fluttering in my chest.

"I didn't care if you did." The timbre in his voice combined with the thick foreign lilt has my eyes closing and my heart lurching into rapid rhythm. For years I dreamt of hearing his voice, and for years I've replayed echoes of his soft murmurs during our most intimate moments.

"So why didn't you show up?"

"It wasn't necessary."

"You mean I'm not worthy of a handshake? Or at the very least a little gloating on your part."

"No gloating necessary. I'm well aware of your position to deny me this. But you never cared about his company."

"Why now? Why did you wait so long?"

"I wasn't sure I wanted it anymore."

"What's changed?"

"Nothing, except deciding I did."

Despite my mission with my own career, I haven't so much as touched Roman's company since I inherited it because, though I hold my grudges close, it was never supposed to be mine for the taking.

"This was supposed to go down years ago. What happened? Did you take pity on a dying man?"

"Plans changed."

Quietly exhaling, I turn and lay eyes on him for the first time in six years. It's a shot to the chest which robs me of breath and ricochets when his eyes collide with mine. In those few seconds, I'm engulfed in flames, my lips parting slightly as we take in the other, at a loss for words.

He's cruelly beautiful, as he's always been, even more so now. He's larger than life in the outdated office. His dark suit clings to his physique, his build just as magnificent as it was years ago when I felt his naked flesh under my palms, and our breaths mingled.

No memory I have did him justice. From the surreal ember color of his eyes to the cut of his jaw, to the majestic strength of his nose, down to his light crimson lips, he's spellbinding. And just as I recognize the fire in his eyes that I've longed for with every beat of my betrayed heart, they cool considerably before slicing like diamonds down my form.

"I see we're going with an openly hostile reception. I would think this would be a good day for you, Tobias. A celebration. You won."

"I won nothing." His tone sends a chill down my spine.

"I've been well, thanks for asking." I take a step toward him to engage, and he stiffens. "You're going to give it back to them, aren't you?"

One sharp nod.

"They deserve it. I won't fight you on that."

Another nod as he sweeps me as if he's trying to make sure I'm unharmed. I'm fucking not.

"But I won't let it go fully, either."

He snaps his eyes to mine. "Can't you just be done with this?"

"In the last six years, I've been no burden to you. I did what was asked of me."

"I told you not to come back, Cecelia. I meant it."

"Yeah, well, sorry about the inconvenience, my father died. I have business here."

"Your father died two years after you left; you didn't show up then. But if you want to use him as an excuse, then let's get this over with so you can go."

I square off with him. "Sorry. I no longer take orders from you."

"You never did. And this doesn't have to get ugly."

"Except it will because I won't be manipulated by you again. And I want answers."

"Let it go. We were foolish people then, who did stupid shit. Your part in it ends in this room."

"Stupid . . ." I draw the word out. "Well, I've definitely felt that over the years."

333

His nostrils flare as I draw closer, the energy between us crackling with each step, making it harder to breathe. Volatile eyes scour me before he shoves his hands in his pockets. "Do you want an apology?"

"Now *that* would be worthless. What you did to me was unusually cruel, don't you think?"

"It was necessary."

"Necessary . . . no, I don't like it. And cruel might be mild in comparison to what it was. Merciless might be the better word. But I've tried really hard not to hold it against you because it came from a place of pain. At least it did *at first*."

His jaw feathers with irritation and my palm itches to slap and soothe. Physically I can feel every emotion rolling between us, but I want so much to break this tension because it hurts.

His voice is barely a whisper when he speaks. "What do you want?"

"I want you to talk to me. Grant me a conversation."

"I have nothing to say."

"I have plenty."

His nostrils flare. "Then let's hear it."

"No," I say softly. "I don't think so. Not this way. Not with ears on the other side of that door."

"This was a mistake," he barks out and runs a hand through his hair, ruining the composed look of it. "The deal was—"

"We're still in negotiations," I snap, striding toward him in anger. "You plotted and schemed using me as a ragdoll, and *you're* the one who's aggravated? I'm not going to deny you this, but how dare you stand there and have the audacity to act indignant about it?"

"Again. You were never supposed to be involved in any part of this. From day one, I told you to stay the fuck away. But you didn't listen."

"And you stayed away?"

He levels me with his response. "It meant far more to you than it did to me." Inside I'm dying, his words hitting as hard as he intended. I glance back out the window to keep him from seeing the sting. Tension thickens as he speaks from behind me. "Everything has moved on without you."

"Good to know."

"Just sign the papers and go home. You'll be a rich woman."

That comment has my focus back on him, my glare full of the offense I feel. "Money means absolutely fucking nothing to me. And I'm a successful woman already without this deal."

"I'm aware."

"Are you?" I cross my arms. "Is that part of moving on?"

"We're not going back there." His voice is steel, the edges of the blade slashing across my chest. Why can't I let go of this man that so clearly despises me? I had suspected as much, but now it's blisteringly evident. In a way, I cost him his brother, as my father did his parents. Maybe he has every right to hate me and vice versa, so why can't I hate him back?

Electricity sparks the longer we share space, and I can feel the increase in the thrum between us, while he tries to feign indifference. But it's still there. And how I wish it weren't. How I wish that fate or Karma or whatever it is that decided to tether us together would disappear and release me, release us both. But it's there, and it's so loud, it might as well be the pound of a drum.

This, *this* is why he didn't want to be in the room with me. Our connection is in our chemical makeup, an unexplainable bond. It was our undoing years ago, and it ate us alive. It's every bit as strong now. It's so easy to put my finger on the why of us when every part of me is buzzing in awareness.

"You want to keep this civil? Fine, indulge me. How is Sean?"

"*Married*. Happily. He runs the garage now. He's got two kids."

I swallow. "T-that's, that's wonderful." I cross my arms over my chest. "Are you still close?"

"No."

"Why?"

His eyes ignite, and this time, it's take no prisoners. "I'm done here," he snaps, picking up the pen and holding it toward me. "Sign. And go home."

"No. I think I'll hang around for a bit. I've got old friends to see. How is Tyler?"

He takes an aggressive step forward. It's almost as if he's in pain staring back at me. Greedy, I eat the feel of it up because being within feet of this man has heightened my senses to a point I didn't think I was capable of anymore.

He reads me easily.

"Times have changed. This is the last thing that ties us."

I tilt my head. "Is that so?"

"Just fucking sign," he orders in warning. "I want to be done with you." I flinch, and for the first time since he entered the room, his eyes soften, but I'm already hemorrhaging.

Hate him. Please hate him.

"Sign," he utters, his voice low. It's as close to begging as he'll get.

The air stills the longer we square off, and I know he's with me. We're both fighting the draw, fighting the shift between love and hate. The longer we're in the room, the more it blurs, and the angrier I get. But I'm not going back on the promise I made myself.

"I want the truth."

"Prepare to be disappointed."

"Meaning?"

"Don't push me, Cecelia."

"Don't push you? Oh, you silly bastard, it's about to be a shoving match," I grit out, lifting my chin. "I deserve answers."

The door opens, and Ryan steps in. Tobias's glare lands on him, but Ryan's eyes are on me.

"We okay in here?"

"Fine," I answer quickly, though I'm anything but. I'm coming apart the more the seconds tick past. "We just need another minute."

Tobias doesn't spare Ryan a word as the two have a silent but loaded moment before he closes the door behind him.

Tobias looks back at me incredulously, before shaking his head in disgust.

"What?"

"Of course, your fucking lawyer is in love with you."

"He's a dear friend I trust, and he's the best at what he does. In fact, he's about to put your balls in a vise, so you might want to play nice. This *is* business, and I'm keeping my silly heart out of it, you taught me that, remember? And who better to teach that lesson than a heartless man?"

He slides the documents across the table.

"Sign it."

"No. I don't think so. Not *this* contract. Draw up another where I have a twenty-five percent stake in the company. And if you don't, I'll take the next offer for bottom dollar, and you'll never have this fucking plant." His eyes light with fury, but I don't bother to celebrate, I'm defeated in a way I didn't think was possible. Coming here was the biggest mistake I've ever made because seeing him again has wrecked both me and my chances. I still feel it, every ounce of it. The truth will never set me free. I'm not in love with a memory. I'm still in love with the man standing in front of me. And that truth unleashes an anger inside me that's been building for years.

"You might have made it easy for yourself by once again exiling me, but you destroyed that stupid naïve girl with your selfish shit and war games. I circled the drain for years wondering how I could have meant so little to you. I've lost half my fucking sanity trying to battle my way back from what happened, and that's because of the way you shut me out and left me dangling in the dark, completely alone."

I begin to shake with anger.

"I lost him too. And then you saw to it that I lost everyone else." His eyes sweep me, and I see a flicker of guilt, but it's not nearly enough. It never will be.

My tone is just as frigid when I finally lift my chin to my maker. "But that girl grew up, and she's angry about the cards she got dealt by *your hand*, and she wants her pound of flesh. You can have the company, but you won't ever, *ever* cut *all* ties to me. I've been serving the sentence you passed for years, suffering in silence, and it's time you start serving yours." My voice rattles with fury, my hurt and hatred emerging from the river of lies he left me drowning in. "You thought with this, you could wash your hands of me? *Tough shit*. You don't get to break ties with me, not now, not *ever*." We're so close at this point I can see the dark tint and curl of his long lashes, the divot beneath his nose, the faint freckle on the corner of his lower lip. I can smell the rich scent of his skin.

"I'll give you what you want when I have my answers." I grab my purse and jacket and palm the handle of the door. When I glance back at him, his eyes are predictably on me. "That's my counter-offer. Take it or leave it. I guess the question is now, how bad do you still want it?"

Jerking the door open, I gesture to Ryan, and he joins me at my side, his eyes darting over my shoulder as I stride toward the lobby.

"What happened in there, Cee?" He helps me into my jacket, his gaze darting between the lobby and where we stand.

"Negotiations." I'm still shaking as he ushers me into the parking lot toward my car.

Once I'm behind the wheel, my body goes slack as he looks over to me, his eyes wide. "Jesus," he says, looking as bewildered as I feel. "Who the fuck is that guy?"

"Just a part of my history I need to put to bed."

"I physically felt that, Cecelia. I felt the tension in that room."

"Yeah, well, he thinks you're in love with me."

A long beat of silence has me turning his way.

He rakes his lower lip with his teeth before lifting deep-blue eyes to mine.

"I am. And I've never been so jealous of another man in my life."

I gape at him. "Ryan . . . you aren't serious . . ."

"Don't beat yourself up about it. I gave up on you a long time ago." He nods toward the building. "And no man alive can compete with that."

"I never . . ." I search for the words as guilt gnaws at me. He's always flirted, even in front of Collin, but he's had a dozen or so more girlfriends since we broke up. He sees the guilt in my eyes and shakes his head.

"Want to feel better?"

I nod.

"I've fucked my way through half of Atlanta."

"That's more concerning than anything."

"I'm also the reason there's a high turnover of assistants."

I glare at him. "Marcie?"

"Yep."

"Damnit, Ryan! She was my favorite."

"Mine too, which is why I bent her over your desk just for spite."

"You're a pig."

"I know. My penis has not been faithful to you. When it gets hurt, it has a tendency to self-sabotage. Feel better?"

"Kind of."

We share a smile.

"I do love you back, you know?"

"We're good," he assures as he pulls up his phone. "I want more background on this asshole."

I cover his phone with my hand. "Don't. Promise me you won't. Promise me."

"Why?"

"Because I know all I need to about him. And he's not the enemy."

"Fine. But I hate him."

"I do too."

He lifts a brow. "No, you don't."

I turn to him, my eyes stinging. "Ryan, he owes me, and I'm here to collect. And the only way I can do that is if this deal goes my way. This is really important to me."

He grips my hand and kisses the back of it before letting go. "I've got you."

"Thank you." Turning the ignition, I freeze when I see Tobias standing in front of my hood on the sidewalk staring directly into the car, his lethal gaze on Ryan before drifting to me. In the next second, he disappears down the row of cars and out of sight.

"That wasn't scary at all," Ryan speaks up next to me. "Should I expect to see a bloody, decapitated horse head in my hotel bed in the morning?"

Chapter Thirty-Three

S TILL IN MY car, I sit out another bout of freezing rain in the front of the house as silence lingers on the other side of the line.

"Christy? You there?"

I glance down at the phone in my lap and see the call is connected, the seconds ticking by.

"Chris—"

"Let me get this straight." I hear the swish of her bath-water. "Three days ago, you called me to help you with the seating chart for your posh, high society Atlanta wedding, and today you're in Triple Falls because you had a dream, tore up your wedding dress, broke up with your fiancé, decided to sell your father's business to a man who ripped you apart, and shortly after your college boyfriend confessed he was still in love with you?"

"Yes, I know it sounds crazy but—"

"*Crazy?* No, crazy would be a downgrade. This is a late-season *Grey's Anatomy* episode. Everything but the kitchen sink."

I'd dropped Ryan off at his hotel, and though he said we

were okay, I knew he turned down dinner due to our awkward drive back to town. He'd all but ignored me by answering emails, but I felt the distance. Had I been so oblivious to his feelings?

"I feel awful."

"Everyone knew he was in love with you. I saw his face when Collin proposed, and it was so sad."

"Now I feel worse."

"You didn't lead him on, but damn, how I miss having boy problems."

"You have the perfect husband."

"He left the toilet seat up last night and didn't flush. I fell into the toilet and woke up both my children, and we all screamed until dawn. I'm still not talking to him."

I can't help the laughter that bubbles up. The world I left seems so far away now as I gaze at Roman's front door.

"I've really lost it this time, haven't I?"

"No, you did the right thing."

"You think so?"

"No, Collin is gorgeous, funny, charming, and your equal in every way."

"I hate you."

"You love me. But if you don't love him enough to marry him, you shouldn't marry him."

"I do love Collin, just not the way I love *him*."

"It's unhealthy."

"I know."

"That man has caused you nothing but pain."

"I know."

"He wrecked you."

"I know. And when I saw him today, I swear to God,

my whole body lit up. I didn't imagine it, Christy, none of it."

"And did he feel the same way?"

"Even Ryan said he felt it."

"He said that?"

"Yes."

"So, I'm guessing after six years he still holds a grudge because you slept with his brother?"

Lies, all lies I told in lieu of the truth I can never confess.

Even so, part of me thinks that's some of the reason why it was so easy for Tobias to keep his distance and let me go.

"What *are* you doing, Cecelia?"

"I don't know," I say as the day catches up with me. I picture Collin in our house, staring at the wedding invitations I left stacked on the table. Tears gather and fall at the thought. I can't imagine what he's thinking or how he's feeling.

"What have I done?"

"You threw your life away for a man who doesn't at all deserve you. Babe, a better friend would have you admitted."

"I know it seems crazy, but I have to see this through."

"Go back to Collin. He'll take you back."

"I told him the truth."

"You what?!"

"I had to." And today was all the proof I needed. It was there. Healthy or not. It was there, everything I felt for him, and I can't deny it. Especially now.

"Jesus, Cecelia. What did Collin say?"

"He hung up on me. And I don't blame him."

"What a shitshow. Look, I know I was joking, but are you okay?"

"No. No, I'm not. But what am I supposed to do? I can't

continue living a lie, and that's all I've been doing. It's not fair to either of us and today . . . I got my answer. Not that it's the one I wanted, but it was there. It was still there. I hate that I'm still in love with him. I hate that being within feet of him had the same effect on me."

"Do you want him back?"

"I don't want to love him," I whisper hoarsely. "Stupidly, I thought . . ."

"Thought what?"

"I thought I would see him, and my adult brain would kick in and reason with my stupid heart."

"That you would see him differently, and it would put your feelings in perspective?"

"Exactly."

"But that's not what happened."

"No."

"Well, I love you. And if this is what you feel you need to do, and where you need to be, then do it. I'm behind you, and I'll be here. Just try to get some sleep."

"I will. I Love you."

"Love you."

Making my way up to the bedroom, I feel the weight of the day take its toll. For years I've imagined this day, seeing Tobias again and finally being able to unleash some of my anger while gaining the upper hand. But it never works out like I imagine it would. And with him, it never will. But Christy is right. If I ever had a chance of making it with anyone, it was Collin. And despite my emotions winning and the realizations I've been faced with, remorse wins as I pull my engagement ring out of my purse, slip it on my finger, and cry myself to sleep.

Chapter Thirty-Four

R YAN SIPS HIS coffee and eyes me over his laptop. "He's going to blow a gasket when he sees this. Daily morning meetings? Moving headquarters temporarily to Triple Falls, and, are you serious?" He points to the list of conditions I handed him.

"Yep."

"You sure he'll go for this?"

"Yep." And he will because he thinks he'll win. Tobias is overconfident when it comes to me, always has been. Despite the kick to the chest yesterday, I'm determined to keep it business.

Ryan types a mile a minute as I kick back with my coffee, a smirk on my lips.

"You're determined to piss this guy off."

"Like I said, he owes me—either way, we're selling. Go ahead and entertain another bid. Make sure he catches wind of it."

"Aside from you, what's this guy's interest in the company?"

"It's personal."

"You're infuriating."

"That's exactly what I'm hoping for."

"Shooting it off now." He sits back and eyes me. "What exactly are you hoping to gain here?"

"Perspective."

"And you need it. Why?"

I glance down at the ring on my finger. "Because I need to atone for what I've done."

"How so?"

"People got hurt because of us. People are still getting hurt."

"This is about a breakup?"

"Not exactly."

"For fuck's sake." He slams his computer shut and shoves it into his satchel before standing.

"Ryan, I'm sorry, but I can't—"

He snatches his jacket and pulls it on. "I'm going for a walk."

"Ryan—"

I move to go after him when my phone buzzes in my pocket, a local area code, and a number I don't recognize.

"Cecelia Horner."

"Do you think this is fucking funny?"

I can't help my smile. "Good morning, Tobias. I'm looking forward to working together."

"This isn't happening. I've given in to all your other demands."

"All except one. The only one that matters."

"You do realize you're fucking with the wrong man." Not a question.

"You don't think I know who you are or what you're

capable of?" I hiss walking to the corner of the lobby where I'm not heard and look up at the surveillance camera, knowing his eyes are on me.

"Ezekiel Tobias King, born Ezekiel Tobias Baran, July thirtieth nineteen eighty-four, thirty-seven-years old, son of Celine Moreau, and adopted son of Guillaume Beau King. A US transplant at age six, you were orphaned at age eleven along with one brother, Jean Dominic King, who died at age twenty-seven, no autopsy." I swallow away the ache with every word.

"You went to France at age sixteen to attend IPESUP prep school to ensure your acceptance to the prestigious HEC Paris to earn your business degree. You spent your time wisely recruiting and vetting old relatives to build an alliance for your cause. After graduating, you started your company, Exodus Inc, and went public with it four years ago. The net worth as of the close of business yesterday is sitting just below two billion dollars. Just after you formed your company, you began to search for your last living and close relative, your birth father, Abijah Baran, a French Hebrew and member of Parti Radical until he was diagnosed with schizophrenia at age twenty-eight. Six years ago, you found him. Shortly after, you had him committed to a mental institution, Centre Hospitalier Sainte-Anne, in the 14th arrondissement in Paris, where you visit him annually. A fact you've hidden from everyone in your life. His association with certain extremists and his mental disease no doubt one of the reasons why you never married and have no living heirs, and a large part of the reason for your secrecy. That and the fact that the only thing you have ever truly fucking cared about in this life is your immediate family, your personal vendetta against Roman Horner, your ambitious agenda, and getting your goddamn way." I lift my chin to the camera. "Know your opponent, Tobias. Your move, *King*."

I hang up and walk outside to spot Ryan halfway down the square and decide to give him space because I can't give him answers. I know how he feels; I'm fighting tooth and nail to get my own.

"Cecelia, is that you?" Crossing Main Street, I turn to see Melinda racing toward me, her eyes wide.

"Hey, Melinda, how are you?"

"As I live and breathe, girl, you only get more beautiful, look at you," she says as she grips me to her in a hug. I hug her back just as tightly before she pulls away. "You're just gorgeous. All grown up."

"Thank you, you look great."

"That's because I just spent a hundred dollars on my hair." She runs her hand through it. "And don't BS me. You just left without a word. I was so worried about you. And when you didn't come back for your father's—" She reads my expression and falters.

"I'm sorry, I had some personal things come up and just took off."

"Are you staying long?"

"For a little while. Not long."

She lights up. "Well, we have a wedding in the family coming up. You remember my little niece, Cassie? She's getting married! Can you believe she's so grown up? Seems like just yesterday I was telling you about her baptism." As always, she easily sorts through her phone and lifts a picture.

"She's beautiful."

"She is, and he's so handsome. Are you doing anything right now? Come on, let's have lunch."

Searching the street for any sign of Ryan, I come up empty.

"Sure."

Her eyes light up.

"Perfect, I know just the place." We walk Main Street, Valentine's decorations in almost every glass storefront, remnants of early morning snow beneath our booted feet.

Dizzied by her conversation, she guides me into a restaurant as she tells me about an upcoming play she's in. Once seated, a basket of bread is placed before us, along with two glasses of water and a menu. It's when I see the logo on the front of it that my heart stops—The Pitt Stop.

"You catchin' feelings for me, Pup?"

I trace the letters with my finger and look up past Melinda's shoulder as she rattles on about the plant. Rows and rows of pictures of the Roberts family line the walls, and I strain to study each one; when I manage to find one of Sean in his early twenties, arms crossed as he leans against his Nova, his hazel eyes shining as he smiles for the camera.

My heart explodes into rhythm as my eyes begin to burn. Melinda reads my expression. She glances around and then back at me.

"Oh, honey, I wasn't thinking, I really wasn't. Are you okay being here? I guess I should have asked, but by the size of the rock you're sporting on your finger, it looks like you moved on and moved on *well*."

I glance down at the diamond on my finger. It's a little ostentatious in size, but all I see when I look at it is the love in his eyes when Collin presented me with it at our company Christmas party. Before I can answer, a young waitress takes our drink order. I rattle off iced tea and, unable to resist, I stand and tell Melinda I need to use the restroom.

I spend the better part of ten minutes studying the walls, every glimpse of him excruciating. He got his looks from his mother mostly, his build and smile from his father.

Years of photos of my first love line the walls, from little league to his prom along with family shots with celebrities who've dined here over the years. I search and search for recent photos and find none, knowing they're in the restaurant somewhere, and cursing the fact that I'll be obvious if I search for them. I hadn't flinched when Tobias told me he was married, but I felt it. And the knowledge now feels like nails dragging across my chest.

Sean has a wife and two children. He married. He moved on as he should've.

I am happy for him. And a little jealous.

It's hypocritical, but I am. I only want to remember the time when he was mine. It's my God-given right not to know how happy he is.

No matter how unconventional, we had something good until everything went to hell. I was in love with him, until he was ripped away from me.

The dreams that I have that star him are sometimes the hardest. The love I had for him was pure and untainted. I don't know how to measure love in totality. I only know how to love them individually. But the love that I feel for Tobias is too hard to separate from any other man. My contempt for him exceeds any other as well.

I search one more wall, simply for the capability of acceptance and come up empty. Maybe it's best I don't see them.

Old wounds threaten as I wash my hands and meet Melinda back at the table and dine with a lump in my throat.

I'm a creep.

I shouldn't be here.

But I can't pull myself away. So, I pick at my food, I listen to Melinda talk, and when we check out at the register, that lump turns into a boulder. Over the cashier's shoulder is a picture of a little boy with hazel eyes, like those of his father. He's beautiful in a way that has me staring long after is appropriate. Once we've paid, I break from Melinda's hug on the street, promising to keep in touch just in time to catch the first tear with my scarf.

When I reach my car, I see Ryan standing next to it, his arms crossed, his ocean eyes softening as I walk up to him. I know my mascara is lining my face, and I don't bother to hide the new tears that shimmer in my eyes. He approaches me and slowly lifts my scarf to help wipe the smudges from my face.

"You know one of the things I love most about you is that you have no idea just how beautiful you are."

I scan his handsome face with regret. I know that if I hadn't have moved to Triple Falls when I was nineteen, Ryan would probably have been my first real love. Maybe Collin would have been my second, and I wouldn't be so absolutely fucked.

"I fell in love one too many times before I got to you."

He pulls me to him and wraps his arms around me. "He agreed to the terms, we sign tomorrow," he whispers hoarsely. "I'm here as long as you need me, but when we conclude our business here . . . please consider this my notice of resignation."

Chapter Thirty-Five

THE NEXT MORNING, after signing the papers with Ryan and setting up my temporary office, I drive back to the cemetery. I wasn't here for the funeral, and that regret eats at me daily. The grey cloudy sky holds as I lay my jacket down and kneel before his headstone, setting my cell phone down after hitting play on Pink Floyd's "Wish You Were Here".

"Dominic, do you have any idea how hard it is for a twenty-six-year-old white woman in a power suit to get weed in this town? The discrimination is real, my love." I pull one of the joints I rolled from my pocket before adjusting myself on my jacket. "And you thought *I* was guilty of judging by appearance. People practically ran from me." I let out a laugh. "And then I remembered you mentioning Wayne from the deli. Nice guy. Still works there." I fire it up and take a long pull as the music lulls me into a more peaceful state.

For endless minutes I recall the rainy days we spent in his bed reading, the flash of teeth he gave me when he knew no one was looking. The soul he revealed to me in bits and pieces capable of something more. The longer I dwell where he rests, the more I become convinced he knew his time on earth would be short.

We both know I was never going to make it to thirty, brother. Take care of her.

He knew.

"What do you want for the future?"

"Nothing."

He refused to let himself hope for anything. A true soldier, he wanted as few people as possible mourning him. And he'd let me love him. I was the girl honored enough to get close to him in a way few others did.

I reach out and palm the freezing stone. "God, I miss you. I miss you all the time. I'll hear a song you played for me or read something good, and you're the first person I want to tell." Unable to handle the sting any longer, I let the tears fall at will.

"Motherfucker or not, I saw you. I saw you. I *knew* you. And I grieve for you every damn day. You lose, Dominic, because there's not a day that goes by that I don't mourn you." I hiccup, my chest burning as I finally put a voice to years of pain. "Why? Why couldn't you just wait for help?"

Breaking apart, the bitter wind adds a sting to the tears on my cheeks as more fall. It's then I perk up with realization. I've felt it enough times to know, and it's undeniable, tangible, it's distinctly him.

"I know you're there," I say, taking one last drag of the joint before tossing it into the grass and standing. I turn to feel the inevitable jolt the minute I see Tobias just outside of the gate, watching me. It's evident he's been there a while, his face tinged red by the wind. The sight of him agonizing. He looks every bit like the polished man I met. Volatile amber eyes rest over the smooth planes of his face, his square jaw set. His thick, ink-colored hair is swept back, not one lock out of place. His suit cloaked by a long grey trench coat and leather gloves. Do I still know him? Every bit of our eye exchange tells me I do, but that he will never admit it.

We stare off for endless seconds before I finally speak. "You want to know why I'm here?" I turn back to the grave. "I never left."

The gate squeaks as he walks through and stands next to me to peer down to where Dominic lies. And for several minutes, I know our collective thoughts are all about him and the moments before he left us.

Raw ache spreads through my chest as I try to imagine what it was like for Tobias to bury his brother. As I try to imagine the crowd of people I grew to love all those years ago, who were gathered here collectively mourning his passing; it was something I was deprived of.

"I have to believe that forgiveness is possible, because if I don't, if I don't . . . Tobias, I won't be able to live like this, I can't live like this anymore. I want so much to make peace with the naïve girl I was. Not to blame myself for what happened but—"

He shakes his head as if to refute the idea.

"I want so much to move on as you all seem to have," I admit. "I do, but it's been impossible for me. I never got the chance to say goodbye," I say, choking on my words.

Briefly, his stare flits with emotion before his expression grows cold and unforgiving. It's everything I expected and nothing I would ever want.

"I'm here for the same reason you are. To mourn him. To

miss him. I have a right to be here." His empty stare rips me to shreds. Part of me wants to retreat safely back into the life I had just days before, to beg Collin to forgive me, and take back the future I destroyed, but I know better. And the reason is standing in front of me, a shell of the man I once knew.

"You need to go home, Cecelia."

I huff, gathering my jacket from the ground and sliding it on. "You should know that's the last thing I'll do."

"You never could make things easy."

"So, we *are* blaming me?" I take a step toward him, and his nostrils flare as though the mere scent of me is repulsive. I take that hit to the chest, knowing I may never get more than this.

"I should have been the one to die that night," I press, "do you hate me because I didn't?"

"I don't blame anyone but Dominic for his decision."

"I don't think you mean that."

"I do. It's not your fault. But I say a lot of things I don't mean when you're around me. That stops the second you see yourself out."

To be so close to him now without touching him is devastating. In a matter of minutes, the longing I've felt for years intensifies ten-fold as I linger in my own manicured shell, holding onto the high for the split second he allows us in close proximity. He feels it too. I know he does. I lost my heart the minute we connected on a molecular level. Somewhere between the games we played and the love I gave him, I lost a lot more.

One mistake, one night, it cost us all.

It's clear he doesn't trust me. Maybe he thinks I have an agenda.

And to a point, I do.

But it's obvious now that agenda was the same pathetic attempt to liberate myself from his hold. And all of that hope disappears the longer he glares at me, the more I become swept up in his volatile depths. He taught me everything I know. And together, he and his brothers taught me love in every degree.

But this man hosts the hottest fire.

I'll love him my whole life, and I'll despise him too for what he took away, for the way he discarded me, shunned me, cast me out. And I allowed it because of the price he paid, but I've been paying too, and it's time he knows it. I turn and face him fully.

"I loved him."

He drops his gaze. "I know."

"But not the way I loved you."

His eyes snap to mine. I know it's not the time, but I have no idea if I'll ever get the chance again. I never told him, not once, but I'm now in the business of truth. I have absolutely nothing left to lose.

"And whether that matters or not, I *deserve* to grieve him. And I deserve answers from you."

"I don't want you here."

"Have you ever?"

He averts his gaze, and I catch his eyes. "How about we blame the fucking secrets. Because *those* seem to have done the most damage."

He turns on his wingtips and crashes through the gate, and I follow hot on his heels. "You denied me all of it! All of it! I deserve this damn conversation, Tobias! And I'm not leav—"

He closes the door to his newer model Jaguar, and in seconds he's tearing out of the parking lot. I race after him, scrambling to start my Audi. When I gun it out of the parking lot, I swear I feel the presence of a cool dark cloud envelop me. Tobias shoots down the road, trying to outrun the past, our mistakes, me, and I stay on his tail before I gun past him over double yellow lines, and my lips lift in victory.

"Should have bought an Audi," I snark, speeding well past his view and gaining good ground. Banking on him following on the straightaway, I go wide, giving myself great lengths before I slow bank on the shoulder and pull the emergency brake, correcting the wheel, so we're head-to-head. In seconds he's racing into view and slams on his brakes coming feet from killing us both. He gapes at me through the windshield, his eyes wide with surprise.

"Like that? Your little brother taught me that hat trick. *Your move.*"

He glares at me for another second before pulling onto the shoulder and flying out of his car. The minute I'm out of my door, his hands shoot out, and he grips my upper arms, anger rolling off him. "Are you out of your fucking mind? You could have killed us both!"

"Well then, I'd guess I'd be putting us both out of our misery," I retort.

"Whatever you're thinking about, forget it." He's so close that I can feel the fabric of his jacket. His smell invades my nose, and nostalgia hits like a lightning bolt, but I remain defiant.

"I can't forget it."

"You need to go back to your life."

"Just talk to me, that's all I want."

"I'm going to say this once. That was *then*. There is *no* now."

He releases me as if touching me burns him.

"You're still the same smug, obnoxious, overbearing bastard you always were."

"No." His tone is acidic. "I'm *much worse*, and I always get my way. You might remember a lot, but you seem to have forgotten that."

He turns on his Italian leathers and walks back toward his car.

"You lured me here with that offer. You knew I would eventually want to rid myself of the burden when you didn't make good on taking it from him. Why didn't you go after him?"

He pauses his walk and turns to me. "What does it matter? It's mine now."

"God, you're ridiculous. You must hate the fact that I've grown up, and I won't be manipulated by you *ever* again."

"I got what I wanted. So, your point is moot."

"Not entirely," I taunt. "I'm holding you up to your end until you give me the answers I deserve. I've lived in the dark long enough."

We face off just feet apart, and I know he sees the resignation in my face. "Just go home, Cecelia." He ducks into his car, slamming his door before he speeds off.

Chapter Thirty-Six

I TOSS OFF the duvet, covered in sweat, my limbs aching as an agonized cry leaves my lips. I'd chased Sean through the trees all night, begging him to stop, but he just kept running, and he refused to look back.

"Damnit!" I hurl my water bottle across my room, and it smacks the wall before landing on the carpet just in front of my moonlit French door, the remaining water steadily leaking out.

It's my subconscious I'm constantly battling. Waking hours are far easier, but every night or every other, in some way, I grieve one or all of them.

And it's pathetic because they're almost always dreams of rejection.

I beg, I plead with them not to leave me, to love me back, to forgive me. Just for once in these dreams, I want to be angry, to tell them that they're liars, that they never deserved me, or my loyalty, my devotion, my ever-faithful heart. Still, it's always them I'm chasing after, begging their forgiveness, begging for absolution, begging for my feelings to be returned.

Even with the strength I display on the outside during my waking hours bringing grown men to their knees in my business dealings, in my dreams, I'm forever weak. And my mind won't relent in making me remember that it won't reason its way back into the truth of today, not yesterday. Unable to keep the effects from trickling in, I dial the number and pray she picks up.

"Talk to me," Christy says in a sleepy voice.

"I'm only getting worse. This place is only making it worse."

"I'm here."

"I'm sorry," I sigh, eyeing the clock. "I know it's late."

"I have a baby sucking on my boob, and I'm watching Insta Videos; trust me, I'm not mad."

"Kiss him for me."

"I will."

We sit silently for a few seconds. She's waiting.

"I'm such an idiot. Everyone has moved on."

"I'm your best friend, and I'm telling you that you went robotic the minute you got back from that godforsaken place. You haven't been the same since that year. And I'm not saying I don't love you and all your malfunctions, but I see your face when you think no one is watching. You had three boyfriends who screwed with your head and your heart, one of whom died in a car accident, and you never got to grieve him properly."

Guilt gnaws at me, but the secrets I have to keep.

"Can I ask you something, Cee?"

"Stupid question. Of course."

"Did you get pregnant?"

"What? No. Not at all. Nothing like that." I'm weak. I

can't talk to her this weak. I've been holding my secrets with me safely for too long. "It was just another bad dream. I'll be fine."

"Look. Eventually, I'm going to run out of kids to steal my sleep and suck my tits into something scary, which means murder for you someday when you wake me in the middle of the night. I want you to be happy. If that doesn't include a future with Collin, fine, if it's going back to the scene of the shitshow to make peace, fine, but make sure it's for *you*, Cecelia. You've suffered enough at those bastards' hands."

"I will."

"Good. Remember why you left."

"Trust me. I can't forget it."

"And don't forget who the fuck you are. CEO and all-around badass. You make grown men cry every day."

"Thank you. I love you."

"Love you, too."

I manage to get through three-quarters of my presentation, and I can feel his heavy stare on me. It's our first morning meeting. Tobias has already fired everyone on the board. Together, we have the task of turning the plant from a corporation structure to employee-owned. I won't bother to ask him what he's doing with the other plants, because I'm sure once he sees my plans for this one, maybe he'll make similar changes to the others. Ryan sits at the table along with one of Tobias's assistants, Shelly, as I go through the presentation—I worked half the night on—a step-by-step plan specific to the Horner Tech to right the wrongs of the past. It will give the faithful workers incentives along with better healthcare and retirement options. "Their lives won't change overnight, but oh, what a difference a year can make."

I pause after voicing that thought aloud, feeling the full weight of the attention of a man I was sure only existed in my dreams.

"Cee?" Ryan asks as I stand there, completely wrapped up in the memory of a warm summer night filled with toe-curling kisses, wine, of lightning bugs, of a magical place we created where no one else existed, and we recognized each other.

"Cee?" Ryan prompts again as I try to find my place.

"Sorry." I clear my throat, feeling fire lick the side of my face and down my neck. I haven't spared Tobias a glance, but the entirety of the outdated boardroom has been crackling with energy since he entered it.

"Within the next year," I continue, "not only will we have given the employees incentives to stay, but we'll have created and budgeted for *twelve* new supervising positions."

"I already have plans in place." It's the first time Tobias has spoken up, and my eyes lift to his.

"I just wanted to give you some options. This is what I do."

He doesn't waste breath with his retort. "I've been doing it longer. Is that all?"

"Okay, let me word it better," I snap. "Plan B is what's happening."

Ryan speaks up, biting Tobias right in the ass. "It's a condition of the contract."

Tobias doesn't spare Ryan a glance and gives me a dead stare.

"I'm creating jobs, not ruining your plans."

"Debatable," he counters and stands.

"I have fifteen minutes left," I object. His eyes roll over my form-fitting pantsuit. I may have spent a little more time than usual on my appearance this morning.

"You're doing what you want, why does it matter if I'm here?"

"Your presence at these meetings is also in the contract," Ryan counters as Tobias finally shifts his focus. And the result isn't pretty.

"You going to lick the bottom of her stilettos when she's done here?"

"She's not into foot kink," Ryan retorts with a sure smile.

Tobias's eyes drift up to mine, the look in them enough to condemn me. And now he knows I've slept with my lawyer. I glare at Ryan, who shrugs, giving me a thorough and appreciative sweep Tobias does not miss.

"Gentlemen, tuck your penises away and take a breath," I snap. "This isn't about who has the most authority here. This is about thousands of workers and their future and what's right for them. *I* don't have to be right. Let's just come to an agreement on what's best for *them*."

Shelly speaks up. "Agreed. What we have planned is very similar; I'll cross-reference our prospectus with what you've got, and we can work together to get the kinks out."

"You're speaking out of turn," Tobias scolds her.

"I don't lick shoes or wipe asses, Mr. King, that's why you hired me." She doesn't miss a beat. "Cecelia, I think this is brilliant, and since *I'm* the one who'll be getting this information together and out to the masses, I would love to hear your last fourteen minutes."

I bite my lips to hide my smile as Tobias's eyes narrow at Shelly before he takes his seat. "Floor is yours."

I can practically hear his thoughts—*your move*.

Ryan chuckles, and he and Tobias stare off for a second before they both turn expectant eyes back to me.

And this is just day one.

Fuck.

Chapter Thirty-Seven

I CAN'T HELP my smile shortly after our meeting when Tobias walks into the office across the hall from mine. Floor-to-ceiling windows create no barrier, giving us little privacy so he can't, at all, avoid seeing me during working hours. I feel his hesitation as Shelly guides him through the set-up of his workstation. I feel a lick of heat from his stare before he finally takes his seat. Transitioning from corporate to employee-owned isn't a matter of signatures or a one and done. It will take weeks of careful planning to work out the details, and I plan on using the time wisely.

He can't avoid me. But he's damn sure going to try. Hours later, we duel on our keyboards, and every so often, I feel the lift of his head and the weight of his stare. He's been listening to my phone conversations all day, his door open. I have loose ends to tie up before I can entirely hand the business over to Collin, who also isn't speaking to me. He's had his assistant email me with questions about the pressing matters. And I get it. I understand. But it still stings.

Ryan has been planted in the office next to me for most of the day, and the crackle I feel brewing only intensifies as the hours pass. But I forge on, intent on using all my tools to make the transition smooth and beneficial to the employees. Because I've been in their shoes, literally. Ryan heads to the breakroom for another cup of coffee when I crack my neck and look up to see Tobias working diligently on his laptop. His shoulders tense the minute he feels me eyeing him, but he keeps at a steady pace. He's in a pinstripe suit today that makes him look regal, like an old-world gangster. It's so fitting. He's so perfectly manicured that he looks completely out of place in the dump we've been stationed in. The bottom floor has a distinct stench of mold, and the ceiling tiles are heavy with residual water and stained brown. I decide to shoot off an email to Shelly to see if we can find a little wiggle room in the budget for a cheap remodel. I've just sent it off when Ryan strides back into the office, our coffee forgotten.

"Cee, we got him. Jerry Siegal." I wince as Tobias's head snaps up from where he sits, and Ryan hands me his cell phone. I go to speak, but Ryan jerks his head, insisting I put him on speaker.

"Hell no, I'm not missing this."

And I can't deny him this. We've been working on this for a solid year. Feeling the livid eyes of the man across the hall, I shake off the ill-feeling it gives, unwilling to let it get to me, and hit the speaker button.

"Jerry, how are you?"

"You fucking bitch," he seethes on the other end of the line as Tobias stands and walks over to the doorway of my office. I turn my back on him and begin a slow pace behind my desk just as Shelly walks in with an arm full of folders.

"Don't be such a spoilsport, Jerry. You'll serve no jail

time. You can take that neglected wife of yours on a long vacation. She seems to need it after, what? Her second suicide attempt this year? You really should be spending more time at home."

"I'm going to fucking end you, Horner."

I glance at Tobias, whose eyes are blazing and smirk. "I'm afraid you'll have to get in line, and it's a long one. Growing by the minute."

Ryan sits in the seat next to me, sporting a shit-eating grin as Jerry continues his tirade. "It's not enough your snake of a father—"

I wave a hand though he can't see me. "Roman saw you for the sucker you were and made moves on you because you were weak prey. So, instead of licking your wounds, being innovative, and coming back a more worthy adversary, you decided to one-up him and became even more of a waste of human space. I'm guessing your phone is lighting up right now with investors ready to back out. You might want to use this time wisely instead of making idle threats."

"I'm going to—"

"Like I said, you'll have to get in line." I lay my hands on my desk and look directly at Tobias. "And let's make one thing perfectly fucking clear. I am not my father, and I'm not his daughter and one more threat from you, and I'll finish the job he failed to do." I cut the line as Ryan shakes his head and stands, we exchange an amused look before bursting into laughter.

"We did it," he says, beaming.

"Couldn't have done it without you," I reply. "All right, you know the drill. Just make sure we're covered."

"On it," he says, pulling on his jacket. "And I'm going

to grab us a bottle. Something fancy. That French wine you like. What's it called?"

I swallow, unwilling to look at Tobias. "Louis Latour, but you won't find it here."

"I'll find something," he assures. I don't miss the cock salute Ryan and Tobias share before he walks past him. I finally lift my gaze to Tobias, who looms in the doorway, looking like he's about to splinter into flames. I'd nearly forgotten Shelly, who eyes the two of us from where she lurks just behind him.

"I have no idea why I came in here, so there's my excuse to leave."

As soon as she's out of earshot, Tobias steps inside and slams the door so hard the windows rattle.

"What in the hell do you think you're doing?"

"My job."

"Cecelia, you don't fuck with Jerry—"

"Oh, but you were. You were making moves. I beat you to it. You should stay and celebrate with us."

"He's not the guy—"

"He's exactly the guy," I argue. "The *head*, not the foot. Your words. I know what I'm doing. I have all the makings of a federal case being couriered to his desk right about now to ensure I live to fight another day. Something happens to me or anyone within my company, or any others close to us, he goes to prison for *life*."

"It's fucking dangerous," he snaps, taking two strides in, placing his thick fingertips on my desk.

"I'm aware I'm stacking up enemies. I do what's necessary to ensure my safety and the safety of those who work for me. But this is my side gig, and it's none of your business.

369

And who are *you*, of all people, to preach to me about what I do under the radar?"

"I gave that information to you in confidence," he snaps.

"Dear Daddy's old business partner needed to be put down, Tobias. So, I used the information for good. You can't honestly tell me you weren't aware of what I've been doing all this time."

"Those were little fish."

"Only the minnows you were aware of," I counter. "The ones I purposefully fed you. When it comes to me these days, you *don't know everything*. Not anymore."

"Jerry's not just the fucking head, Cecelia. He's the neck too. You can't snap the neck and not expect—"

Scowling, I shake my head. "I *expect* opposition. I expect someone to best me. And at some point, someone will," I repeat his words from years ago. "I'm also aware that what I don't know *will* hurt me. But I'm playing the game, I'm on the board, Tobias, and have been for years. I don't need or want your permission to do it. And I damn sure don't want your advice. It's my decision which heads to hunt."

"You're asking for war."

"I declared it long ago, and I'm already in battle. I came out guns blazing because it's the only way to do it. I'm playing my part."

Seconds pass as we stare off, and I swear I see a swell of pride in his eyes before it disappears.

"This is what you saw in your father's boardroom all those years ago."

I nod. "I dreamed a thousand dreams, but this was the first one."

"You didn't tell me." He has the audacity to sound hurt.

I step around my desk and cross my arms, leaning on the edge of the desk next to him.

"Sorry if it's not the part you decided for me to play when you sent me away to live out some other fictional reality." I huff with contempt. "What exactly did you see for me after I left here? A two-car garage, a picket fence, a tire swing out front? I'll have all that when I'm ready, but for now, I've taken my position. And *that* head was *mine* to take. I have it on good authority Jerry's the one who sent Miami."

"Jesus Christ." He fists his hands at his forehead.

"Take it up with anyone you want, but don't preach to me about what's dangerous." I push off my desk. "I made friends with dangerous. We're intimate now. We're in bed together. The Beretta in my purse has *real* bullets. I paid for it with *real* money. In *my club*, we know the worth of a woman's intellect. And *fuck* a fort, I want them to *see* who's taking them down."

Tobias grips me by the neck, his eyes roaming my face. "You want a pat on the back? You want my approval for making stupid moves?"

"It wasn't a stupid move. It just wasn't yours." We're so close now, anyone who came in would feel the whirring. Reaching back, I release his fingers one by one, and he allows it before I step away. "Rest assured, Mr. King, that was my last move for some time. I've been thinking a lot about my other dreams."

He eyes the ring on my finger and turns before throwing open the door and marching over to his office. Confused, I watch him rip a box open before he flips his office light off. A second later, he comes back into my office and slams a bottle of Louis Latour onto my desk. "I guess congratulations are in order."

I don't bother to correct him. "Don't suppose you have a corkscrew?"

He leans in, his tone lethal. "If you keep fucking with me, Cecelia, I'm going to make this hurt."

I shrug. "Of course, you will."

He turns and strides out of my office and out of sight. Sitting by my desk twisting the ring on my finger, I stare into his dark empty office. And the next day, it stays empty.

Chapter Thirty-Eight

"HORNER," THE JAILOR calls just as I finish out my fourth hour behind bars.

Ryan eyes me through a small window as I sign for my possessions and account for them in a plastic bag before I'm buzzed through another door. It's only when we're outside that his lecture begins.

"What the hell are you doing?"

"What do you mean?" I ask, tugging my coat tightly around me.

"Don't play stupid. You got arrested for going a hundred and three in a fifty and caught with nearly an ounce of weed. What do you call that?"

"A fantastic Thursday afternoon?"

"This isn't funny!"

"Depends on who you're asking." I frown. "And that was some damn good weed. I guess I'll have to go back to that deli."

Ryan blinks at me like I just shot him.

"I was just feeling nostalgic."

"Who in the hell are you?" he asks, eyeing me.

"Relax, you can get the charges dropped. They didn't even fingerprint me. It was a power play. He wanted to send a message."

"You mean—"

"Shhh," I laugh, darting my eyes left and right. "Dare not say his name."

"Cecelia, this isn't funny. I looked into him. He owns half this town, including the hotel I'm staying at."

"The police too. And I'm aware. And I asked you specifically *not* to do that."

"So, you are aware Exodus Inc—"

"Very."

"He's a bigger player than Jerry was."

"Operative word for Jerry being *was*," I counter.

"I don't trust him," Ryan grabs my elbow and escorts me to the parking lot.

I sober. "Neither do I."

"Then why are you poking this bear?"

"I told you, he owes me."

"He had you thrown in jail. I don't think you should plan on collecting."

"I will. Don't you see it's working?"

"Yeah, I can see how you would think that," he snaps sarcastically.

"Tobias is a different animal. But I need you to trust me."

"This town is starting to freak me out."

"Feeling eyes on you everywhere, huh?"

"It's not funny.

"Oh, but it is. I've got him right where I want him."

"Only if that's annoyed."

"Exactly."

"I really hope you know what you're doing."

"I do. Kind of."

He sighs. "I can get the possession charge dropped, and the ticket reduced to something less criminal, but you aren't getting your car back."

I pause my walk. "What?"

"There was a van on the road, and so they accused you of street racing. They're impounding your Audi for a minimum of thirty days. I may be able to wipe the charges, but small towns like this will suck you dry with penalties to make their quota."

"It's fine."

"It's not fine, that was fucking reckless. What are you doing?" he asks as he escorts me to his car. I go to take the keys, and he jerks his head. "Hell no. You're lucky you got to keep your license."

"Fine." I sigh and get in when he opens the passenger door.

"This is not like you. What is happening here?"

"I'm sorry, Dad. Let's just pay the fines, and I'll figure a car out."

"I've already got a rental lined up. But, Cee—"

"I had a moment," I admit sheepishly. "It was stupid. It's over."

Once behind the wheel he regards me carefully. "You've been having *moments* since we got here."

"I know, okay? I know. I've just been feeling a little restless lately."

"What exactly happened here?"

"Too much to explain, and too unbelievable for you to imagine."

I turn to him, resigned. I trust Ryan with my life. He's

the one and only person who's helped me with my side hustle in bringing the most notorious down. He's proven himself time and time again. "Am I really losing you?"

"Yes. Answer the question."

"I did answer you, just before you resigned."

"This shit right here is why I'm not changing my mind."

He starts the car and takes off, driving me toward my father's house.

"I don't want to go back there."

"Tough shit. You need to really think about what you're doing. You've all but declared war on a man who does nothing but glare at you."

"Haven't noticed." I stare out the window as clusters of evergreens pass in a blur. "I'm sorry for the trouble."

"It's fine, Cee, just, I'm worried." He glances over at me. "Just tell me how I can help fix the *real* problem."

"You can't. No one can. He knows what I want, and until he gives it to me, I'm stuck here in limbo." I cover his arm with my hand over the console. "You can go home. I'm set up here now. I have to see this through."

"Look at what just happened. You think I'll leave you here to deal with it alone?"

"It's the only way to deal with it," I say, resigned. "It's time, Ryan. I've got to do this myself."

I turn back to the passing landscape and see we're already on the long road back to the house. "Our business is concluded; it's all personal now."

I can feel his blue eyes on me but decide not to acknowledge it as he pulls up to the gate, and I give him the code. He whistles in appreciation as we draw closer to the house. "Nice."

"It's a great big fucking lie."

He frowns. "What do you mean?"

"I mean there's no life inside that house. It's haunted. Want a tour?"

"I do, but I won't."

"Why?"

"Because I'll try to kiss you. And you won't let me."

"Ryan—"

He grips the wheel, irritated. "I fucking hate this. I hate the fact that I have to go home and find another job." He turns to me. "But I will. And I'll find another woman to love. A more beautiful woman, a smarter woman, a woman who isn't in love with someone else. Should be easy," he drawls sarcastically.

I lean over and kiss his jaw. "You will find her, Ryan. I know you will. Don't settle. And when you resent me a little less and love her a lot more, please reach out to me. I already miss you."

"Are you sure?"

"Yes. I've got me. You've done your job."

He shakes his head. "This doesn't feel right. I can wait."

"I'm under his protection here. He'll be hard-pressed to admit it, but you don't have to worry about my safety. Trust me. I'm not. Go home. Find that job, but take a salary until you do. But I know someone who could really use you."

"It won't be the same."

"Collin needs you more than I do right now."

He nods. "Way to guilt me, Cee." He runs a hand over his jaw. "Fuck, I feel like my band is breaking up."

"It's just life. People come and go. But I don't want to

lose you, totally. Not you, Ryan. Promise me that you'll eventually reach out to me."

"I will. I was going to stand by and watch you marry another man. I promise we're good." He runs his hands along the steering wheel before bringing his dejected gaze back to mine. "I had to try, didn't I? Isn't that why you're here?"

I nod. A piece of my heart breaking. This is the damage I've caused by just showing up to Triple Falls. By setting Collin free. Another casualty to add in the wake of my reckless heart. "I love you," he says with surety. "No matter what."

"Love you too."

Defeated, he thumps his head back on the rest and turns to me. "Now get out of my car, you reek of weed and teenage angst."

Smiling tearfully, I step out and stare up at the house. Feeling my hesitation, Ryan speaks up from where he sits behind me.

"He loves you, you know." I turn back to where he sits. "Not that I'm encouraging this shit because let me make myself clear, I hate him. He's a pompous, French asshole. But no man can rage that much over a woman who means nothing to them. He's fighting it."

"Thanks for that."

"I would wish you luck, but the asshole is toast."

If only that were true. Then it might make all my sacrifices worth it.

"Call me when you land?"

"I'll text you." He drops his gaze as I step away from the car.

Ryan's been in my life for years, and I can't imagine not

seeing him on the regular. I've dismantled my life, my company. People I love and work for because of a fucking bad dream, because of a past I can't outlive. And my resentment only grows.

The gravity of it strikes me as I close the passenger door and he drives off, granting me the freedom, per my request, to face this *alone*.

Your move, Mr. King.

Chapter Thirty-Nine

THE FIRST FOUR days of the following week, Tobias avoids me at all costs by locking himself in his office when he decides to show up after missing every morning meeting. I don't bother to call him out on it, because it's pointless. Regardless of his intentions to block me out, Shelly and I have spent endless hours going over the financials and programs to be set in place. And for the most part, we've accomplished a lot. If I left now, I'm confident she would see it all through. Tobias has been working on similar ventures most of his career, but I'm not quite done yet, and it's my loyalty to the workers that will keep me here to see it through. But the fact that he's avoided me so artfully makes my mission that much harder. But even on the days he keeps his office sealed, I can feel his curious stares and the weight they hold. I have no idea what it's going to take to get my answers, but the more time that passes, the more I'm starting to believe I'll never get them. And for that, my anger only grows.

Desperate for a friendly face, I park my rental and exit the car, locking it up before I make my way through the door. A bell jingles at my arrival.

"Be right there," she calls from the dressing room. The shop has changed in appearance; newly renovated, fresh paint on the walls, a new and improved logo. As I search the rack for new dresses intent on helping her make her quota for the month, I smile. It's good to know some things haven't changed.

Tessa rounds the corner, her focus back on the woman in the dressing room. "Let's try a size up." She turns in my direction. "Feel free to look arou—" She stops mid-step, mid-sentence when she spots me in the middle of her shop.

"Hey, Tessa. Been a long time," I smile, giving her a little wave a second before her eyes drop. She bites her lip before walking past me to a rack. When she finds the dress size she's looking for, her eyes again lift to mine. "How are you, Cecelia?"

I revive my smile, baffled by her initial greeting. Is she angry I left without a goodbye? It's not like we were girl-friends. We never ventured out together.

"I'm good. In town for a few weeks, and I wanted to stop by and see how you're doing."

She dips her chin. "Good. Give me a second."

Maybe I expected too much, but her reaction was not at all what I hoped for. Rattling with uncertainty, I sort through a rack, grabbing a few dresses in my size before she reappears. Her hair is a little longer, but she looks very much the same. Curvier in the hips but still a stunning blue-eyed blonde. She's got a bit of color despite the winter temperatures. And before she saw me, she looked . . . happy. She approaches me, just a little shorter in stature, and addresses me with a lifeless tone.

"So, who are we dressing you for today?"

I frown. "Just me. I haven't been back in ages, and I just really wanted to see you and stop by and pick up a few dresses. I love what you have in here. How is business?"

"*Business* has been good for a *really* long time," her words are laced with a little contempt. And I feel the stab as she eyes me. "You look . . . incredible."

"Thank you." I almost want to make my reply a question because of the way she said it.

"You always were gorgeous." This is not a compliment.

And I'm no longer hurt, I feel insulted. And I'm not as beat around the bush as I used to be. "Tessa, have I done something to—"

"I'm ready, Tessa," the lady calls from the small dressing room, exiting the door. "Come see what you think."

Tessa's eyes roll over me before she tears them away. "Some people just don't know when to give up," she mutters, "I'll be back."

Briefly, I consider taking cover before she does return. The last thing I need is another confrontation with someone I once considered a friend. But the way she's regarding me, it's as if I'm raining piss all over her parade.

I pick out a few more dresses as Tessa checks the woman out. I step up to the counter with an armful, and she rings me up. It's the diamond on her finger that draws my attention while she bags them, and then it dawns on me.

Oh, Karma, you disloyal bitch.

When I tried to play matchmaker with her and Tyler years ago, I'd been vetting her for the wrong man.

"Tessa—"

"Tyler wasn't the one who walked in my shop after you left. It's Roberts now," she says, lifting biting blue eyes to mine. "We named our son Dominic. He'll be four next week. Baily is two. We named her after his grandmother. But you never did get to meet her, did you?"

Fighting the lump in my throat, I shake my head as Sean's wife holds out her hand. "That'll be one seventy-three."

Fumbling with my purse, I hand my card over as she cashes me out.

"Tessa, I didn't realize—"

"I often wondered what I'd say to you if you ever came back here." Her tone is no longer full of accusation, but curiosity as she walks around the counter with the bag in her hand. "I guess it shouldn't matter that you got him first, only that he's mine to keep." There's not a trace of fear or malice in her tone. She's confident in her marriage.

"I'm nothing but happy for you both."

I bite my lip as she hands me my bag. "You should grab another dress on your way out, on me. It's the least I can do. After all, you're the reason I have my family."

Emotions warring, I rip my eyes away. What can I say? There's nothing to say. I feel more like an outsider than I ever have.

Sean's wife.

She's probably in on more secrets than I can possibly imagine. Speechless, bag in hand, I turn to leave, and she stops me by speaking up.

"I'm sorry, Cecelia. You didn't deserve that. But I just can't look at you without thinking about the beginning." She lets out a labored breath. "It took me a long time to get close to him. At one point, I almost gave up. And when I found out it was you who . . ." our eyes lock. "I guess I started to resent you a little and your place with him. All those days I dressed you . . ." she shakes her head as if clearing the memories and shrugs, but I feel the weight of the act. "Small towns can be a bitch, right? But that was a long time ago. I can't fault you for being with him, can I?"

Tears threaten as I look back at her and imagine her struggle to try and build something with a man who was closed off due to the loss of his best friend and the woman who he felt betrayed him.

"I don't know what to say." Guilt eats me alive, and she gives me a solemn nod. I palm the handle on the door. "You have to know I'm no threat to you. I would never—"

"*He* would never," she corrects me confidently. "But he's not why you're back."

She knows.

She knows my history. And I could give her a number of reasons for my sudden appearance that has nothing to do with her husband, but she's no fool, and she's not out for blood.

"Be careful, Cecelia. You know well not everything is what it seems to be."

It's not a warning. These are words of caution from an old friend. She's throwing me a bone, and I accept it. She's not threatening me, but she clearly resents the fact that I'm here.

And she's not alone.

I say the only thing I can as the winter wind whips at me from where I stand with the door partially open. "Take care, Tessa."

Chapter Forty

Heavily buzzing, I enter the dark, dank bar as a flood of memories come rushing back. Not much has changed. The floor littered with the same small round tables and cheap wooden chairs. The walls glow with a slew of neon signs. The only addition is a thinly carpeted stage and karaoke machine set up next to the jukebox.

"Cecelia?"

Behind the bar, Eddie stands scrutinizing me. I greet him with a smile as visions of the past swim in my head. "The Boys of Summer" by Don Henley drifts from the jukebox as if welcoming me back to that time, in this place. The lyrics haunting, fitting, wrapping me up inside them as I sink back into the history I lived here.

"Hey, Eddie."

"You shouldn't be here," he says as I approach the bar. "He won't like it."

No question of who *he* is.

"Yeah, well, I have an issue with management, and I think it's time we settled it. I'll have a Jack and Coke."

He slowly shakes his head while toweling off a pint glass.

"You really aren't going to serve me?" I blow out a breath of frustration. "Really, Eddie? I thought we were friends." I should know better by now. I'm starting to go blind from the gleam of the "Scarlet A" on my chest. I left Tessa's dress shop feeling like the Whore of Babylon. From the reactions of the people I used to feel safest with, I've been reduced to nothing but an old hood groupie.

"You shouldn't be here, Cecelia," he repeats.

"Don't worry. I brought my own." I pull my half drained brown bottle from my purse and lift it for him to see.

"You can't bring that in here."

I pull out my wallet and place a hundred down. "Then give me one."

Reluctantly, he pulls a bottle of Jack and a glass up from behind the bar, and I slide the money over. He shakes his head, refusing it. "Thanks, Eddie."

"He's going to have my nuts for this."

"But you're good at keeping secrets, aren't you?"

He grunts, and I push the money toward him again. "Can I have some change?"

He exchanges the bills in the cash drawer. And I take a few of the singles and stuff the rest in his tip jar. "Good to see you, too."

I lift the bottle and glass, and he stalks off to tend to a man perched at the bar while eyeing me with warning.

A warning I ignore.

I set my things at the table closest to the jukebox, tumbler in hand, and search through the endless music and pause when I see it.

"Keep on Smilin'" by Wet Willie. The song Sean and I danced to in the street. I searched for it the day after the festival and kept it on repeat for days—reliving those short minutes we spent together before he left me without a word.

And I'd just had a run-in with his wife.

His beautiful wife, who he has two children with.

I toss back a good amount of liquid, trying to extinguish one burn with another. Why in the hell do *I* have to be the one to pay the highest cost for our shared past?

Because it's the way it is.

Because I'm the villain.

Because I'm the one encroaching on the reality of now with my hang-ups over the past.

I punch in the numbers and glance around the mostly empty bar, before shrugging off my blazer and taking my seat.

When the music starts to play, my eyes instantly water.

I can't seek him out now, and I'm terrified to run into him. Terrified of what his reception will be. If it's half as scalding as his beautiful wife's, I don't know if I'll survive it. The floodwater that separated us years ago is now stale, murky, and unrecognizable. No way to wade through, no way to get around.

I can't go back there. I can't move forward without my answers. I thumb my engagement ring and decide to box it in the morning. It's going to be the most painful step to fully let go of my future—of Collin—before I make peace with the past. But that's the order of things, and it's time. I didn't come back to drown. I came back in search of my kick. Lost in my thoughts, a masculine scent invades me before a familiar voice whispers in my ear.

"Can I have this dance?"

I turn my head, and my jaw drops when recognition kicks in. "Tyler?"

"Hey, Cee," he says softly, his eyes filled with warmth where he towers above me, his hands on the table. Stumbling back, I leap from my seat and lunge for him; he catches me easily, pulling me into a bear hug.

I hug him so tight he coughs out a chuckle of surprise. "I almost didn't recognize you in a suit."

"Hey, girl, hey," he croons softly, tightening his hold.

I pull away as his eyes glitter over me and tears sting my eyes.

"You have no idea how happy I am to see you."

He grins. "You are ten times more lethal than when I met you. You are fucking beautiful, woman."

"Thank you," I say, soaking him in. He's got a scar on his chin now. It's white, old. I run my finger along it. "What happened?"

"Battle scars," he says softly. And I wonder if it has anything to do with the last time I saw him, but I dare not ask. He shakes off his coat and takes a seat.

"I can't stay long."

"Drink?" I pour some of the whiskey into my glass and thrust it at him. I'm not above bribery for just a few minutes with an old friend.

He takes the offered glass and tosses it back, eyeing me the whole time.

"You know he's coming, right?"

"I don't know that. He probably won't bother. He's refused me at every turn. All I want is a conversation, and he won't even give me that."

"You being here is dangerous, Cee."

"My father is dead," I whisper quietly. "It's all *over*. I've signed over the company, and I'm here to tie up loose ends. Have another." I pour and push the drink toward him.

He smirks and accepts the whiskey. "Despite the growing population, this is still a small town. Your return is big news. You have a few people nervous."

"I've kept my mouth shut, and you damn well know it. I'm not here to spill hood secrets. I'm here to get answers."

"I know that, and you know that, but prying eyes don't know that." He lifts his chin, and I see a few of the men scattered around the bar eyeing us both. I meet their curious gazes one by one, unflinching, and bring my eyes back to Tyler.

"Oh, I'm aware. I just had a run-in with *Mrs.* Roberts."

He winces.

"Yeah," I say, sipping straight from the bottle. "It went a lot like that."

"And so you're here because?"

"A drink?"

He lifts a brow.

"Fine," I say, tossing more whiskey back. "Maybe I'm here to pick a fight."

"Cecelia, he's changed."

"We all have."

He slowly rotates his tumbler on the table. "I'd be lying if I said I wasn't happy to see you. But this won't end well."

"Damnit," I say, slamming the bottle down. "Fuck him. Okay? He's not the only one who lost. Don't you think I deserve answers?"

"You know better than to look for those."

"Why? Why does *he* get to be the one to decide?"

"You know why."

"I'm staying put."

He eyes me with concern. "Can I help?"

I shake my head adamantly. "I deserve them from him. He's the one who condemned me to hell." I can hear the anger in my tone. "He owes me, and I'm not leaving without answers." I swallow and shake my head. "I miss them," I say, lifting another shot to my lips. "Being here has made me sentimental, and I'm well aware I'm not wanted, but the day you put me in my Jeep . . ." our exchange reflects the pain of the memory. "You're in the know, but you can't imagine how being in the dark feels after all this time."

Pure guilt shines in his eyes. "Things got too fucked up. We didn't want it falling back on you."

"Don't think for one minute I'm not grateful. You saved my life. Dominic . . ." I choke on his name. "But it doesn't change the fact that I deserve answers."

"I guess I can't argue with you," he sighs. "But some things are better left in the past."

He lowers his gaze briefly as he continues to rotate his glass.

"I was sorry to hear about Delphine."

He sobers considerably before he pulls the bottle out of my hand and refills his tumbler. "You gave me a gift when you brought me to her house that day."

I just wanted to thank you.

His words from our run-in years ago, when Tobias and I were in the kitchen. Delphine is what he was thanking me for.

"You got back together?"

He nods. "We got nearly two years before she died in my arms. I can't even tell you how much those years meant. She got sober, and she fought hard. It was the most blissful time of my life." He swallows, his voice raw when he speaks. "But I won't ever regret it. And it's because of you that I had that time with her. She told me I healed her just before she passed." His Adam's apple bobs painfully. "She wasn't afraid."

A tear slides down my cheek as he looks through me, somewhere in the past with her. "I'm so happy you got that." I take the glass from him and pause it at my lips. "I want the same thing, you know? Some peace of mind after all that was lost."

"I'm pulling for you," he says. "But just tread lightly."

"I've done that long enough," I say defiantly.

He stands and kisses me on the cheek. "Gotta run."

"No, please no, stay," I beg. "I'll buy you a bottle of your own. I'm a rich woman now. Did you hear?"

He nods, pity lacing his gaze.

"Don't look at me like that. I'm fine."

"If you say so. Please, just be careful."

"I'm not afraid of him."

He flashes a boyish grin. "You're still the same insanely beautiful, smart-mouthed, hard-headed woman you were years ago."

"You act like that's a bad thing."

"I really have to go."

I stand and pull him to me. He wraps his arms around me, and I press off my toes and whisper in his ear. "I missed you too, ya know. When I left, I feel like I lost you, too."

"Same," he whispers before releasing me.

"Please stay. One more drink?"

"I can't. I'm flying out of Asheville in an hour."

"You don't live here?"

He shakes his head. "I haven't in years."

Years. "Are you going to tell me what you've been up to?"

"Little of this and that."

I roll my eyes. "I don't know why I asked."

"It's always better if you don't."

"I would say, don't be a stranger, but I know better." He pulls me into his hold one last time and releases me. "I wish you well, Tyler, be happy, okay?"

"I've got your back, Cee. *Always.*"

"I know."

He winks, and like most of the other men in my life, he disappears.

I shake my emotion away, knowing I'm being watched. Pouring another shot, I wrap my hand around the glass lifting my middle finger, my intent for those prying eyes clear, and swear I hear a chuckle come from a few of them. Another sip in, it becomes easier to ignore the watchful gazes of the men lining the bar.

Minutes pass, and I kick back, rocking to my music, to Sean's music, my limbs growing heavy with the buzz. Within the next few minutes, I'm digging through my purse, pulling out Sean's Zippo. I flick it open and closed, eyeing the guy closest to me a table over.

"Hey," I say with a smile.

He returns it. "Hey."

"Look, I know this might seem out of the blue, but would you happen to know where I can get a little weed?"

He grins and lifts from his chair, his beer in hand, and walks the few feet over to get to me. "I may be able to help you," he says, his eyes lighting as I scan his arm. No ink, and completely ignorant he's just stepped in a ring of fire.

"Oh yeah? How much?"

"Free, if you smoke with me."

I shake my head, regretting my decision to start the interaction. Ryan is right: I'm being stupid and reckless. But after today, I'm finding fewer and fewer fucks to give. It's the look in the stranger's eyes that has me on edge. "That's *not* what I'm looking for."

"It's all good. I don't bite."

"Well, *I do*. And I'm saying no, thank you. Forget I asked. It was a bad idea."

"Sounds like a good one to me."

"Trust me. It's not."

He inches closer, his eyes roaming over me, and I know he hasn't heard a word I've said.

"Seriously, never mind." As he draws near, my sixth sense kicks in, and bells begin to ring in warning. "I mean it, stay away from me."

"Don't be like that," he says, setting his beer on my table and leaning toward me with a clear look of intent. "We're just getting to know each other."

"Jack," Eddie speaks up from where he stands behind the bar, "you don't want to mess with that one."

"Yeah, Jack," I say, a faint if not imagined itch stirring on either side of my spine. "You should go."

Jack eyes Eddie and then me before pulling back, contemplating the warning while picking up his beer, but he's too late. Standing at the entrance of the seedy bar is the most lethal and beautiful of devils, and he's brought hell with him, the summoned flames dancing in his eyes.

Chapter Forty-One

I SLOWLY STAND, the chair scraping the floor behind me as I prepare for war. "Jack, there's an exit behind the bathroom," I whisper hoarsely. "You better take it."

Jack stands frozen as his threat sets into motion. Head dipped, an Armani-tailored imp, he moves toward us in a cloud seeming to create a wind of his own, his powerful arms extended, his menacing movements barely traceable as cocktail tables start to fly and explode on either side of him.

Flip. Flip. Flip. Flip. Flip. Flip.

Tables somersault and burst into splinters as if willed so by some invisible force as he makes his way toward me, punishment promised in his eyes while he leaves nothing but destruction in his wake.

Oh, fuck!

I've never seen him so angry. Terrified, I turn to Jack. "Jesus! Go!"

Jack's white as a sheet when he turns to haul ass toward the dark hall leading to the exit. I swallow as Tobias draws near, thankful for the whiskey thrumming through me, steadying my shake. He reaches me just as I lift the tumbler to my lips before he bats it out of my hand. The glass falls with the force of it, smacking the side of the table, the amber liquid splashing on my slacks before the tumbler shatters at my feet. It's then I realized the bar has cleared and the music's been cut off.

"I take it you aren't in the mood to dance?"

"I told you to leave."

"Come now. We should be celebrating. We're business partners."

"What the fuck, man," Eddie says as he surveys his destroyed bar, righting a table.

Tobias glares down at me without an ounce of regard for Eddie and his horribly renovated bar. "You need to leave. I'm not asking anymore."

"Or what?"

"Stop playing fucking games, Cecelia."

"You're the one acting like a child. I came here to have a few drinks."

"What do you want?"

"The truth! I want the truth! I want to know what happened!"

His jaw ticks as his acidic glare cleaves me to pieces.

I lift the bottle in offering. "Sure you don't want a drink?"

He slaps it from my hand, and it joins the pile of rubble on the floor.

"I mean, I know you're more of a gin man, but that was uncalled for." His face remains granite. "Jesus, Tobias. I just want to talk."

Murderous eyes roam over me, and my body responds to every inch his gaze sears over. He's so fucking beautiful, and his anger brings me back to the long nights we spent

395

exorcising our hate for the other in much better ways. He's aged incredibly, and I find myself aching to pull him closer, even in his furious state.

I lift my palms to his heaving chest and leave them there. His nostrils flare, but he allows it. "Do you ever think of me?"

"No."

"Liar," I drawl, with a watery smile. He grips one of my hands painfully and steps away from my touch.

"This is not a game."

"I know," I say softly. "There's a death toll. What's it up to now? Did you include me? Did you add us both in?"

My words seem to strike him where intended, and he darts his eyes away.

"Because I've been slowly dying every day since I left."

His jaw flares, and my fingers itch to touch it, to soothe his anger. He reads my thoughts, sneering down at me.

"You're drunk."

"I just want to talk. Please, *please*, talk to me."

He grabs my purse from the table and finds my keys before taking me by the arm like a child and making his way toward the back exit.

"Wait, please, Tobias, hold on." I grab my purse from him and gather the envelope of cash I withdrew this morning and set it on the table before addressing Eddie who's gazing around the bar with a helpless expression. "Sorry, Eddie. This should cover it." The look in Eddie's eyes tells me I won't be welcome back.

Tobias doesn't waste a second, dragging me past the bathroom before we burst through the back door. He unhands me as I stumble in my heels. The minute the night air hits me, I turn back toward the building and vomit.

"Putain." *Fuck*. Tobias pulls my purse out of the line of fire and steps forward, gripping my hair.

"It's just nerves," I say through a dry heave.

Another curse as I wretch again, and he unhands me, disappearing behind the door before it slams next to me. Completely empty, I pant, disgusted with myself that I can't keep it together. Being here, seeing him, his reaction to me, the emotions it's stirring is too much. It's like constantly being struck with a wrecking ball.

Tobias comes back a minute later with some bottled water, unscrewing the cap before he thrusts it toward me.

Humanity.

He's still in there. Somewhere.

I take the water and sip, looking up at him.

"Don't look at me like that," he snaps, pulling his cell phone from his pocket.

"Like what?" I nod toward his cell. "What are you doing?"

"Getting you a ride home."

"Why bother? I'm sure you would just love it if I disappeared over a cliff."

"Always so dramatic."

I tilt my head back against the brick and laugh. "You just destroyed a bar, and *I'm* dramatic?"

Tobias turns away from me, pulling a pack of cigarettes from his pocket before lighting one up.

"I wasn't planning on driving."

He doesn't spare me a glance when his call is connected. "Hey, get a blue light at the bar."

A pause.

"A ride." Pause. "Cecelia."

I faintly hear a voice on the other end. "They aren't a taxi service. You take her."

Sean.

"Get someone here, *now*."

"All tied up right now, *boss*. Deal with it."

Sobering, I walk over to where he stands. "Is that Sean?"

Silence on the other end of the line.

"I'll figure it out," Tobias snaps, ending the call and taking another drag.

"Since when do you smoke?"

"This?" he asks, before blowing out a plume of smoke. "*This* is just to keep my hands occupied to prevent myself from strangling you."

"Har har," I counter. "You never smoked when we were together."

"You mean all of the *five minutes* we were together?"

"Don't act like I don't know you. It's insulting."

He draws on the cigarette and glares at me.

"So, you have the cops in your pocket now, huh? Well, thanks for getting my car impounded, asshole. And if this isn't a game and you're not playing, then why the shady move?"

"You have no fucking business speeding around smoking dope."

"Last time I checked, my father's urn is sitting in his mansion."

"When are you going to fucking grow up? You need a reality check."

"Oh, trust me, this trip down memory lane has been nothing short of sobering. But if I'm going to suffer through it, I'm going to numb as much as I can, because no one seems to want to help me out here, you've made sure of it!"

"That's your cue to leave. But you seem to be missing those."

"And just who in the hell do you think you are telling me where I can and cannot be? You might own half the businesses in this town, but you don't own *me*. You think *I'm* childish? How childish is it to tell me I can't take a turn on your playground? Especially with the price of admission tattooed on my back!"

We glower at each other for endless seconds before he draws on his cigarette and tosses it, grinding it out with the heel of his glossed shoe.

It's the sound of a car door opening and closing that cuts our argument, drawing both our eyes to the source. All words fail me as a gorgeous, dark-haired woman approaches, her eyes on Tobias. She's polished from head to heel, her hair dark spun silk, a curtain of it draped over her shoulders.

She's stunning.

Stunning. And familiar.

"Alicia?"

Her eyes flit to mine. "Hello, Cecelia."

"I almost didn't recognize you." Though her smile has some genuine warmth, her brown eyes hold some grudge as she weighs the situation.

"It's been a long time," she concedes. "You look well."

My hair is plastered back with sweat, and I know I'm white as a sheet. There's vomit on my heels. She's being kind, cordial. The same sweet disposition of the girl I met all those years ago but . . . not at all a girl anymore. I'm still reeling from the change in her. She carries herself in a majestic way as she makes her way toward us, a far cry from the reluctant teenager I met years ago.

"Hey," she greets Tobias with a tone of familiarity.

His gaze softens as he addresses her. "Almost done here."

My hurt lurches in my chest as Alicia moves toward him, placing her hand on his jaw before leaning in . . . to kiss him. It's brief, but it's enough. The sight of it knocking the breath from me like a sledgehammer. She pulls back, and Tobias looks down at her, his eyes glittering with affection.

"Take the car," he says softly, and she nods.

"See you at home?"

Tobias nods in reply. "Sorry about dinner."

"You'll make it up to me," she whispers, "you always do."

My insides clang together as I watch their intimate exchange. Apart, they're stunning. Together, they're devastating. She grew up in the life, and she seems to have it together in a way I never will. She's perfect for him. The type to keep her calm despite any circumstance, to keep her emotions in check, a strong silent support. A true queen.

And I'm willing to bet she's never slept with his best friend or his brother.

I die a thousand times before she turns back to me, not at all intimidated by my presence, and that undoes me. I feel the stab soul deep. It's like losing him all over again.

"It was good to see you, Cecelia."

I can only nod, as white-hot jealousy eats me alive before she saunters away. She starts his Jag and makes her way out of the parking lot, and I stare after her for several ragged heartbeats before my eyes drift back to Tobias. My voice fails me for a handful of seconds before I finally speak.

"She's beautiful."

He nods, watching me closely.

"Good for you," I rasp out. "I was supposed to get married in two months, but I broke it off before I came here."

He slides his hands in his pockets, his expression unintelligible.

"I can see myself home. You should get back to her. I'll figure it out."

"Come on," he says, moving toward me, and I shake my head, refusing him.

He pulls my keys from his pocket, gripping my elbow. I jerk my arm away and he groans out in frustration. "Just get in the fucking car, Cecelia."

My chest screams for relief, but I know tears won't ever be enough to alleviate the unbearable ache.

"Were you going to tell me about her?"

"No point."

"Why? Because you knew it would hurt me? That's what you do best."

"This doesn't have to get any uglier."

"But you love seeing me in shreds. And you love to be the one to do it. So why hide her? You had to know how much it would hurt me."

He lowers his gaze.

"Look at me, you bastard!"

Blazing eyes flick to mine. "It's been six years, Cecelia. What did you expect?"

Not her. *Anyone but her.* Anyone but a woman capable of making him happy, of being the *right* woman at his side. Anyone but a woman who deserves him, anyone but a worthy woman. He scans the parking lot and clicks the fob to locate my rental. He wants no part of this conversation.

"She didn't fall for or fuck your brothers," I say, and his head snaps up. "She had a crush on Sean back when," I continue, "but I guess that's a minor offense compared to *me*."

Agony. Pure agony. It's nothing like I've ever felt, which surprises me because I thought I'd felt it all up until this point. I can only imagine it's nothing compared to what he felt when he witnessed and heard my confessions for the two men closest to him after the fact.

I was a fool to think that my sexual exploits wouldn't have consequences. They were fools to think so as well, but I seem to be the only one paying for them.

Either way, it's a punishment that I. Can't. Handle.

Not in my state, not with so much alcohol in my veins.

"I don't know what I expected."

Tobias comes for me as the threatening tears finally fall. "No." I shake my head over and over. "I left my fiancé. I left my whole life . . . I'm so damn stupid," I say as the first tear falls.

"Cecelia, don't—"

"What must you think of me now?" My breath hitches as my heart scatters at my feet. "Have you ever once missed me? Have you ever wondered what would have happened between us had it all gone down a different way?"

"I'm not doing this." He closes the space, gripping my elbow again and unlocks my rental with the fob before he ushers me inside, tossing my purse on my lap before leaning in to buckle me in.

"I've got it," I snap, clicking my seat belt before he rounds the car and gets behind the steering wheel.

He turns over the ignition, and I lean back cradled in the leather and just stare at him, utterly lost. I feel too damn much and always have. I don't care if he sees it now. Let him. My foolish heart brought me here, and it's been completely drained of all hope. So be it.

Because if he's truly moved on, if he loves her, if he's happy . . . I suffocate in my skin as I look over at him. He didn't want me to see her, or maybe he's glad I did. Maybe he's never taken me seriously because of my past with his brothers. But for me, what Tobias and I had was sacred.

Exposed and raw, I watch him in the dim blue cabin light as he turns out of the parking lot and onto Main Street.

"Tobias—"

"Just go to sleep."

"I've slept enough," I sniff, as tears I can't deny begin falling one after the other. "I was asleep my whole life until I came here."

"Cecelia," he sighs. "It was a long time ago. Everyone has moved on."

I reach out and tentatively stroke his jaw with shaking fingers, unbelieving he's sitting next to me. The minute my touch lands, his eyes close briefly. "It wasn't that long ago. Do you love her?"

"Love." He tilts his head, withdrawing from my touch. "It's always about love with you."

"That's why all this started, isn't it? The love of your mother, your parents, the love of your brothers, a promise to protect each other, and the ones who couldn't protect themselves." I swallow, my words coming out dry. "But you keep throwing me in the fire when I'm the one who loves you most."

He snaps his gaze toward me and stares at me for long seconds before focusing back on the road.

"I wish I could move on," I sigh, turning back to stare at the dark road ahead as we pass the rest of the city lights. "Collin, that was my fiancé, he didn't deserve what I did to him. I'll never forgive myself for hurting him."

I run my fingers along my cheeks, but it's useless. I'm not wasting a second with him. It's time to confess.

"That first year was the hardest." I turn in my seat to face him, my cheek resting on the fabric. "I got on the highway no less than a hundred times, on my way here, back to *you*. And the whole time, I prayed you were on your way for me too. That you didn't mean it when you sent me away, that you were grieving, and you didn't mean it when you told me not to come back."

Silence.

"School saved me in a way. In the summers, I fled to France. I explored every part of that country. It was a dream. I fell in love. It was everything I hoped it would be." I swallow. "I saw a few familiar tattoos while I was there. But you wouldn't know anything about that, would you?"

Silence. Not a single tell.

"I even took a trip to Saint-Jean-de-Luz. Your finish line is beautiful, Tobias. A dream." His expression remains stoic. "I was hoping so much that you *were* watching. Hoping that you were proud of me," I sniff as years of sadness and longing creep up on me. It's only been a few weeks and I'm unraveling. I was nowhere near prepared for this.

"See, in my *new* life, I couldn't make a move without you in mind, hoping every day you saw what happened mattered to me, *changed* me."

I study his face carefully, and he gives away nothing.

"I threw myself into school, into my plans. By the time

I graduated with my masters, I'd already started my company. I did it mostly for me, but the whole time I had you in the back of my mind. Hoping that you saw what I was doing was honoring Dominic." I stifle a sob and collect myself enough to speak. "Even though you all refused to let me in, I wanted to play my part." Throat burning, I get lost in the years I spent away. "Then Collin came along, and he was so . . . gentle, so understanding, sexy, so . . . safe to love, and I let him fall for me knowing . . ."

Tobias drives on, his expression impenetrable as if he's not even listening, but I know he hears every word.

"I wasn't the lonely girl anymore. I had a life, a business, friends, and a fiancé who adored me. I did everything I was supposed to do. I took all those steps to ensure I had a full life, a life I forced myself into because I had no choice."

He pulls onto the road leading to the house, and I will myself to finish.

"So, day by day, I lived this life, hoping it would be enough, praying that I could forget this place, forget you, hate you, but at night . . . when I dream—" an angry sob bursts out of me as the full weight of my fate overcomes me with grief. "The dreams won't let me forget. I've tried everything, and I can't move on. I can't. So that's why I came home, and you, God, I thought if I could just face this, it would make me stronger, braver, but all it's made me is a bigger fool." I shake my head. "I'm not supposed to admit this to you because of how pathetic it makes me, but I've been riddled with grief and guilt since I left, and I'm done lying to myself." I run my sleeve along my nose and gaze over at him to see him looking straight at me. "Because the life I truly want doesn't have a thing to do with perfection.

It's the farthest thing from safe, and the man I want is anything but gentle."

And, with that, I pass out.

I rouse to the feel of his hands. A faint caress on my breasts as he slowly unbuttons my shirt.

"Tu penses que tu peux juste revenir après tout ce temps et dire de telles choses . . ." *You think you can just come back after all this time and say these things . . .*

I stifle my moan as the silk is drawn away, leaving me in my lace bra. My nipples pebble under his breath as his hands faintly roam, the lightest brush of his fingers sending tsunami pulses up my spine. I fight the alcohol fog I'm drifting in and out of to bring myself back to him.

"Je baise mon poing tous les jours en pensant à toi." *I fuck my fist to you every day.* He unbuttons my slacks and slowly pulls them down. "Et je te déteste pendant tout." *And I hate you the whole time.*

Briefly, he buries his head in my neck, his warm, nicotine-laced breath stirring every memory of intimacy we shared. My limbs tremble as I rouse from my whiskey coma and fight myself to keep from clutching him to me. But I opt to play comatose, my obliterated hopes sparking with every word he speaks.

"Tu dis mon nom quand tu jouis?" *Do you call out to me when you come?*

Yes.

"Tu ne peux pas être ici. Je ne te laisserai pas voler mon âme une nouvelle fois." *You can't be here. I won't let you steal my soul again.*

I love you. I love you.

He runs his thumbnail beneath my lower lip. "Tellement belle." *So goddamn beautiful.*

Yours.

"Belle et destructrice." *Beautiful and destructive.*

Pot and kettle.

I hang onto every word like a lifeline, while the strength of the whiskey latches onto me, threatening to pull me back under.

"J'allais bien." *I was doing fine.*

Liar.

He lifts me, unfastening my bra, and pulls it away.

"Putain. Putain." *Fuck. Fuck.* "Tu es en train de partir. Ça n'arrivera plus." *You're leaving. This isn't happening again.*

Thick fingers trail up the sides of my breast as a low moan escapes me. His fingers still when I open my eyes. His are brimming with anger, lust, and resentment. I gaze back at my reflection in his flames.

"T'aimer m'a rendu malade et je ne veux plus jamais guérir." *Loving you made me sick, and I don't ever want to get well.*

I let sleep take me.

Chapter Forty-Two

I WAKE TO the sound of howling wind outside my window. I lift from unrestful sleep to see two Advil on my nightstand along with a bottled water. I down it all, the split in my head enough to have me contemplating spending the day in bed. Pulling on my robe, I opt for fresh air, moving onto my balcony through the French doors. I take in the early morning, the blanketing clouds gathering in the horizon and drifting closer. The chill in the air has me shivering where I stand when awareness pricks, and I glance over the railing and spot Tobias on one of the loungers next to the covered pool. He's still in last night's suit and a black wool trench coat. Reclined back, a lit cigarette pinched between his fingers, with his eyes closed.

He never left.

Despite the chorus of drums in my head, I dress quickly into warm clothes and make my way out onto the deck. I approach quietly and take a seat in the lounger next to him and drink him in. He's thirty-seven now, and at the time we were together, I thought we were ageless. Time didn't exist then, and time has done nothing but complement his bone structure, his build, his unparalleled beauty. It's then I recall his words from last night, his touch, the subtle but possessive strokes of his fingers, his heavily veiled affection for me as he undressed me from my soiled clothes.

I simply gaze at him, knowing he's aware I'm there. He pulls on his cigarette and lifts to sit, his eyes opening but focused on the textured cement beneath his feet.

"My first clear memory is of a red coat," he says softly. "It had black toggle buttons. It was hanging next to the door when my mother snatched it off the hook and wrapped me in it, fastening the buttons one by one. I could tell she was terrified."

"N'aie pas peur, petit. Nous partons. Dis au revoir, et ne regarde pas en arrière. Nous partons à l'aventure." *Don't be afraid, little one. We're leaving. Say goodbye, and don't look back. We're going on an adventure.*

"But she was scared. And when the doorbell rang and she answered it, a man I'd never seen smiled down at me."

"Beau? Dominic's father?"

He nods, flicking ash off his cigarette.

"He said he was taking us to America, and we were going to be happy there. He gathered us and the few belongings my mother packed into his car, and we left. That's all I remember about fleeing France. Being in that coat, my mother's fear, the red-headed stranger, and boarding my first plane."

He runs a hand down his shadowed jaw.

"And we were happy here, mostly. But my mother missed France horribly when we got to America. She didn't contact anyone. It was the price of fleeing from my father. Back then, he had a lot of connections and it was too risky. Over the years, I would catch her crying while sorting through old pictures, mourning her family. Her mother especially. But she loved Beau King, and it was easy to see. And he was good to me, strict but good. He saved us. She would tell me constantly that he saved us. And I believed her. The only memory I had of my real father was that day I told you about."

"Saint-Jean-de-Luz."

Another nod as he puffs on his cigarette.

Snow begins a lazy drift from the clouds above, and I sit idle, too afraid to break the spell.

"Not long after, her belly grew, and then one day, they brought Dominic home." His smile is faint, but it's there. "At first, I despised him. I didn't want to share my mother's attention." He gives me a sheepish grin. "So, I put him in a Tangelo orange box and took him out to the garbage. I put a can of his formula and bottle in there with him so he wouldn't starve."

"Oh my God." I can't help my laugh, and he chuckles with me.

"When she realized what I'd done . . . Well, it's the maddest I've ever seen her. I was spanked raw, but she never told Papa."

He shakes his head, his smile lingering. "The next day, my mother insisted I hold him. She set me up in her rocking chair and placed him in my arms."

He looks over to me, but he's a million miles away. "He was mine. From that minute on. He was *mine*."

I nod, a hot tear sliding down my cheek.

"Our English was pretty bad the first few years. We struggled quite a bit, and we were not at all prepared for the culture shock. I think Mom considered America the Wild West at the time. She was paranoid, and rarely let me play outside. She and Papa would have fights about it, and she would always win. She was so stubborn."

"Sounds familiar."

Tobias rolls his eyes, and I can't help my answering laugh.

"I hated school, kids being kids and shit, they made fun of my accent, my clothes. When I'd go home, I would take Dominic into my room. And I would play him music, my mother's old tapes."

This confession has my heart aching. The music. His mother's music.

He tosses his cigarette and slides his hands in the pockets of his trench coat, his thick hair falling along his forehead with the sweep of the wind. "He was the happiest baby. Constantly smiling, laughing, and he rarely cried. For a time, he was the one who made things okay. He helped us cope so much those first few years. He was such a joy. And eventually, things got better. Mom let me play outside. We adapted."

He sighs, eyeing the pack of French cigarettes lying next to him.

"My mom would always come home from the plant exhausted, but she rarely complained, but Papa would talk about the boss who robbed his employees, and they would fight. She would tell him to leave it alone.

"Je ne lui fais pas confiance. Il y a quelque chose dans ses yeux. Il est mort à l'intérieur." *I don't trust him. Something in his eyes. He's dead inside.*

"She used to beg him to drop it, tell him they were there on a work visa that Roman had helped them get, and they should be grateful. But Papa wouldn't let it go. He started leaving us alone at night, and often. I didn't pay close attention to everything, but they had horrible fights sometimes. I remember one night well because it was one of the rare nights Dominic was inconsolable."

I reach for his hand, and he runs it along his thigh, denying me. I ignore the sting of rejection.

"My parents were not the type to fight behind closed doors, so I would lock Dominic in the closet with me in the hall just outside their bedroom so I could keep an eye on my mother. Papa was never violent, but he was aggressive enough to scare me."

I cough out my sarcasm, and he looks at me pointedly. "Shut up."

"You got it, *apple*."

"He wasn't my birth father."

"But you are very much Beau's son."

"That's true." He lights another cigarette and inhales deeply.

"Papa started to talk to me after that. I think he was starting to resent Mom for not understanding that he was trying to do something good, not just for us, but for the other people who worked at the plant. He would take me on walks and give me long speeches on what it meant to be a man. To look out for others. I didn't think anything of it. I just thought he was trying to raise a good son."

"Do you think he knew that he was in danger?"

"Looking back now, I think he was losing faith in his hopes for building a life here. Nothing was going as he planned. They were exhausted, not gaining any ground." He inhales some smoke. "And then the meetings started. They happened in our townhouse, every second week of the month."

"The brotherhood formed there?"

Tobias nods.

"Frères du Corbeau." *Brothers of The Raven.* "I didn't pay much attention because I was only eleven. But one night, I got bored and hid on the stairwell, having decided to listen in. A few of them were calling for drastic actions. Delphine was one of them. You know she's the one who got my parents the job there."

I nod.

"She was on board with Papa. A few fights broke out that night, and my mother surprised everyone by standing and speaking out. I'm guessing it was the first time."

"C'est la peur qui va nous garder en colère, nous garder confus, nous garder pauvres. Nous devons cesser d'avoir peur des hommes comme eux, des gens qui profitent de nous. Si la peur vous arrête, la porte est grande ouverte. Nous ne pouvons pas compter sur vous." *It's fear that's going to keep us angry, keep us confused, keep us penniless. We have to stop being afraid of men like this, of the people who take advantage of us. If you're going to let fear stop you, walk out that door. We can't afford you.*

"I know now that, at one time, my mother was an activist, much like my birth father, and when she had me, she stopped her involvement. I think my papa's disappointment in her and the reason for their fights is that she refused to fight along with him. After she spoke, only one person left that night. The next week my parents died, and no one at that plant was talking. No one knew a single detail about what had happened. But Delphine found out the shift supervisor who wasn't even on the floor when they died, got a raise and a promotion shortly after."

"Confirming Roman's guilt." My stomach drops.

"That was the assumption. After that, Delphine took us in. And that's when Dominic started to cry, and often."

Snow begins to settle silently, coating the grounds around us.

"We grew up dirt poor. In some pretty shitty conditions."

"I saw."

Tobias pauses, eyeing me. "Her piece of shit of a husband left her a few months before my parents died. She drank a lot and was heavy-handed at times, especially with Dom when he started to act up. It wasn't all bad, but it . . ." he sighs. "Well, you saw."

I nod, batting a tear away.

"A few weeks after we moved in with Delphine, we got a curious visitor."

"Sean?"

"Yeah," he says softly. "He was younger, but he just kept coming around. He and Dominic took up together fast, and I was often in charge of watching them and walking them to and from school." Tobias shakes his head, a soft smile playing on his lips. "He was a fucking mess. His hair was always jacked, always. He was a dirty little shit, always hanging from the trees and never going home until way after dark. He used to sneak into my room at night, and the three of us would go off into the woods. He was fearless, even at five years old. Almost every morning, he tore off the clothes his mother had dressed him in and put on the same raggedy shirt. He refused to follow rules, even back then."

We share a smile.

"Tyler came along just after. We didn't have much at Delphine's, but we made do. And the men from the brotherhood never forgot my parents and were our saving grace. They would come by and give us treats. Sometimes they would send clothes and money by mail—little things to help us along the way. My aunt would allow it, and not long after they died, she started hosting meetings in her home. The more time that passed, the more time I would sit in. Delphine was far more extreme. Her ideas on how to fight back were argued about, but for the most part, she was the leader. There were only a handful of the originals left by then. Most of them had died out or left the cause because of what happened to my parents. But the more I listened in, the more I became involved, and on my fifteenth birthday, I stood and spoke for the first time."

"And they listened."

He nods.

"Right before I left for prep, I was running the meetings, networking to get more people. And Sean and Dom were starting to pay attention. My plans for the brotherhood had grown exponentially. I would come back home during the summers to be with Dom and Sean, who were slowly becoming more involved. Dom was taking over meetings and running the local chapter by the time I returned after my sophomore year of college, and that was the first time I laid eyes on you."

That's when Tobias lifts his eyes to mine and looks at me, really looks at me for the first time, and I feel it down to my toes.

He pulls out my library copy of *The Thorn Birds* beneath his jacket. It fits easily in the palm of his hand. My eyes widen with shock.

"You were there when I stole it?"

"Dominic lived at the library. It was his favorite place in the world to be. He despised Delphine most days because she was a nasty drunk, and escaped there when he wasn't out gallivanting with Sean. I was there to pick him up, and I ended up browsing while I waited for him. You were a row over when I spotted you, and I didn't pay you much attention until Roman walked up behind you and told you he would buy you books, and you didn't need to rent them. You rolled your eyes and called him a 'butt munch' under your breath before you stuffed this book in your pants."

Stunned by his confession, my eyes drift to the book in his hand.

"It's when I saw you that I knew you were just a kid. Innocent in this and with no knowledge of who your father truly was or his fucked-up business dealings. I knew you weren't close. He ushered you out, and I followed you both out to the parking lot. You looked so miserable, but you wore this faint smile on your lips. Like you were happy about your silent rebellion in stealing the book."

No doubt I was. It was the last summer I spent with Roman before we became estranged. Tobias runs his fingers over the tattered binding of the book. "You were just a kid, and I vowed that day to keep you out of it. I kept close tabs on you after, and when you didn't return after that summer, I assumed it was for good."

I rub my hands together. "So did I."

"Dominic was still in school, and I wanted to give us time to gain strength in numbers before we made any serious moves. Sean was already running the garage we bought with Dom's part of the settlement and heading up the meetings there. Dom secured his place before he left for college, and he made damn sure everyone knew of it. And Sean held it all down while we were both away."

Snow continues to drift between us, and I shiver in my jacket as Tobias stands and crushes out his cigarette. "I was twenty-four when I made my first million, and I began networking on a corporate scale by the time Dominic graduated high school. Tyler went into the service. Sean kept it together here. So, I spent my time between here and France, strengthening the network, finding old relatives to help us. By my twenty-fifth birthday, we were more of an international movement, not a small-town organization. And for a while, I lost sight of our original goal. So had everyone else, and over the years we only got stronger."

"And then I showed up."

He dips his chin.

"By the time you came back, we had hundreds of members in all combined chapters, and we were growing by the day. Dom had graduated MIT and made it his mission to eradicate future money problems by stealing chunks at a time from white-collar thieves that I hand-fed him, all the while stocking our arsenal and recruiting more brothers. It was only a matter of time with Roman, but when you got here, and Sean and Dominic discovered you, they moved in, thinking they had you under control."

I nod, knowing that story all too well.

"Now you know I was searching for my birth father, which is why I was distracted in France."

I nod.

"By the time I got to him, he was too far gone. I'll never really know who he was."

"I'm so sorry."

"It's fine." His eyes drop, and I know it's anything but fine. "I just couldn't leave him the way I found him."

"You did a good thing."

"Did I?" He swallows. "I don't know. The way my mother spoke about him." He shakes his head. "I don't know."

"He's being cared for, that's a good thing."

He runs his teeth over his lip and eyes me, and I know that part of the conversation is over.

"When I found out what was happening, of how they were hiding you, I flew home to handle it. And fuck—" he runs his hands through his hair, and it's all I can do to keep from touching him. His guilty eyes roll over me, and he darts them away.

"Their punishment wasn't just about you. I had to remind them of why we'd started this in the first place. I sent them to live with one of the partners I trusted in France. He kept them focused, let them in on everything I'd been building while I refocused on our original plan. I was one move and a handshake away from taking over when you and I struck our deal."

I'll still never be able to place how I should feel about the betrayal on all sides, nor the guilt of being Roman's heir.

Tobias sighs, setting the book on the lounger and clasping his hands together between his thighs. "I understood your need to care for her, Cecelia. And you had been through enough already. And I railroaded you out of anger when I returned. You were never supposed to be a part of this for good reason."

"You keep saying that, but that's not the way it played out."

"No, because I allowed myself to get lost in you the way they had."

I bite my lip, eyes stinging.

"I found myself wanting so much to protect you from it all because you were so innocent. The first time I saw you, you were just some kid who had no idea her father was crooked, and that's the way I always pictured you until the day I came to you at the pool."

Everything changed the minute our lives collided.

He keeps his eyes lowered, his dark lashes blinking the snow away. "You were the most terrifying thing I'd ever seen in my life. You went from the awkward bratty kid to the most beautiful, most vivacious fucking temptation I've ever come across. I was so mad they discovered you *and* hid you from me. And then I was run over when I walked up and was confronted by the most infuriating damn woman—" he shakes his head—"but it felt like a punch to the gut knowing . . ."

"Knowing I was with them."

He nods solemnly, his voice bittering with every word. "I kept my distance and kept watch over you. I had no intention of anything happening. But when you came out in that clearing calling their names, wearing that necklace, I got angry all over again. Mostly because I'd kept you safe and away from us for all those years and you went headfirst into a trap that was never supposed to be set. Sean thought he was doing the right thing by bringing you in. Dominic was so hardcore, he didn't give a shit if you got hurt, *at first*."

"They warned me. They tried, but I didn't care," I admit freely.

"I knew you weren't built for this back then," he whispers

heatedly. "Even though you told me you knew what you were getting into, you didn't. I saw the reality set in on you the night Dominic died in your arms. I don't know," he exhales. "Maybe I didn't give you enough credit then, but that was a lesson I never wanted you to learn, and now, *you* . . ." his voice breaks with more resentment. "You were never supposed to be a soldier in a war I declared."

"They made me one. And how could I not step up with *you* as an opponent? You are just as guilty."

We share a sad smile.

"Please tell me what happened that night."

His expression dims as his eyes dip once again.

"That afternoon, I received a tip that Andre and Matteo had accepted a bid and were coming for Roman." His eyes lift to mine. "That tip came from your father."

Chapter Forty-Three

I GAPE AT him.

"He knew about you?"

He slowly nods. "Shortly after he called me, we met in his office in Charlotte. I knew Matteo and Andre well. Andre was one of my first recruits. And when they made a hit, they made it personal. I knew they would strike Roman at home either here or in Charlotte. As soon as I found out, I had to make a fast decision to play my hand and plan an extermination. There was already a divide in Florida, a loyalty struggle, and it came to a head and presented itself at the perfect time. So, Roman and I struck a deal. In exchange for your dad's pull with the local police and media, I told him I would eradicate the threat to him and his daughter and clean up the mess if he kept it quiet."

"He knew about you the *whole time*?"

"I'm not sure when he caught on, but I underestimated him. Nevertheless, he didn't get to where he was by being oblivious. It took me a while to figure out he'd been onto us for some time. It occurred to me after the first few weeks of staying here that he'd all but pulled back completely on security. Why would a man worth so much leave his only heir so vulnerable? After years of keeping eagle eyes on you, which he did, suddenly he was leaving you in his mansion, *alone?* It didn't make sense."

"He knew about my involvement with you?"

Tobias nods. "Not only that, he was aware of our plans for him. But you were the middle ground, and he'd already made plans to hand the keys over to you."

"Why would he agree to any of this, trust you, knowing who you were and your intentions?"

His eyes bore into mine. "Because that day, I told him I was in love with his daughter."

I barely have a second to absorb it when he speaks again.

"When he discovered our weakness was his only daughter, he allowed us in, and knew that it would stall my plans if not rid me of them entirely."

"He used me as bait to save his company?"

"He didn't have to." The implication of that hits hard. "It happened naturally. Sean leapt the minute he discovered you. All Roman had to do was sit back and watch. It was a little bit of a gamble on Roman's part, but he knew how valuable you were and that you were protected by us. It was a stroke of genius, really."

Snow covers me, and I brush it off, ignoring the chill seeping into my bones. Tobias stands and shrugs off his jacket.

"I'm fine," I say in irritation, but he wraps it around me anyway.

"But you're wrong if you think his company was the only thing he was set on saving."

"Don't bother," I say, burrowing into his jacket.

"He was fucking terrified that day, Cecelia. Terrified enough to call me in. He didn't have enough security to protect both places. He was asking for help."

I look up where he hovers and see pity.

"I don't give a damn about Roman." I ignore the concern in his eyes. "Just tell me what happened."

He runs a hand through his dampening hair and nods. "Though we knew Florida was coming, I had no idea they were coming in hot like that. I didn't have enough intel, and neither did Roman. So, I put out an all points to the brotherhood and fucking flew back from Charlotte scared out of my goddamn mind because you had gone off the rails when you discovered you were marked."

The garage. The night I'd enabled them. I'd sabotaged my own safety with that stunt by slashing their tires and cutting off all communication with them. I'd thought about it long before now but didn't realize the gravity of just how bad I fucked up by declaring war on the people determined to protect me.

"Everyone was searching for you, *everyone*. And Dominic and I met at your house. We only had a small crew with us because of the search and sent them to border the property. Dom kept you distracted in your bedroom while I watched Miami pull up ten cars deep. I put in a call to Sean to get everyone back here, but we were too late."

"Andre and Matteo were already in the house," I say.

Tobias swallows, sorrow etched in his eyes. "I've gone over it and over it, and the only conclusion I can draw was that they were in the garage. That's the only place I didn't check after driving Roman's car home."

"That's why it was here."

"I was trying to lure them in." Sorrow-filled eyes lift to mine. "I assured Roman his daughter was safe. We had millions in the bank, unlimited man-power, and still, we weren't ready for a bunch of fucking thugs from Florida."

It was my fault. I'd flattened all their tires in my tirade and then sent them on a wild goose chase to find me. It was my fault they were scattered out in the mountains that night looking for me, in an attempt to *save me*. I was the cause of the loss of those precious seconds needed to save Dominic.

"I'm so sorry," I cry out hoarsely, and he shakes his head, grabbing my hand in his and rubbing a soothing thumb over the back of it.

"*Sorry?* About which part?" he asks, before dropping my hand. "About the fact that you were *used* on both sides as a bargaining chip between the men you loved and *trusted*? About the fact that you had *no idea* who you were giving your trust to, and that you could *never* have anticipated the chess moves being made all around you? About the fact Dominic lost his life because he was too fucking *stubborn* to think critically before he acted out as the hero?"

The ache in my chest grows unbearable as he shakes his head in anger.

"Hear me. *Really* hear me. I don't blame you for Dominic's death. I blame him. And I blame *myself* for putting all of this into motion. You're right. I wanted my fucking way. I wanted your dad to suffer, and it cost me my brother—what was left of my family. The only one I will never fully be able to forgive is myself."

"Tobias, you can't live like that."

"Those motherfuckers turned their back because of money.

Money, of all things, Cecelia. And I'm the one who let them into our ranks because they were a necessary evil."

"You aren't responsible."

He shakes his head. "We got too confident. Dominic got too heavy-handed with power. I got too wrapped up in the business end, in searching for my father, and . . ." He gives me a pointed look.

"In me."

He moves to kneel in front of me.

"You know, you were right in a way. We were a bunch of kids who built a fort together, but we didn't know how to use it. We weren't ready."

And there it is, all of it, the truth. The truth I've been begging for, the truth I've blindly been living alongside him. The truth that sets him free and liberates him from me.

And it's crippling. This knowledge. He studies me for a solid minute as I take it all in.

"Thank you." I reach for him, and he jerks away, stands, and looks down at me expectantly. He held up his end of the deal. Though he's not saying it, I know he wants me to hold up mine.

"Is this really what you want? You want me to leave? You want me out of your life?"

"Did you hear a word I said?"

"Every single one."

"Then you shouldn't be fighting to stay. You should be running."

"I would, except you left the best part out of your story."

He draws his brows and shakes his head. "Don't."

"Us. That's the best part. Our part." I move toward him, and he steps out of reach. "Tell me what to say, what to do."

His voice is gravel when he speaks. "Give me my brother back."

I sniff, my fight building even as he delivers precision blows. "That's the one thing I can't do."

"Then keep your word and leave."

"You do blame me."

"No, Cecelia, I don't. But I won't make the same mistakes again."

"It wasn't a mistake."

"It was, and you know it."

"Tobias, I've been with you the whole time. None of my life from the time I left to this moment has been real. This is the most I've lived since that night. This moment, where I tell you I still love you and you tell me I'm a mistake. But I don't believe you mean that." I lift my chin. "I'm not running away because I know you don't believe it, either. I'll take any life with you over the one I have. Don't throw me away. Don't turn me away. Don't do it again."

He begins to pace in front of me as I call his bluff.

"I heard every word you spoke last night. You still love me."

"Tu me rends tellement fou!" *You make me so goddamn crazy!*

He thrusts his hands into his hair and then cranes his neck to glare at me. "And just how do you see this playing out? You think I'll what . . . *marry you*?!" He shakes his head as if it's a ridiculous notion. His cruelty knows no bounds. "You think we're just going to ride off into the sunset, that we both can forget? Too much has happened; you shouldn't forgive me. You won't forget the things I have done to you. *I* can't forget the things I have done to you, and to my brothers. Everything got too fucked up, and everything has changed." He takes a menacing step forward and looks down at me with resignation. "We don't get a happy ending, Cecelia. We just get an ending."

"And why does it have to be this one? We can—"

"You're still fool-hearted enough to think that love and sex are some sort of fucking answer. That's your problem. You yourself said you were never objective enough to distinguish truth from the fiction in your head. Love and sex don't help *anything*. My brother loved you. Was in love with you when he died to protect you, and so was Sean. What exactly did that help? *Nothing*. It solves nothing. It fixes nothing. It causes problems and complications. You're blind if you think otherwise."

"No, you are. Because they knew I loved them back. And I can love them for who they were to me and what we shared, just like any other woman with a past lover and friend. But time didn't grant me the gift of separation. I got my experiences, my education, all at once. And it wrecked me. But I won't regret it. I won't regret any of it. I won't apologize for it. Because it's *not nothing*. And you'll just have to fucking accept it. But that all fell away the first time you touched what wasn't yours to touch, and you knew damn well what it was then and what it is now. And it's *not nothing*!"

Snow begins to pour heavily from the sky as I fight for his stare and win.

"It's everything, Tobias. It's everything that's important. If I'm hanging onto something, then it's that. *You* taught me the difference between truth and fiction, and you made damn sure I knew where your place was." I beat my chest with my fist. "No matter how we came to be, we were and still are. You stole my heart, and you let me love you with it, and you made damn sure I knew where its home was. You want to play innocent now, paint me the whore who got in the way, well, that's you being a coward, and really too fucking convenient of an excuse. You lying bastard, you knew exactly what you were doing."

"I didn't know! I didn't know! I didn't know! I didn't know seeing you a foot away from them the minute they came back would fucking destroy me the way it did. I hated knowing . . ." he slams his hands against the side table and roars before flipping it over, his eyes wild with jealousy and fear. Fear for admitting what it's taken years to admit. "I didn't know how fucking possessed I was until I saw the way they loved you."

I stand deathly still as he lifts livid eyes to mine.

Unexpected calm washes over me. "I'm still yours, Tobias."

He shakes his head, a war raging inside of it.

"I was always meant to be yours. You said so yourself before everything went to hell. And they knew it when they saw us together, just like I did, just like you do. That's why my mind won't let me forget, that's why my heart continues to torture me. It doesn't matter how it happened, but make no *mistake*, you made it happen."

His nostrils flare, but his eyes soften considerably. "You need to let go of the romanticized image of us in your head. We were never anything more than a mistake. A mistake we both paid enough for. Let it go. Let *me* go."

"Do you love her?"

"I trust her! I respect her!"

Both of those blows land, sending me spiraling into

unimaginable hurt. But his truth is so clear, the part he left out, and it's the only comfort I can take.

"But you don't love her."

"I'm *with her*. End of."

"Not end of. You can talk in absolutes all you want, but your hold is still as tight as it was. I feel it. Every single fucking day, I feel it. You haven't let me go no more than I have you. I don't want your forgiveness because you will never have mine. But I'm yours. Whatever parts of my heart they claimed they keep, they have their place with me, but you own the rest. All of it, including my mind, my body, and the fractured remnants of my soul. You're the victor, and these are your spoils, but you're too much of a fucking coward to acknowledge it, to accept me, to accept us. You're hiding behind your precious purpose and your brother's death. You didn't win me by default, Tobias, I was already yours, you made me yours *before* your brother died."

He jerks back as if I've slapped him, and in a way, I have. It's guilt we're both battling, and the imaginary line he's drawn that says we aren't allowed to have the other, not after what we lost.

"One of us has to say it. We knew. We knew what we found, and we didn't know how to handle it because it started in a way that it shouldn't have—with the betrayal of two men we both loved. And you think you can't or don't deserve to be with me because of this guilt, but this is our reality now, and you aren't the only one who lost. He's gone, Tobias, and he's not coming back, and we can't change that any more than we can the truth that we still love each other."

"Damnit, Cecelia. Let it go!"

"Dominic knew, Tobias, he told me he'd never seen you so happy just minutes before he died."

Tobias shakes his head, his eyes glazing as I step forward.

"I came back to make peace, to grieve his loss, to get answers, but I realize now that I also came back to claim the life I want, with you, because despite the guilt, I know we deserve to live out the rest of our punishment together. We're the only people who can heal each other. I'm not saying it will be easy, I'm not even saying it will work, but we deserve the chance to try. Because despite it being the cruel truth, it was real, more real than anything I've ever felt. More real than your need for revenge or your promises to any other. Right or wrong, my place is with you, and you belong as much to me. Just admit it."

He jerks me hard into his grip, his fingers curled around my jacket, his eyes filled with emotion as tension rolls off his shoulders. I can feel the break in him, the bleed.

"I love you," I say softly. "It's not too late."

"Cecelia?"

I freeze as his gaze shoots past my shoulder and he releases me, stepping away, turning in the direction of the voice.

Collin.

Chapter Forty-Four

"COLLIN, WHAT ARE you doing here?"

"I'm your fucking fiancé." He slams open the gate, anger evident in his features as his glare flits to the man standing next to me.

"You were, you *were* my fiancé."

Tobias's eyes roll down his form as I move to intercept Collin, who's stalking toward us, his eyes narrowing in pure accusation.

"So, it's you, then?" he says, his posture possessive, threatening in a way I've never seen.

I can see the amusement in Tobias's eyes as he sizes Collin up.

"Collin, stop," I intercept as he approaches and place a hand on his chest. "What are you doing here?"

He lifts his chin toward Tobias. "What is *he* doing here?"

"We were just talking."

Collin charges past me and squares off with Tobias as a surge of apprehension rolls through me. I do my best to get in between them as a sick smile crosses Tobias's face. "Heard a lot about you."

"Ironically, I hadn't heard a word about you until recently," Collin retorts, his accent riddled with condescension.

Tobias's smile grows, and he gives Collin a slow wink. "I'm a best-kept secret."

"Collin," I interject, "please go inside. I'll meet you there."

Collin turns to me. "You think I'm scared of this, this—" he snorts—"thug in a suit?"

Tobias's laugh is maniacal. "I can see why you like him. He's funny."

"This stops now!" I move to wedge myself between them and know the effort is futile.

"I was just leaving," Tobias says, stepping away, his gaze darting to me and zeroing in on the ring resting on my finger. "It's your turn, Cecelia."

My turn, my turn to keep up my end of the bargain. He wants to leave it like this?

Hell no.

"We aren't done talking," I snap before turning to Collin. "Please wait for me inside."

"No need, she's all yours," Tobias says, twisting the knife in.

Collin rips his gaze from me, barking after Tobias who is barely a step past him. "Make sure you recite that to yourself on the way home. Or better yet, write it down," Collin snaps. "That is, if you can spell."

"Tobias, no," I groan in anguish just as Collin yelps when Tobias pins him to the snow-covered lounger. He lifts a clenched fist to his line of vision before playfully popping Collin on the nose with his knuckles. Bright-red blood starts trickling out of his nose as I rip at Tobias's shoulders.

In one cruel move, Tobias has completely emasculated Collin.

Tobias shrugs me off easily as he leans down just an inch away from Collin's gushing nose. "How does it feel to know that when you were fucking your future wife, she was thinking of me?"

Collin's eyes bulge and water as he looks at me over Tobias's shoulder, utter devastation etching his face.

Enraged, I pound on Tobias back. "Damn you, let him go!"

"I've got that *thug dick* she craves," he sneers, sliding his crotch along Collin's stomach as I rip at his shoulders as he leans in. "Can you make her come with just a finger and a whisper in her ear? I mastered that." Tobias glances over at me, his eyes lit before turning back to Collin, hauling him off the lounger and righting him to stand before straightening his jacket. "If you needed some tips, all you had to do was ask."

Tobias's eyes go dim, all traces of humor gone. He brushes Collin's shoulders as Collin glares at him, nose gushing. "Don't insult me again, pretty boy, or playtime will be over." Tobias releases him and turns to me. "Take him home, and while you're at it, *stay there.*"

"You're such a horrible bastard."

"I never claimed to be a good man," he says, taking long strides toward the gate. "Not once. That's part of the story you made up in your head." He smashes out of the gate, and I call after him.

"I'm not leaving!"

"Yes, you are."

As if out of thin air, a car pulls up and Tobias slips in

the passenger side. They tear off out of the driveway through the dense and heavily falling snow, disappearing out of sight.

I turn back to Collin, who glares at me from where he stands, holding his bloodied nose with his hand.

Fuck.

I bite my lip to fight a smile as I slide another tampon into Collin's nose. He's the polar opposite of Tobias with light, feather-soft blond hair, deep-blue eyes, a runner's build, lean and muscular, but absolutely no match for the blunt force he just thrust himself up against.

And I love him all the more for it. He'd charmed his way into my life with his British quirks and devoted friendship before he smuggled his way into my heart. And I do love him for his patience, for his caring, for his understanding, for the man he is, and the friend he's been.

And, in return, I've been selfish.

He looks up to me utterly baffled, his English accent muffled by the tampons clogging his nose. "This is not funny."

"I know it's not. I'm sorry you're hurt, but I told you not to mess with him."

"Who in the *hell* is he?"

"More than a thug in a suit, but man—" I can't help my smile—"am I glad you said it."

"This is the man you still claim to love?"

I slowly nod, knowing the truth is hurting him.

"Why?"

"I wish I knew. I would stop it in a heartbeat and walk

down the aisle to you if I could. But I don't deserve you. And I never did."

"He didn't fight for you, not at all. He told you to leave."

He killed for me, made deals with his enemy for me. Protected me at the cost of losing his brother, all the while denying himself his own happiness.

"He's sacrificed more than any man should for me."

"How so?"

"It's a long story and not mine to tell." I scoop up the blood-splattered paper towels and feel Collin's eyes on me as I clean up the table.

"How is it not yours to tell?"

"Because I came into it long after it started."

"We were the best of friends before we dated," he reminds me, incredulous. "And you never told me *any* of this. Just that your father died, and you weren't close. How have you lived this whole other existence here without my knowledge? How do you have this whole past that you've never even hinted to? I thought I knew you, Cecelia."

Guilt, so much guilt mars me as I gaze down at him. Another victim of my sordid tale. "It was a year. Just *one* year, but it changed everything for me.

"Sometimes, a lot of the time, I wish it had never happened, but regardless, it made me who I am." I kneel before him. "I'm so sorry. I am. I never meant for you to know about him. Or any of this, but this is who I truly am. And the woman you met is me as well. I'm just built from more than I let on, and I'm tired of hiding the other parts of myself."

"Because you were promiscuous?"

"That's not everything, that's not . . ." I sigh, "I should have never admitted that to you."

"I'll be hard-pressed to forget it now."

"And I'm so sorry. So sorry for that. But I did it so you would never have to face him, to avoid *this* situation, because I am the bad guy. Feel free to paint me any way you want to our friends. I'll deserve it. Trust me. I've condemned myself enough trying to live with it. But in doing so, I've denied myself the freedom to want what I want."

"And it's him?"

"Yes. But Collin, what you and I had was special. It was built on the right things: friendship, trust, mutual respect. It was healthy, and I'm so grateful every day for what we had together—for you. I didn't take your proposal lightly, and I should have thrived in our relationship, but I didn't. I was hiding behind it."

"And you're here to, what, to win him back?"

"I don't want to hurt you any more than I have," I say, gripping his hand. "I don't want to keep telling you things that you'll hate me for."

"And if he refuses you?"

"He is, and he will continue to, and I'll have to live with it, but I won't ever put anyone else in your position again. Hurting you was my rock bottom and the end of my denial."

"And he's a good man?"

"He's a very *complicated* man, that's for sure. But he also happens to be a man I can't stop wanting no matter how complicated he is."

"So, you're really ending this for a man you may never have?"

I stand and run my hand through his hair before cupping his jaw. "I hope you'll believe our breakup is for more than me. I broke our engagement because you deserve a woman

who can forget her past and be solely yours, and I truly want
you to be happy."

"And what about your happiness?"

"I don't know, Collin. I guess . . ." I repeat Tobias's words.
"I don't get a happy ending. I just get an ending."

Collin slips on his jacket, destroyed after hours of sorting
our lives out, after more tears and arguing and one last attempt
by him to take me home. And as I follow him out to his car,
I acknowledge that my life back home is truly over. After a
painful negotiation, he's moving me out of our home and
putting my things in storage. Once I leave Triple Falls, I'm
moving forward, not going back. There'll be nothing to go
back to. The life, the lie I lived for years, is over. He pulls
away with my ring in his pocket, and I stand staring after
him for long minutes, mourning the loss of him, stuck in
the truth.

Chapter Forty-Five

IT'S BEEN A week, another lonely week of driving through hills and valleys, of talking to Dominic where he rests, of sorting through memories. I drive by the garage daily but never stop. With the transition nearly complete, especially with Tobias's surprising cooperation, I know my time is almost up. Maybe it's closure I sought out, but after all that's happened, knowing the truth of the lengths he went to, the truth of his feelings for me then and now, I'm hard-pressed to just up and leave, to fully let it go. But he's made his decision, and he continually makes it every day keeping me at arm's-length.

But my foolish heart refuses to forget how torn he was the night he drove me home. The words he spoke, the way he touched me, he wanted to touch me. He said things to me I could only dream of hearing.

He still loves me, but he refuses to let himself.

Guilt. Guilt separates us, but it was our mistakes that made us.

But he still wants me, despite our mistakes, despite our history.

Even with the gorgeous woman who waits in his bed.

But he is with her.

And he's with her *now* as he walks through the door of the restaurant. Stunned by their sudden appearance, I sink in my seat, lifting my book higher, my gaze just over the edge as my waitress approaches with another glass of wine.

I send up a silent prayer, hoping the hostess seats them as far away from me as possible. But I can't look away as Alicia smiles at him over her shoulder as he slips off her jacket.

It's hell on Earth watching them function like a couple. I lift my glass, gulping down half the contents to fight the raging jealousy stirring within me.

Though we had played house for nearly a month, we never had the luxury of being in public. Once we let our hostility go and embraced the other, they had been the most fulfilling weeks of my life. But his choice is clear tonight as he wines and dines her, and my appetite disappears.

I thank my waitress when my pasta is set in front of me and curse my fucking luck as they're seated in a booth adjacent from me.

Tobias is facing away, but Alicia can get a clear view of me where I sit at a two-seater, *alone*, next to the window facing the street. I flip a page in the book I'm no longer reading and lift my fork, the food flavorless as I force myself to chew and swallow. Alicia beams at Tobias from where she sits while rocks form in my throat.

Fuck this.

Lifting my hand to summon my waitress for a box, I knock my wine over. It spills to the carpet, and I'm thankful for the lack of sound, but it's too late. Alicia's eyes find me as I shuffle to stand, pulling my napkin from my lap to blot the carpet. Except it's not my napkin, it's the tablecloth I mistake it for, and now my dinner has joined my wine. It's from the floor that I see a flash of flame as the candle on my table tips before it sets the cloth on fire.

I hear the terrified cry of a woman to my left as I lift my water glass to douse the flames. Thankfully it goes out, but not before setting my book alight. Before I can lift the linen to snuff it out, I'm pushed out of the way, and it's done for me. Spiced citrus wafts through the air as I curse fate. Curse my inability to make a silent and smooth exit.

I can't look at him. I refuse to.

"Thank you."

His dark chuckle rumbles, lifting the air between us with the sweet sound. "You're far less smooth than you were at eleven."

"That's clear."

He lifts the half charred, half soaked book in his hands.

I glance at it, chest aching, utterly devastated that it's now just another ruined piece of my history, *our* history. Tears threaten, and I sniff them back as I gather my purse.

"It's just a book, Cecelia."

But it's not, it's the last piece of me that clung to hope. It's more than a simple possession, and he knows it. Finally, I lift my eyes to his, fire and water collide, and in them, I see those days we spent in his enemy's house. The days and hours we talked, laughed, fought, fucked, and made love while he whispered things to me that made me breathe differently. "Yeah, it's *nothing*, right?"

"Oh my God, are you okay?" My waitress intercepts as she dips to gather the dishes from the floor.

"I'm so sorry," I say softly, my eyes fixed on Tobias. My words meant for him. He absorbs them. "J'espère que je pourrais . . ." *I wish I could be . . .*

"Be what?" Tobias asks softly, his words wrapping around my heart, the gentleness in his gaze stealing my breath.

I know Alicia is watching our exchange, but I refuse to look away.

The waitress stands after collecting some of the mess from the floor. "I'll get you a new cloth, wine, dinner." She laughs softly. "Sorry, I can't do anything about the book."

"That's not necessary. And to be honest, the mini-series was better," I joke, a shitty attempt at masking my pain, but the shake in my voice makes it clear, "and I was just leaving."

She looks at Tobias, her eyes widening as she drinks him in.

He's beautiful, isn't he? He's my thorn, and with him, I sang the sweetest song.

"And losing him," I say aloud, finishing the thought, taken fully by the seconds that pass, and he lets me in, *truly* lets me in, his gaze just as filled with longing, with our shared history. He remembers. He remembers us. He remembers everything.

"Pourquoi la vie est-elle si cruelle?" *Why is life so cruel?* I ask him, my eyes glazing.

"Is that French?" My oblivious waitress asks, busy with her task of trying, in vain, to right everything in my tilted world. "It's beautiful."

"How much do I owe? Because I don't think I can afford to pay much more," I ask somberly, addressing the man in front of me.

"Nothing, honey. I'll take care of it. You didn't eat."

Tobias swallows, clear conflicted emotion in his eyes as I open my purse and place some cash on the newly covered table, my gaze still locked on his.

"I'll get your change," she says, taking the offered cash and glancing between us, her face sobering as we stare off into our past.

I shake my head. "All yours."

She thanks me and leaves us standing and staring. And that's what we do as the seconds pass, getting our first good look at each other as the haze of hurts we've been harboring finally clears and for the first time, see the other past it.

"Maybe I shouldn't have come, but I just wanted to see . . ." A lone tear slides down my cheek as I fail to gather myself and shake my head. I glance down at the book and fold his fingers around the charred pages. I give a self-deprecating laugh as tears cloud my vision again, and I admit my greatest truth.

"Je suppose que je serai toujours la fille qui pleure à la lune." *I guess I'll always be the girl crying for the moon.*

Tobias is still standing at my deserted table with the book in his hand when I push out of the doors and into the freezing wind.

Chapter Forty-Six

I SHOOT UP in bed, my latest dream leaving me exhausted as my limbs protest, remaining heavy with sleep. Attempting to clear the haze, I see the tell-tale double flash of lightning out of the French doors.

The thunder must have woken me.

Breaths evening out, I try to remember the dream and am thankful when I come up empty. But the air around me, the heat in my cheeks, the fast breaths coming from me make it clear it wasn't harmless.

My dreams seldom are. I've failed in every way to free myself of them.

Pound. Pound. Pound.

That's not thunder.

Leaping from the mattress, I search the room around me and come up empty.

Now isn't then, Cecelia. Get the door.

Rattled, I slip on my robe and grab my gun from my purse, trying to shake myself free of the fear.

Now isn't then, Cecelia.

The longer I stay, the distinction of past and present are

becoming clearer, and I'm relatively safe. I'll never be the girl incapable of fighting or attempting to save myself again. I've been an armed woman since I left Triple Falls. Collin and I got into a ton of fights over my selection of small guns. I always won.

Pound. Pound. Pound.

Rain batters the house, washing the new snow away as I keep my gun lowered, padding down the staircase.

Ding. Dong. Ding. Dong.

"Dominic, no!"

I inhale a calming breath as I reach the front door and look out to see headlights shining through sheets of rain. I can't make out the car.

I scream out as the bang sounds again, and he hears me.

"Open the fucking door, Cecelia."

I flip on the porch light as the hairs on my neck rise. He pounds once again, and I open it to see Tobias drenched from the rain, his eyes glossy, his expression stone. He's dressed in the suit he was wearing at dinner, the tie around his neck pulled loose and hanging, his glossy dark locks drenched.

His eyes drink me in, pausing on the gown he bought me years ago before he takes an aggressive step forward, and then another, until I'm backed against the foyer table, my hand outstretched behind me for support.

He glances down at the gun in my hand and, in one swift move, slaps it out of my grip. It slides across the floor and lands with the barrel pointed against the wall.

"You idiot! The safety was off!"

"You're unarmed now, and *that's* what you're worried about?" He staggers forward, his posture searing with intimidation. He's been drinking, and he's furious.

"You won't hurt me."

"Won't I?"

"What's wrong? What happened?"

"You happened. Why haven't you left?"

"Why does it matter? I'm not doing anything to you. I'm not bothering you."

"Your presence bothers me!"

He's soaked through, the water dripping down his profile. I lift my chin.

"Tough shit."

He glares down at me as the sky lights up behind him, and thunder rolls in the distance.

"You won't hurt me."

"Think again." He grips my face so tight I know I'll have faint bruises tomorrow. "I told you to leave it alone. But you just couldn't. When are you going to understand we were nothing but a weak moment?"

"So much of nothing you've been at the bar rehearsing this speech for how long?"

He jerks my robe open, and I slap at his hands.

"Go take your shit out on your girlfriend. I'm not dealing with this."

"Not dealing with this?" he hisses, sliding a thick finger down the strap of my nightgown before jerking it free and exposing one of my breasts.

"Think of Alicia, Tobias. This isn't right." I push at his chest to no avail. "You aren't *that* man."

"No, I'm not. You made sure of that."

"What in the hell are you talking about?"

"She was a good woman who deserved all the attention I could give her."

"You broke up?"

"She seems to think we have unfinished business. I agree. I say we finish this." He rips at my gown and unveils my other breast before roughly cupping it.

"Stop it, Tobias, we've played this game before."

He knocks the empty vase off the table behind me, and it shatters on the floor. I jerk my chin from his grip. "Stop it, you bastard! Stop it. We're better than this."

"No, we're not. *This is* who we are." He presses me against the table, his weight and strength pinning me. "This is all we are. And this—" he pinches my nipple painfully, sending a shot of lightning to my core—"*This* is why you're here, right? Waiting for me?" He rubs his hard length along my stomach as I hold in my whimper. "Well—" his voice drips acid—"here I am."

"This is how you want to play it? Fine." I push at his chest, and he stumbles back. I lift the hem of my nightgown, unveiling myself in nothing but panties, and toss it down. His eyes roam freely, lust hazing out some of the anger. His nostrils flare as his thick hair drips, the droplets falling over my breasts and sliding down my stomach.

"You don't scare me, Tobias. You never have. That's what pisses you off the most."

"No," he leans, and I inhale leather, citrus, and rain. "What pisses me off the most is that I let you go because I *don't want* you anymore, and you're too blind to see that."

"No, what pisses you off the most is any woman you find won't *ever be me*."

He releases my jaw and dips his head, biting into the flesh of my breast, and I cry out, ripping at his hair as he pierces the skin, before drawing me into his mouth.

I don't have time to blink before I'm pushed onto the table, and he's jerking my panties down my legs. I gasp as he runs his erection along my thigh, his fingers tightening around my throat.

"How many nights have you touched yourself thinking of me, closed your eyes and thought of me while your fiancé was fucking you?"

"Every night," I hiss, clawing at every part of him to get him closer, "every night." He pauses his assault, glaring down at me.

"You're right. You're sick. This, *we*, are fucking sick. And it isn't going to end the way you want it to," he seethes.

"I know," I gasp as he presses a finger inside me, his grip on my neck tightening as I hoarsely cry his name. I'm soaked, so much so that I feel his cock twitch through his slacks when he finds me needy.

Lightning flashes behind the open front door as he finger-fucks me ruthlessly while the thunder rolls in. I push off his jacket while he drinks from my neck. Slowly, he lifts his head as thirst pools in his fiery depths while he crowds me, our eyes connecting as he unbuckles his belt, jerking his cock from his pants while I yank off his tie. His hands cover me, mapping my body, his touch damning, branding as I rip at his shirt.

He stops my movements, flattening me to the table with his palm as he runs the head of his cock through my slit before he drives into me, burying himself in one thrust. Once locked, he hangs his head and curses as I cry out, reaching for him.

And then he's moving, his mouth taunting me with a kiss he refuses to give as he wildly fucks me, savage and without care, his anger unyielding. His strokes are unforgiving as his face twists between anguish and rage. Lust swallows me whole as I call out to him again and again, begging somewhere between heaven and hell. The slapping of skin, our connection consumes me whole, fueling my desire as I start to shake with the build. He pulls back, eyes lit, and thrusts into me to the hilt, his hands covering my breasts, his need taking over. He angles his hips striking along my walls, restraining me with just the pressure of his palm.

"Tobias," I call out, as he tears into me, possessed by anger while giving into us.

He groans as he finally releases me, pushing my thighs wider as he drives in. He leans over, gripping my neck and lifting me, his grunts and exhales hitting my lips. Our mouths collide, his tongue diving deep as he kisses me and kisses me. I shudder around him, my core clenching as I moan my release into our kiss. My orgasm seems to unleash him as he fucks me deep, pinning my hands beside my head. Inching the table forward with each thrust. I take his brutal licks because it's what he needs and what I want. His anger, his passion, the proof of life that still beats in his chest. His regret and resentment for the love I still harbor for both the man and the monster that dwells inside him.

It's possession and reclaiming. It's too much of everything he can't get past and can't forgive either of us for. Flickers of torment cross his features as pained grunts escape him.

"We are nothing," his voice cracks with his lie.

"You love me," I counter. "You still love me."

He roars as he comes, forehead pressed to mine before spilling the rest of himself on the table between us. Chest heaving, he backs away, while jerking up his pants. The porch light blankets us in light as he retreats, his face going ashen as he gathers his jacket and the state I'm in—torn, bitten, and flushed from my orgasm. His face twists in anguish before he hangs his head at the threshold of the door.

I gather myself from the table. My limbs still shaking, but I manage to keep my voice steady. "It takes a queen to love and understand a king. Did you think this would break me? You made me!"

His silence is answer enough.

"You really thought that would do it? Would change what I feel for you and get me out of your system? You should know better than that, you fucking fool!" I wrap myself in the ruined silk.

He palms his mouth, frozen on the doorstep, unshed tears in his panic-filled eyes, a plea on his lips when he speaks. "Please leave, Cecelia. I can't give you what you want." Shadows of our undoing sneak in, casting darkness over his features, his eyes wild and haunted while an agony-filled groan escapes his throat. I see it then, the ironic truth: I might be strong enough, but he's not. He turns and stalks out, leaving the door open.

Chapter Forty-Seven

THE NEXT MORNING, I pace the house, my core sore, throbbing, as I contemplate my next move. I know I have to go. I know what needs to be done. I'm trying to break through a door that's long closed and sealed shut.

I will leave, for the both of us. I'm only hurting us by staying. I admit to myself I had hoped we could put it behind us, never Dominic, but all of the heartbreak and deception. We were torn apart before we had a chance to be. His unreasonable anger with me I can't fully understand. It was horrible circumstances that ruined us that night, and I now know that the easiest way for him is to blame our relationship as a whole and deny me for himself as penance. And I get to share in that punishment no matter how much I want just a measure of absolution.

In a haze, I find myself in my father's room. When I lived here, I never, not once, was curious about his living quarters. It was just a part of the house I never dared enter aside from the night Tobias showed up injured. Entering his room now, I see the room of a stranger. The whole of it covered in floor-to-ceiling windows, offering a spectacular view of the mountains. His furniture is simple, elegant, dark mahogany, and void of much life. Aside from the fading smell of lemon polish, it remains untouched. Just the way he left it the day he died. I open his chest of drawers and lift some of his socks before pulling out one of his T-shirts. I've never known my father's smell. He never hugged me, held me. Never. He wasn't that man. That thought saddens me as I inhale the laundered shirt. And then it occurs to me.

Roman died without a single soul mourning him, not even his only daughter.

His cover-up of Dominic's death had settled my fate with him. I never spoke to him again after that, and he rarely ever reached out.

And if I'm not careful, I might not have many who mourn me when my time comes.

But from what I knew, we were two different people who live and lived completely different lives. I'm still reeling from the fact Tobias swallowed his pride and met with him, told him he loved me, swore to keep me safe all the while protecting him, a man who covered up his parents' deaths, accidental or not, and gave him money in return.

Tobias got the same consolation I did.

Money.

The most necessary of evils that can completely change a person for better or worse.

My mother lives comfortably now, but she's grown used to it, and it's brought her no greater happiness. It never brought my father any either.

And for me, it is an insult. I hate it. I hate the power it gives to those who don't deserve it, and the lives it steals for those who are a slave for just a little of it. I hate the greed, and the thirsty deeds done to acquire it, and the fear and the bitterness it inspires in those who don't have it.

I hate everything it stands for.

It's not a God, but a runner-up to blame for a lot of life's cruelties.

I lay on Roman's bed, on the stark white comforter, and stare up at the ceiling. Despite my need for something—closure, or just the necessity to grieve properly because I was denied—I've caused more damage to myself.

But I asked for it.

And now I'm lying in the bed I made.

In truth, I got some of what I came for: answers. And I fight myself to be satisfied with that.

Last night, getting physical with Tobias only opened an old wound and helped us bleed out a little faster, but the truth is, we are *bleeding out*. He'd ended his relationship, but that meant nothing if he couldn't accept us. And his words and actions last night only told me he never would.

It is love, but it's love lost, no matter who's to blame, and it's time I face it.

Fighting with him brought me back to life in a way, and having him inside me, no matter how angry he was, was proof that nothing or no one can take his place. His touch will forever be the only touch I'll ever want.

I turn on the bed and gaze out the window wondering why the men in my life could never embrace or fully trust the love I harbored for them.

Had I made it so hard?

Briefly, just briefly, I imagine what my life would have been like if I'd had a father. One who loved me as a father should. Who did more than support me financially.

I never had it rough as far as life went.

But when it came to a father's love, I just . . . never had it.

I don't want to feel sorry for myself.

But just for a few seconds, I do. I mourn that girl who grew up knowing she was an obligation.

A low-lying simmering anger trickles into my subconscious. I lift to sit on the edge of the bed as it starts to engulf me whole.

Fuck them all.

All of them.

I wasted my heart—wholly, completely. I wasted it, and it will never be mine again. I'll never be whole.

I want to take back the years I spent hoping and praying for some returned affection. For the days and nights, and years, and months and hours and minutes, I questioned myself, my existence, and lost myself in them all.

I resent my father and my love for him.

I resent the men who made me.

I wish I never met any of them.

"FUCK YOU!"

In a burst of anger, I clear off the top of Roman's dresser scattering mail and his cologne bottles.

Just as fast as it comes, it ebbs, but it's there, it's always been there, my pride, my self-respect, all that I had put aside just to give my fucking heart a chance.

And for what?

I'm a lover who got nothing in return but a broken heart and tattered self-image. I betrayed myself for the chance of being loved.

"No more! No more!"

It was never worth it.

But I am. I am worth it.

I didn't ask him for anything, but why did he have to make it so fucking painfully clear that he didn't love me?

I'm the daughter of no one.

How could my mother love a man so cruel?

How could I follow in her footsteps and fall for a like-minded man whose agenda and role in life came first over my affection?

Money. Power. I'd give it all up just to make myself whole again.

The smell of cologne permeates the room, and I open one of the windows before I kneel to pick up the glass from the broken bottle. I open his bedside drawer to place the pieces in and see a letter resting underneath a watch box. I study the thick envelope and pull it from beneath the box. The note atop of it is addressed to me.

Cecelia,
I'm everything your eyes accused me of being. You were
better off.
  Forgive me,
  Roman

I pull it out and open it. In seconds I recognize the writing. It's from my mother.

Roman,
I'm sorry I bombarded you the way I did. I've humil-
iated myself in a way I'll never be able to forget. Please
forgive me.

I came back after all these years to apologize. To thank you for all you sacrificed for me while carrying hopes of the girl you banished from your life.

You still haven't married. And that gave me hope. I always secretly wondered if my lingering feelings were returned. I hope you'll forgive me for reaching out to find out.

But I can see it now. I need to give up.

I can still remember our time together so vividly. It seems just like yesterday I was starting at the plant, and you walked in, and we just stared at one another.

You saved my life, in more ways than one with the way you took me in, the way you cared for me.

I've never known that kind of love before you and haven't experienced it since. And every single day, I wonder if it meant as much to you. I couldn't face the end of us. I still haven't recovered from losing you, and I never will.

But I feel I stole your life from you with that horrible secret. One I would do anything to take back. My conscience eats at me daily, that I locked that door. It was my fault that fire started and my stupid judgment that caused such great loss. If only you had let me claim responsibility, if only you would now, I'd take it a thousand times over if only to set you free of the burden you carry.

And yet you never once let me step forward and never will. And I'll never understand it. The only conclusion I can draw is that at one point in time, you did love me enough to save me, to make sure our baby was safe, and I'll remember you that way.

Our daughter is so beautiful. She's thriving, and I know it might be hard for you to look at her and see the mistake you made in loving me, but please try to open up, Roman, and show her the man I fell in love with.

When you look at her, I hope you feel at peace with the reason for your sacrifice, because I've showered the piece you gave of yourself to me with the love I will forever feel for you.

D

I read the letter over and over, calculating and recalculating the timeline, all the while praying for the facts to change.

My *mother* killed Tobias's parents.

My mother.

Not my father.

Horner Technologies was a chemical plant twenty-six years ago. She made a careless mistake and killed two people. Accident or not, my father covered it up.

The only thing Roman Horner was guilty of was being a cheap, shrewd, and unethical businessman.

I race to the bathroom and empty my stomach before sinking onto the cold tiles.

Chapter Forty-Eight

I PULL UP to my mother's house, a large three-bedroom on a lakeside lot. It's not at all ostentatious, but the garden reminds me a lot of my father's as I round the house following the music that drifts from an outdoor speaker. I find her there amongst the bare branches with a glass of wine by her side. Timothy is leaning over her, as they exchange words, pressing a kiss to her temple before he spots me over her shoulder. His greeting is warm, as is his smile.

"Hey there, Cecelia. Didn't expect to see you today."

My mother shoots from her chair, a ready smile on her lips as she turns to me. "Hey, baby. I was just thinking about calling you."

"Glad you're in the mood for conversation." Her smile fades when she sees the look on my face just before I pull the letter from my purse.

"What's wrong?"

Timothy stands and eyes us both as I make my way toward her. She flicks her attention to the letter again a second before her face goes ashen and turns to Timothy.

"Give us a minute to catch up, babe?"

Timothy nods and eyes me, clearly sensing the situation. "Will you be staying for dinner? I'm going to put a few steaks on in a bit."

"No, I have to get back, but thank you."

Tension fills the air even with the overabundance of it already between us as Timothy takes his leave, and my mother reaches for a cigarette, lighting it up as she watches me closely.

"My letter?"

"Why was I safer?"

She blows out a plume of smoke, pulling her sweater tighter to her. She lifts the bottle of wine in offering, and I shake my head.

"I'm not here to catch up."

"I see that," she swallows. "Give me a second."

"To think of more lies?"

Her eyes drop as she lifts the glass to her lips and takes a hearty drink.

"Why was I safer?"

"Your father was the most beautiful man I've ever laid eyes on. Truly. Not one woman in that plant went a day without fantasizing about him, I'm sure of it. And I was one of them."

"Answer my question."

She gives me a sideways glance, her tone biting. "Do you want the whole truth or a quick answer?"

"How could you? How could you let me believe he didn't want me, how could he?!"

"Because it was safer that way."

"And you think he loved you?"

"I know he did, as he loved you."

"He made us go without all those years! He regarded you

like you were nothing, treated you horribly. You call that love?"

"I call it penance. Sit down, Cecelia."

I walk up to where she stands, her scars shining in her eyes as she pleads with me to listen to her.

I take one of two seats that case a small garden table in between and grab her wine.

"Fine. Talk. And I swear to God, Mom, if you leave anything out, this will be our last conversation."

I don't miss her faint, pained smile. "You're so much like him in a way. Eyes that convey so much and at the same time cut so deep. But you're horrible at hiding your feelings. You have too much heart to be anything but a beautiful and loving woman, no matter how much it hurts. I like to think that's me I see."

"I don't consider it a blessing. I'm nothing like you."

"Oh, baby, you're so much like me. You love blindly and foolishly, and there was no way to keep you from experiencing it for yourself. I knew when you were little, you'd inherited my heart, and there was no way to keep you from loving the way you were created to love. There was no way to stop your heartbreak. You think I haven't seen the change in you? You think when I look at my own daughter, I don't notice you've been irrevocably changed by it? I taught you exactly about the heart you have long before you gave it away."

"Don't credit yourself for being a parent to me the last seven years."

"I deserve that. And a lot worse. But it's your father who saved me from that fate."

"Tell me."

She stubs out her cigarette and faces me. "He was a bastard: hard-nosed, straight-edged, power-hungry, money-hungry, and damn near impossible to penetrate. At first, I thought I was just a distraction for him, you know? And he made me believe it for a time. He was too focused on creating an empire to worry about a nineteen-year-old who had no future other than that damn plant. I knew it was stupid. I knew it was reckless to love him the way I did, and God did he make me question my sanity on more than one occasion. But then, one day, everything changed. It was as if he gave himself permission to love me back. We hid our relationship well. Your grandmother was oblivious. It was hard. In fact, I only confided in one person the whole time we were together. A gorgeous French woman by the name of Delphine."

I damn near let the glass slip from my hand but manage to bring it to my lips and take a large sip.

"We bonded because she felt out of her element; she had moved from France a few years before, followed a man to America, and married him. But the first time she showed up to work with bruises . . . I could just tell she needed someone to confide in. And honestly, with your father, I did too. He was so secretive, so hard to love. It was as if we both needed permission to love them and found it in the other. As wrong as it was, we were both victims of our foolish hearts. We became great friends."

She swallows and pulls another cigarette from her package.

"She was the only one who knew?"

Mom nods, taking the glass from me.

"That night . . . the night of the fire, Roman and I had a huge fight about . . . you. He didn't want me to keep you, and I refused to let him strong-arm me into aborting."

"So, he never wanted me. Big surprise."

"Not in the way you think. It had little to do with him not wanting to be a father."

"That makes no sense."

"Cecelia, you came for an explanation. One you deserve. Let me talk."

"Fine."

"We fell hard. We were very much in love when you were conceived. So much so I thought . . . I thought him proposing was a real possibility. But it happened so fast. So fast. One minute I was his distraction, the next, he made me feel like his obsession. And it was the best I've ever felt in my life aside from the day the doctor put you in my arms."

She flicks her ashes as I soak in the still water of the lake.

"Back then at the plant, there were a few labs, with specific and strict safety guidelines—and newly trained—I just wasn't thinking. That fight we had was horrible. I thought your father a monster that night; questioned all my reasons for loving him. I couldn't believe just how multifaced he was." She swallows, and her eyes water. "Anyway, I was distracted. Distraught, so much so I just wasn't aware of anything or anyone around me. I was tormented about the idea that he wouldn't have me if I kept you. I was so in love with him, I considered it—it was only a split second, Cecelia, but I did. And I hated him for it."

I keep my silence though her words sting.

"Love will make you a complete idiot, and I'm no less guilty of being a slave to it than any other woman." She takes another sip of wine. "So, I was working that night with a few other technicians who were on break. I just wasn't . . . I wasn't all there. So, when I messed up, I tried to contain it—in the event of a fire, you're supposed to evacuate, and lock the door. That sets a chain of events in motion that isolate the threat. I followed protocol, not realizing I wasn't alone in the lab. So when . . ." she turns to me " . . . I didn't see them. I thought I was alone. The minute they appeared at the door, there was an explosion. I didn't know . . . by the time I was made aware they were there—it was too late. I can still see them screaming, pounding on the door a split second before the blast. I can still hear their panicked cries. I watched it happen."

I close my eyes, the image of Tobias and Dominic's parents pleading for their lives as my mother stood panicked on the other side of the door.

"I called your father first, and Roman was upstairs—he was the first there and sent me away immediately—he refused to let me take the blame. I was almost three months along."

"But it was an accident. Why couldn't you come forward?"

"At first, I thought it was a knee-jerk reaction to protect me, but it was for a different reason altogether. He took care of it—all of it. And refused to give me the details or his reasoning. He was so . . . adamant about it. And he's a man you don't question. For months I wondered what in the hell he was thinking . . . until after you were born."

She takes a long drag of her cigarette. "After the funeral, I quit the plant at Roman's insistence. But I swore the day I saw Delphine on the opposite side of those caskets, she just knew. She looked at me in a way I knew she knew. She was outraged; she wasn't privy to the details of the investigation and stopped talking to me when I clammed up when she questioned me. I feigned ignorance. Roman and I tried to move on, but it was the beginning of the end. He moved me into an apartment, away from my mother. I thought it was so we could have the freedom to be together, but shortly after, he slowly started to freeze me out. We were never the same after that night. But it was you who kept us glued together. Sometimes he would look at me—at my belly—and I could see so clearly he wanted to be more, to mean more to the both of us. Sometimes, I could see a hint of us again, but other than an occasional visit, he'd all but ended our relationship."

"He felt guilty?"

"I know he did. He bore the brunt of it. This secret had the ability to bring all he worked for crumbling down around him."

"But if you had just admitted to it—"

"He didn't want to take the chance."

"I don't understand why."

"Because he didn't want anyone to know about us."

"So, you *were* his dirty little secret?"

"No, my love, you and I were his biggest fear. I knew he was a cold man. I knew he was ambitious in his business dealings, but I didn't know he had others keeping close tabs on him. He'd made enemies with old business partners, and he didn't want anyone knowing."

"So, you fought because you were pregnant?"

"I wanted you. He didn't. And I didn't fully understand why until three months after you were born."

She blows out a breath.

"Your father came to see you for the first time that night. I can't tell you how hard labor was alone, thinking he didn't want to have anything to do with us, didn't care enough to see you come into this world. He ignored my calls, my pleas for him to come, and I truly hated him for it, but I had you as consolation. You were everything beautiful about us before things got ugly. The day you turned three months old, I fell asleep in your rocker after putting you in your crib." Her eyes are somewhere in the past as she speaks as if she can see it vividly. "I woke up in the middle of the night to see Roman standing and staring into your crib, and there was no denying it. His eyes were so full of love. And that's what it was for him, something I experienced myself the day our eyes locked the first time. It was love at first sight for the both of us the minute we saw you. I stood and went to him, and it was the first time since the fire he let me in and see him. That moment was beautiful, and I'll never forget it. He stared down at you with so much reverence, Cecelia, a father's love. But it was when he reached for you that he went pale." She looked over to me and swallowed. "When he pulled back the blanket to hold you for the first time, there was a loaded gun in the crib next to you, situated in an unmistakable way."

"A threat?"

"A warning of retribution." She looks out to the lake and back to me. "I went ballistic when I saw that gun, and I checked you from head to foot. I've never in my life been so terrified. It was then I knew he was distancing himself from us for my protection and yours. He didn't want you because he knew having you made you a target. That was when I realized just how much he'd been hiding from me. As careful as he was, I knew immediately who was responsible for that threat."

"Delphine."

Mom nods. "I killed her family with my foolish mistake.

But not once had it occurred to me that she was capable of anything like that. I assumed her grudge was my connection to Roman. And so I told him. He was furious."

She takes another steadying breath.

"That night, he held you for the first time in his arms for hours before he looked up at me and point-blank told me we were over and that he didn't want us anywhere near him. I fought him on it, but with that image of that gun in your crib, it didn't take much to convince me.

That night, we agreed that I get a court-ordered paternity test and take legal action in order to gain child support. He said it would look more convincing if you seemed an obligation on paper, in essence making you seem like a bastard child. Since we'd already been discovered, he was sure the best thing we could do was to try and make it seem convincing. He'd hired the best lawyer possible so he would have to dole out as little as possible."

"And you agreed to it?"

"There was a loaded gun pointed at my baby's head. Of course I agreed to it. I let him break my heart. I let him treat us like his dirty little secret. I let go of him and all ties because he was a dangerous man to love. And we were dangerous for him to keep. That was our deal."

"So, you moved us here, and never spoke to him after?"

"I didn't hear from him for three years. Not a word. And every conversation after was about you and negotiated visits. Roman made it a point to be as cruel as possible in our exchange. He was paranoid. He refused to even look at me the first summer I dropped you off."

"That's why he sent me to camp on my first summers with him?"

She nods. "He hired men to watch us twenty-four seven. We were under constant surveillance. Do you remember Jason?"

I nod. It was one of my mother's longer relationships that ended when I was in middle school.

"He was one of them?"

She nods. "It just sort of happened."

"How convenient."

"It was. I felt safer with him there. But my reasoning for starting it was entirely selfish."

"You wanted a reaction."

Mom nods.

"One I never got." She frowns. "Something must have happened that last summer you spent with him. Another threat, I assume. He caught wind of something and refused to take you again until he took you in. And even then, he'd made it seem like a business transaction."

"That's why he contacted me by email?"

She nods. "A paper trail to anyone watching."

"Why, why didn't you tell me?"

"Because it kept you safe."

"Why did you go back to him after all that time?"

"Because for nineteen years, I loved him. For nineteen years, I pined for him. For nineteen years, I paid for my mistake, and I just had to know. I had to know if he regretted it. If he at all felt the same about me. He cruelly turned me away when I went to him, but at your graduation, a few months later, I caught him looking at me. Timothy was by my side, holding my hand, but Roman looked at me in a way I knew I wasn't alone in what I'd been harboring. It was still there, between us, the man I fell for was still in there. And I knew. I just knew. A woman knows these things. And it was when he looked at me like that . . . it felt worse than not knowing. It destroyed me. But it was all he had left to give. Just those few seconds in the crowded stadium."

"Jesus, Mom."

"I thought about that look every day. I still think about *him* every single day. Was he a good man? No. But he is the man I'll die loving."

"And you think that's fair to Timothy?"

"It hasn't been fair to any man, and sometimes the guilt eats me alive, but what would you have me do? Timothy lost his first wife, and I know at times he feels the same guilt that I do. We all don't end up with the one we hoped to. He doesn't resent me any more than I do him. We've made peace with it. And we're happy." She turns to me. "We are happy. We're content."

"Content is not love."

"It is our version of it. I don't think Roman would have made me happy. In fact, I know he wouldn't have. Doesn't make my feelings for him less crippling."

"This is . . ."

"Roman loved you, Cecelia, he did. But he was a hard man to love and be loved by. Impossible. And it wasn't just my mistake that cost us. It was his. He needed to own a piece of the world. There was some insatiable drive inside him, and it was his ambition that made him enemies, that cost him his family. All of his wealth wasn't protection enough for him and the damage he'd already done."

"Don't make the same mistake she did."

I set her wine glass down and stand. "You're right, Mom.

I inherited your heart. And don't flatter yourself about it, because it's been nothing but a fucking curse."

"I know that too." She reads my posture and pleads with me from where she sits. "Please don't go, Cecelia. Don't go away like this."

I stare down at her and shake my head. "You've been lying to me my whole life."

"If I would have told you this when you were younger, you only would have subjected yourself to his rejection. He loved you the only way he could, from afar."

"It doesn't make it okay! I treated him horribly. You couldn't even come clean when he was dying?!"

"He didn't want you there."

Stunned, I stare at her. "But you were?"

"I sat by his side and kissed his lips before he passed."

"Jesus, Mom!"

"He didn't want you there because he didn't want you feeling guilty because you didn't deserve to. He didn't want absolution. He *was* an absent father. He chose to build his kingdom over the both of us. He was incapable of voicing his feelings or expressing his true emotions. You wouldn't have gotten the reunion you wanted."

"I should have had the choice!"

"You had a choice. You met the man he was. That was Roman. Let me be clear. There were no deathbed confessions. That's not who he was."

I remember the day he stopped me at the foot of the stairs, his eyes pleading with me to see him past his mistakes. But I'd begged him in that boardroom and got nothing but a whisper of the same look.

"That house he built," she rasps out, "it was a daydream

we shared when we were our happiest, every last detail of it down to that garden which was meant to be mine. He punished himself by building it; a sordid monument to what could have been."

I furiously wipe the tears from my eyes.

"It's taken me twenty-six years to forgive myself, Cecelia. And I will serve out the rest of my life only truly loving one man. Don't get me wrong, I love Timothy, so much, he's good to me, and I've given him all I have left to give, but your father was the love of my life. Whether or not he deserved it. We truly don't get a choice."

"Do you have any idea what keeping this from me has cost me?! Do you even care? Of course you don't. You were too busy wallowing when I needed you most. You were selfish. He was selfish."

She reaches out and grabs my hand as I glare down at her. "I care. Cecelia, I love you with my heart and soul. I did what I thought was best for you. We both did. You, too, are the love of my life, and I'm sorry I was selfish, and I'm sorry I got sick, but I hope one day you'll forgive me, that you'll forgive us both."

"I have to go." I pull my hand away, and she nods, her eyes glossing with fresh tears.

"Please don't do what he did. Please, Cecelia, don't shut me out. I can't lose you too."

"You aren't the only one who's paid. Don't you get that?"

Her brows draw as I shake my head at her utter ignorance. "I've paid *dearly* for *your* lies, for *his* mistakes, and I still am."

"What do you mean?"

The decision comes easy.

"I guess we all have our secrets, Mom." Stalking off, I make a beeline for my car. It's when I slam my door I catch sight of her gazing on at me from the side of the house, and I tear out of the driveway.

Chapter Forty-Nine

U RN IN MY hands, I stand at the edge of the garden and try to imagine what it would have been like to grow up in this house. Images of me running around as my parents sat and watched me play. Posing for pictures with my prom date under the canopy of wisteria as my mother snapped away while Roman eyed him in warning, demanding I be home by curfew. Coming down the stairs on Christmas morning to open presents next to a crackling fire. In my year here, I remember more than once picturing a family here, a happy family, and thinking the house had gone to waste, but that's precisely what the house represented—the life we could have had.

"You were the first man to break my heart, and I guess it's fitting. But you didn't have to. You didn't have to punish us both. I came here to collect your fortune, but I would give every dime back for just a few minutes with you. Just to tell you I may not ever understand you fully, but in discovering what you did, I felt like your daughter for the first time in my life."

My breath hitches as I remember my dream from last

night: a little girl reaching for her father's hand over and over only to come up empty.

"But I refuse to be the coward you were. That's what you taught me. I won't make your mistakes. I'd rather be reckless and in love than die safe without a real legacy. And it has nothing to do with money or position. I think that's what you realized. I just wonder when you did." I crumble a little where I stand. "At least I now know you were capable, and that's something. But you didn't build this home in vain. This is the place where I was the happiest I've ever been, so I'm sharing it with you." I open the urn and scatter the ashes in the whipping wind; they catch on a gust and carry for a few feet before dispersing amongst the withered branches of the vines. And for a brief moment, I picture Roman in the fully bloomed garden, mourning the woman he loved and the daughter he abandoned, and with that image, I make peace with the house, haunted by the family that never existed.

The ground rattles with another coming storm as I make my way toward the grave. I study the headstones next to Dominic's as I grieve the people I feel I now know; two lives my parents took, creating two orphaned boys who would grow up angry, confused, and set on vengeance. My future lovers, teachers; two men who loved me wholly and sacrificed themselves to keep me safe.

It's all wrong—all of it.

I let myself mourn as I kneel at Dominic's grave, my hands on the frozen ground.

Grief engulfs me as I sob out my apologies.

Dominic's beautiful face flashes across my thoughts.

And with the rising of the wind, I swear I feel him, a cool blanket that envelops me as I finally ask the question I've never dared to. "Forgive me? Please, forgive us."

"*Make him happy.*"

"*Take care of her.*"

Would he be angry to know neither of us did what he asked, what he wanted? Neither of us honored his sacrifice. Instead, we let his absence be the reason for our demise.

"Il ne me laisse pas l'aimer. Il ne me laisse pas essayer. Je ne sais pas quoi faire." *He won't let me love him. He won't let me try. I don't know what to do.*

"I'd give anything to go back, to be braver. I was so scared. I was such a coward, and you died. You died . . . I never got to tell you how much I loved you. How much you meant to me, how much you changed me. How much I respected you. You were so brave, Dominic, and so strong. I was so privileged to know you. To love you. As much as you tried, you were never a forgettable man. I will miss you every day of my life." I press my hand to my chest.

"Attends-moi mon amour. Jusqu'à ce que nous nous revoyions. Jusqu'à ce que nous puissions sentir la pluie sur nos deux visages. Il doit y avoir une place pour nous dans la prochaine vie. Je ne veux pas d'un paradis où je ne te vois pas." *Wait for me my love. Until we meet again. Until we can feel the rain on both our faces. There has to be a time for us in the next life. I don't want any part of a heaven where I don't see you.*

At the gate, I glance back at his grave one last time.

"A bientôt. Merci." *Until then. Thank you.*

Chapter Fifty

I CLOSE HIS office door behind me just as he ends his phone call, his eyes blazing down my body in careful inspection before he darts them away. Guilt.

He stands and swallows, turning to look out his window. He has a view of the top of the plant and most of Triple Falls. It strikes me then that I feel indifferent about him taking my father's place. In a way, it seems just.

"I came to you yesterday, and you weren't there."

Did he think I left? From the looks of him, he did. But I don't let it deter me.

"We need to talk."

He turns to me, sliding his hands in his tailored pants. "Did I hurt you?"

"You know you didn't."

He looks back out the window. "I don't know anything."

"I think we both know that's a lie."

He scoffs—silence and tension lingering in the room before he speaks up softly. "Cecelia, I'm sorry. I had no right at all to—"

"If you're going to apologize to me, look at me."

He hasn't slept, his jacket and tie are nowhere to be seen, his shirt is wrinkled and unbuttoned. He looks as defeated as I feel. He opens his mouth to speak, but I stop him.

"I let you because I always have. It was a decision. I wanted it. Maybe I was waiting for it, Jesus, I don't know. But it doesn't matter. I'm leaving."

He swallows, and I see the faint dip of his chin.

Once upon a time, I was a lonely girl who met a lonely king, and we both suffered from too much pride and oh, how the reckless have fallen. Between my romantic notions and his aspirations, we deceived ourselves, and all I feel now is sorrow.

Sorrow for the three orphans who were left to battle it out for themselves due to their parents' mistakes.

And that's why I'm here, to address the boy inside the man and give him the explanation he rightfully deserves. But how in the hell am I going to convey this to him? Tell him that he built an empire based on a lie? That our lives collided because two people fell in love, and one of them made a mistake, which started a war. A war that has *everything* to do with me.

"I have to tell you something."

Tobias studies me closely, and I know my face is paling. As much as I resent him, the guilt is riddling me.

"I . . ." I shake my head furiously and pull the envelope from my purse.

"Cecelia." An order.

The words burst from my lips. "My mother started the fire that killed your parents. It was an accident. A horrible accident."

I watch him carefully for a reaction, and he doesn't so

much as flinch. Instead, his eyes fill with curiosity. "How do you know that?"

"I found a letter from my mother to Roman." I hold it out to him. "I went to Georgia yesterday and spoke to her. It's all here, her confession. It was written a few months before I moved to Triple Falls. This letter is the *reason* I was here in the first place. It's the truth, and you deserve it."

He lifts the letter and studies it briefly before placing it on his desk.

"You aren't going to read it?"

"No."

"Then you should know Roman did it because she was—"

"I know."

I'm shaking so hard it takes me a second to understand his reply.

"Wait, you what?"

"I know. Roman told me the day I met him."

"The day you met him . . . you *knew*?" Anger slashes through me, and I cough incredulously, refusing to shed another tear. "And you didn't think to share that with me?"

"It was one of the conditions of our deal."

"Your deal?"

My purse slackens on my shoulder as my posture slumps from the crash of adrenaline. "You son of a bitch." I rip my eyes away and walk toward his office window, staring out for several seconds while I try to wrap myself around it. "Damn you, I've been sick trying to figure out a way to confess this to you." I turn back to see he's close.

"Feel better?" He offers a weak smile.

"Jesus, Tobias. I didn't think I could hate you, but . . ." I fight every surfacing emotion.

"You should. You should have all along."

"But I didn't." I feel numb. Close to numb, but he'll never win in completely desecrating my heart. It's the one thing I've kept despite all the loss, hurt, and betrayal. It's the one thing my father never allowed himself to give over entirely, and that Tobias battles to keep out of reach from everyone who's loved him, especially me. But it's not because he doesn't love me, it's because he can't lose me. I can't be another casualty in his war with life.

That's what broke us.

History is painfully repeating itself.

And I saw it the minute it happened, the second he snapped. It was the look on his face when I held his dead brother in my arms. Equivalent to that of Roman seeing a loaded gun pointed at his infant daughter.

The look he gave me before he walked away from me was one of utter resolution.

Love will never win with men like Roman and Tobias.

He would rather lose me in life than risk my death, my blood on his hands.

It's the coward's way out. His resignation to leave his heart out of it. To leave me out of it.

But I'll never let mine grow cold despite the damage done or the havoc it's wreaked. And for that one victory, I'm thankful the blood still runs crimson, still beats faithfully in my chest. I study him carefully and can't find a single trace of resentment.

"I don't understand how you're so calm."

"I've had years to deal with it. To put it all in perspective. I don't have many regrets. I'm still doing what I was meant to do regardless of the reasons it started and—" he lets out a long breath.

"And?"

"And the night I met with your father, my war with him ended."

"But you still bought his company."

"Because the board is full of corrupt pricks who constantly robbed their employees; he was one of them, and it was a good deal."

"So, you were never going to tell me?"

"I knew it could destroy your relationship with your mother."

"I'm so fucking lost," I say hoarsely before I let out a disbelieving laugh. "And with you, I always will be."

"That's why you need to leave, Cecelia. This place has never been good for you."

"Stop blaming the place. It's just a fucking *place*. It's the *people* in my life who've deceived me and robbed my sanity. I can't believe you knew."

He leans against his desk, clasping his hands. "Even though your dad was crooked as fuck for covering it up, he didn't kill them in cold blood. Instead of losing my shit over it, I was glad. I was glad I didn't have to hate him anymore because it meant I could keep my promise without resenting you for it. Until . . ."

"Dominic died." I can barely hear my own voice. I don't know how I'll ever look at my mother the same way. Maybe I won't. Maybe I'll disappear on her the way she did me. I've suffered horribly because of her secrets. Maybe I'll punish her for the years I've spent in purgatory to make sure she is taken care of. For years after that, I've been trying to piece myself back together while she's lived in luxury with her fucking silence. Maybe I will hold it against her, for the life my father lost covering her mistake, and for the explanation I deserved about his absence.

Tobias speaks up. "The truth is my parents died in a horrible accidental fire started by a very scared and pregnant teenage girl."

"And you forgave her?"

"I had to. One day maybe you will too."

"I don't know how much forgiveness I have left in me."

He silently nods. Even though he looks defeated, there's a calmness inside him, one I haven't seen in years.

"You seem . . . different."

"Seeing you . . . you coming back here has stirred up shit . . . shit I've been avoiding for too long."

"Well, I hope you make peace with it. Life is short; Dominic taught us that. But my opponent was never invisible." He keeps his gaze steady on mine. "You were always going to be the one who got the best of me. You knew it, I knew it, and I still fought it. But I'm giving myself a headstart by giving you my queen, so, there's your check."

Silence. And I don't know why I expected anything more.

"One thing's for sure," I say, "no matter how hard I fought it over the years, *I am* my mother's daughter." Confusion flits over his features, and I nod toward the letter. "Read it. It's the same pathetic shit. I ended up living here all those years ago because my mother had the audacity to try and come back and win the heart of a man who didn't love her enough to let her in on his secrets. Who couldn't forgive her enough for being young and reckless. Who punished her for horrible mistakes he himself helped liberate her from, all the while loving her from afar because he refused to trust her enough to make her own decisions. My father slammed the door in her face. And it ruined her. It's poetic justice, really."

"Cecelia, I've never hated you."

"Yes, you have, and I can't afford to care. Loving you is way too expensive, and I'm not paying for it another minute. You've stolen enough from me, the rest I let you take, and you can fucking keep it."

For once in my life, I'm okay with letting love lose.

I'll forever be a foolish romantic, chasing the high, though no high will ever compete with the one I felt with him. It ends here.

I don't know how to be both powerful and in love, and that's my downfall.

We had our song, and it's time to take us off pause and let the rest of our story play out. The way it was always going to.

Meggie fell for a priest. I fell for a prophet. We declared war on their calling and cause, and neither of us won.

But I'm keeping my love story, not because it included both martyr and sacrifice, or because it's the story I wanted, it's because I would never rewrite it. And I would live it all over again just for the chance to sing with him.

"I've finally found my reason to hate you, Tobias." His eyes snap to mine. "Not because of our past, not because of the way you've pushed me away, but because of the way you're punishing us both—the same way Roman did. Love isn't an inconvenience, it isn't a mistake, and the danger makes it all worth it. I walked through fucking fire for you. I survived hell *for you*. You don't deserve me. You *never* deserved me, not at all. But I deserve you. *I. Deserve. You.* But it's the king I deserve. It's the king I want." I clench my fists. "I loved the bastard I met, the thief that stole me, and the king who claimed me, but I refuse to love the coward. I *hate* the coward."

Ripping my eyes from him, I pull another envelope from my purse and toss it at him. It thuds against his chest, falling to rest on his wingtips. "An addendum to the original contract that will negate my shares in *your* company. It's over. Ties broken. I'm *letting* you win. Goodbye, Tobias."

My heart nags me with every step I take away from him, begging me to make it whole as I quietly close the door behind me.

Chapter Fifty-One

"SHOULD SELL FAST. Especially at the asking price. Are you sure you don't want to start higher?"

I shake my head as she plants the "For Sale" sign into the ground before securing it into place with a rubber mallet.

"I'll contact you at the number you gave me."

"Thank you."

She glances around. "Such a beautiful place."

"It is." I can't argue with her. It was a place built for a family. A blueprint that stemmed from unrealistic dreams of two people who spent a moment in love, meant for a family who never had the chance to exist.

Two dreams died in this house, but the foundation of those love stories is spectacularly similar. And now it is a reminder of all that was lost.

A fucking Greek tragedy with a Shakespearean twist.

And for all my efforts, I can't at all renounce my name. I'll forever be the Capulet without a Romeo.

There's no gypsy to relieve us of our curse, no apothecary with a quick solution. All that dwells here is a painful history repeating itself.

And so the story goes.

All are punished.

I nod as she secures the lockbox around the door when I spot the envelope tucked into it.

"I'm going to take off, but I'll be in touch. I'm taking Melinda to lunch for referring me for the listing."

"Please tell her I said goodbye, and thank you for your help," I say absently, taking the envelope in hand, thumbing the contents inside.

My heart lurches at the weight of it.

Several minutes later, I collect my bag as my car pulls up. With one last walk through the house, I lock it up, leaving the key in the lockbox.

One last order of business and my life will again be my own.

Exiting the cab, my bag in hand, I hear the recognizable guitar licks of southern rock, lighting up at the sound of the familiar music. Just as I approach the bay, the sun beams from between the clouds, and I take it as a sign of encouragement. Insides rattling, I peek into the garage and see him hunched underneath the hood of a BMW.

The clanging of tools and an exhaled curse have a smile upturning my lips. I study him briefly, at least what I can see—dark jeans and greased tan work boots.

"Excuse me, sir."

"Be right with you," he replies sharply, his tone having nothing to do with me and everything to do with his frustration. My smile widens.

"I'm new in town, and I was just wondering if you knew where I could find some trouble to get into around here?"

His body tenses unmistakably in recognition before he slowly lifts, his upper half coming into view before he darts his head around the hood, and hazel eyes meet mine in an agonizingly familiar tug.

He's still golden, his skin drenched from the endless sun that seems to wrap around him. Though his hair is cropped shorter, I can still see the tint of platinum sneaking through his thick threads. He looks so much the same it steals my breath.

"Trouble?" he drawls. "Oh, I think I should be asking you since it just walked into my garage." He studies me a beat, then two. And then I see his decision.

He's striding toward me all swagger before he whisks me into his arms and whirls me around like not a single day has passed. Cedar and sunshine, and Sean. The smell is distinctly his. It has my emotions warring as I inhale as deep as I can before he lets me back on my feet. Deep creases line the corners of his eyes as his smile lights up, filling me to the point a fast tear forms and falls.

For seconds, we look over the other, and I latch on to it with all my might, feeling him slip away the second his memory kicks in, and the light in his eyes dims. The pain leeches onto my chest as he steps away and pulls a rag from his pocket to start wiping his hands.

"Heard you were in town, Pup."

"And you still didn't come to see me."

"Wasn't sure if I wanted to, or if I should."

And there it is, the grudge; some for me, some for what happened. But for those seconds, just moments ago, he remembered me, remembered then, remembered us, before everything went to hell. I should be grateful he acknowledged it, but all I feel is . . . loss.

"Yeah, well, the wolf sought me out *first* so you couldn't protect me this time."

"I never was good at it anyway," he says softly.

"You were too busy making me tough."

I don't miss the flare of pride in his eyes. "I did a hell of a job with that."

I take a step back, unable to stand the fact that he's still within reach and yet so far away. Years away, a lifetime away. A lifetime I'll never get back.

"Heard about all that ass-kicking you've been doing."

"I had someone pretty incredible pry my eyes open with a crowbar, so I can't take all the credit."

"The hell you can't."

"I'm not going to, so let's leave it at that." I glance around. "So, this is you?"

"Yeah, old habits die hard. As much as Tobias tried, suit life isn't for me."

"Yeah, I can see that. Do you still go hiking?"

"Not as much anymore. But I get out when I can."

"A wife and two kids."

His smile reaches his eyes before they dart away, and I bristle where I stand, utterly clueless about how to let him off the hook. He made the decision not to see me, and I need to respect it. "I'll go, but I . . . I'm guessing this came from you?" I pull the envelope from my pocket and open it, knowing what's inside. He watches me intently as the key falls to my palm.

"It's mint. I checked it out. Brakes are good." He glances over his shoulder at the car. "He would have wanted you to have it."

"I want it so much. Is that wrong?"

"Not at all. It's yours."

I glance over to where Dominic's Camaro sits and back to him. "Do you really believe that?"

He pulls a cigarette from his pack. "You were the only one who loved it as much as he did. Title's in the dash."

I nod toward his cigarette. "You should quit that."

"So I've been told, a thousand times," he says on an exhale, his tone thawing by the second.

"She's beautiful, Sean, really."

"Yeah." There's nothing but pride in his voice. "She is."

"I'm glad you found . . ." I shake my head, a blush of embarrassment threatening as he exhales a cloud of smoke past my shoulder. My fingers itch to trace the small scar where his lip ring use to lay. "Well, I should probably—" I hitch a thumb over my shoulder—"I have to be some-where." We both know it's a lie, and his telling hazel eyes call me on it, "and thank you again for this, it means a lot but . . . mostly, I just really wanted to see you . . . it's been a long time."

He nods, his gaze dropping to his boot as he stomps out his cigarette. "It has."

"I wanted to reach out so many times—" my voice starts to shake when I sense his hesitation. "I just . . . I couldn't . . . come home without . . . I just, I'm so glad you seem to be doing well. That's so good."

Do not cry. Do not cry.

I let myself get one last long look at him and let out a shuddered exhale. "It was so good to see you; take care, Sean. And thank you," I say, lifting the key.

"You too," is all he says as I back away and grip my bag,

rolling it away from him while burning the memory of him into my mind one last time.

Legs shaking, I make it to the Camaro as the sun slips back behind the clouds, as if mocking me. Peering inside the car, I steady my breaths and grip the handle before I open the door. The smell alone has my eyes watering.

"You might be trouble. But you're still more. *A lot more*." The rumble of his voice has me glancing over my shoulder toward the road so he can't see me break with his words. I don't look up as he walks over to where I stand, frozen on the side of the car. Lungs burning from the sobs I'm tamping down, I keep my head turned, my gaze averted, knowing I won't be able to look at Sean again without letting him truly see what I'm feeling.

He brushes the hair away from my shoulder as I fight the onslaught of emotions his gentle touch causes. How many times had he touched me this way? Visibly shaking, I white knuckle the door frame to keep myself from buckling.

"I just . . . really wanted to see you."

"Can't do that if you aren't looking at me." He gently takes my chin in his hands and turns me to face him, and my tears spill in rapid succession. In his eyes, I see the remnants of the man who looked at me not so long ago with nothing but adoration, love, lust, and longing. I see it all in those seconds, the love we had, the love we distorted, our friendship, our season together—my golden sun. So much to say, and the fear I may never get it out, that he may never want to hear it.

"I still think about you, Cecelia. It's impossible not to."

Unraveling, I bite my lip to control my shaking jaw. I still feel so much for this man. But this is the part I swore I'd let myself have, let myself feel, let myself confess. I owe it to both of us.

"I can't tell you . . ." I let myself get swept away by his gaze and the vulnerability he's allowing me to see. His eyes are swimming with our memories, more than that, with love. He's giving me more precious seconds, and I can't for the life of me look away or deny his gift. "I-I-I . . ." I swallow. "Me too." The floodgates open, and emotions overwhelm me. Sean was the first man I ever truly loved, and one of the most beautiful men I've ever known. "Are you happy?"

He gives me an easy nod, even with his eyes brimming with emotion. "So fucking happy, Pup. I am."

"G-g-ood. I'm so . . . I just, I never got to say goodbye," I choke out. "I never got to say goodbye and—" I sob in my hands briefly and feel his arms surround me. "You were my best friend, more than that, so much more. Everything got so fucked up, and I just, God, I missed you for so long. You were my first love, and I loved you, Sean. I really loved you. And I'm sorry. I'm so sorry."

"Fuck that," he murmurs, pulling my head to his shoulder. "I'm sorry. I'm so fucking sorry I never reached out after it happened, I'm sorry I let him get between us, that I wasn't man enough to . . . I blamed you, but it was easier. I fucked up too. But I was so . . . lost, so fucking lost."

"I know," I whisper, "me too."

"I never wanted you to hurt, I hope you believe me," he whispers to my temple.

I nod, gathering my fragments and ash and trying my best to get it together. "I do. And if you're happy . . . that's all I want."

"I've got a wife I don't deserve and two beautiful kids I

never, ever thought I'd be capable of loving the way I do. I named my boy after Dominic, and the little bastard acts just like him. It's a curse, but I'll always have a piece of him," he drawls, his voice laced with regret, and longing. "Just like I'll always have a piece of you—" he strokes my back in the soothing way I've missed for so long—"And you will always have a piece of me." He pulls back and cradles my face in his hands.

"But I can see it. You still haven't let go. You have to let go so you can get your happiness too. You were never to blame. Never. And I know if Dominic could, he would tell you the same. It was his decision. And he loved you." I nod and nod as he wipes my never-ending tears. "I regret a lot of shit from back then, a lot, but I don't regret you. I loved you then and now, and I always will."

Our eyes lock as a part of me rips while a larger part of me heals. I feel the first stitch and the sweet relief that comes with it. He leans in and presses his forehead to mine, our pained breaths mingling. "Deep down, even though I have everything I'll ever want, more than I could have ever expected for myself, some part will always wish it was me."

"I'm sorry," I whisper as tears coat my lips as I gaze up at him. "I sometimes wish I would never have met him, never laid eyes on him."

"Don't be. It played out the way it was meant to. You were always supposed to be his secret to keep."

It's the first time I've hated his honesty, hated the truth. "You know I'll always love you, too."

He lifts his chin, eyes shimmering with our mistakes. "Yeah, I do. *Go.*"

He releases me, his gentle gaze probing, begging me to

do the same. I nod and step away as he widens the door, and I slip into the car.

In the next breath, I'm turning over the engine as he stands outside the window. I don't look at him, but I know he's peering into the car, stuck in the past with me, where I brought him, remembering me, remembering *us*, regret as heavy as his hand that lays flat on the window. It's when I put the car into gear and check the rearview that I see the glint of something familiar, something that once belonged to me. Lifting my hand, I pinch the symbol between my finger-tips, tempted to ask the question but deciding it's better left unanswered. I release the necklace hanging from the rearview just as Sean steps away. I refuse to look at him, for fear any resentment slips back into place. I'm taking his love, all that he could spare me as I pull away, hopeful he recognizes the piece of me he will forever own.

It was a decision to come and face the ghosts of my past, to free my truths, and I've done it, I've slain it all, and yet the relief is heavy. Gripping the steering wheel, I sit idle at the highway mulling over a direction.

My eyes lift to the grey mist smoking through the mountains in the distance when a thought occurs to me. I click the signal and floor the gas, every mile I tread getting a little easier, every thread of wind whipping through my hair filled with bittersweet release. I lift my phone and hit play. The opening lyrics to "Keep on Smilin'" by Wet Willie, lulling me into a state of peace I haven't felt in years. I may be leaving, but I'm taking all of them with me. Gunning the car, I shoot toward the highway, thankful: thankful to have felt, and experienced love in every degree, for the gift of knowing it, for every memory I'm taking with me. For the love I had and lost, and the burning reminders surrounding me, charred into me, telling me that, no, I'll never be that woman who can let go of the past, but I can take it with me.

With Sean's music filling the air, Dominic's buzz at my fingertips and feet, I pick up speed over the county line, just as the sun peeks back through the clouds. And then I'm flying. The wings on my back, I decide belong to *me*. And with them, I free myself.

Chapter Fifty-Two

Eight months later . . .

"WHAT'S HE GOING on about now?" Marissa asks, sliding the register closed with her hip. I glance over my shoulder to see she's looking up at the TV before turning to warm up the coffee of the man sitting at the counter. "Will there be anything else?"

"No. Thank you," he says, failing to catch my eye as I lay down his check. It's his third time coming in this week. He's handsome, but I know better. I'm nowhere near ready—one day.

One day.

Maybe.

The second time I left Triple Falls, I gained something I never thought I'd have again, faith.

It's contradictory to love in the way it doesn't destroy you. You can have a little of it or a lot, but it can't tie you up in knots. Faith is a healer, and it gives birth to hope. And hope is my next step, but I rest easy in faith.

"Cee, two sunny," Travis, our short order cook calls as I

retrieve the plate and deliver it to the older man propped on the stool. He nods toward the television, unwrapping his silverware. "Turn that up, will you?"

I glance at the TV to see it's another presidential address. The second in the last week from our new elect last fall. He was sworn in as the youngest president ever to take office.

"Jesus, it's like 2008 all over again; our money isn't safe anywhere," the man says, shaking his head.

I grab the remote and turn up the TV before I cash Mr. Handsome out, laying his change and receipt on the counter. Briefly, I think of Selma, and a smile crosses my face. Except I don't bother to steal from this owner; it's my name on the paychecks.

Oh, the irony.

"Just more bullshit. More promises that won't be kept."

Billy, a grumpy regular who's tapping ketchup on his scrambled eggs, grunts out his agreement. "I don't like the look of him. I can tell he's a crook."

Laughter erupts from me. "Is it his suit, his haircut?"

Billy looks at me like I've grown an extra head, and I shake my laughter away and refill his coffee as he thumps his sugar packet with his finger, one, two, three times. I swallow the sting it causes and speak up as I pour, "You know, we're still a young country, as in two-hundred-and-forty-plus years *young* versus others a thousand or more years old. Maybe, one day, we'll get it together."

Mr. Handsome nods, eyeing me reflectively. "Never thought of it like that."

"Yeah, well, I'm just a messenger," I whisper, mostly to myself.

"He's a quack," Marissa says, and this time I do burst into roaring laughter. She gives me the side-eye. "What's so funny?"

"Nothing."

I glance up at the TV at the new president discussing the newest shitstorm on US soil. In the past six months, unbreakable banks have gone under, federal judges have been fired, and President Monroe has cleaned out his entire cabinet and replaced ninety percent of the White House staff. In essence, he cleaned house, and nobody likes change. I like to keep an open mind. Briefly, I read his assurances in closed caption. It's much of the same, of how our country will survive, band together, overcome our odds, and come out stronger.

It's the words that everyone needs to hear, but words that are equally as deceiving. But as I look closer at his surroundings, it's the man to the right of him who gives me pause before that pause gives way to electric shock.

I pick up the remote and hit rewind.

"*Hey*, I was watching that," Billy protests.

"Sorry," I whisper faintly. "Sorry, just a second. It'll play-back."

When I've gone back a few seconds with a clear view, I hit pause and cover my mouth.

"Oh my God." I would know that face anywhere, that hair, those eyes, and if he were smiling, that dimple.

Tyler.

Marissa rounds the corner, eyeing me. "Cecelia? What? What is it?"

I drink Tyler in amongst the line of a few standing guard behind our President and scan him from head to foot; his posture tight, his eyes are drawn sharp, watchful, his face stoic. The man standing guard doesn't much at all resemble the jokester I know and love. But it's him. It's Tyler.

Tyler is guarding the President.

I can't even form words as everyone at the counter stares at me with odd looks. I give myself a second, and then another.

I clear my throat and shrug. "Nothing, I swear, I thought I saw a ghost. Sorry y'all." I hit play and barely hear Marissa. "He's okay-looking, I guess, but he *could* use a tan."

Hand visibly trembling, I manage to set down the coffee pot, shaking in revelation.

They're everywhere. The banks, the stock market. All of it. It was them.

They've infiltrated the fucking White House.

I don't know why it surprises me, but the sight of Tyler standing in such an esteemed position has me utterly astonished. Palms sweating, I try to gather my wits and fail.

They've done it.

They're still doing it.

And it comforts me so much. I feel safer knowing whatever agenda they have. It's the right one. A pride-filled tear threatens, and I haul ass through the service doors to the kitchen and tuck myself in a corner near the baker's rack.

"You sons of bitches," I whisper, covering my mouth, my smile widening as I shake my head and tears fall freely down my cheeks. Inside I feel hysterical.

After a few minutes and a few deep inhales, I school my expression and walk back out into the cafe addressing Marissa.

"The deposit is on my desk—could you possibly take it today?"

"Sure, love, you okay?" Concern covers her features.

"Fine. I . . . just want to get home early and let my dog out. There's a storm coming and he's afraid of them."

"No problem. See you in the morning, sweetheart."

Sweetheart.

It's odd how that word can be used as a weapon or term of endearment. Dominic used it once or twice. But I don't look back anymore with resentment. It's pride I feel now when I remember my time in my parents' life choice purgatory. It's not the hard times I think of. It's hiking with Sean or watching Dominic read, or sipping wine while gazing at fireflies underneath the night sky with Tobias.

It's love I had, and love I took with me.

And it's my greatest strength. It's my true superpower.

Feeling the rumble of thunder, I exit the café and make it halfway to my car when I feel the air still. I search the parking lot and come up empty before giving myself a second to rationalize the static is nothing but the coming storm. I bat away the part of me that wants to mourn in disappointment. I've done enough of that. My tears have long since dried up.

I'm living the life I chose—day by day. No expectations, little responsibility. No ambitious quest, no fight with my conscience. Simple. Uncomplicated. A life I refuse to waste looking in the rearview. I took a monotonous role not to pay penance, but for peace of mind and the ability to think about what I want moving forward. I want to be okay with simplicity, the kind that entails honest work and aching feet. It's humbling if anything, and for the first time, it makes sense to me. I want to smile while doing it.

And some days—most days—I do.

I don't begrudge my past anymore for the future I have. It's wide open, but for now I'm keeping it simple until I come up with a different plan. Purse strapped over my shoulder, I take strides toward my car and climb in. Buckling in, I frown when I see the window on the passenger side is rolled down. I don't remember leaving it that way. Thankful I missed the storm, I turn the engine over. I jump back in my seat when "K." by Cigarettes After Sex bursts through the speakers.

I haven't heard it in years, not since the day I blasted it out in the woods . . .

I jump out of the Camaro and do a three-sixty, scanning the parking lot.

"Only one other has a key to this car, and it won't ever be used."

No. No. No.

The haunting melody drifts through the window of the idling car, bringing me back to a day where my life forever changed.

Frantically, I search the parking lot again and come up empty. I did not and would not have had that song playing. I peek in to see it's connected to Bluetooth and pull out my phone furiously, closing out my apps, but the song continues to play. It's not my phone it's connected to. I press my hands to the hood. Warm.

Is this another game?

I can't stomach anymore.

I laid us to rest—the past. I left. I did what he asked. What the hell is the point of this? I scan the small shopping center again, and it's then I spot Tobias stepping out of the A&P, a grocery bag in his hands. The sight of him in dark jeans and a T-shirt is foreign but electrifying. His posture is relaxed, but his brows are drawn in concentration. I know it the minute he realizes I'm standing there, and he tenses and stops mid-step, a second before his amber eyes lift to mine.

He rakes me from head to foot as I cross my arms and whistle.

"Wow. Not only did you steal the car for a joyride, but you decided to go grocery shopping *after*? You've got some balls on you, and your arrogance knows no bounds."

I don't miss the twitch of a smile as he approaches, and then it's gone. I tear my eyes away, my pride only taking me so far. He's so fucking beautiful, and in a way that snatches sanity. I can't afford to lose an ounce more.

"I knew you took it."

"It was a parting gift from Sean. And rightfully yours if you want it, but please . . ." I rasp out hoarsely. "Don't take it."

"I get my way, no matter what. You know that, and you weren't supposed to get off until four."

"Well, I took off early, and I guess I shouldn't put it past you to snake the one possession I care about." I duck into the Camaro and kill it, slamming the door after retrieving the key and my purse. "All yours. Now I really do hate you. Are you happy?"

"No. Not at all. You're a waitress, who gave up millions of dollars, and are living in another bum-fucked town in the middle of nowhere, Virginia. You think that makes me happy?"

"I don't care what that makes you. *I'm happy*. I love this town. And I'm not penniless. I own that café and the house I'm living in. You think I'm really dumb enough to give away every cent? I grew up poor. I'll never be that damn generous."

Confusion flits over his features. "You own it?"

"Technically, my mother does."

"Why Meggie's?"

I damn near laugh at the fact that he hasn't put it together. *Men.*

"It's a long story."

He frowns. "Do I know it?"

"Intimately, *and* as an outsider."

"Are you going to give me a straight answer?"

"It'll be *my* secret to keep." I glance up at him. "The presidential address shook me a little. That's why I took off early."

I don't miss the clear swell of pride in his eyes. "Caught that, did you?"

"All that time I thought I was playing on your board, and you'd already switched to another. Seeing Tyler standing there . . . Gah, I can't tell you what that did to me. It's remarkable, truly what you've done, what you're doing. In my wildest dreams . . . I consider myself lucky I get to watch it unfold." I deflate. "I just wish you would have let me in . . ." I shake my head. "Doesn't matter."

"You're getting every dime back, Cecelia."

"I'm fine."

"Look. At. Me."

"Nope. You see, I don't have to. Let that sink in a minute."

"Cecelia—"

"You weren't supposed to know about the money. It doesn't matter about the money. It's where it should be, back in the hands of people who worked for it. You'll see to it that the rest is used in a way that matters. I know you will."

"You think I wouldn't notice that much money? Look at me, Cecelia."

Our eyes meet, and I curse the zing that runs through me. He's the man I knew, and yet so much has changed. But one thing never will. Our connection—it's our connection that keeps me captive no matter how much of a free woman I preach to be.

When I finally give him the full attention he seeks, there's something in his eyes I've rarely seen. They swell with emotion when they sweep me.

"I've come to claim what's mine. And you know it's not the fucking car."

He sets the bag down and steps toward me, and I take one back. "In that case, you're better off trying for the *car*."

I don't miss the twitch of his lips. "You're going to make this hard?"

I widen my eyes. "No, I'm going to make this *impossible*."

He takes another step toward me. "Good. I expect opposition. I expect retaliation. I expect to be surprised because of human nature. Case in point, the interruption that is *you*. But make no mistake, I *know* my opponent."

"I'm done with you."

"No, you aren't."

"Smug, arrogant, ignorant, and completely clueless. You think I'll take you *now*?"

"No, I think I'll have to walk through hell daily for months to come, but I'm willing to try and earn admission."

"You're wasting your time."

"Debatable."

"This isn't cute. I don't find this amusing. You're out of your depth. Save your bullshit."

He swallows, his eyes filled with a rare fear, all amusement leaving him.

"Then, how about a little honesty?"

"That was a joke, right?"

"No."

"Well, I'll never believe you."

"It was real," he says. "All of it. It was real."

"Stop," I say, dropping my gaze. "You can't do this."

"Please," he rasps out. "Please look at me."

Jaw clenching, I lift my eyes.

"Beau taught me that a 'real man' stakes his claim and won't let *anything* or *anyone* come between him and what he can't live without. And I was ready for that. I was prepared for it. I was ready to fight my brothers tooth and nail, to fight you every day until you forgave me. I had a thousand dreams ready with you in every single one."

He tugs me to him, trapping me in his hold and slowly lifting my shirt from where it's tucked into my jeans before sliding warm palms up my back and running the pads of his fingers along my wings. "This—" he palms my back—"it's the fucking worst thing I've ever done to anyone, but—" he swallows—"you are the only thing I've ever stolen for myself. I let jealousy fuck up the beginning, and losing Dominic ruin the rest," he admits, his gaze imploring. "When I saw him in your arms, when I saw how terrified you were, I couldn't handle not knowing if I would lose you next. I couldn't fucking handle it. I've never been so terrified in my life. You were all I had left. But I wanted you then, and I still want you. But more than that, I wanted to deserve you. I couldn't take *any* of it back. I felt like the worst man alive. I did things that you should *never* forgive me for. And I couldn't believe that you still loved me when you came back, after all the hell I put you through. I couldn't believe you still looked at me the way you did, that same look." He shakes his head in disbelief, sliding his thumbs along my back. "Maybe this isn't a happy ending, but it's okay if we deal with whatever it is . . . right? I'm sorry it took me so fucking long, but I never, not once, expected you would forgive me—want me again." Tears fill his eyes. "We can't bring him back, you can't forgive me for everything, but we can fucking try to be . . . whatever it is we're cursed to be. I don't care how fucked up we turn out as long as I've got you."

"W-w-hy—" I clear my throat—"why now?"

"Because loving you made me sick as fuck and losing you twice has made me terminal. I don't want to live out any ending that doesn't include you."

I palm his chest and push. "Tobias—"

"I've only begun to prove myself to you. Let me. Please let me. If you never tell me you love me again, I'll deserve it, and I won't even ask for it. Not ever. But it's your heart that I want most, Cecelia, not your beautiful face or your body, it's your heart that I'm drawn to, it's your heart that's the most beautiful thing about you, it's your heart that makes you my most worthy opponent." He buries his head in my neck. "Please. God, *please*, Cecelia, let me finally love you the way you deserve." He pulls back, his words sneaking past my armor, through the fabric, and into the skin before driving straight into me.

I shake my head at my idiocy. "You forced me to let you go. You're asking too much of me."

"You think I don't know that? You think I haven't tried to talk myself out of this to spare you my greed?" His eyes lift to mine. "I sent the proposal to buy Horner Tech the day after you got engaged. It was my *only* move. And when

I got no response, I thought you ignored it because you had truly moved on. It was one of the worst fucking days of my life knowing that another claimed you and you accepted. Even though I was with Alicia at the time, I make very bad decisions when I get jealous over you, and that one I decided was a selfish decision after the fact. A weak moment. A coward's play, but I could never fully commit to her." He places my hand on his chest. "You gave me a choice the day you left, to play coward or be king." He releases me, pulling a chess piece from his pocket and places it in my palm. "And you were right, you've always had the heart of a queen, but you have to know, earning your love will be the *only thing* that will make me a king."

I study the piece in my hand—the piece from my father's board. A piece I hadn't realized was missing. The night I arrived. The gin. He was there.

I blow out a frustrated breath. "You are an unimaginable bastard."

"*Your* bastard," he adds, a faint smile simmering on his thick lips though his eyes are etched with worry. It's need I feel pouring from him. And for one caution-free second, I let myself celebrate it. His fingers massage my skin as he cradles me in his arms, his eyes imploring with a gentleness that has me aching.

His heart pounds against mine, willing me to obey and no amount of lies I tell it, will it believe. This man is the only one capable of giving it to me. I'll forever be its slave. He searches my face, his eyes glistening. But I won't make it so easy for him, not until he earns it.

"We'll fight all the time."

He grins. "I know."

"You're a lunatic for marking me."

"I know that, too."

"So, are you done?" I ask fearfully. Because if that's the truth, it's the biggest lie he will ever tell. The brotherhood is his whole identity. Any other life would be living a lie. "Because I don't want you to quit for me. That's not who you are."

"I'm on an extended leave of absence for now, and I've fucking earned it."

"I won't let you quit."

"I won't let you let me." He runs his hands up and down my sides, his voice full of determination when he speaks. "If you leave, I'll come after you. If you change your mind, I'll change it back. I'll fight so fucking hard for you every single day, so you never question if you made the right choice."

"No more secrets between *us*, Tobias. No more convenient omissions, no more games, no more protecting me because you think it's best, we both make the important decisions."

He nods. "I swear."

"Well, you're a *liar*."

This earns me a faint smile. "And you're the only woman who's ever called my bluff."

"So, once I've put you through months of hell, we'll be in this together?"

"Oui." He slowly nods. "We always have been, haven't we? Whether we wanted to be or not."

I nod just as he expels a stressed breath and crushes me to him, his kiss lasting a blissful eternity. He delves deeply into my mouth, running his hands along my back. When he pulls away, I can feel some of the tension leave him. "Fuck." He drops his head. "Thank you. Let's go home."

I draw my brows. "And where's that?"

He picks up his bag and shrugs. "You tell me."

"So, you *have* been sleeping in the woods this whole time?"

I don't miss his smile. "Maybe."

"I have someone there, you know. You'll have to fight with him for your place in bed."

"Is that so?"

"Yes. And he's just as much of an evil overlord as you are. French, too. You're in for a fight."

"I can take him."

"I'm not so sure."

I move to go to the passenger side, and he shakes his head and corners the trunk.

I draw my brows. "You're letting me drive?"

We lock eyes over the top of the car. "I trust you."

Three words.

Three words I never, ever thought I'd hear from Tobias King. More potent than any other words he could ever speak to me. I feel the weight of them as I gather myself in the driver's seat, and Tobias climbs in, biting his lip to hide his smile as "Father Figure" sounds out when I turn on the car. I study him closely, his expression . . . content, his eyes filled with affection when he turns to me.

"I *do* trust you, and respect you more than any other and I heard you clearly, Cecelia. I always have. That mark was supposed to be a promise that I always would."

My future has no more room for tears. I've shed enough for both our lifetimes. But I can't help the one that sneaks away, with a foreign tinge to it that reeks of elation. And it terrifies me. Tobias reaches over, gripping my face.

"There's something else you should know."

He rubs his thumb along my cheek. "I did watch. That night you told me you hoped I was watching. I was. I have been the whole time," he whispers softly, "I couldn't look away."

A sob bursts from my lips as he draws us together, our foreheads touching. "I'll make it up to you. Every day I denied you, I denied myself. I'll make up for it for the rest of our punishment. *Je t'aime*, Cecelia. I love you so fucking much. Mon trésor." His kiss isn't gentle. It's claiming, damning us both to the other for eternity. A punishment I'll gladly live out and see through to beyond our lifetimes and the next. When he pulls back, I glance in the back seat.

"What's in the grocery bag?"

"Breakfast. Ingredients for French toast."

I lift a brow. "Debatable. Cinnamon?"

He dips his chin. "Two bottles."

I can't help my smile. I buckle my seat belt and put the car in gear and glance over to him. "Fair warning, my place isn't exactly a palace."

Not a palace but a waking dream.

A vision I had the night Dominic told me he wanted nothing for a future. A vivid dream of a long driveway lined with Bradford pear trees that bloom white in the spring. A driveway that leads to a house on top of a hill floating in the middle of the mountains. A small house with lots of built-in bookshelves, cozy reading nooks draped with soft plush blankets and throw pillows. And behind it, a garden filled to the brim with every imaginable scent and color. I'd searched for nearly a month before I found something resembling what I dreamt of. The day I closed on it, I painted the front door blood red. And then I stocked the fridge with a rare wine. My last touch was adding my French Bulldog, Beau.

After a long day at my café, feet aching, I sit in my garden with music drifting from every room of my house to where Beau and I sit on the patio overlooking new blooms. It might not be Roman's palace, but it's a *real* home—lived in. Comfortable. Untainted by secrets and lies. Aged, but untouched by the unforgiving world surrounding it. A sanctuary.

Tobias leans over and runs a finger along my lips and down my throat, his eyes igniting with promise. "Does it have a stove where I can make you breakfast?"

"Yes."

He trails his touch down along my breastbone as my pulse begins to rocket.

Heavily lashed eyes sear into me as he whispers over my lips. "A bed where I can make you come, and often?"

"Yes."

He presses his lips to mine and pulls back. "Then what else do we need?"

"Nothing."

His smile cracks along with the sky, and it starts to pour; sheets of rain beat down on the windshield when I pull up to the main road and click my signal.

I turn to Tobias as he eyes the water pounding on the hood and looks back to me. We share an ironic smile.

We most definitely aren't riding off into the sunset.

He shrugs. "First of many. Merde, c'est nous." *Fuck it, it's us.*

"It's not a storm, Tobias," I say, looking up at the sky. "It's a blessing."

Acknowledgements

First and foremost, I would like to thank my readers for your continued support, which means so much to this writer. My life is so richly blessed by you.

A special thank you to my extraordinary patient line editor, Donna Cooksley Sanderson, without whom I'd be lost as a writer and human. This series would not be what it's become without you, and neither would I.

Thank you to my content editor, Grey, for the gentle nudges and creative pushes. Your extra is exactly what I needed to complete this series. You're amazing.

A huge thank you to Maïwenn Bizien for translating all the French in this series. There's no way we could have done this without you.

Thank you to my betas for your priceless feedback, and to my proofing team, Bethany and Marissa. Without you, getting these books published would have been a much harder feat.

Thank you to the rest of my KLS PRESS Team, especially Autumn Gantz, Bex Kettner, and Christy Baldwin. You three are lifesavers.

Finally, thank you to my incredible family and friends for your unlimited support. No matter what world I venture into, you are with me.

THE FINISH LINE

Read on for an extract from the final book of The
Ravenhood Trilogy

'I was never really insane except upon occasions when my
heart was touched.' – Edgar Allan Poe

Prologue

TOBIAS

Age Forty-Four
Saint-Jean-de-Luz, France

"Viens ici, Ezekiel," Come here, Ezekiel. *I walk over to where he stands, his hand lowered, a round, brown seashell with a flat bottom resting in his palm. When I go to take it, he moves it out of reach.*

"Qu'est-ce que c'est?" What is it?

"Un clypéastre, un dollar de sable. Lorsque tu en trouveras un, garde-le. Et lorsque tu seras prêt, alors tu le casseras. Mais tu dois le faire bien au milieu pour pouvoir en récupérer son trésor." A dollar of sand. When you find this, you keep it. And only when you're ready, do you break it. But you have to do it right down the middle to claim the treasure.

"Quand serai-je prêt?" When will I be ready?

He ruffles my hair. "Tu le sauras." You'll know.

*

Standing on the shoreline, I skip rocks along the foamed waves flooding in at my feet. I never recalled the whole conversation from that day my father brought me here, only the look of the sea, a glimpse of sand, the flash of early sun peaking behind him, and the strange shell in his palm. It was on my last visit to the institution that he recalled our discussion verbatim during one of his rare and lucid moments. He told me the story of his son, Ezekiel, and repeated our exchange that day with surprising clarity just minutes before he asked me to search for him.

Whether it was a sign, or fate, or something else playing a factor, I found a sand dollar on the beach in pristine condition the day I broke ground on the house. Though he didn't jog my memory until years after, the why of what drew me to keep it when I found it was made clear. Somehow without knowing the details, I knew the significance of it.

It's ironic and cruel how the mind works, mine especially. Some memories I re-live regularly but would do anything to forget, the details so vivid, so ingrained, it can be torturous. While others, the memories I hold most dear, at times evade me. But it's my fickle memory that planted a seed that day and instinct that had me hiding that shell—that makes it all the more meaningful. And it wasn't until I looked up the significance of the 'treasure' that I understood his state of mind that day, a state very much like my own mindset now.

We were never close due to my mother fleeing from him because of his temper and mental illness—a diagnosed schizophrenic—but I feel some connection to him now. However, I've been fearful since the day I found him decades later, covered in his own shit and rambling frantic

French at any stranger who passed him on that street in Paris. Seeing him in that state gave way to trepidation that one day I would suffer the same fate—that everyone who claimed to care for me would eventually abandon me—due to mental illness and lack of control. A fear that crippled me for years and kept me from investing, in believing in people fully.

To me, love was always conditional—until her.

My mother never fully understood the extent of my father's illness. It's my belief now that she assumed he'd just gone mad. Although that's partly true, it wasn't by conscious decision. It wasn't as if he'd let some dark side of him take over, which I believe was her stance on him up until the day she died. It was sickness that claimed him and the fear of inherited sickness that's plagued me for so long.

But at this stage in the game, the odds and my age are in my favor that I will never suffer his fate.

Retrieving the sun-bleached stone from where I hid it a lifetime ago, I start toward the winding cliff-side staircase that leads to my finish line. It's more apparent than ever that it was never the house I was waiting for. It was today, this moment of clarity—a day where my head and heart are no longer at odds.

If I had to sum up my life, my journey in one word, it would be today. I did it all for this moment. The irony is, I never knew through my plotting and scheming a day like this could exist for me. Fate threw me the cards while Karma had its wicked way with me. Luck was never factored in, but it came through for this opportunist enough to know that at times, it was present, and during others it had abandoned me completely.

Noted, luck. And fuck you for it.

But if I have to measure my life against the uncontrollable powers of what could be, at any time, for or against me, I'll have to bat them all away. I'll have to choose something else to measure my life by, a different entity all together, a cosmic force to trump all others, *her*.

Without her, my purpose would feel meaningless, as would this day.

Because she wasn't wrong. We, what we have and what we have found in each other, is all that matters. The path I traveled to get here would amount to nothing without someone to reflect on it with. And there's no better story-teller, no better reflection of my worth than in the eyes of the woman who shared in my journey and helped me navigate my way through the worst of it.

She's my mirror, my judge, and has revealed herself as my sole purpose. She brought direction back to my deadening soul when I lost my way, and she continues to guide me back, a star too bright to ignore, no matter how far I stray.

There's no more strength in life than a man's purpose. For so many years, I thought mine was something else entirely—until she showed me the truth. I always considered myself a lone traveler until she blazed her way onto my path as my opponent, my lover, teacher, confidante, and best friend.

Any significant sum of every day I've spent on this Earth will always amount to her.

If I would have succeeded in throwing my purpose away, if I were successful at self-sabotage, I wouldn't know such a complete feeling existed. I would have never found such peace inside myself. The panic would have seized me long ago and made me sick to the point of no return.

The minute I step through the door of the house, I won't ever look back on the cruelty of the path or how many steps I took alone. Instead, I'll appreciate each bend of the journey, aside from a single blow so fucking merciless, I'll never be able to shake it off. Not ever. A loss so painful, there won't ever be a day it won't hurt.

My brother.

Her savior.

An irreversible scar that will never fully heal and proof of my weary travels. I'm halfway to the top of the cliff when my phone rattles in my pocket.

Lady Bird is in the nest.

However, I've already sensed her nearby. From above, I hear her shout my name as she races through the house, clear panic and excitement in her voice as I begin taking the stairs two at a time, heart thundering.

"I hear you, Mon Trésor," I reply, hastening my steps, chest pounding, the delicate offering safe in my hand. *I will always hear you.*

Already choked up with emotion, I nod at the two Ravens standing guard at the back of the property as I pass and enter through the back door. Beau greets me with his typical cock check before he allows me to run my fingers over his ears. I've learned to tolerate him over time, despite the fact that he's still ridiculously territorial over our woman.

"Bonjour, you greedy fucker."

Of all the planning I've done in my life, this is the idea I've obsessed most about coming to fruition. But if Beau's here with her, that means not only did she get my text, but she clearly understood the double entendre.

Meet me at the finish line.

Though I've never set foot in this house and have refused to without her, I pay it little attention as I stride past the wrought iron staircase railing, knowing exactly where I'll find her. I've dreamt this dream a thousand times over the years, and both my heart and head know the way.

A light breeze guides me down the long, Spanish-tiled corridor, past the sand-textured caramel walls. The house is just a few rooms short of a mansion, but fitting enough for a queen.

The details I soak in through passing are few because my sole focus is far more appealing. There's nothing but fire and need in my hammering chest, which is beating as hard as it was the last time I came to her with a request. Then, I was just as fucking terrified. Terrified she'd refuse to take me back. Terrified she believed my lies. Terrified I believed them for so long, I convinced myself they were true.

Twelve years ago, I forced her out of my life. In doing so, I lost myself, my purpose, my meaning, and my fucking mind.

Over half of those years I spent without her were due to fear, guilt, and self-condemnation.

Today, I come to her a changed man because of the years we lost and because of the years that brought us here. She may not have believed my lies, but I always believed *her truths*, in her love, in the surety of her heart.

Because she saved me.

Earning her and her heart has been my greatest accomplishment, making it my most prized possession.

A treasure any worthy thief will try to steal.

A treasure many *have* tried to take and failed. Because I made fucking sure of it. Before, I would never have gloated about such a feat of winning her because of the cost. Before, the guilt made it impossible to make such declarations.

Before . . . was too fucking painful.

I was selfish then, as I am now with her, without much apology, because the need outweighs the guilt—mostly.

After forty-four years of life, I'm positive she's the only thing I can't live without.

And for the next forty-three, I will *never* love another.

She's loved many. That's the nature of who she is. It's what shaped her, but I've been greedy with my heart, and it has one sole owner. Nothing has, or could ever, compare to what she stirs inside of me.

My selfishness, my ambitions, my jealousy, and greed almost cost me my future, cost me her.

Since she accepted me back, I've spent every single minute of our time together paying penance while biding my time for this day.

Sentence served.

My time is up, and I'm officially a free man.

Which is exactly why I have to find her. Right. Fucking. Now.

Napalm desire, along with the ache in my chest, has me

hastening toward her as Beau struts next to me, determined to be the first to seek her affection.

"Fuck off, mutt, she's mine for the rest of the night."

Beau continues to prance next to me, ignoring my order. It took over a month to ship him here and another six weeks in quarantine to get him to the house. Now it seems he's already staked his claim as the head of it.

"Go. Now. Or I'll never cook you another steak."

His ears perk as if aware of the implication of my threat, and he stops when I do, circling at my feet. Snapping my fingers, he returns my gaze, unphased, before he struts off.

Fucker.

When I reach my destination, I find her exactly where I thought she'd be, perched on the balcony, her long, breeze-blown hair tangling around her face. Her hands lay flat on the thick clay ledge as she gazes out at the sparkling sea. She's dressed in white, the silky material dipping low in a V on her back, exposing every inch of her spine. Her skin golden from the sun, but it's the sight of the delicate wings along her shoulders that gets me hard. My thirsty eyes drink her in with a mix of desire and relief.

Getting her here was the final step of countless many.

I wait for her to recognize I'm near, and within a second of me standing at the door, I see her tense in awareness. Furious, watery, dark-blue eyes find mine as I take her in, emotion clogging my throat.

We've come so far since that day in the parking lot in Virginia, where all I had, literally, was the shirt on my back, an apology that would never be enough, and the fight she stirred within me to win her, to keep her, to reclaim what I stole all those years ago.

And we've come so far.

So. Fucking. Far.

From then to now seems like a lifetime ago.

In a sense, I've been waiting . . . but as of this moment, it's over.

In a matter of seconds, I will have done everything I set out to do. But it's the first day of my sentence that comes to mind when I breach the doorway and charge toward her. In the flash of the seconds it takes to reach her, I re-live it all.

Discover the TikTok sensation:
The Ravenhood Trilogy

Kate Stewart's Ravenhood Trilogy is a sexy,
unconventional modern love story, a fresh take on
Robin Hood, full of breathtaking twists.

Flock

The deal is simple: all nineteen-year-old student Cecilia
Horner has to do is survive a year in the small town of
Triple Falls, living with her estranged father. But everything
changes when she meets sexy bad boys Sean and Dominic,
both of whom have the same raven tattoo . . .

Exodus

Cecilia is reeling from the discovery that Sean
and Dominic are members of The Ravenhood,
a secret group of vigilantes. But at the head of the society
is The Frenchman, a man she has every reason to hate . . .

The Finish Line

The Frenchman has lived most of his life in the shadows.
His life's ambition has always led in one direction –
revenge. But he's determined to have it all: to settle old
scores, and win back the woman he loves . . .